Master Wu's Bride

by
Edward C. Patterson

Master Wu's Bride
by

Edward C. Patterson

Dancaster Creative
www.dancaster.com
edwpat@att.net

First Kindle Original Edition, February 2016
Copyright 2016 by Edward C. Patterson

All rights reserved. This book may not be reproduced in any form, in whole or in part (beyond that copying permitted by U.S. Copyright Law, Section 107, "fair use" in teaching or research. Section 108, certain library copying, or in published media by reviewers in limited excerpt), without written permission from the publisher.

Other Works by Edward C. Patterson

No Irish Need Apply
Cutting the Cheese
Bobby's Trace
The Closet Clandestine: a queer steps out
Come, Wewoka & Diary of Medicine Flower
Surviving an American Gulag
Turning Idolater
Look Away Silence
The Road to Grafenwöhr
Are You Still Submitting Your Work to a Traditional Publisher?
A Reader's Guide to Author's Jargon and Other Ravings from the Blogosphere
Oh Dainty Triolet
Pacific Crimson — Forget Me Not
The Twinning of Vincent Cassidy
Mother Asphodel
Little Vin at Dreamland

<u>*Nick Firestone Mysteries*</u>
The Sapphire Astonishment
Old Friend Cane

<u>*Farn Trilogy*</u>

Belmundus – The Farn Trilogy – Book I
Boots of Montjoy – The Farn Trilogy – Book II
The Adumbration of Zin – The Farn Trilogy – Book III

<u>*Southern Swallow Series*</u>
The Academician - Southern Swallow Book I
The Nan Tu - Southern Swallow Book II
Swan Cloud – Southern Swallow Book III
The House of Green Waters - Southern Swallow Book IV
Vagrants Hollow - Southern Swallow Book V

<u>*The Jade Owl Legacy Series*</u>
The Jade Owl
The Third Peregrination
The Dragon's Pool
The People's Treasure
In the Shadow of Her Hem

Translations from the Book of Odes are by James Legge, The China Book Company Shanghai 1879

To

Elaine Taylor

Colleague and Friend, whose support has been solidly and keenly felt

Acknowledgements

The idea for *Master Wu's Bride* stemmed from a short story I wrote in the 70's called *Master Wu's Ghost Bride*, which contained the kernel for the protagonist's journey. This I later distilled into a flash story of 500 words entered into a contest at *Whim's Place*, an on-line site run by Betsy Gallup, publisher of *anotherchapter.com*, where *The Jade Owl* first had appeared. The piece, *Chi-lin and the Cup*, won 2nd place and a cash prize. I have reprinted that piece at the end of this work.

I returned to Chi Lin late in 2014 and pondered it for some time, deciding to expand the work to capture life in 15th Century Ming China. I reasoned it had contemporary relevance, especially pertaining to living conditions for women in traditional cultures. I decided to cast the work entirely in a woman's point of view, a decision not to be taken lightly, especially since I would need to experience, firsthand, the sensibilities of women, including the adaptability of rights denied and the physical ramifications of pregnancy and childbirth. It was enlightening to stroll, even at a half-wavelength, in Chi Lin's shoes.

I am indebted to my many female friends who described the joys, bitterness, frustrations and management of the inequality between the sexes, which still pervades society. For a man to get his head around morning sickness and other lady ailments are details every man should ponder before pressing the myth of male superiority. Of course, in marrying these elements to my background in Imperial Chinese culture, I hope to spark my readers with some level of understanding of this journey through womanhood, a journey still traveled by most of the world's women today despite the passage of seven hundred years.

I also owe a big thank you to my friend, Margaret Stevens (Peg) for her constant support and word wizardry as she applies her eye and experience to my little army of words and commas (and lack of commas) and chapters and stuff as it flows, sometimes without structure, into semi-baked molds. Peg has stuck with me as an adviser and reader through my entire published career.

Edward C. Patterson
February, 2016

Ming Dynasty China

1373 - 1405

Table of Contents

Part I: Purple Flowers (1372-1375)

Chapter One: A Dash in Time

Chapter Two: Yan-cheng

Chapter Three: The White Cockeral

Chapter Four: The Hall of Silver Silence

Chapter Five: Husband and Mother-in-law

Chapter Six: Evening Shades and Shadows

Chapter Seven: The Crawl of Industry

Chapter Eight: New Acquisitions

Chapter Nine: Mending Things

Chapter Ten: Moon Cakes and Guan-yin

Chapter Eleven: Inspecting the Ji-tzao

Chapter Twelve: The Master Speaks

Chapter Thirteen: Gentle Rain and Lanterns

Chapter Fourteen: Reunion

Chapter Fifteen: Plum Wine

Chapter Sixteen: Growing Pains

Chapter Seventeen: Winter Measures

Chapter Eighteen: Full Blossoming

Chapter Nineteen: Spring Toward Summer

Chapter Twenty: Mistress Purple Sage

Chapter Twenty-One: Dismissing the Shadows

Chapter Twenty-Two: Tai-feng

Chapter Twenty-Three: Assessment

Part II: Queen Crane (1399 — 1405)

Chapter One: The Salt Goddess

Chapter Two: Chi Lin and the Mei-ren

Chapter Three: Passing the Torch

Chapter Four: The Cold Palace

Chapter Five: Infringement

Chapter Six: A Different Arrangement

Chapter Seven: Siblings

Chapter Eight: Last Settlements

Chapter Nine: The Grand Director

Chapter Ten: Serenity

Reprint: Chi-lin and the Cup

Master Wu's Bride is a work of short fiction. Names, characters, places and incidents either are products of the author's imagination or are used fictitiously. Any resemblances to actual persons (living or dead), events or locations are entirely coincidental.

Part One — Purple Flowers (1372-1375)

Chapter One

A Dash in Time

1

"It is time, mistress," the gruff servant said. "The porters are approaching and you have not even made an effort."

Chi Lin sat beside the courtyard pool, her aging eyes closed, fearing what she might see in the waters if she could stretch so far as to peek. The air was filled with jasmine, the aroma reminding her of the best days, if she could count them. She had sniffed both wonderful scents and more horrid within these walls. The house had been home and prison, but she did not care to distinguish one from the other today.

"Mistress," the gruff servant said again. "Let me prepare you for her coming."

Chi Lin opened her eyes. The sight of her handmaiden, a woman nearly as old as herself, did not favor her today. Still, she knew she had to prepare. It was a duty and a privilege. But she preferred to sit by the pool catching the scant breeze pressing a promise across her canyoned cheeks. She stirred, but stopped short of standing. She reached into the pool, brushing the surface. Her hand jostled a lotus blooming above a swollen *koi*, her fingers trying to recall another pool, a dream of days past. She dared to take a peek, her rugged reflection rippled, hinting at younger days and a better complexion, despite the layers that painted her now. She shivered, but in that recall she eased to dreams of long ago, separating her from dark days — days of toil and fearful nights; and yet it was in this place, not far from the lotus pool that her hardships had blossomed. Now her fingers broke the surface sending ripples to the *koi* and sweet tidings to the lotus.

"The duck pond," she murmured.

"Again the pond," Mi Tso-tze said. "No time for it, mistress. No time."

Chi Lin shook her head. She closed her eyes again, recalling another reflection beside another pool — her father's duck pond, no *koi* nor flowers, but the tingle of minnows and an old catfish lurking on the bottom. There she would come and watch the moon's reflection as it set, and then waited for the sun's face to shine again. Then it was not a vigil, but a dash in time, between her studies and her chores, when she fretted on the departure from her father's house and her golden fate in a rich neighbor's estate — the House of Wu.

"Do not sleep, mistress," Mi Tso-tze nagged. "The priest will scowl."

"Let him scowl," Chi Lin muttered. "Let him wait. He has waited before."

"When?"

"Ah, yes. Before you had entered my service."

Chi Lin could hear Mi Tso-tze chuff, but ignored her. She remembered the time beside the duck pond and in the barnyard. She missed her mother, who had taught her to play the lute and to sing ballads to the moon. On the banks of the *Ti-shui*, her mother had sat beside her and her sister Chi Tsai and contradicted the world, telling her daughters tales of women who changed their times. Beyond Chi Lin's father's house the world was stern and regulated. The Ming dynasts poked their fingers in every *mu* of land. Wars ensued, breaking the old order — a barbarian order. Now warlords became ministers and a bandit became the Emperor. The era of Hung Wu had been proclaimed and a new order stalked the land. Chi Lin's father, Chi Ming, was called into service and serve he did — and long. But now the old scholar retired to his books and paintings, teaching his son the character forms. Chi Ming the scholar believed his daughters could master such things as *the Spring and Autumn Annals* and *The Book of Odes*. He encouraged their curiosity, despite the bans. But Chi Ming's only son was cripple-born and could not contribute much to the household. Heaven had cursed the scholar with two daughters, whom Chi Ming prized above all.

"Do not sleep, mistress," the gruff servant said. "It is time. The porters are approaching and you have not even made an effort."

Chi Lin snored.

2

"It is time," her sister called. "The porters are approaching and you have not even made an effort."

Chi Lin sat by the duck pond, her hand sweeping the foam, disturbing the frogs. She kept her eyes shut, her sister's voice yet another distraction from sadness. Chi Lin longed for her mother, who was lost to different waters — *the Yellow Springs*. Mother played her lute and told her tales to the ancestors now. Chi Lin thought her mother could have soothed all concerns on this day. No moonrise or sunset reflections could do it. No other family member could.

Sister Chi Tsai was practical, more intent on housework and tending the cowcumbers than musing over frogs and minnows. She had had her chance for family honor, but declined the opportunity. It was never discussed. Brother Chi Sheng was kind, but preoccupied with his studies. When asked, he offered kind words and adages from the Classics. As fond as Chi Lin was of the aphorisms of Masters K'ung and Meng, she was stirred more by the poetry of Su Tung-po and Po Chu-yi. When asked, her father provided guidance but only from precedent. But precedent could not console her now, because, when the sun's arc reached the third watch, Chi Lin would retire to the cottage and don the red dress, because today was her wedding day — an act of duty, with dim prospects. This she knew because her future father-in-law had sent a bouquet of *ma-lan* flowers — a dreadful message for any bride. Today, unlike her sister, Chi Lin would bestow honor on her household.

"It is time," her sister called again. "The porters are approaching and you have not even made an effort."

Chi Lin sighed, her hand still wet.

"I wish to stay here and admire the ducks."

"You know that is impossible."

Her sister was dressed in a drab gray robe tied with a plain green sash. She would not attend the wedding today. No need. Such distractions as sisters were superfluous at such events. Chi Tsai hopped along the stone path until she reached the pond. Although a pretty maiden, she scowled now, shaking her head.

"It is a good match for our family. It brings us needed honor."

"But no more than that," Chi Lin snapped. "It also brings a *ma lan* bouquet."

"It is the way with the world. Mother once told us . . ."

"I know that tale. It chills my heart."

Her sister relented, hunkering down, her scowl easing into a half-smile.

"In a rich household you will have many pretty things and dainty food. You shall sit by your own pool all day and splash the ducks. Perhaps you will be permitted to read between your duties."

"I am not about such things, Chi Tsai. You enjoy tending to things. I am not accustomed to it. If my life will continue as it is here, why should I not remain here?"

"Because the dowry is paid and Master Wu waits."

Chi Lin scowled now. She knew what waited.

"When the chair comes," Chi Lin replied, "fill it with the dowry, but leave this bride behind."

Chi Tsai stood, shaking her fists.

"You have always been as stubborn as an ox. You must do your duty or no house in the county will favor us again with an offer. You shall wither on the vine. I know this too well."

"*We* shall wither on the vine, sister."

Chi Lin wept, her hand diving into the pond. She felt the minnows kiss her fingers, perhaps trying to console her.

Chi Tsai turned away. Chi Ming approached.

"What is the delay?" he said, approaching cautiously. "Why is the red dress still on the bamboo pole? Why is the veil bundled in the sack?"

"She is as stubborn as an ox, father," Chi Tsai grumbled.

"Ah, my daughters. Do not quarrel over such things as marriage. It is a day for celebration. I lose a daughter and, Heaven should know, I am joyous in that." He looked to the sky and nodded. "Such riddance is a blessing to any father." He then leered at Chi Tsai. "I shall handle this." He then whispered to Chi Lin. "I too am heartbroken at your departure, but let us not give Heaven an excuse to sweep our good fortune away."

Chi Lin knew that fortune had once graced the House of Chi, but the Emperor was as fickle as he was powerful. He had called all his ministers into the Imperial courtyard one day, accused them of ingratitude and had a thousand heads removed on the spot. On that day, Chi Ming was ill and had made an excuse. On the next day, the Emperor had a change of heart and halted the purge. Still, all those who served, served no longer — no longer enjoying Heaven's behest. So Chi Ming retired to this county town and lived on his neighbor's good will.

"I shall obey, father," Chi Lin said, nodding. "But it is unfair."

"It is a woman's lot," her father said. "How bad could it be in the House of Wu, even when they send the *ma-lan* flowers and deck their walls in snowy silk?"

Chi Lin stood, her sister guiding her. Her brother, Chi Sheng, had hobbled across the threshold on his crutch. He rarely emerged from the house, but he was anxious. He would not be going to the wedding either, cousin Chi Fa being sent in his place. His crippled leg prevented his journey and it would be improper for him to be carried in a chair — a blow to his sister's honor.

"They will be here soon," he called. "We should not delay."

Chi Sheng had commanded the house staff to gather the balance of the dowry — a chest of cash, seven goats, three pigs and a fine ox, as well as twelve bolts of finely woven silk. The servants loaded the carts and assembled the livestock. Chi Sheng was efficient, in charge of the household accounts. He assured that the ceremonial incense always burned and the ancestral tablets were properly honored. Now he waved his hand for his sister to hurry. Chi Lin loved her brother, but the circumstance did not capture her sandals with gratitude. Instead, she shuffled to the house setting about her duty with a heavy heart.

3

Beneath the red robe, the bride wore white, a doff to the purple flowers. The silk reminded her of the act's cruelty — the heavy cloth her husband would never see. Quickly Chi Tsai covered the skirts with rich crimson brocade, draped in three layers.

"There, sister," she said. "Only you know that it is there."

"I and *Guan-yin*."

"The goddess knows everything," Chi Tsai said. "You cannot complain to her about such things. She rules your destiny and cannot be bought, no matter how many prayers you make or sticks you burn."

"I do not believe that," Chi Lin said.

"Believe what you will. It does not make it so."

Chi Lin sighed, but received both sisterly chiding and the red blouse as roughly as the rude, white undergarments. She was already hot in this dress and would be hotter still on the road to Yan-cheng. The salt bogs would fill the air with bitter fragrance to accompany the mosquitoes.

"Must I wear so many layers?"

"Do you wish to void the contract?"

Chi Lin did not, and yet she did. At least, for her part it was void already. But her family depended on this connection. Perhaps her father might find a post in the Ya-men again. It was a daughter's sacrifice, but Chi Lin remembered her mother's words.

"A woman's lot in life is to ease our men folk to positions that will make the ancestors proud and give hope to those who carry the family name."

Suddenly, her brother was on the threshold.

"You are not allowed here," Chi Tsai snapped.

"I do not see why I should not hasten slow women when time is lost on the horizon. The chair has arrived and the drummers too."

Chi Tsai turned on her brother, but did not dare push him. In his unsettled condition, any push might tumble him. Instead, she opened a fan and waved him away.

"He can stay," Chi Lin said. "I will miss him when I am tucked away beneath Master Wu's roof."

"And you will not miss me?" Chi Tsai asked.

"I will. Although I will not miss your rules of order."

"If you have learned nothing else in your *xien* filled life, Chi Lin, you must remember the rules of order. The day tells us where and when we should be, how we should prepare and how we must fulfill."

"No space for idle dreaming?"

"Just so. You have had your days of idle dreaming. Now you must find your way in your husband's household."

For Chi Lin that was like being a flower boat unmoored in a whirlpool. She could not guess the rules of order in such a house — a gentry estate in a busy town. But since she did not die in the night, she guessed *Guan-yin* had decided a daughter must fulfill her role. Fulfill the sacrifice.

The drums beat and a half-dozen *xiao* flutes bleated competing with the goats.

"Let me see," Chi Tsai said, inspecting her sister's face.

The powder had been applied quickly, the eyes given an underscore and the lips a vermilion coat. It would suit. So Chi Tsai hoisted the heavy robe onto her sister's shoulders and tied the sash. The headdress was fitted and the veil prepared.

"Leave it be," Chi Lin said.

"What bride would go out with her face revealed?"

"I would see the sun. I would see our father's face once more."

Chi Tsai hissed, but gave in. She guided Chi Lin over the threshold and through the kitchen. Carefully the bride swept over crockery and dust until she crossed the high threshold barring demons from the inner sanctum. The sun was bright, reflecting her white face like the moon's borrowed light. She squinted. The veil would be a comfort after all. Chi Lin saw her brother inspecting the dowry and paying the musicians. She noticed three bannermen toting red flags to signal the nature of the procession. The animals were restless, except the ox, who winked at her as if he knew nothing more than that he was destined to yet another field or perhaps a roasting pot. The pigs were oblivious. Beside her father stood Cousin Chi Fa, a mature man, who was dressed in his best robes, his sandals tied with yellow ribbons and his hair coiffed in a tight bun, a spatula holding it together. His cap was an old official's bonnet, secondhand, but suitable. Upon seeing Chi Lin, he nodded and pointed to the chair.

The bride's chair was plain and smaller than she expected. Bright red and wrapped in crimson bunting, it was nothing more than a carry chair lacquered for the occasion. But it would do, she supposed, as long as the porters did not drop her in the road. A makeshift awning covered the vehicle to assure no one saw the bride before the household did. Her father approached.

"Come, come, my daughter. You are as ugly as ever." He winked, and looked to Heaven. "Was ever a man so cursed? But somehow I will miss you and perhaps I will see you again, if not here for a visit, at the *Yellow Springs* beside your mother's tablet."

She gazed into her father's eyes — eyes dewy. She loved this man, whose kindness and sponsorship gave her the privilege of letters and painting and hours of going beyond what her sister called *the rules of order*. He had forgiven her lapses in mending and cooking and feeding the chickens. Perhaps her brother's ailment had allowed her a special place. But that place now evaporated like the water in the salt marshes that hugged Ting-hu Prefecture's monopoly. She saw those salt marshes in her father's eyes. She bowed.

"Now, now, daughter," her father said. "You will be a mistress in a great house. No need to bow to me. True, I am your father.

True, you owe me much. But you have paid me well with smiles and giggles and hugs."

He turned away and disappeared over the high threshold.

"No time for sentiment," Chi Tsai snapped.

She had not noticed her sister's presence. She thought Chi Tsai had drifted off to feed the pigs. But Chi Lin realized she would also miss the nattering of this constant in her life. Suddenly, the world was red, the sun dimmed by the heavy brocaded veil. She could not see to get to the chair, but a hand touched hers.

"Thank you, brother," she said.

"It is me," came a voice. "Chi Fa. I hope the feast will not be curtailed because of your *ma-lan* bouquet. In times like these, they withhold the full feast and make do with cold gruel and scallions."

"If it does not suit, cousin," Chi Lin replied. "I am sure you can return here and kill a pig."

"Yes," Chi Fa laughed. "Yes, that would do. Not that I think the Wu family would cause an insult to the Chi or risk endangering the contract. The dowry is handsome. But you never know with the press of taxes and the squeeze of the magistrate. There are always concessions. Always concessions."

Chi Lin took Chi Fa's hand and trusted that he could deliver her safely into the chair. His words lay heavy on her heart, as heavy as the *ma-lan* bouquet, which she had thrown in the wood pile behind the mulberry shack. Still, there were always concessions and when her foot engaged the marriage chair, Chi Lin was making hers.

Chapter Two

Yan-cheng

1

 The forests had long since disappeared in Yan-cheng District, the briny flats having eaten the roots of all but the hardiest yews and pines. Even then, the surviving trees bowed to the bogs like servants to *Guo Po*, the river god. Between cattails and water bamboos, the red-crowned crane reigned, strutting through silt, looting salt from salamanders and frogs. The wild was King Crane's domain, the dammed zones champions of the Imperial monopoly — barriers and breakers demarking the ponds, dikes affording paths for salt workers to rake residue from the sun-resurrected brine and saline. The air was redolent with industry, water bugs clamoring the banks and mosquitoes dancing on ponds in search of crimson nourishment. Still, the cranes reigned, their trumpet call signaling the brood to create twig nests in bamboo hides, a sad attempt to preserve their plumage from some official's cap or a display in gentry *ke-tings*.

 The cranes arose with the sun, their dance marking the wild with elegance and perhaps with more industry than the workers who hewed salt from the boggy bottoms and through evaporation towers. It was ever thus in Yan-cheng, for two-thousand of years or more; and none but cranes worried about the ever-shrinking fen. Surely the salt merchant, who held the privilege, did not. Surely the bent backs cutting through the brine, did not. Surely the Hung Wu court, which managed well without bending backs, did not. And certainly Master Wu's bride, enclosed in her bride's chair, ported across these dewy meadows, did not. Only the cranes said as much, calling to one another, sounding throaty concerns and prancing like fleas on a glassy surface. Perhaps *Guo Po* on high witnessed their distress. More likely he ignored them as much as *Guan-yin* ignored Chi Lin's plight. Perhaps a ghostly groom would show pity on her and allow the chair to reverse its course.

2

 Chi Lin choked, the heat stifling her, enclosed in her prison chair. She had traveled in this chair before — before it was red-lacquered and repurposed with awning and drapery. Then a cool breeze had shown up and kissed away her perspiration. But not on this day nor in this state. Chi Lin had lifted the veil to breathe more freely, but that did not relieve the heat's press. She pushed the curtain aside — a breach, but if she had not, she might have fainted. A slight breeze paid a brief call, but it smacked with the salt beds' bite. She peered out. A serving boy pulled the pigs along to the constant drum beat and the occasional flute bleat. Chi Lin supposed it was useless to hail her progress to the multitude of laborers in the marshy spread. They would not be attending the ceremony. What would they care? At least the drumming gave them a working rhythm. So Chi Lin's passing was not an entirely wasted contribution.

Chi Lin leaned further out, daring to push the drapes aside. She could see the town gates — crenulated walls, blacked with time's passage and charcoal burning. The drum tower stood sentinel to the ages. Over the roof's sharp down and upturn, Chi Lin spied the Yan-cheng Ya-men's distant façade, the Prefectural seat, where the magistrate and superintendent kept courts as proxy for the Hung Wu Emperor. It was in that place her father had served until summoned to the capital. In those days, the family remained at home, but enjoyed the honor of service. Chi Lin's mother kept servants then. Mulberry was harvested and silk spun, providing a steady source of income. It was not so very long ago, yet it seemed like ancient days. The sight of the Ya-men stirred memories.

The curtain rattled.

"This is madness," Chi Fa snapped. "You are not a proper bride if you do not keep to your place."

"I am sorry, cousin. The air is . . ."

"That is part of it," Chi Fa said, closing the curtain.

"But it would be good to see Yan-cheng."

"You will have time enough for that."

Chi Lin was not sure this was true.

"You are stern with me," she dared complain.

"That is my part, daughter of my uncle." Silence ruled, except for the drums. Then the curtain rattled again. "I will tell you what I see and, if you keep to your place, I will allow you one glimpse of the Wu mansion when we come to it. Is that agreeable, cousin?"

Chi Lin grinned, although Chi Fa could not see it.

"It is."

"Good. Not that there is much to see now, except the gate and drum tower. You already have seen them."

The chair swayed to the rhythm. Blended with the salt stink and the abysmal heat was oxen gas, the beast having decided to let free his morning hay. Chi Lin gagged, but did not make a fuss, fearing another round of chastisement. The flutes played steadily now. Then the curtain rattled again.

"It is busy here, cousin. We are passing water vendors and cowcumber sellers. There is a tea house and a pleasure den, which I will not describe, not that I could not, but you are delicate. Those who visit such places are rough."

Chi Lin giggled. Chi Fa's face peered through the drapery crack.

"This is no laughing matter, cousin. The world is seedy as you shall know. Best stay clear of such places." The drapes shut. "Ah, now, there are flower sellers and a great market hung with meats of all kinds. Can you not smell the aromas?"

Chi Lin could, but they did not liberate her from the enclosure's stench. However, to see flowers would be a treat. How she wanted to burst free and enjoy the blooms. Her cousin continued to describe people and wares along the market street. Then he whispered.

"The Ya-men. Bow your head, cousin, so Heaven knows that a lowly woman passes His Majesty's place of sacred authority, may He live ten-thousand years."

Chi Lin bowed and even returned the veil to its place. She could feel the Imperial force. She knew its power. She knew its wrath. She knew its changeability.

The flutes ceased, and so did the drumming as they passed the Ya-men in silence. When they resumed, Chi Lin knew they had passed the place. Then, and only then, did she lift the veil.

Her cousin was silent now. She wondered what she was missing — gentry houses to be sure, and the merchants' quarter. A cook shop was definitely passed because she inhaled streaming buns and, a little later, the aroma of roasting pork. She also heard voices — well wishers. Her procession must have approached the Wu homestead, the neighbors and tenants expressing respectful regards.

The chair halted.

"One glimpse," Chi Fa whispered.

Chi Lin pushed the curtain aside slightly and was stunned. The road was lined with hundreds of folk, all heads bowed. The man nearest her chair looked up and gave her a toothless grin. At first she started, but remembered she would only get a glimpse. She looked ahead to the walls of Master Wu's estate, which gleamed golden in the sunlight, except for a long white banner imposingly draped along the breadth of the parapet, ending in a dozen white, flapping pennants. Chi Lin gasped, recalling her bouquet. She had had her glimpse, and returned to her place to avoid her cousin's further chastisement.

"Thank you," she said.

"We proceed."

3

Chi Lin entered the House of Wu, the gates opening to her. A grave silence descended on her procession when they crossed the threshold into the first courtyard. Chi Fa's whispers were quieter still.

"This is a grand place, cousin," he said. "The yard is wide with many blossoming trees and fine pots with golden moss. Water runs in a rockery and there are peacocks. A dragon wall I see, the likes of which I have never seen before. The beast has four claws. Impressive."

Chi Lin did not much care if the dragon had four claws or two. As for the vegetation, she was sure she would tire of it within a day. However, the rockery enticed her and peacocks were an uncommon bird.

The sun suddenly disappeared when the chair proceeded under a covered walkway. The light returned again and again, as they processed through many courtyards and moon gates.

"Where are we?" she muttered.

"Be calm. The place has many rooms — fine rooms and courtyards. There are attendants everywhere. Surely Master Wu was a great man."

"But such silence. Not even the peacocks call."

"A mixed blessing. But your journey is at an end."

The chair halted.

"May I escape the chair?"

"Stay still until you are summoned."

Chi Lin desired to bolt. She wanted to run free, her unbound feet fleeing through the invisible rooms and courtyards. But the silence bore its tension down her legs, paralyzing her in interminable waiting. She scratched her nose beneath the veil, the powder having turned to paste, itching her face. Suddenly, the curtain parted — the front portion, giving her a clear view of the main hall and its wisteria-kissed moon gate. Near the portal stood four *fa-shr*, Taoists priests no doubt by their high feathered caps and their white and red ribbon-dotted robes.

Also in the courtyard stood three women, all older than Chi Lin. They came to the chair to leer at its passenger. These were Master Wu's other wives, come to inspect the fourth wife, although their approval or disapproval would be too late. The wives wore unadorned white silk robes. The first wife stood tall. *Severe. Unbending.* The other two wives were assisted by handmaidens because their feet were bound. They tottered precariously over the cobblestones.

The first wife poked Chi Lin with her fan, raising the veil slightly, inspecting the face. She then looked down to inspect the feet.

"Free of the lotus pads," she proclaimed. "Good. You shall be a worker." She turned to the others. "No porcelain beauty this. The mistress shall be glad in that."

Chi Lin, uneasy with this assessment, noticed the other two wives listened intently to the first wife, preserving seniority's strict form. The first wife sneered at Chi Fa, who was all bows and homage. She then snapped her fan and led the other two wives away. They would not be attending the ceremony. Their participation in the service had ended.

From the hall emerged a plump official — the magistrate of Yan-cheng. Chi Lin knew him as Po T'ai-kuan. He was once an under clerk to her father, but he had managed to survive the purges and now thrived. He was famous for wearing the finest robes even for the most menial functions. This day was an exception. The Wu family was too important in Yan-cheng to overturn protocol. So, Po T'ai-kuan wore a simple white robe over a red lace undercoat, his hair wrapped in an unadorned black turban. He approached the chair.

"Daughter of Chi Ming," he said. "Your actions will not be forgotten by Heaven or the Ya-men. Your tablet shall stand in its proper place and will assure the lineage of the House of Wu and the House of Chi." He bowed, holding his heart. "I am privileged to escort you into the *ke-ting* and to affix the seals."

The magistrate's leer made Chi Lin's skin crawl. His tongue swept his teeth as if he wished to be the groom or at least sample the groom's privileges now that such privileges were blown to Heaven.

"Master Po," Chi Lin said, sweetly allaying her disgust. "I am honored by the courtesy."

Po T'ai-kuan turned to Chi Fa.

"Your duty has been fulfilled. You are discharged, Master Chi. The ushers will show you where to store the tributes and to take refreshment."

Chi Fa bowed, probably happy knowing that he would be fed, although he would have preferred a wedding feast and wine enough to assure a carry-chair home.

The four priests began a simple dance, rattling hand drums and chanting a prayer. It unsettled Chi Lin further, especially when Po T'ai-kuan latched his hand to hers, tugging her forward to the threshold. There she paused.

"Say the words," Po T'ai-kuan coaxed.

She knew the words. She had dreamed of the day when she would say them. But now they were shallow acknowledgements to a contract, and nothing more.

"I come to the edge of the end of my life in the House of Chi," she said, her voice breaking on the words. "I am suspended between the worlds. Is it Heaven's wish that I enter the House of Wu?"

"It is," came a masculine voice from within.

Chi Lin bowed, and then crossed the divide between her old life and her new one, not knowing what she would find in the Wu household tomb.

Chapter Three

The White Cockerel

1

Wu T'ai-po was long the head of the household, old but steadfast in his position as the holder of two Imperial salt monopoly certificates — one granted and one bestowed. The granted certificate made the household rich because the Wu family oversaw the individual salt work holdings, the *ji-tzao*, and distributed this commodity through the local Ya-men for a fixed, but profitable, amount. The pledge made the Wu family wealthy, the old man doing little more than holding the precious document, while his tenants fulfilled the terms. The monopoly rights would be passed to Wu T'ai-po's eldest son, Wu Hung-lin, whose wedding was today, his fourth wedding and, indeed, a curiosity for the family. The *granted* salt certificate would pass through Wu T'ai-po's eldest son and onward until the end of time or the end of the blood line, whichever came first. The *bestowed* certificate was outsourced to a merchant guild, which transported the salt to the border regions where it supplied the Ming Imperial armies. It was lucrative and made the Wu wealthier still. This trade was overseen by Wu T'ai-po's second son, Wu Liang-tze, who lived in a nearby villa and fulfilled the certificate terms through minions. Wu T'ai-po's third son, Wu San-ehr, was a captain to the Hung Wu Emperor's fourth son, Prince Chu Di, and lived at the northern garrison near Yen-jing. But it was to the first son, this Wu Hung-lin, whom Chi Lin would marry today.

Three wives preceded Chi Lin, each a floral acquisition across the threshold. First there was Mei Lo, the Jasmine flower, who gave Wu Hung-lin two sons. She commanded the other wives under the stern guidance of Wu T'ai-po's wife, the Old Lady of the House. Second was Ho Lien, the Lotus blossom, a dainty maid who Wu Hung-lin discovered in the tea house and brokered as a bride to satisfy his lusts. She gave him two daughters, which served no purpose beyond expense. The third wife was Lan Hua, the Orchid flower, a frail child, whose dowry could not be shunned at any cost. Always ill at ease in the house, Orchid rarely emerged from her quarters unless summoned by Wu Hung-lin, an effort which yielded but one child — a daughter, who just began to scurry under the household's feet. Chi Lin was the fourth and, although she was not named for a flower, she bore the name Ma Lan, the Purple Sage because of the sad bouquet Wu T'ai-po had sent her — the bouquet she had left behind.

Master Wu Hung-lin was an obedient son and a scholar in a house of gentrified merchants. His commands, although subservient to his father's and a shadow to the Old Lady's, held sway in the household. He had great expectations for this household. He would inherit the *granted* monopoly certificate as would his first son. He had expected to father many more sons, and thus he commissioned the marriage broker to find him a fourth wife, one which the *fa-shr* found worthy to bear sons — a pretty woman with unbound feet, who possessed intelligence. Master Wu had two dull but pretty wives to suit his fancy, and his first wife was formidable enough, but could only discuss local gossip and the price of scallions in the marketplace. No. Wu Hung-lin would have himself a wife who could play a round of *Xiang-ch'i* and gracefully lose the match. Lotus could play the *p'i-pa* and, when coaxed, Orchid could sing. Jasmine was a nag at times, but she could be relied upon to curb his sons of base manners. But to have an intelligent woman, who also knew her place, would be delightful. This woman, the daughter of a retired official, came to his attention through Magistrate Po T'ai-kuan, who knew the man and had seen the daughter. The marriage broker was set upon the match. The bride price was not exorbitant and the dowry was fair, although paled compared with Orchid's. So, at forty-three *sui*, Wu Hung-lin was to marry again.

No one knew how the demon crossed the threshold, but it did. An evil mist crept through the portal and past the dagger-mirrors and kitchen gods. It crept silently through the six courtyards until it found Master Wu Hung-lin's quarters. There it hovered, an invisible cloud sucking the air from the room. He awoke sweating, hardly able to breathe. Then a rash developed followed by a fever. By the time the physicians arrived, his face was covered with pustules, his body convulsing. By the time the doctors applied their balms, the *fa-shr* were called to exorcise the demon. Wu T'ai-po donned a mask and came to his son's bed. The Old Lady caressed her son, cradling him as only a mother could. Jasmine, Lotus and Orchid were called to pray to *Guan-yin* for their husband's recovery. His sons, Lin-kua and Chou-fa, burned prayer paper at the ancestral shrine. But the demon prevailed.

Master Wu Hung-lin breathed his last, never making it to year forty-four. It was then that Wu T'ai-po sent a message to the Ya-men that the wedding would proceed for the bride and dowry's sake. No sense breaking the contract or risking the bride's position in her own ancestral shrine. An unmarried woman lived a hard life and died an outcast. So Wu T'ai-po made the arrangements and sent Chi Lin the purple bouquet — the Purple Sage.

2

Chi Lin stepped over the threshold into the *ke-ting* to endure her Ghost Wedding. The groom would be there in spirit. She was happy his corpse was absent because she heard that in some cases families only regarded the ceremony sanctioned if the groom attended in the flesh — rotting stinking flesh. She had never seen Master Wu, but preferred to wed his effigy since she was compelled to seal the marriage bonds. As she crossed the threshold, she was overtaken by heavy jasmine aromas meant to purify the *ke-ting*. Haze veiled the few attendees, mostly *fa-shr* chanting prayers, sounding more funereal than celebratory. On a table sat a portrait of her husband — a fine painting destined for ash. White ribbons framed it. To Chi Lin's eyes Master Wu was comely and would have made a pleasant, but old, bed partner. But she would never know. A cockerel was caged beside the effigy — a white cockerel. It was drugged or it would have been pecking for freedom. A flame and wok would soon liberate it.

Paper pastries, shoes and a red silk bed were among the wedding presents set before the table. The priest presided, but in the shadows an old man sat beside an old woman.

"Daughter," the man croaked. "It is with mixed blessings we meet, but be assured you will be treated as my son's wife for as long as you breathe the Wu house's air."

Chi Lin was unsure of the meaning because, as the wife of a dead man, she would be denied his touch in bed and giving birth. Her purpose here, besides dowry and her own position in his ancestral temple, escaped her. Still she bowed, her hands deep beneath her crimson robe sleeves.

"You come of your free will," Wu T'ai-po stated.

"I do," Chi Lin replied.

"It is a good thing for your family that you do. *Guan-yin* smiles upon you today."

Chi Lin doubted that. She had prayed for two weeks and still she was here, voluntarily bound by the opinion that if she had not donned the bride's gown and come, she would lose her standing in family and community.

The Old Lady stood. She was stern, like a wood block left out in the rain. She marched to the Cockerel.

"My son awaits his bride," she snapped.

Chi Lin bowed. Her master may have been a ghost and his father, her benefactor, but this woman promised to be her whip if she did not please her. The Old Lady rattled the cage, the bird jumping beyond its dosage.

A plate of rice cakes and a cup sat beside the portrait. The priest, continuing his prayers, broke the rice cakes into crumbs, feeding them to the bird. Some crumbs were reserved, the Old Lady sweeping them into her brittle fingers.

"For you," she said to Chi Lin.

Chi Lin revealed her hands, taking the crumbs. They were dry on her lips and tasted awful. She had difficulty swallowing and suppressed a cough. Heaven watched, after all.

The priest lifted the cup, splashing the milky rice wine at the cockerel. The bird was not prepared for the bath and crowed — a morning call in the afternoon. As anticipated, the Old Lady took the cup, swished it, and then handed it to Chi Lin. She stared at this woman and imagined the commands that would come from this old festering head. Chi Lin was leaving a life of study and observation replaced now with her mother-in-law's unpredictable whims. If the Old Lady appeared easy or kind, Chi Lin would have dismissed concerns. But the Lady of the House had a cat's leer. With gnarled hands, she extended the cup.

"Drink," she commanded.

Chi Lin hesitated, drawing a leer from both the woman and the priest.

"Drink."

"No second thoughts, my daughter," Wu T'ai-po carped from his shadowy perch.

This was not a question, but a command. So Chi Lin took the cup and drank, but not too deeply.

3

The rest of the ceremony was swift and predictable. Chi Lin's hand was tied to the cage by a red silk cloth while the priest chanted the final rite. Drinking from the cup she became Master Wu's fourth wife, Purple Sage, the Ghost Bride. Where there should have been congratulations, there were death prayers. Where a feast would be attended by lusty friends of the groom, there were cold vegetables set out for the priests, which Chi Lin was invited to sample. Where the wedding presents would be shown to the household with pride, instead the effigy painting, the paper apparel and the silk bed were solemnly marched to the Wu ancestral hall, where Wu Hung-lin's two sons ceremonially burned each item and chanted prayers as the smoke brought the gifts to their father on high. The sons were coached carefully by their mother Jasmine since neither boy was old enough to know these things — Lin-kua being twelve and Chou-fa eleven. Upon seeing the new wife, they bowed, called her Auntie and went about their business. Jasmine, Lotus and Orchid smiled wanly, but did not offer congratulations. The only consolation was that this new wife would not contribute to the baby pool, and thus was a side dish to the household's main course.

From the beginning, Chi Lin felt like an outsider. Her father-in-law inspected her, grinning and nodding as if he would like to try her out. But he was a safe bet, old and bound by strict rules. The Old Lady ignored her at first, but then ordered three servants to escort her to an inner court — a barren pavilion within a moderate size courtyard. As Chi Lin walked over the sunless cobblestones, the Old Lady was carried beside her. Then they halted before the room.

"This will be your place for now," she snapped. "There is much to do and you shall do it. What you do not know, I shall instruct you. Remain here until you are summoned. You will find it pleasant enough, I am sure. You can improve it when you earn your place."

Chi Lin bowed. Questions bubbled to her mouth, but before she could express a single one, the Old Lady snapped her fan and the servants whisked the chair back through the gate, lost within the Wu estate.

Chi Lin sighed. She did not even have someone to help her out of the red gown. She slowly approached the verandah of the pavilion, climbed the stairs only to sit on a stone bench before the threshold waiting to muster the energy she needed to enter. She looked to the sky — gray sky now, pillaged by the occasional black cloud from the salt pots. Her hand sought the pond — an imaginary pool, which would have calmed her spirit, but her hand struck cold stone and nothing more.

"Remain here until summoned," she murmured.

Chi Lin could not summon her own legs to lift her off the bench to explore the room. She was never so lonely in life. She longed for her sister's nagging and her brother reciting the classics. Where were her father's patient supplications to Heaven and his wink to his daughter's beauty now? She wondered whether she would ever see her family again. Then, across the threshold scurried a curious creature — a short man dressed in gray, barefoot, with his eyes downcast to the cobblestones. He approached her quickly, bowed, and then crossed the threshold. She turned to the darkness inside the room. Suddenly, a lantern glowed within and she had light — light from a silent servant, who clattered about her quarters.

Chi Lin was no longer alone.

Chapter Four

The Hall of the Silver Silence

1

Chi Lin's first encounter with her new home was not happy. Nor was it curious, because there was not enough light inside the hall to fully show her the place. A small rope lamp was lit near a cabinet bed, which may have been best in quality in days past, but was surely threadbare, cloaked in tatters and draped in worn gauze. The barefoot man shuffled nearby trying to light a brazier. He paused, looking up at Chi Lin.

She was startled at his appearance. Old and squint-eyed, the servant twitched in his pause before continuing his attempts to light the fire. He briefly stopped to point at a low chest near the bed. Chi Lin approached it. Dusk's grey light streamed though a window illuminating another corner while her eyes adjusted. Soon the place was sufficiently revealed to depress her. It was a sad place, dust laden and fading. The walls were papered with wisteria flowers, but the buds had long been smudged with age. The plastered characters of past events were torn, crimson now violet, yellow now puce. The hall was redolent of sour grass and mold.

"See what the beauty has left you," croaked the old servant, still pointing at the chest.

"What beauty?" Chi Lin asked, cautiously

"The second wife," the servant replied.

"But the second wife lives."

"Not young Master Wu's second wife," the servant laughed. "Old Master Wu's second wife. She was called Peony."

"Where does she live now?" Chi Lin asked.

"Dead," the servant said. "We had hoped new life would come into the Hall of Silver Silence, but when young Master Wu died we knew that it would remain as it is." The servant turned toward Chi Lin, cocking his head. "My old woman said, *Lao Lao, when the new one comes, she will make do with what is there and no more.*"

"Lao Lao?"

"Lao Lao." The servant laughed, stood, and then bowed. "I am Lao Lao, mistress. Me and my old woman are your servants. We come attached to the Hall of Silver Silence. We are as fast here as the carpet and the bed. But look, look. See what the beauty has left you."

Chi Lin, puzzled by this curious servant, complied. She went to the chest, a cloth covered container closed with ivory fasteners. It was easy to unfasten the buttons through the loops, but the cover was stuck, most likely having been closed for a very long time. But Chi Lin managed, raising considerable dust in the effort. She was struck by the tantalizing aroma of camphor, and then realized the box contained neat stacks of apparel — robes, undergarments, vests and caps.

"These are for me?" she asked Lao Lao.

"For you, the wardrobe of the second wife."

"But will they fit?"

Lao Lao cocked his head again, examining Chi Lin's frame.

"It is hard to say until you remove your bridal vestments, but you appear to be the same in stature."

Suddenly, the bride's clothing was oppressive — more so than before. She longed to shed them.

"Is your old woman about, Lao Lao?"

"She is, but will not come today." Lao Lao paused, rubbing his hands. "She is worse on some days than on others. Today she remains on her mat."

Chi Lin was sad for this woman she had not met, but wondered how a servant so unwell could remain in service. She shrugged her shoulders.

"I can help," Lao Lao said.

"You are a man and not my husband."

"Your husband is a ghost. He will be of no use except to watch over you in the night. And I am an old man and have seen many things — many things indeed, none of which can stir me now. I am as safe as a child."

"But would it be fitting, Lao Lao?"

"Who is to say and who is to see. You will not see the Old Lady of the House in this place, and Master T'ai-po is saddened by this pavilion. Too many memories. It is less fitting for a father-in-law to come to his daughter-in-law's dwelling than an old fart of a servant to play the help maiden to the mistress of the Silver Silence."

Lao Lao laughed, but then bowed. Chi Lin sighed, but began to disrobe.

"Choose for me something suitable for bed," she said.

"These are fine garments, mistress," he said. "The sleeping attire is already laid out at bedside."

She looked and it was true. A faded blue silk shirt and short-skirt were neatly folded beneath the overhang. She supposed they belonged to the second wife also.

"Also hers?" she asked.

"Everything in this place, mistress, belonged to Peony — Mistress Hung Hua," he replied. "The other wives would not touch them — ghost clothing that they are. But a ghost bride is welcomed to them."

Chi Lin felt angry at this. Was she to be relegated to the realm of the dead? Would she live her days in this house as a rejected specter?

She let the bridal robe drop and stepped over the heap. She did not care now who saw her, her shift also dropping. She heard Lao Lao gathering the fallen garments, but she did not see whether he properly cared for them. *She* did not care. As far as she was concerned he could burn them in the brazier. She would never wear them again. She tossed the veil, which had been tacked over her shoulders, to the floor. The mice could gnaw at it for all she cared. She reached for the sleeping garments — rich and fine beneath her hand — a crimson rose embroidered along the hem. The silk slipped on with ease. It was a perfect fit.

"I shall inspect the contents of the box tomorrow, Lao Lao," she said. "Secure it, if you please."

Lao Lao rattled to the box, closed the lid, and then secured the bone ties.

"It will be good to see these garments walk again, mistress," he said. "My old woman had maintained them well — skilled as she was with the needle and thread."

"And now?"

"Now is the time that winter touches our hands and heads. She is as white as I have become. And she is blind. I often ask her to use the bell when she comes and goes, but she is afraid the Old Lady of the House will be distressed and turn her out to beg."

"That would be cruel," Chin Lin said, sitting at the edge of the bed.

"It may happen yet. *You* may want to send her away. You may want to send *me* away also."

"Why would I do that when you are the only voice I may hear in the world of ghosts, as you tell me?"

"My old woman's cooking is not good any more, as you will taste; and when she does attend you, she might step on your toes."

"I am more tolerant than most people, Lao Lao. This place distresses me, but do you see me making a fuss?"

"A fuss?" Lao Lao said as he folded the bridal robes. "If you want to see a fuss, you should see the other wives. They hate me and ignore my old woman. The first wife does not address us, nor should she, but the other two remain like painted dolls in their pavilions, demanding fine food and other dainties. That is why they only managed daughters."

"They managed a husband's touch, Lao Lao. I shall not have as much."

Lao Lao bowed deeply.

"Forgive Lao Lao, mistress. My tongue has no mind and speaks without thinking."

"It does not matter," Chi Lin replied. "Second and third wives are always baubles."

"Fourth wives also, mistress, when they have their feet crammed into golden lotus slippers. Lotus and Orchid need help standing. They walk on a cloud. Give me a full footed maid. Give me . . ." He stopped, staring at Chi Lin's feet. "Again, my tongue, mistress."

"Your tongue is loose, but it says truth. My feet will allow me to get about."

"Your feet will force you to work, mistress. That is the way of this place. The Old Lady of the House likes industry within these walls. The first wife is exempt. Sons, you know. The other two are hobbled. So I am sure you will be assigned tasks. It is the way of the place."

Chi Lin reflected on this miserable servant. He was like a history book. Although honest and, in that honesty, brutal, he might prove a keynote to the way of this place. She longed for her old life and her father's gentle voice, her brother's industrious study and even her nagging sister. But there was nothing she could do. She was destined to this fading hall, the dusty bed, the makeshift fire and the one open window to the world, unless she regarded Lao Lao as a second window, one that she wanted to shutter now.

"I am weary, Lao Lao." she said. "I would sleep."

"Shake the clacker if you need me or my old woman," he said pointing to the rattle hooked to the bed.

"Thank you," she said.

Suddenly, Lao Lao's face brightened — a man not having been thanked in an age, now kneeling before a new mistress, one who might ease his mind in his dotage.

2

Dreams would not come for Chi Lin, weariness having taken her within seconds of clamping her neck into the headrest. When she awoke, it was still dark and she thought she saw a strange creature near the bed cabinet. In the scant light she recognized the form as old and bent, perhaps Lao Lao again. But when the creature tripped and stumbled about emitting low curses to the shadows, Chi Lin knew it must be Lao Lao's old woman. A bitter odor drifted to the bed. Chi Lin hoped it was not the food being shuffled to the table. Perhaps it was old-lady smell. But soon, after the woman departed, the odor lingering, Chi Lin realized it was breakfast.

She sat bedside, her feet dangling, still hoping that this was a dream that would not come. Yet as the sun rose, the gray light filtering through the window gauze, Chi Lin knew the Silver Silence Hall was her legacy — the inheritance for the Purple Sage. She hopped to the low table, peering into a watery bowl of sorghum, dotted with shattered plums. Beside this was a kettle of water and a tea bowl, the leaves strewn in the depths.

"I could not eat that," she said, sniffing the porridge.

He nose wrinkled. The sight of it offended her. She was accustomed to rice congee — nothing rich, but rolled carefully by Chi Tsai and poked with cinnamon sticks. This slop was clearly stewed by a sightless woman, who might have lost her sense of smell also. Chi Lin took a cloth and covered it. The tea would do. She poured the water into the bowl and waited for the leaves to steep. This was an accommodation, because the ceremony of boiling the leaves was a ritual observed in her father's house. She would teach it to the old lady or assume the tea duties herself. But this would do for now. Perhaps Lao Lao could fetch a steamed bun when he made an appearance.

While Chi Lin waited, she peered through the window. A pool stood at a distance — a lotus pool with no lotus, just weeds and broken tiles. She wondered if it held water. Then from a hovel near the courtyard wall, Lao Lao emerged, went to the pool, opened his robes and performed his morning relief.

"More than water in there," Chi Lin muttered, and sighed. "No ducks either."

The tea was ready. She took it quickly, and then went to the clothes box to select the attire for the day. In the morning brightness, she explored an array of fine garments, each more beautiful than the next. She had never been one for finery, but she supposed as a married woman in a monopoly holder's house, she would need to be presentable. Her eyes caught a turquoise jacket with matching skirt and shawl. A robe would surely be within. It would suit for today, although she wondered who would pin her hair, her sister having done that for her all her life. She could manage it, if she could find a brush and varnish.

"Mistress," came a voice on the threshold. "My old woman shall help you dress and adorn your hair."

Chi Lin turned about seeing Lao Lao and the old creature he called his wife. She was huddled over a cane, her rheumy eyes squinting about the hall perhaps looking for her new mistress.

"Approach," Chi Lin said. "Let me see you."

The old woman tripped, tapping the cane before her, looking about until she spied Chi Lin. She smiled, and then bowed.

"Have you selected, mistress?" she croaked. "Or shall I do it."

"You could not see the box," Lao Lao chided. "But you can manage buttons and hair."

Chi Lin smiled and reached for the old woman, who shied at the touch.

"I am too low for such kindness, mistress," she said, and then looked over at the table. "Was the porridge to your liking?"

"I shall have some later," Chi Lin said, as brightly as she could. "The tea served well. And . . . and if there is a steamed bun, that would be fine as well."

"We can do that," the old woman stammered. "I can get the basket going. But what have you decided to wear? You will be summoned for sure after you pay your respects."

"Stop bothering the mistress," Lao Lao snapped. "Help her dress. I will fetch the hair things."

Chi Lin stood near the box, while the old woman rustled through the jacket and skirt, muttering what sounded like *her favorite, I remember. Her favorite.*

"Lao Lao, what is meant by *being summoned*?"

"You will have household chores. The Old Lady of the House will speak to you for sure and tell you what is expected. It is not for me to guess."

"And paying my respects?"

"To your husband, mistress."

"You must burn the incense and red paper," the old woman muttered as she slipped the undershirt over Chi Lin's head. "It is a daily thing that you do, no doubt. But we have never had a ghost bride in the House of Wu, so I can only say what I have heard."

"She thinks she knows everything," Lao Lao said. "It is a fault you will need to come to know and forgive, I hope."

Chi Lin spun about as the jacket and skirt jostled on her. The garments were far from straight, so she had to snug them while the old woman sought slippers and robe. The robe would make the entire ensemble hot, but if she was to be summoned, she needed to look her best. She was pleased with the garments and her old dresser amused her, drawing her from darker thoughts.

"Do you have a name?" she asked the old woman.

"I have one. Do not bother your head about it. I come when you call."

"But when I call, who should I call?"

The old woman laughed.

"Just wave and say, *Come, you* and I shall manage to come, if I can see my way clear."

"Which she cannot," Lao Lao added, bringing the brushes and pins.

"But I must call you something."

The old lady sighed.

"Snapdragon," she said. "You can call me Snapdragon, if you need a name."

Lao Lao laughed.

"That is nicer than the flowers I recall."

The banter continued, while Chi Lin's thought drifted. She felt the brittle touch of Snapdragon's fingers through her hair, the bun being formed, and the varnish applied. The first pins stuck true, grazing her scalp, making her wonder how her head would appear.

She was quite surprised when Lao Lao lifted a hand mirror showing her his old woman's blind handiwork. Chi Lin looked presentable — more than presentable.

"A jewel perhaps," Chi Lin muttered.

"There are hair baubles, mistress," Lao Lao said. "But I would not advise it."

"Not on the first day," Snapdragon whistled. "The Old Lady of the House is fussy about such things and must approve what dangles from your quills."

"And face paint is not encouraged," Lao Lao said. "When a rouge pot is sent to the hall, it will be sign enough for what you may smear. Besides, you are too pretty to wear a mask."

"Is she?" Snapdragon asked.

"She is, but to say more will incite Heaven to jealousy."

Chi Lin laughed. She was ready to venture into the bleak courtyard and pay her respects to her husband, a ritual she would perform every day for the rest of her life.

Chapter Five

Husband and Mother-in-law

1

Chi Lin knelt on the temple cushion before the ancestral shrine. Wu Hung-lin's effigy was newly planted beside a prayer scroll to the Jade Emperor. The incense had burned out overnight, but the sharp orange blossom aroma still lingered. The brazier burned low although maintained by the shrine attendant, whose sole job was to manage the shrine. He was nowhere to be found, but somehow Chi Lin felt his eyes watching from behind a rock blind. Chi Lin clapped three times, and then bowed, first to *Guan-yin*, and then to the Household god, who was Wu Xin-fei, an ancestor from Tang times, a great scholar and courtier, who first brought wealth to the house by marrying a Li princess of the twelfth degree and receiving a dowry enough to build a home south of the capital. Many Wu ancestors followed in Wu Xin-fei's footsteps, a long line of obedient sons to the Empire, both the native one and the foreign invaders. Such history Chi Lin knew because her father was insistent that she learn it before crossing the Wu threshold, but she cared little for it. She only bowed out of respect. Perhaps the old patron god might be on her side when the rest of the family ignored her.

Chi Lin reached for a joss stick, lit it in the brazier, and then tucked it in the sand before her husband's totem. She bowed and clapped, and then burned the red paper prayer with the hope the sentiments arose to his soul in Heaven. She squinted through the smoke to observe his portrait. She had seen a similar one well enough during the brief ceremony, but the room was dark then and the white cockerel a noisy pest. Now that she had a quiet moment to reflect, she could see her husband's features were comely. He was older than she; much older. But if he had lived, he would have demanded sons and she would have complied. He was not so old and withered to be shunned in bed. She would have welcomed him freely and without regret. Yes, he was a handsome man; mature, but a maiden's delight.

Chi Lin sighed.

"My lord," she whispered. "I fear because you are gone and I am a ghost bride, my place has been set aside. If you could speak to your noble ancestors on my behalf, I would be most obliged. We were both denied the marriage bed, but I would have given you many sons. To show you this, I live here and honor your parents as my parents, and come to your shrine to thank you for choosing me as wife."

Chi Lin bowed, burned another red paper prayer, and then clapped three times. Suddenly, she felt she was being watched. Perhaps by the shrine keeper. She turned to see two black marble eyes staring at her. It was a girl, perhaps three or four *sui* in age, looking up, her head resting on folded arms.

"You pray?" she asked.

"Yes," Chi Lin replied, cocking her head.

"They say you are the ghost bride," the girl said, cocking *her* head to match Chi Lin's. "I have never seen a ghost bride."

"Now you have," Chi Lin replied. "Are you lost?"

"No. I live here. I am Pearl. My mama is called Lotus."

"Does she know you are here?"

"I come here sometimes to smell the smoke. She does not care. The *amah* watches me and my sisters. She does not care either."

Chi Lin shuffled to her feet, approaching Pearl. But the girl darted to the rock blind.

"I will not hurt you," Chi Lin said.

"But you are a ghost," Pearl replied. "They say ghosts eat little girls."

"I am a ghost bride." She pointed to Wu Hung-lin's portrait. "There is the ghost."

"That is papa." Pearl frowned and shook her head. "He died. He was nice to me. He came to our hall and mama would sing for him. He would laugh and tickle us." She frowned again. "But he died."

"Yes, Pearl. I am his bride but have never met him. You must tell me more about him."

"But you are a ghost."

"Do not bother Mistress Purple Sage," snapped a high pitched voice from behind her.

Chi Lin turned. Standing there was a tall woman in a stately robe, but had unadorned hair and a servant's badge, three gray ribbons sweeping from her right shoulder. She bowed to Chi Lin, and then stepped closer to Pearl.

"Child, where is your *amah*?"

"She is asleep. She is always asleep except to feed us."

"She should be more attentive to your doings," the woman said. "You should not be conversing with your elders. You should be learning to sew with your sister."

"It hurts my fingers, and you are an elder. You speak to me all the time."

"Enough."

"She meant no harm," Chi Lin said.

"She never does, but must learn her place. Children can grow wild and, in this household, they seem to do so,"

"My brothers are wild," Pearl objected. "They do anything they want."

"But they do not bother Mistress Purple Sage."

"They would," Pearl said. "But they are afraid of ghosts."

Pearl stood tall, bowed to Chi Lin, and then scurried away.

"She meant no harm," Chi Lin said, bowing to the woman.

"No need to bow to me," the woman said, pointing to her badge. "I am Willow, and nothing more than the Old Lady of the House's maid. She sent me to fetch you. Come."

Willow turned brusquely about and walked to the courtyard gate. Chi Lin quickly looked to her husband's effigy, nodded, and then followed at a near trot.

2

As Chi Lin followed Willow through four courtyards, each busy with servants, energetic in their work, each nodding to the ghost bride as she passed, she was not sure how to respond, so she returned the nod not wanting to insult any one. She also noticed the careful landscaping in these courtyards, nothing like the shambles of her own courtyard. The pools were pristine, water flowing over rock hides; buckets of cabbage plants and tea flowers were carefully placed along cleanly swept walkways. The Halls were laced with wisteria and trumpet flowers. The entrances sported wood carved plaques heralding their names — Blue Heaven, Crimson Blossom, Golden Oak and, finally, and the most prominent, Jade Heart.

"Look smart, mistress, if you please," Willow said over her shoulder. "We approach the Hall of the Jade Heart where the Old Lady resides with the Master."

"Will she see me?" Chi Lin asked.

"She may, if she is so inclined. But if she does not, I will instruct you in the days work."

Chi Lin said no more. The Old Lady of the House was a queen within these walls. If she was moved to give an audience to a fourth wife — a ghost bride, she would order it. If not, she would allocate her message to someone else. Chi Lin thought if she entered this hall and did not to see her mother-in-law it would be a slight of tremendous proportions. Willow perhaps was trained to answer questions concerning the great lady's schedule without commitment. It was not Willow's place to make commitments.

The threshold was being scrubbed by a plain servant, a man of strength. But he hid his face, so Chi Lin was unable to assess his age. He immediately curled into a subservient ball to allow Willow to pass. He muttered something to Chi Lin, but she could not make it out.

Inside, she was overcome by the fresh smell of lavender. It was too potent to ease her to thinking sweet things about her mother-in-law. It evoked sanitation and sterility. Her eyes squinted in the dim hall, looking for a throne or a magnificent chair. Instead she saw four women sitting in a circle, sewing. Willow left her at the edge of this circle.

Silence prevailed, until . . .

"So you have come to work," the Old Lady of the House said from her seat in the circle. The women were mending sandals, their fingers accosting the soles deftly. "Do you mend shoes?"

Chi Lin was not sure this question was meant for her. She hesitated until the old woman looked up, frowning.

"I have never done so, mother to my husband," she replied.

The woman shook her head, pointing to another woman, the one beside her. They were all serving women as Chi Lin could reckon by their shoulder badges. That woman stood, bowed, and then withdrew. The old one pointed to the chair.

"You begin now," she snapped.

Chi Lin took her position beside her mother-in-law, who thrust a small red shoe into her hands.

"Your father was remiss to not have someone teach you to sew sandals," she snapped. "But no matter. Look here." She took the needle hook to her own red shoe, poking it into the last. "You push in and pull out, loop twice, and then pull out again. Tighten and . . . no, no. Give it here." She repeated her sentence frowning at the remaining servants, who sported grins. "You try again."

Chi Lin followed the old woman's example, but missed the second loop.

"I will learn well, mother," she said.

"You will practice, but . . ." The woman looked to the servants. "About your business. There are tables to repair and chairs to straw."

The two servants put their shoe work aside and disappeared into the hall's shadows. The old woman grumbled, but snapped the shoe from Chi Lin's hands.

"There is plenty of work for you and much to learn."

"Yes, mother of the husband."

"Yes, remember that. You are a useless acquisition, but it was not your fault the demons crossed our threshold and took my son to *the Yellow Springs*. Still, you will not contribute a son and that was your intended purpose. Jasmine has produced heirs and has the place of honor below me. Lotus has given us expense — daughters, as has Orchid. But both are baubles in this house, acquired for pleasure, for a man's jaundiced eye. They served their purpose, but are now an expense. They are tiny hoofed and cannot work. But you, Purple Sage, you are full footed and look strong enough. Your dowry was meager, but was acceptable in the contract. Still, a barren wife can be nothing more than a chore mistress and an auntie to her husband's other children. So you shall earn your keep."

"I understand, mother of my husband."

"You will honor him every day, learn to sew and mend furniture, assist with daily meals and, when the time comes, act as go-between for tenants and the master's rule of law."

"I understand, mother of my husband."

"No need to understand what you must do because you must earn your keep. But you are my son's wife, and so, unlike the servants, you will have respect, although you are the lowest member of the household. You know it to be true." She reached beside her chair into a small satchel. "Here."

The old woman withdrew four silver ingots placing them in Chi Lin's hands. Chi Lin bowed, touching the shiny buttons to her forehead.

"The Hall of Silver Silence is in disarray. Your husband meant for it to be repaired and made comfortable for his wife. Use these wisely, because you cannot expect more. You may also wear a purple flower in your hair and a *tzi-jing* jewel in your pins — only one, and a small one. I would prefer you wear purple robes, but I suppose you must make due with Peony's cast-offs, so I shall tolerate other colors."

Chi Lin bowed again.

"Now, try again to sew the slipper, Purple Sage and by night fall you will have mastered the first of many chores."

Chi Lin squirreled the silver ingots into her sash purse, picked up the slipper and tried again. By nightfall, her hands would be blistered and her back sore, but she would master the first of her many chores.

Chapter Six

Evening Shades and Shadows

1

It was a long day with few breaks in the sewing for Chi Lin. Lao Lao's old woman came quietly to the threshold to deliver a steam bun, which was brought to Chi Lin, who dared not stop to eat it until her mother-in-law set her own work aside to tend to the kitchen staff. By that time Chi Lin's belly sang a rumbling tune, which the steam bun hardly quelled. It also confirmed that Lao Lao's old woman needed lessons in steaming buns. A light repast from a different quarter was brought, no doubt on the Old Lady of the House's orders — jasmine rice with plums, a small ration of mashed pork and a sliver of bitter melon. It was much to Chi Lin's delight and she ate it like a serving girl, which quite fit the moment. When her mother-in-law returned, she chastised Chi Lin lightly for not finishing the shoes allotted. This did not discourage the woman, because she ordered another basket of sandals for mending. She also delivered a constant lecture on the quality of the stitches and how, in time, Chi Lin would need to embroider lion faces and lotus blossoms on the children's shoes — an art to be sure, but one she would be expected to master. Between the craft talk came the reminder that she was a ghost bride and needed to earn her way, expense that she was. Soon this mantra was lost on Chi Lin. She could think of nothing more than the four silver ingot buttons hidden in her sash purse and the improvements she could wrought on her living quarters with such a sum. It offered hope.

At one point, the other women returned from their furniture mending and continued sewing — robe tatting, sash hemming and cap refinements as well as the never ending shoe and sandal mend. *How many feet did this household have?* Chi Lin thought. But they all ceased working when the Master of the House, Wu T'ai-po, visited the work hall, mumbling his greetings, but ignoring their work as men were disposed to do. He stared for some time at Chi Lin, her face demure and downcast. He inspected her with eyes only, no words exchanged, not even with his wife. Silence spoke louder to the occasion. He came to see his daughter-in-law but it was not seemly for him to speak with her, so he just made her uncomfortable, and then nodded to his wife, leaving just as spontaneously as he had arrived.

By nightfall, Chi Lin was alone with another cup of rice and three ripe cherries, carefully eating them, avoiding any stain to the shoe cloth. Then Willow appeared to escort her back to the Hall of Silver Silence, where she was met on the threshold by Lao Lao and his wife. A modest meal sat near the cabinet bed — more steamed buns, bean curd and a bowl of cabbage. Chi Lin was too hungry and tired to be bothered with it. She was hot and sweaty, wishing a basin of water more than slimy cabbage and bean curd.

"Lao Lao," she said.

"Yes, mistress."

"Is there water?"

"Boiled on the table."

"Not to drink, but to bathe."

"Is that wise, mistress? It is not a bathing day."

She turned, and sighed. Lao Lao bowed, disappeared over the threshold and soon returned with a basin of water and two lotus pods. He set the bowl near the bed, and then retired.

Chi Lin stared into the water, the light reflecting her tired face. It was clean water, not drawn from that dirty pool. She wondered about the source and how it might be made more available. At this thought, she retrieved the silver ingots, rolling them between her fingers. She decided the first repair would be to the pool. It would be a reminder of home and the duck pond she loved so. Gazing at the silver she had many thoughts for its use. Perhaps a floor rug and a place to keep her hair brush, a dressing table perhaps. The walls could use some new paper and beadwork; and the bed, mending. It creaked. The underbox was useless for storage and there was a crack in the cabinet leg. As she examined that crack, she cocked her head. She expected a cricket or mouse to emerge, but then she had a thought.

"It will do," she said.

She took the four ingots and wedged them into the crack until they disappeared from sight. She then turned to her bath, dipping the lotus pods into the basin, the chilly water caressing her hands.

Chi Lin slipped her robe down halfway and opened her sash. Peony's blouse was hot and sticky and peeled off like a second skin, exposing her breasts to the dim light. The air felt good — delightful. She splashed some water on her chest and squeezed the dripping pods over her cleavage — refreshing and invigorating. She closed her eyes as she rubbed herself, dreaming of a place where she could have been instead of the place where she was now. The pods were her consolation, the husband who would never touch her. It was a maiden's dream, a poor one, but fleeting as the cool water rolled between her breasts.

Suddenly, she heard giggling. Her eyes flashed open to see small heads peering through the window — three little girls and two not so little boys. Chi Lin dropped the pods and pulled up her blouse.

"Why are you here?" she snapped.

The children giggled. One, a boy of eleven, reached in, his hands outstretched.

"We come to say hello," he said, while the others laughed.

"It is not proper at your age."

"How are we to learn about ladies if we cannot see them without their robes?" the other one quipped.

Chi Lin stood, holding her robe tenaciously.

"Go. Shoo. It is not proper."

The boys disappeared, but the girls remained. She recognized Pearl and assumed the other two were her sisters.

"We can watch," said a squat-nosed tot (not Pearl). "We are not boys."

"No," Chi Lin said. "It is not proper."

Suddenly, the girls' heads careened about, terror in their eyes. They gurgled, and then disappeared. Chi Lin was glad to see them go, although on some level their behavior amused her. But she was puzzled by the fierce look on their faces as they departed. Then she heard a different sound. *Clopping*. An approaching horse.

Lao Lao appeared on the threshold, bowing curtly, and then quickly approaching.

"Go, Lao Lao," Chi Lin said. "I am not finished my bath."

"Yes, mistress, you must finish it now. It is over. He comes."

"Who comes?"

Lao Lao came closer.

"Liang-tze," he whispered. "The second son. You must be careful."

"Why?"

Lao Lao set the basin aside and dared to pulled Chi Lin's robes closed tight.

"He is to be watched with care, mistress. He is the Tiger of the Wu clan and . . ."

Chi Lin was confused, but had little time to listen to an explanation. The Tiger was on her threshold.

2

Wu Liang-tze stepped over the threshold and stood in the dim light. Chi Lin nodded her head, but quickly raised it again to see this man, her brother-in-law, who came unwelcome to her hall. He was dressed in black leather riding trousers and a short robe. A sword was slung haphazardly from his belt. He wore a dark blue turban, a throwback from an earlier time. Chi Lin could see the resemblance to her husband, but also a crucial difference. While Wu Hung-lin's portrait displayed a gentle countenance, kind in most respects, Wu Liang-tze squinted and boded peril beneath his mustached lip. He exposed grim teeth, less tiger than dog.

"I have come," he said, his voice raspy, a defect groomed from shouting orders, no doubt. "It is my right to inspect my brother's bride."

Chi Lin stood, and then bowed.

"It is late, brother-in-law. Is this proper?"

"Do not speak of propriety to me, ghost bride. You are fortunate that I speak to you at all." He strode to the table and glanced at the cabbage and bean curd. "Peasant food, I see. I suspected my brother lowered his sights with this choice. But no matter. He is dead and you are baked into our walls." He laughed, and then turned to Lao Lao. "Why can I see your face, servant?"

Lao Lao crouched into a ball. Liang-tze picked at a piece of curd, tasted it, and then spit it at the servant.

"I am sure you are welcomed to eat my lowly repast," Chi Lin said.

"My dogs eat better." He cocked his head and inspected her. "Why not open your robe so I may see what my brother never saw."

"Please," she said. "It is not proper."

"Perhaps not. But who are you to say, ghost bride?" His eyes swept to the floor. "Big feet. The other two wives are dainty footed, to my delight, now that I can entertain them with my wit and good looks. But a big footed peasant girl is not much to my fancy. But my brother was not one to chose without reason. What special gift have you brought?"

"Just my dowry, brother-in-law."

"No jewels or serving ladies?" He peered at the clothes chest. "I know that piece. Is that all you harbor here? Peony's cast offs? I would not touch those because she would haunt me as she haunts my mother. But surely my brother had intended to repair this old heap of a ruin. Come, come. Where is it?"

Chi Lin shivered. He wanted her silver ingots? How did he know about them? She cast her eyes down, but away from the crevice in the bed post.

"I have no such gift, brother-in-law. I am as you see me."

"But I do not see you. Uncover. I demand it. Uncover, at once."

Chi Lin felt a cold shiver run through her spine. She dared not defy this man, a man to whom she just favored with a lie. He appeared a dangerous sort. He could beat her and throw her out naked in the courtyard and no punishment would be meted to the second son of the Master of the House. So, slowly she let the robe fall, and slipped the under blouse away allowing her breasts to become a feast for his eyes.

The tiger growled, his hands just short of touching her. But he stopped and turned to the servant.

"You," he shouted. "Open the chest and dump it out."

Lao Lao fidgeted with the bone slips, and then lifted the cover. He then began to toss Peony's clothing to the floor, while Liang-tze rumbled through them looking for Chi Lin's treasure. When he came to a small jewel box, he carefully opened it, expecting something wonderful, but frowned.

"Peony's," he grumbled. "My brother is a disappointment." He threw the box at Lao Lao, and then turned to Chi Lin, who was shaking now. "He indeed left you with nothing more than this old shit house and the second wife's underwear. I would pity you, except you will thrive here, no doubt once you have earned your keep. My mother is stern, but fair. She will insist on keeping up appearances, which will benefit your sagging breasts and your peasant feet. Cover up!"

Chi Lin quickly pulled the robe up and shrank away to the window. Wu Liang-tze snarled at Lao Lao, but knew better than to strike him. Purple Sage may be to his disliking, but she was the fourth wife and deserved this lowly old piss ant to wait upon her.

Liang-tze nodded to her.

"I leave you, sister-in-law . . . for now."

She curtsied as he marched to the threshold. He paused, looked back, and then spat. The tiger was gone.

3

Chi Lin collapsed to the bed, weeping. Lao Lao did not console her, but managed the clothing into neat stacks and reclosed the chest. When he turned to his mistress, she was kneeling on the floor, her hand poking into a chink in the bed cabinet.

"Mistress," Lao Lao said. "He is a brute. We are lucky he does not live here, but in the Villa. He was tossed out when Master Hung-lin married Mistress Jasmine." Lao Lao's eyes rolled. "He could not be trusted in the house. He is a rover. He has three wives, but I suspect they never see him. In the tavern, they say, he is always at the House of Perfumed Beauty or the Sojourn of Heaven's Eye. Two of his wives came from the pleasure houses. I am surprised he does not have twelve wives from . . ."

"Please, Lao Lao. This is indelicate."

"Yes, mistress, but true. You must know to beware the man. Be glad, for now, that he does not like your breasts and despises your big feet." Lao Lao suddenly frowned, and then bowed. "Forgive me."

Chi Lin smiled. This servant was refreshing in his honesty, but pitiful in his embarrassing statements.

"I am glad also for my big feet, and not just for warding off the attentions of my brother-in-law." Her hand favored the bedstead cranny. "He is unpleasant. I am glad he does not live here."

"Mistress," Lao Lao said. "If that break in your bed is bothersome, I will have it repaired tomorrow morning."

"No," she said. "No. It is fine." She smiled. "In fact, I am of glad of it, because I *have* had a gift from my husband."

"Truly?"

"Our secret, Lao Lao. Our secret."

"Who would I tell? My old lady?"

"Tell no one, but I will be able to afford some repairs, beginning with the rock pool."

"I would begin with the roof, mistress."

Chi Lin looked up. The roof looked fine to her.

"The rock pool would give me some place to relax after chores."

"But when it rains, you will be glad that the roof has been repaired."

She laughed. This man knew the state of things better than she did. Some silver must be reserved for roof repairs. She patted the crevice, and then stood.

"I am weary. Very weary. And tomorrow will be as wearisome."

"You must sleep, mistress. You can tell me of your great plans tomorrow."

"The plans must evolve slowly, Lao Lao. Slowly. If my courtyard and hall are suddenly beautified, what would my brother-in-law think?"

"He would think you were not truthful."

"He would buzz about me like a bee on a flower. I must remain humble, quiet and unattractive to his eye."

Lao Lao grinned.

"You are like her, mistress. Most like her."

"Who?"

"Second wife Peony," he said. "But take care in that resemblance, because the Old Lady of the House *is* haunted by her. In that the second son spoke the truth, and he mostly lies and does not care who knows it."

Lao Lao bowed out of the hall. Chi Lin sat for some time, despite her weariness, starring out the window. Finally, she finished undressing and gathered Peony's bed clothing loosely about her shoulders. With her noggin laid back on the porcelain pillow rest, she closed her eyes.

"Father, how I miss you," she whispered, and then visited home in her dreams.

Chapter Seven

The Crawl of Industry

1

When Chi Lin awoke after a restless sleep, her fingers pained beyond belief. The tips were sore and unfendered. She crabbed them to the daylight and wondered whether she could hold a needle again. But she needed to earn her place. Complaints would be unacceptable. Beyond the needle pricks, her head still dwelled on the ugly face of her brother-in-law and his untoward intentions, which were unclear, beyond fleecing her of her meager household silver. To that she had more thoughts, agreeing that the roof would be a priority. If she improved the interior of the hall, it would be quite useless if ruined in the first heavy rainfall. The pool could wait. She exercised her fingers — her aching fingers.

"Wake up," she said. "You must keep alive for my mother-in-law."

She laughed, but then sighed. The ubiquitous bowl of morning mush was waiting on the table beside the tea bowl. Her thoughts again went to her brother-in-law's visit, the ugliness of his face and the blackness of his mood. While her prospects were not bright in the House of Wu, the chance visitation of Wu Liang-tze was terrifying. She could not mention it to anyone for fear they would think her disrespectful to the second son, and yet his reputation was such she was sure any complaint would fall on sympathetic ears. Yet no one would help her against this frightener of women and children. He was the second son, after all, and was curbed by few protocols.

"I must live with it," she said, getting up and heading for the morning congee and tea.

After eating and dressing, she wondered where Lao Lao was. Perhaps his constant presence was a short-lived thing — the first days with a new mistress, and then only when summoned. But she knew the way to the ancestral shrine. So without further assistance, she poked through the dawn's light into the courtyard and made her way to greet her husband. Perhaps she could report his brother's conduct and he could tell the other ancestors. They could curb Liang-tze of his ways if banded together in a ghostly dream.

But she was sure Wu Hung-lin knew his brother's wicked ways already. Was not Liang-tze removed from the main household, not to be trusted with the other wives?

Chi Lin burned incense first to Guan-yin, and then to the household god. She was careful not to spill ash on her purple robes because she wore them today as a courtesy to her mother-in-law's wishes. She even had the small purple gem dangling from her hair pins. She clapped three times, and then bowed to her husband's totem.

"I have come again, my lord," she said. "But you can see that I have. In your bright eyes I hope I am acceptable. I will regale your spirit as long as I have breath and will honor your name." She clapped again, and then burned red paper prayers. She knew she was being watched, this time by two sets of small eyes. "If it pleases you, my lord, breathe your healing *ch'i* upon my aching fingers so I might please your mother in the work. I did my best yesterday, but I fear that pain might steal away my zest today." She bowed again. "And may you keep your spirit fixed upon your daughters who come to spy upon me." She turned abruptly to the two girls. "Pearl. I see you are no longer afraid of the ghost bride."

Pearl moved closer, but the other one hid her eyes.

"I have brought my sister Jade to see you."

"But she saw me last night," Chi Lin replied. "Am I more fearsome when dressed and in your father's presence."

"He is dead," Jade said. "Are you dead too?"

"Do I look dead?"

"I cannot tell," Jade replied.

"She is not dead, silly," Pearl said. "You saw her last night washing her bonies. Ghosts do not have bonies, you know."

"How do you know?" Jade asked. "You do not have bonies."

"Neither do you. Are you are ghost?"

Jade stuck out her tongue at Pearl, but suddenly paused. Her eyes grew wide. Pearl turned also, and both girls scurried away. Chi Lin knew that Willow had arrived.

2

"Purple Sage," Willow said, as she escorted Chi Lin through the courtyards. "Today you will visit the First Wife, Mei Lo, who is called Jasmine. You will see her in the Blue Heaven Hall."

"Am I to sew today?" Chi Lin asked.

"Perhaps. If my mistress commands it. But she wishes you to meet Jasmine and learn about the Silk *ji-tzao*, which all women of the house must learn and attend."

Chi Lin grinned. Perhaps her fingers would be spared today. She wanted to make so bold to ask Willow a question, but then remembered that Willow was a servant and not to be obeyed except when issuing the Old Lady of the House's commands. So Chi Lin became bold.

"Do you work with the silk also?"

Willow did not answer at first. Then she halted, and turned, bowing slightly and grinning.

"I know the art and have practiced it since my childhood. Now, not so much, because my mistress has deemed me worthy of attending her. But even my mistress has worked with the silk. It is an enterprise central to the house. All the tenants have silk *ji-tzao* and send two thirds of their cocoons here for reeling to subsidize their requirements for the salt *ji-tzao*. Salt and silk." She bowed. "Yes, it is salt and silk in this house. None are exempt. All work for the benefit of the monopoly."

"Thank you," Chi Lin replied.

Willow turned again, progressing through the courtyards. She remained silent. Chi Lin asked no more questions.

The yards were busy — sweepers and toters, planters and scrubbers. Men servants rushed about with baskets, while maids hastened with bed linens and clothing, some for the main hall, while others rushed to the halls of the three wives. Chi Lin saw workmen repairing flagstones and recalled that her quarters needed the most repairs. The task would be daunting. She remembered the young worker from yesterday who caught her attention as he repaired the threshold, although she did not glimpse his face. However, she thought she saw a man of his stature crossing the main courtyard. He was tall and muscular. He had a manner about him that was distinguished as if he was raised to be something more than a servant. Nevertheless, it was a momentary thought, which she soon put aside, because they now stood before the Blue Heaven Hall.

The hall was similar to her own abode except it was not a shambles, but a fine painted structure — turquoise and gold with green trim. The porch was surrounded by a yellow balustrade and everywhere there were sprigs of pine and willow. Pots of blue-green cabbage lined the stairway and long vines of firecracker flowers draped from roof to ground.

Chi Lin followed Willow into the room, which, like its owner, was redolent of jasmine with hints of camellia. The walls were covered in silk brocade and beadwork. On the floor, a vast peacock rug. A sandalwood partition separated the sleeping area from the *ke-ting*, which contained ebony chairs, a table and a throne-like couch. On this couch sat Jasmine, the first wife. Chi Lin had met her on the day she had entered the house. Then Jasmine appeared aloof, inspecting Purple Sage with the eye of an appraiser. Now was no different. She sat like the lady of the house, which she was not, but her demeanor aspired to it, or so Chi Lin thought. But Chi Lin did not begrudge Jasmine her place. She was the first wife and had given Wu Hung-lin two sons, one of which was the heir to the Imperial Salt Certificate. Both sons were here now — chest high youths slouching at either side of their mother.

Chi Lin curtsied to the First Wife.

"Am I in the presence of Mei Lo?" she asked.

"You are, Purple Sage. I favor you with this meeting so you may begin the task." She rose a little on her chair, but did not offer Chi Lin a seat. "Willow."

"Yes, mistress."

"You may wait outside."

"Yes, mistress."

She then pushed her sons forward.

"These are our husband's sons," she said. "*My* sons. The first is Wu Lin-kua, the heir."

Chi Lin curtsied to the taller child, who looked nervously at his brother.

"What is wrong?" Jasmine snapped. "Mistress Purple Sage is your Auntie, now. Bow like a gentleman."

Lin-kua bowed, but still appeared nervous. Chi Lin suspected he worried whether she would say something to his mother about their encounter last night — a window peek and a pair of breasts.

"And this is Wu Chou-fa," Jasmine announced. "He is second, but still a legacy to the house. Bow to your Auntie Purple Sage."

Chi Lin curtsied to his bow.

"Fine sons," Chi Lin said, eliciting a smile from Jasmine.

"They are," she said. "Scholars also. Of course, we will not press you with their accomplishments as you will be denied the honor of sons. But all Wu Hung-lin's wives are honored aunties." She clapped. "Now off to your studies. Master P'ing Chin does not tolerate tardiness."

The boys bowed curtly again, and then scurried off. Chi Lin remained nervous in the silence that followed. She was not sure whether it was her place to speak to Jasmine. But this woman was a woman after all and not her commander. Jasmine ranked higher, but was here to facilitate, not to order her about. So Chi Lin became bold again.

"P'ing Chin is a fine scholar," she said.

"Oh. You know P'ing Chin?"

"He was a student of my father's and worked in the Ya-men as an underclerk."

Jasmine frowned as if the acquaintance did more to downgrade P'ing Chin in her eyes than raise him up.

"I did not realize your father was a scholar."

"*Is* a scholar," Chi Lin replied, nodding to assuage the contradiction. "My father was at court, but was excused after His Majesty's evaluation and adjustment of government officials,"

"I know no such thing and neither should you," Jasmine said. "It does not add to your status here."

"I am sorry to mention it, but a father's history should be cherished by all his children."

"Just so." Jasmine stood abruptly. "It is time for you to come. Follow me."

Jasmine strode past Chi Lin, who managed to follow her over the threshold. Willow waited outside, and then also followed. The three women formed a feminine train heading for the silk *ji-tzao*.

3

A high hedge surrounded the silk barn and the mulberry grove. Two dozen or more workers tended the bushes, or so was Chi Lin's rough accounting. Their backs were bent over the baskets, where leaves were collected. Some climbed ladders to the uppermost branches cutting the tenderest flanges. As Jasmine engaged the pathway, those whom she passed bowed. Chi Lin knew these bows were not for her as she had not earned her place yet. Still, perhaps the obeisance was for the entire company rather than just the First Wife. Near the barn were trellises, each protected from the sun with green paper awnings.

Chi Lin was amazed at what she saw, for each trellis was crawling with worms, chubby grayish white larvae waddling along on strings and branches. Each trellis was attended by three women, who fed the beasties mulberry leaves by hand. The only men here were workers who tended the strings and repaired the trellises. Chi Lin noticed the youth who she thought she had seen yesterday, the one who had repaired the threshold to the Jade Heart Hall. She had not seen his face then, but his body drew her attention, as it did now. He had a sweet face and, upon seeing her, he smiled, but then quickly changed his mood to the stern countenance of a man focused on his work. Chi Lin's heart jumped.

Jasmine halted before this trellis.

"This is where you shall work," she said. "But first I will show you how these babies live and grow to be farmed for the house's great benefit." She picked up a mulberry leaf, and pointed it at a cluster of worms. "These are special babies, Purple Sage. For these worms have molted three times and are on their fourth molt. It is then that their cocoon can be useful, and only then."

Jasmine touched the leaf to the worm and it wiggled, its tiny jaws greedily consuming the leaf until its mandibles neared Jasmine's fingers. She snatched another leaf and fed it again.

"It is a simple task," she said. "But if your hand is unsteady, the worm will not feed and if it does not feed, it will not molt. At first you will find that it takes to it well, but as the hours pass and your hand tires, it might abandon you, which is unacceptable." She tossed the leaf aside, and pointed to the many cocoons that were ripe for gathering. "When they are perfect, the best are taken."

Jasmine turned abruptly and marched into the barn, Chi Lin and Willow trailing in tow. Here the air was acrid and bitter. Chi Lin choked.

"It is not a pleasant odor," Jasmine said. "But you will grow accustomed to it in time. You will be thankful that you will start outdoors feeding the beasties."

Chi Lin cupped her hand over her mouth to filter the stench. It scarcely helped. Still she was amazed at what she saw. Vats of boiling liquid, bubbling and, inside the vats, the cocoons. At intervals, servant women ladled and drained the cocoons, which were bright white and dripping.

"We do this until the gum is boiled away," Jasmine said. "Then the cocoons are propped in the feed bowls."

Jasmine picked up a cocoon and, with her fingernails picked at loose stands, the fibers frizzing in a cloud above the egg shaped object. She then drew the strands out until they formed threads. She placed the cocoon's cradle into a feeding cup and hooked the strands through button holes, joining these strands to other strands. Here, a woman rotated a four spoke wheel, drawing the strands onto the reel. Chi Lin recognized the woman. It was the Second Wife — Lotus, who sat on a chair to preserve her bound feet. She nodded to Chi Lin.

    "Lotus has a fine hand and spidery fingers for this work," Jasmine said. "It comes from playing the lute in the House of Pleasure."

    Lotus nodded again, but remained silent. Chi Lin noticed the Third Wife, Orchid, propped on a distant chair spinning a similar reel. Evidently this important task was the prerogative of women of rank. However, Orchid did not look well or pleased with the work.

    "Will you teach me how to reel the silk, Jasmine?" Chi Lin asked.

    Jasmine did not reply. Instead, she walked toward another area, where the second reeling was undertaken and bolts of silk thread were readied for the loom. She whisked her hand in a demonstrative manner, and then marched back to the feeding zone.

    "You shall begin," she said, depositing Chi Lin at the designated place, where Willow stood now as a place marker.

    The First Wife was gone leaving the Fourth Wife to her new labors among the trellises and mulberry leaves.

Chapter Eight

New Acquisitions

1

Feeding worms all day was less wearisome than sewing, or so Chi Lin thought. Perhaps it was easier on her sore fingers, the chubby recipients of the mulberry feast gentle in their bite. She grew less steady after a small lunch of tea, a bun and cold cabbage hearts, and her legs became strained by the time Willow came to fetch her again.

"The mistress wishes to see you," Willow said.

Chi Lin smiled.

"Come see," she said to Willow. She continued to feed a worm. "I call this one Bright Eyes, because he always finds the tip of the leaf. And that one is Dumpling because she is so fat."

Willow grinned and picked up a leaf, feeding it to Dumpling.

"It is not good to take them to heart," Willow said. "When they climb the branch and spin their cocoon, you will never see them again. When the water boils, they die in their cradles."

"This I know," Chi Lin said. "It is their sacrifice to our betterment. But I am happy to befriend them and make them fat before they meet their misfortune."

Willow stared at Purple Sage as if to see her for the first time. She fed another leaf to Dumpling, and then nodded.

"It is time."

Chi Lin stepped away from the trellis, her legs buckling slightly now that they were released from their constant position. She placed the mulberry basket aside, and followed. She wondered how she would find any place within this great house without Willow as guide. The servant, who at first was stiff and formal, was now friendlier, easier in gait and disposed to speak at will.

"You have spoken of your father," Willow remarked.

"To be sure."

"The First Wife has said as much to the Old Lady of the House."

"Did that displease her?"

"I do not think so. You did not brag of being a scholar's daughter. But Jasmine is proud and may have meant to make less of you by telling the mistress."

Chi Lin sighed. She did not wish to make an enemy of the First Wife, but she supposed if it were to happen, it would happen easily and not through intent. Still, she would be more circumspect.

"My father was a teacher also," Willow said. "Not a high scholar or official, but taught merchant sons to tally and keep accounts. No more." She giggled. "But he would read to me and my sister and write poetry for us."

"Do you read?" Chi Lin asked.

"It is forbidden." She turned in her progress and winked. Still, Chi Lin would need to be circumspect in this. "Still, he read to us."

In their progress they came to a long house and, as they passed its door, Chi Lin saw Lin-kua and Chou-fa inside practicing their writing, brushes held firmly under Master P'ing Chin stern glance. He looked up and, upon seeing her, smiled. She halted.

"Willow," she said. "May I greet my old friend, P'ing Chin?"

"I am not one to curtail you," she said. "But the Old Lady of the House waits."

"I will be brief."

Chi Lin stood at the threshold waiting for the signal to enter, a signal received from P'ing Chin. The boys stirred upon seeing their Auntie Purple Sage. Again the eye exchange told Chi Lin that they worried whether she would report them for last evening's intrusion. P'ing Chin cocked his head.

"Continue practicing," he snapped. "I want perfect strokes. Nothing less is acceptable."

The boys bowed and worked their brushes frantically.

"Master P'ing Chin," Chi Lin said. "I did not expect to see you here. I was surprised when the First Wife mentioned your name."

"True, mistress," he replied. "I am accustomed to tutor official's sons. But the Wu House is mighty and can afford my services. These boys are very tiresome, I must say. Your father would have thrown them into the sea."

Chi Lin grinned, but was fearful that P'ing Chin would go so far as to reveal in front of the lads that she could read and write. That would never do, because she was sure they were tattle tongues and would tell their mother. Jasmine would whisper that a serpent of feminine scholarship has invaded the House of Wu.

"They are good boys from what I can see," she said, drawing grins from both. "And I am their Auntie now."

"I have heard as much, mistress," P'ing Chin said. "You are the fabled ghost bride they have told tales about already. I am sure nothing these boys can say is true about you and can be remedied with extra hours of practice."

"I remember my father telling me that you knew such extra time when you were his student."

"We learn from experience. *Your* hand was always fair."

Chi Lin quickly opened her hands.

"Needlework," she said. "Needlework and feeding the worms. That is the ghost wife's handiwork."

P'ing Chin caught her meaning because he rattled his teeth, and then bowed.

"As it should be, mistress. Women's hands are applied to industry and never to . . . well, there have been some, but where has that led us?"

"Nowhere, I am sure." She looked at the brushwork and noticed that Chou-fa's radical was incorrectly missing a stroke and, although compelled to tell him, she desisted. "Fine scholars these, Master P'ing Chin."

"Fine? In time. Scholars? Perhaps when the Lady in the Moon winks at the bay. But we shall work them, we shall."

"Industry, Master P'ing Chin. I shall be about mine and wish you a good evening."

Chi Lin bowed to the teacher, and then stared at her new found nephews. She joined Willow on the path.

2

A covered archway stretched over the path which ran between the school and the Jade Heart Hall. It was a lovely stretch with wooden floorboards that creaked beneath Chi Lin's sandals. The roof was varnished crimson and green with tiger faces carved at the cap ends, the sign that the House of Wu was distinguished enough to receive Imperial permission to sport fine curved tiles and ornamentation. Chi Lin's father had such permission at one time, but lost it, his house needing many modifications to comply with a more common appearance.

Halfway along this causeway, Willow halted, turning almost sister-like to Chi Lin.

"The mistress knows," she whispered.

"I am sure she knows many things, Willow. I do not doubt it."

"I mean she knows you had a visit last night from . . . the Second Son."

Chi Lin's heart jumped, her stomach rolling. Did this mean she was going to be chastised for rudeness? Liang-tze was the Old Lady of the House's real son, after all.

"Am I to be punished?"

"No. I mention this so you know to say nothing about it, even if my mistress hints. The Second Son is not favored, his actions troublesome. He has always hovered about his brother's wives, even though he has his own women."

"I have heard as much on the wind," Chi Lin replied. "Thank you for your warning. I will not mention the incident."

"Just know that she knows and might try to make amends. That is my mistress's way." She paused, perhaps trying to decide if further talk was wise. She swallowed hard, and then said: "My mistress is practical and stern, but fair in all things. She is a good woman although you might need to dig to the foundation to find her softer nature."

She turned and continued toward the hall. Chi Lin paused, watching Willow walk, now many steps ahead of her. Then she closed the gap, happy to have tapped the trust of this servant.

The Old Lady of the House was in her usual place within the Jade Heart Hall, mending shoes. At the sight of the footwear Chi Lin's fingers ached. After a full day of feeding the worms, was she now expected to pick up the needle? Her fingers would rebel. She was sure of it. However, the sewing circle was not present.

The old woman looked up as they entered.

"Purple Sage," she said. "Did you learn much at the Silk *ji-tzao*?"

Chi Lin curtsied.

"Yes, mother-in-law. I spent much time feeding the worms. I saw the process. My sister has spun silk in our homestead, but not on such a scale. Never had I participated."

"But now you know. And the First Wife will be pleased in time, I am sure, when you have earned your place. Tomorrow you shall tend in the kitchen and the day after you will mend tables and chairs. Such skills are impotent to running a house of size and status."

"Yes, mother-in-law."

"Good. I see you wear purple today, which stands out from our mourning white. It is proper that the ghost bride eschew white for an interval. It is proper." She set her work aside, and stood. "Have you decided on how to use your husband's gift?"

"I was thinking of many improvements," Chi Lin said. "But I think the roof tiles need repairing and should be the priority."

"Yes. Practical, I see. Good. I am glad you managed to keep your gift safe."

"Why would I not?"

The Old Lady of the House frowned. Chi Lin knew, thanks to Willow, that her mother-in-law had referred to Wu Liang-tze's visitation. But by answering boldly she had avoided a detailed explanation.

"Young women are foolish," the old woman said. "Who knows how they can misplace silver." She looked to Willow. "Willow."

"Yes, mistress."

"Fetch Gao Lin, and then ask Mo Li to bring a basket of sweet buns here. She will know the meaning."

"Yes, mistress."

Chi Lin was mystified.

"Repairing a roof is not a task for a wife in this house, even though she is the Fourth Wife and a Ghost Bride. You will need a strong arm to accomplish it. Lao Lao has nothing more than a strong tongue. His arms would splinter. So I am sending a man to repair the roof. He is in our service, so you need only pay for the tiles and mortar."

"Thank you, mother-in-law," Chi Lin said, curtsying.

"Be thankful that I am as practical as you appear to be."

Suddenly, a man stood on the threshold, Willow behind him, although she soon disappeared to accomplish her second task.

"Ah, Gao Lin," the old woman said.

The man stepped into the light and Chi Lin's breath hitched. It was the young worker, whom she had seen earlier repairing the trellis. She averted her eyes so as not to raise questions, because he was handsome, although shabbily attired. He went to his knees before the Old Lady of the House.

"I am here, my lady. You have summoned me, my lady. What is needed, my lady?"

"Up with you," the old woman snapped. "I am giving you to Purple Sage to help with repairs at the Hall of Silver Silence. She will tell you what is needed."

Gao Lin looked to Chi Lin, his gentle countenance easing at her sight. He grinned, but then quickly frowned, bowing.

"Yes, my lady. I shall do repairs, my lady."

Chi Lin was not sure what to say, so she said nothing.

"Wait outside," the old woman snapped, and Gao Lin left. "Also, my husband has made an observation that you are too thin and would fade after long, the work being steady and your position, low as it is, still higher than the servants, tenants and journeymen. He suspects you are in want of a good meal, and I suspect it is true."

Chi Lin's stomach rumbled for that good meal. She was not a complainer, but her sister was a good cook with what they had, and meals were regular and tasty. Willow returned now with a short, rotund woman in tow, who toted a basket of sweet buns. Chi Lin could not help think that this woman had eaten more than her share of those sweet buns.

"Ah, Mo Li," the old woman said. "Go with your mistress, Purple Sage, for you are to assist in the Hall of Silver Silence with the cooking."

"But Snapdragon will bite my head off, my lady," Mo Li replied.

"None of your obstinence, Mo Li," the old woman said. "You shall help her or do it all yourself. It is not for either you or Lao Lao's old woman to determine these things. That is *my* place. And unless you wish to be returned to the salt *ji-tzao* on your father's holding, you will manage Snapdragon and supply your mistress with nourishing meals. Do you understand me?"

"I do, mistress. I do."

Mo Li bowed first to the old lady, and then to Chi Lin. She turned quickly and passed Willow on the threshold, not needing to be told to wait outside. Chi Lin curtsied low to her mother-lin-law.

"I thank you, mother-in-law. You have a good heart."

"My heart is as others. It seeks proper management in this house. A wife without a proper roof or a full belly will not serve well here. What would they say in the Ya-men?"

Chi Lin caught this woman's eye. It was the first time their eyes locked. She could read them. She could see the sadness of losing her son and being saddled with a ghost bride, but she also saw the remorse of having a wayward second son who was itching to do mischief. Full bellies and repaired roofs were fine as far as they went, but compensation for the stress of having Liang-tze as a neighbor seemed more the reason here. Still, Chi Lin was thankful.

"We should mend shoes now," the old woman said. "But it is best you take your new acquisitions to the hall and sort them into proper quarters to keep them away from the bugs. I suspect Lao Lao will not be happy with any arrangement made. But we do not live for his happiness. Quite the opposite. Have him work it out, and then inspect the results. You are the mistress of the Hall of Silver Silence. The more you invest, the more it will return to presentability. So go. Lead them to your courtyard and make do with your limited resources."

Willow led Chi Lin out.

"Willow," the old lady called.

"Yes, mistress."

"Purple Sage should know the way by now. I shall join Jasmine for dinner. Go ahead and tell her."

"Yes, mistress."

Chi Lin was sad not to have Willow's company. The servant might have explained to her more clearly the reasons for these new acquisitions beyond the obvious. She might have intoned whether the mistress had taken a shine to her or not. Still, Chi Lin did as she had learned to do during her short residency here. She walked on the proper path, and the proper path this evening was through the dusky courtyards to her own spot, now followed by a handsome, brawny handyman and a fat cook. She was not sure which she liked best, but they were happy acquisitions without a doubt, both providing potential nourishment to a starving ghost bride.

Chapter Nine

Mending Things

1

As predicted, Lao Lao caused a fuss. *There was no room in his hut for another woman and absolutely no place for another man.* Mo Li was unhappy with this and declared she would go back to her old quarters, but Chi Lin interceded. Mo Li would stay with Lao Lao and wife, and as comfortably as they could make her. Snapdragon was insulted that after all these years her abilities as a cook were called into question by the Old Lady of the House. *I was steaming rice before she was born and boiling noodles in the days of her grandmother.* But Chi Lin insisted that it was a kindness to provide Snapdragon with help. After all, her sight was failing, if not failed, and help would ease her aching bones by sharing the tasks. As for Gao Lin, Lao Lao showed him a shambled storage hut fit for little more than crickets and mice. Chi Lin objected, but Gao Lin said he could very well stay there as in any other place. So he disappeared into the shadows, seeking solace in the debris.

Chi Lin heard Snapdragon's complaints all night, her sharp voice drifting through the window. But at dawn, the table was laid with braised pork, soft white rice with sweet plums and properly prepared tea. She wondered where Mo Li had found the ingredients. Were they staples in the shack never to be served unless on feast days? Perhaps Mo Li raided the Jade Heart kitchen for the meal. Nonetheless, Chi Lin ate heartily, not caring for the source of the victuals. It was the best meal she had consumed since her arrival. Of course, Snapdragon boasted that she had prepared it with some help from the useless Mo Li, but Chi Lin knew better.

Chi Lin was cross with Lao Lao for not being more accommodating, especially with Gao Lin.

"A partition is to be set in that corner," she said to Lao Lao sternly pointing to the far end of the min hall. "Gao Lin shall sleep there until the storage hut is made inhabitable."

Lao Lao was all *yes, mistress* and *right away, mistress*, but she could tell he was annoyed. He would remain annoyed and just short of insubordinate for a week. But as the meals were appreciated and Gao Lin began his repair work, Lao Lao settled into a seemingly cooperative mood. Snapdragon was . . . well, was Snapdragon, complaining always, while Mo Li was no better, although she became the more valuable. Chi Lin could dress herself and prepare her own hair. On most days she had completed these tasks before Lao Lao's old woman even stirred. But she understood Snapdragon's position. The woman had served and labored in the House of Wu since she was a child. Blindness and shaky hands were a prelude to a trip to *the Yellow Springs*. Yes, Chi Lin understood.

Chi Lin settled into her routine homage at Wu Hung-lin's shrine. She felt his presence there and became comfortable chatting with him, thanking him for the tender mercies shown to her by her mother-in-law and for keeping the Second Son away from her courtyard. She sometimes thought she heard Wu Hung-lin speak to her on the morning breeze, although she had never heard his voice while he lived. She also looked forward to her morning encounters with the daughters. On the third day, the third daughter appeared with her half-sisters. This was the youngest and shyest — Sapphire by name, the child of the Third Wife. Of course, they were all accounted as the children of the First Wife, who would become a powerful force in their lives, but for now they were still living in their mothers' quarters and under the eye of their *amahs*. Chi Lin had glimpsed both *amahs* at a distance, but had no need or desire to have congress with them. The children had to make a distinction between their Auntie and their servants.

These morning chats made Chi Lin ache for children of her own — even daughters. While the sons were more formal in their life at Blue Heaven Hall and in the classroom, the girls were still too young to be taught sewing and mending. They still played with their dollies and had silly, endearing conversations seeking truth in their surroundings. The ghost bride was a curiosity at first, but soon became an opportunity — their only opportunity to talk with an adult lady, one who did not command them to *do this* or to *act that way*. She did not scold them, but answered their questions about her robes and her hair jewel, her funny feet (their mothers needed servants to guide them). In fact, they wanted to see her feet, which she gladly displayed, wiggling her toes. Chi Lin hoped that the First Wife, whose feet were also fully formed, would spare these girls the pain of foot binding. This depended on whether prospective households were drawn to the lotus footed creatures or wanted working wives in their household. Since the First Wife was not foot bound and the Old Lady of the House had big feet too, perhaps these children would be spared. Chi Lin thought it a good sign that they were not bound yet, since the process began at a young age. But who could tell, and she would not interfere.

Then there was the work. On some days Willow would fetch her — on days where new tasks were introduced or when the Old Lady of the House had a change in plan. But more often Chi Lin knew where she was wanted and arrived ahead of her mother-in-law. In the kitchens, she learned to parse ingredients for the cooks, dicing the vegetables and the meat, rolling the bun dough and plating spices for use in the cooking process. She inspected plates and dishes for cracks and learned to repair tea bowls using lacquer dust and powdered silver. Ceramic spoons were patched with gum plaster and paint hid the cracks. Some items were beyond repair, but Chi Lin learned which ones could be safely chucked into the flower pots for drainage. Table clothes and napkins were embroidered as well and soon Chi Lin mastered the *t'ieh* pattern for edging doilies and bun covers.

In addition to the everlasting shoe repairs and designs, Chi Lin often went to the furniture shack, where the journeymen created fine tables and chairs. Her job was to nurture the older pieces with fresh coats of lacquer and shiny brass works. She learned to carefully fit chairs in need of new webbing with woven rattan and to strengthen them with bamboo slats. Chi Lin found this work more backbreaking than any other, the shack musty and confining. She was glad when her days there were concluded.

She liked feeding the worms, and soon graduated into the *silk ji-tzao* barn to learn how to undertake the first reeling process. She never accustomed herself to the odor, covering her face with a makeshift mask from Peony's wardrobe chest. She was also told that since Wu Hung-lin's death, the inspection of the tenants' *ji-tzao,* both silk and salt, were haphazard. The Master of the House, Wu T'ai-po, was too old to do it regularly and his journeymen were spread thinly over the landscape. Wu Liang-tze had been sent out on occasion, but he managed to scare the tenants with his wildness, especially with their daughters. So the Second Son was curtailed from these duties. Of course, Lin-kua and Chou-fa were too young to undertake it, so it fell to the First Wife to take up the slack. Jasmine told Chi Lin that she would be doing inspection tours once the house ceased wearing white. The neighborhood expected the family to be wearing the white, and since the ghost bride wore purple, she could not travel outside the walls. But when the mourning period for women ended, she could expect to tour. Chi Lin looked forward to it.

2

Life for women in the house was toil, but Chi Lin discovered that when her daily duties were finished, she could reclaim some time for herself, depending on the task and, to some degree, on the whim of her mother-in-law. Chi Lin was permitted to take her meals twice weekly with the household women, although she sat at a separate table. But the meal was the same and, occasionally, someone would speak to her or ask her a question. There was not much conversation, especially since the Master of House usually entertained his journeymen and Ya-men guests in the next room. They were boisterous; especially Po T'ai-kuan, who was a frequent guest, knowing where the best food was served and the finest wine flowed freely. The more it flowed, the louder he got, and there was little room for conversation for the women over the noise.

Still, Chi Lin listened and observed. She found the other wives wanting in manners; Jasmine too proud to do more than sneer, Lotus too precious to wait on herself and Orchid too distressed to do more than pout. The Old Lady of the House, on the other hand, domineering as she was, did keep the conversation circulating by asking her daughters-in-law questions on their industry, health and the state of their pavilions. Of course, she was filled with motherly advice on rearing children, which leaned more on issues on how to control the *amahs*, nannies and teachers. On this score little could be said to Purple Sage. Nor could she contribute anything to it. But she learned much about how these children were growing — their petty quirks and their need for discipline. The Old Lady stressed the competency of her grand daughters so that a good match could be made with the lowest dowry possible. Her grandsons must grow up to take over the business of running the house as soon as they could do it, if not sooner. All the while, servants competed with dishes and plates, bowing and curtsying to their betters, while the boisterous laughter rolled over their heads from the adjoining gentlemen's enclave. When these meals were concluded, the wives departed — Jasmine in her litter, Lotus between her two maid servants and Orchid on the arm of a bent older woman. Chi Lin would then arise, bow to her mother-in-law and depart, thankful for the meal and drifting to her bed in the Hall of Silver Silence.

Gao Lin had made progress on the roof, although he still managed to cross Lao Lao by his presence. Lao Lao grumbled at the impropriety of a worker taking up quarters in the main hall, albeit a lowly corner behind a partitioning screen. Chi Lin generally was too tired to notice whether the man was there or not, although she had admired his beauty from afar as he straddled the beams while replacing the tiles. She had also seen him naked once, splashing himself clean at the courtyard's edge. It was a quick glimpse, but one etched on her mind. She did her best to forget it, if she could. But at night, she would fall asleep quickly; the only evidence that there were more than crickets in the hall was an occasional cough from behind the partition.

Gao Lin kept to his place, but on one afternoon Chi Lin returned to the courtyard to find a genuine feud between her servants. All four were gathered at the pool, Lao Lao waving his hands and Gao Lin shaking his head, while the two women barked away over the cobblestones.

"What is this commotion?" Chi Lin snapped, having returned unnoticed. Her appearance silenced them, all four bowing. "Is this how you act when I am away at my chores?"

"I am sorry, mistress," Lao Lao said. "But your worker bee should not be concerned with repairing the pool when he is supposed to be fixing the roof."

"Perhaps," Gao Lin said, "if I am to follow the order of things. But roof tiles and pool tiles are on the same scale — one up and one down. I do not see where one should be preferred while the other should be ignored."

"That is not your place to decide," Snapdragon said. "The mistress needs a roof. The pool is an eyesore and, if anything, should be filled in with dirt and made to yield beans and peas for the kettle."

"Useless suggestion," Mo Li said. "We do not grow things here. The vegetables come from the tenants. Mistress Purple Sage is not a tenant."

"Then take the pool tiles and put them on the roof," Snapdragon said.

"That cannot be done," Gao Lin remarked. "The roof tiles must be shaped to the contours of the pool — made smaller and neatly trimmed. Pool tiles cannot be stretched, unless you know how, old mother."

"Do not call my wife, *old mother*, you field clod," Lao Lao snapped.

"Enough," Chi Lin said, and they all bowed again. "Gao Lin, it is true that the roof comes first, because the silver is only so much and there are other things to consider."

"I understand, mistress," Gao Lin said, and said no more.

Chi Lin sighed — a deep sigh taking in the uselessness of haggling with servants. If each tended to their own business, such arguments would be avoided. But she knew that at the heart of it this had nothing to do with tiles and priorities. It was Lao Lao squaring off his territory and Snapdragon pushing the newcomers aside. Mo Li was intemperate, but her cooking was too delicious to be cast aside. As for Gao Lin, Chi did not question his intentions. He meant not to cause trouble. He had an idea and was exploring it. So, Chi Lin raised a finger at Lao Lao, and then turned to Gao Lin.

"How would you assess restoring this pool if you were commissioned to do so?"

Gao Lin flexed his arms and moved to the pool's edge. As it stood, the pond was clogged with black mold and mud, not to mention the waste of a thousand mornings. The water, if it be that, was poisoned. No fish could dwell there. No duck could squat. The tiles were broken and many were missing. A large decorative rock arose at the far end, where a trickle cascaded into the muck. Behind it, a sluice poked its way from the courtyard wall and beyond.

"It is filthy work," Gao Lin said. "I am not averse to muck and sludge. If we fill buckets, they can be toted and the waste can be removed. Cleansing the inside will cost nothing but time. The bottom tiles can be patched, while the outer tiles can be repurposed from the roof tiles you have already purchased. I can do this thing easily. The great rock must be scrubbed and the drawing canal needs to be releveled. The water source is from the stream which adjoins the house. The feeder needs cleaning and to be unblocked. Again, it is a removal task. The only cost you will need, mistress is the price of flowers and fish — affordable if the lotuses are young and the fish are not too fat." He bowed. "That is my assessment. Also, we must refrain from pissing in the pool."

Lao Lao scowled, but Chi Lin raised her hand again.

"You are telling me that there is no cost to restore it but your labors, which are already mine?"

"Yes, mistress. And the flowers and the fish." Gao Lin grinned. "These three could give a hand and time would be saved."

"I cannot even see this pool," Snapdragon said. "How would I clean it out?"

"It is reasonable," Chi Lin said. "Lao Lao can give you a hand, and Mo Li could help carry buckets."

Mo Li grunted. Lao Lao spit. But neither went beyond that in their discontent.

"However," Chi Lin added. "The roof must be done first."

"Of course, mistress," Gao Lin replied, and went about it, moving to his bamboo framework, climbing to the roof as easily as a marmoset.

Chi Lin did not chastise the others further. Lao Lao would need to be less divisive. As for Snapdragon, Chi Lin did not care if she slept all day. She understood that the old woman feared for her position, which was ultimately up to the Old Lady of the House, not Purple Sage. She turned to Mo Li.

"Can you make *yueh-ping*?"

"I can, mistress, but Moon cakes are for festivals."

"I have had them at other times. Do we have the ingredients? Can I have three for tomorrow morning?"

Mo Li bowed.

"We have and I can, but it is unusual to . . ."

"I have need of these. Do you doubt me?"

"No, mistress. I shall make them, even if I need to work all night."

"All night?" Snapdragon cackled. "*Yueh-ping* is easy. I can make three *shi* in flat pans for the lantern festival. It is easy. Do not let this one fool you."

Mo Li scowled, but went about preparing for the task. When she left, Chi Lin took Snapdragon aside.

"I have brought Mo Li here to help you, even if you say you need no help. I must be sure she is as knowledgeable as you are in these things."

"So, the Moon Cakes are a test?"

"Yes."

Snapdragon grinned, and then laughed. She nodded and dismissed herself from the mistress' company leaving only Lao Lao standing alone.

"You must be more welcoming of Gao Lin, Lao Lao," Chi Lin said, softly.

"If you say so, mistress, it will be so."

"To say it and do it are two different things. You have been in the Hall of Silver Silence for as long as this hall has stood."

"Longer," he said.

Chi Lin had no notion of that meaning, but continued.

"If our roof is repaired and the pool is restored at small cost, my silver will be able to make other improvements which could bring recognition to this quarter of the house. So unless you can climb the bamboo framework and fit tiles in the baking sun, you must support those who can."

"I understand, mistress. I will make an effort."

"More than an effort, Lao Lao. You must be sincere. As for Mo Li, look upon her as an easement to your wife's old age. She will shield her shortcomings, which, under those circumstances, will never come to the attention of the Old Lady of the House."

Lao Lao bowed. Chi Lin was not sure that he embraced the full weight of her remarks, but she was learning that more than shoes and tables and spoons needed mending — more than roofs and pools. Household peace was more worth the effort and she meant to have it — she meant to keep her courtyard peaceful.

Chapter Ten

Moon Cakes and Guan-yin

1

Chi Lin arose the next morning to the wonderful aroma of Moon Cakes. She knew at once her request had been fulfilled, the almond perfume wafting beneath her nose. She sat up and saw Snapdragon hovering over the table — a basket set beside the morning meal of plum and rice congee, sweet melon and tea. Lao Lao's old woman was like a fox waiting for the mistress to awake and, when she did, paced beside the table as best she could, given her poor eyesight and bent back.

"It is done," Chi Lin said, coming to the table. She whisked aside the basket papers and beheld the three cakes — one red, one yellow and one forest green — each square, with a medallion etched on top — three cat faces baked to a golden brown. "These are perfect."

"You must taste them, mistress to see if Mo Li has passed the test."

"I mean not to taste them, Snapdragon."

"But how will you be able to tell? Your eyes cannot taste them. Your nose can be deceived."

Chi Lin frowned.

"My taste does not matter."

"But how will *I* know?"

"Perhaps I meant to test your patience."

Snapdragon bowed curtly and stumbled toward the threshold. Her disappointment was evident, but from Chi Lin's nose and eyes, Mo Li had passed the test, if ever there was a test. She covered the basket, and poured her tea.

When Chi Lin left the hall, she noticed that Lao Lao had not come. But that was soon explained because she spied him gathering buckets for Gao Lin. When he saw the mistress, he bowed and smiled humbly, and then shook the buckets evidently meaning to convey his attempt at cooperation. Chi Lin retuned his bow with a nod. Then she saw Gao Lin astride the roof beam — the great ridge pole that spanned the hall. He worked diligently, loosening old tiles, carefully preserving them, perhaps to be repurposed for the pool restoration. He was bare-chested and sang a quiet morning song, which may have been too low for Chi Lin's ears, both in volume and in use of coarse lyrics. She had heard such language before, because her father's students were prone to tavern talk. When she listened to them, her sister would become upset and set her course away from the house. Still, Chi Lin knew that young men had thoughts of young women and, when congressed over wine or even the brushes, exchanged stories of conquests and prowess. She thought of these moments as she gazed up at Gao Lin.

Suddenly, his eye caught hers. She held steady for a moment, allowing him to drink in her thoughts, while she caught something unexplained from him. Then she looked away and directed her feet toward the shrine for her morning visit with her husband.

Chi Lin could parse these thoughts and who better to share them with than her husband? So in whispers she confided in him that she would have greatly liked to have caressed him in bed and have gone about the business of making a son. She also hoped he was sorrowful that she would never know his loving touch. She sought not remorse from the dead, because that would not be proper. But she did think of Gao Lin as she gazed on her husband's effigy. She apologized knowing she could not hide thoughts from the ancestors, especially a husband's ghost, but she was sorry only for bringing them to the shrine and not for the thoughts themselves. Somehow, as long as they remained thoughts, they spun natural. Only in the act could they become damnable in the sight of the ancestors.

"Auntie does not burn red paper today," came a small voice.

It was Pearl. Chi Lin turned to see all three sisters — Pearl, Jade and Sapphire. They looked at Purple Sage as if they expected her to entertain them with witty comments or to show them her feet. Instead, Chi Lin placed a finger on her lips.

"Your father has brought you a gift."

The girls jumped up and down, looking about.

"Is it a doggie?" Jade asked. "It would be three doggies — one for each."

"Even one for Sapphire?" Pearl asked.

"I want a doggie, too," Sapphire said, pouting.

Chi Lin raised her fingers to her lips again. Silence fell.

"Do you see doggies?" she asked.

"No," came the collective reply.

"Then the gift is not that." She reached for the basket. "The gift is in here."

She brought the basket before them, raising the papers. Three sets of eyes opened wide. Giggles.

"Moon Cakes. For us?" Jade asked.

"Yes."

"I am the oldest, so I get to pick first," Pearl announced. "I want the red one."

"I want the green," Sapphire said.

"But you get what remains," Jade said. "You are the youngest, and I like green."

Sapphire pouted.

"Now, do not quarrel," Chi Lin said. "Your father will be upset."

"You cannot fool us," Pearl said, taking the red moon cake. "Father did not bake these, because he is dead."

"Ghosts can work wonders," Chi Lin replied.

"But they cannot make Moon Cakes," Pearl insisted, taking a bite. Her eyes lit up. "Oh, this is wonderful. I have tasted this before. Mo Li makes them."

Chi Lin laughed. Jade went to snatch her cake, but hesitated, and then looked at Sapphire's sad face. "You can have the green one," she said. Sapphire reached in, but Jade pushed her hand aside. "But I am older, so I will take the yellow one before you take the green one."

She snapped up the yellow cake, brought it to her eyes, and then smiled.

"Meow," she said.

Sapphire laughed, and then took the green one and mimicked the cat also.

"You are suppose to eat them, sillies," Pearl complained. "They are not toys."

"Or doggies," Sapphire said.

Chi Lin was happy. Mo Li had passed the test, indeed. Their auntie had raised smiles on their faces. But she suddenly cocked her head. Something was different.

"You do not wear the white," Chi Lin said.

"No, Auntie Ghost," Pearl said. "Our *amah* says the time for the white is over."

Chi Lin straightened up. She grasped a fistful of red prayer paper, burned it and bowed to Wu Hung-lin. She was expected in the silk *ji-tzao* today and had tarried too long. But now, with this new knowledge that *the time for the white was over*, she would seek out the First Wife instead since it signaled a change in her prospective work duties.

2

It was clear to Chi Lin that this phase of mourning was over. The white banners on the outer walls were furled and the bunting was in the process of removal. Servants reverted to their gray shirts with black trim, their white vestments stored for the next death. The air seemed fresher — less incense, and the general mood within the walls was lighter. Workers walked at a faster pace, and the swallows chirped in the trees. As the ghost bride, Chi Lin would always be in a state of mourning, but today she had worn spring yellow and wondered if she should change to her purple for contrast. But it was too late for it. She was already entering the courtyard of the Hall of Blue Heaven and heard boyish laughter. It made her glad to hear it.

She stood near the threshold watching Wu Lin-kua and Wu Chou-fa play-fighting. They had shucked the white and wore short robes of green and yellow with matching pants. They shadow boxed.

"I have you, Sun Wu-kung," Lin-kua said, raising his leg to kick his brother. "I am the Monkey-King, the pride of the Jade Emperor."

"But I can leap one-hundred thousand and eight *li* with one jump," Chou-fa said stepping aside. "You cannot defeat me, Monkey-King."

They darted between the furniture and behind the potted plants, and came dangerously close to a table, which held a sculpture of Goddess *Guan-yin*.

"I am up to the challenge," Lin-kua said. "I have succeeded with every task."

"The Pig Demon won against you."

"No he did not, stupid one."

"Yes, he did. And I shall defeat you also."

Chou-fa leaped at his brother, who shifted sharply, knocking into a chair. Chi Lin thought to intervene, but it was not her place.

They were children at play. But where was Master P'ing Chin? He would frown on such physical larks.

Chi Lin crossed the threshold and, as she did, Lin-kua halted abruptly, while Chou-fa thrust again. He managed to hit his brother's hip. Lin-kua's eyes opened wide. He raised both hands and pushed Chou-fa — pushed him into the table holding the status of *Guan-yin*. The table tottered, and then came to rest. However, *Guan-yin* fell to the floor, breaking in two.

"Oh, no," Lin-kua said. "Look what you have done. You have broken mother's *Guan-yin*."

"You did it," Chou-fa protested. "You pushed me."

The boys stared at the statue as if it would come back together again and chastise them. Chi Lin rushed to their side.

"Auntie," they said in unison, bowing, and then kneeling around the statue.

"What is to be done?" Chou-fa asked.

"It is mother's favorite, Auntie," Lin-kua added. "She will punish us with the bamboo rod."

Chi Lin took a deep breath. She thought that perhaps it could be raised, the pieces fitted together and placed on the table. Would Jasmine ever notice it? It then could be repaired secretly. The boys were terrified when their mother crossed the threshold.

"What is this commotion?" she asked, but then saw the statue. "Oh, my precious *Guan-yin*. How did this happen?"

The boys trembled, and were about the speak, but Chi Lin beat them to it.

"It is my fault, sister-in-law." She curtsied low. "I am sorry for your distress. I came and was startled while I waited. I stepped backward and toppled this precious statue."

Jasmine shook, indignantly. She gave her sons a sharp look, and then sniffed, stifling her tears.

"This *Guan-yin* was a gift from our husband. It cannot be replaced. It cannot be made whole again."

Chi Lin looked up.

"Perhaps it can, Jasmine. Perhaps it can. I can send my worker here to repair it. He is gifted with materials. I am sure he could put it to rights."

Jasmine gave her a wan look, and then shrugged. Her hands lifted the upper part of the statue.

"Who has such abilities?"

"Gao Lin."

"Gao Lin," Jasmine snapped. "I would sooner have my own worker try. Gao Lin is a wondering tea spout and I cannot afford to have servant children under foot. No. Not Gao Lin." She sighed. "And why are you here? Why are you not feeding the worms?"

Chi Lin touched Jasmine's robe sleeve.

"I observed that the white has been shunned. You told me that when the neighborhood comes not to expect the household to wear the white, I would assist you with the *ji-tzao* inspections."

Jasmine stood abruptly. She turned to her sons.

"And why are you two here?"

"Master P'ing Chin has a sick headache today," Lin-kua replied.

"He told us to study on our own," Chou-fa added.

"And is my *ke-ting* a place to study? If you were not here to startle your auntie, my *Guan-yin* would be still whole."

She swiped her robe sleeves, and then turned away. Her sons bowed and darted out. Chi Lin was pressed to know what to do, so she stood still and stared at the broken statue.

"It is true you will help me beyond these walls," Jasmine grumbled. "But not today. We must have a journeyman to assists us and porters. I will let you know." She slowly turned, her sad countenance now sporting an imperious sneer. "I . . . will . . . let . . . you . . . know."

Chi Lin bow quickly, and returned to the courtyard. She did not mean to stand poorly in the First Wife's eyes, but she knew that it would be so, if not for this, for some other cause. She was glad to know that she would assist beyond the walls and the prospects buoy her spirits.

She walked sprightly to the moon gate where the path turned to the Silk *ji-tzao*. She would gambol her fingers in the mulberry leaves and feed the fat worm babies as they crawled on the twigs and branches. As she reached the gate, she felt two eyes watching her. She halted, not turning.

"Thank you, Auntie," came a voice, Lin-kua's, she knew because his voice was going through the change.

"Thank you, Auntie," hailed a higher pitched voice, Chou-fa's to be sure.

"Be about your studies," she said softly, still not turning.

"Why did you do it?" came the lower voice.

"You have made mother angry at you," came the higher voice.

Chi Lin grinned. They were good boys and grateful, but puzzled by their elder's conduct. She should let them ponder the answer. But, no. She raised her empty basket, the one that had carried the Moon Cakes.

"Your mother is angry, true. It is a pity. And yet she cannot beat me with the bamboo rod. She cannot."

She lowered the basket, and then drifted beneath the gate, knowing she left two grateful young gentlemen bowing in her wake.

Chapter Eleven

Inspecting the Ji-tzao

1

Chi Lin looked forward excitedly to the time when she would join the First Wife to perform an inspection tour of the Yan-cheng tenants and the salt and silk *ji-tzao*. It did not happen for two weeks after the broken *Guan-yin* statue. Chi Lin suspected that the delay was punishment for taking blame for the breakage. Jasmine did not entertain her during the entire interval, but then, word came that, if the weather held clear, Purple Sage was to present herself to the First Wife to learn how these tours were performed. Chi Lin was not sure whether this would be the tour or just a demonstration, but she was anxious nonetheless and extremely enthusiastic at the prospects.

Gao Lin cautioned her to keep a steady heart and not to show her liking for any task shared with the First Wife.

"Mistress, hear me if you will," he said on the morning before the tour. "I remember when your husband undertook these inspections. He was carried like a sullen idol from place to place before meeting with the *pao-t'ien* elder. It is official dynasty business and not an outing for pleasure."

"I know this, Gao Lin," she replied. "But it would make me happy to sit in my husband's chair and be regarded with respect."

"Respect, yes. But a shadow of our lord."

"It is indelicate to remind me of this, Gao Lin. I have consulted at the shrine and know that, as the ghost bride, I am a household shade. But even a spirit's consort can lift into a respectful mood those who toil."

Gao Lin did not contradict her, but his words were worthy, because she had been thinking of the tour as a lark in the sun . . . until now. Even Lao Lao cautioned her. She would have liked to consult Willow on the subject, but the servant had not been about lately, and, when she encountered her, it was in passing. Chi Lin thought to make bold and ask her mother-in-law about the tour, but feared offending her. After all, the Master of the House had relegated this task to the wives and his journeymen until Wu Lin-kua came of age. Perhaps the Old Lady of the House would have liked to have undertaken the tour and begrudged her daughters-in-law or the opportunity. In any case, Chi Lin kept her silence until the day arrived.

She entered humbly the Hall of Blue Heaven, expecting a lecture from Jasmine and references to the broken statue. But she noticed the statue had been repaired and stood finely on its table pedestal. She thought to touch it, but feared accidentally breaking it again, although it would have been the only time she would have done so. While she observed it, she did not notice that two carry-chairs were brought into the courtyard, one larger than the other, two porters to each. A rider also entered on a tall, gray and white horse. He wore a silver badge about his neck — the Imperial Seal of the Salt Monopoly. Chi Lin knew from this that he was the journeyman assigned to the tour.

"That is Chou Kuai-tze," came a voice from behind.

Chi Lin turned to see Jasmine attended by a hand maiden.

"The horse is a high one, sister-in-law," Chi Lin said, nodding.

"As it should be. We represent the House of Wu in this exercise, Purple Sage. It is best you remember this as we proceed. Our prosperity depends on how the tenants regard us. It is a mutual respect, but we keep them in their proper place."

She offered Chi Lin a small fan, her own being ornate and larger.

"Thank you, sister-in-law," she said.

"It will be handy against the flies and will help ward off the more noxious smells."

Chou Kuai-tze dismounted and inspected the porters, who knelt in place. Once satisfied, he signaled the women to mount the chairs. Chi Lin found her chair precariously small. She hoped she would not fall out.

"*Tiao ba!*" Kuai-tze shouted, and the porters raised the chairs abruptly, still taking care to keep them level. Kuai-tze mounted his steed. "*Ch'u ba!*"

Forward they went, too fast for Chi Lin's sensibilities. She gripped the arms tightly. The caravan rushed through the courtyard and the moon gate. The House of Wu was passing behind them fast. Chi Lin had not seen the outer courtyards since the day of her wedding, but she had no time to drink in their beauty. Soon they were beyond the walls heading toward the Yan-cheng *Ya-men*.

The street was how she remembered it, grayed with age and deeply rutted. Carts bumped in these ruts — carts filled with cabbages and scallions and fruited baskets. Pedestrians raced along beside the chairs and behind the chairs, engines of industry bent on attaining their destinations, wherever the sale of goods or bent backs were needed. Some looked up and regarded the two chairs and the horseman, but this parade was salt monopoly business and no business of theirs. So they just shaded their eyes and continued along their route.

Chi Lin settled in as the porters slowed their pace. Soon they brought the chairs together in such a manner that Jasmine could observe her sister-in-law. She tapped the chair arm with her fan.

"Sit straighter, Purple Sage. Yan-cheng is watching us. We do not want them to say that the House of Wu harbors scarecrows behind their walls. We are the wives of Wu Hung-lin, who is remembered in every household along this way. So do not look like you have been pegged to the arm rests. Appear at ease, but do not grace a soul with your smile."

Chi Lin was not smiling, so there was nothing with which to grace the world. As for sitting up straight, she managed just about sitting in the chair without slipping out. The air was tart with the road dust, the vegetable carts and whatever came from Chou Kuai-tze's horse's backside. The fan was used frequently to wave the stink away. She was glad when they halted and the horse rode ahead. They had reached the *Ya-men*, where the Imperial Commissioner would add his authority to their company.

2

That authority came as a proxy in the person of Lin Wu-luo, Commissioner Ai-lo Wun-kua's delegate. Together with the Wu House journeyman, this was the official authority to carry out the salt inspection. Chi Lin watched as the two men approached, a second horse now added to their company. Lin Wu-luo wore an identical breast plate badge for the Salt Monopoly — a silver plaque etched with the character *lu* with its crossed paths and dabbled dots inside a delimiting box. Chi Lin was impressed. It far outstripped her meager ingots. Jasmine nodded to the proxy, so Chu Lin followed suit. Then together, the porters turned onto the salt road, the two horsemen flanking them now. Chi Lin was happy for this, the horses now better positioned, the stink flowing behind her.

The pace was slower — more a procession. The pedestrians were fewer also, but those that toted their wares at the end of carry-poles, bowed as best they could to the county's best family. They did so now because they were tenants of Wu T'ai-po, to whom they owed allegiance and rent. Soon the *ji-tzao* appeared in the distance — the evaporation towers poised over the pits marking the charcoal filters and the salt gathering process. Jasmine pointed.

"Family Lu," she said. "They are many and industrious. They always meet their obligations with both salt and silk. You will see. They are the favorite tenants and receive larger gifts at New Year."

Chi Lin looked toward the low cluster of houses near the tower. She also noted a silk *ji-tzao* nearby. The smoke sent a thin mist across the road, the acrid brine smell nipping her nose. The Lu may have been the favorite, but they were indeed the smelliest. As the chair passed the pathways to the Lu *ji-tzao*, a ragged nest of children poked their heads up out of holes — new charcoal holes, perfectly fitted for little folk and spidery hands. Four adults waved their hats at the procession, fully expecting to be acknowledged as the *favorite* tenant. They were, because Chou Kuai-tze raised his hand, and then tapped his badge.

The pathways branched at every step, each leading to another *ji-tzao*, the landscape dotted with evaporation towers. Chi Lin had never ventured into this zone, except during her wedding procession, when she was, for the most part, a prisoner in the bride's chair. Her own home was beyond this and her father may have traveled this way to the *Ya-men* and to Yan-cheng market, but Chi Lin had been sheltered from the blight. And blight it was, to her eyes. This was not a painting of gentle hills and flowers, but a scarred plain, marshy and inclined to the sea — an invisible sea, only guessed at by the distant tidal sounds and gulls. Still, this was the source of wealth for the House of Wu, so how scarred could it be?

Some towers appeared abandoned or less worked, at least. Jasmine opened her fan and frowned.

"The Wei Family," she said. "They should be slaves and not tenants."

"Why so, sister-in-law?"

"Why do you think?" Jasmine huffed. "If the Lu is favored and the Wei frowned upon, why do you think it so?"

"They make less salt."

"They make no salt at times and try to pay their rent in carrots and turnips. That the Master of the House allows them to stay on the land is a wonder."

"But he does." Chi Lin smiled. "He is a good man."

"You should never speak about the Master, sister-in-law, especially when your words can be heard by one of his journeymen." She snapped her fan closed and rapped it on the side of the chair. "It is not proper. The porters will gossip. Our father-in-law's good character is of no concern to others. Their opinion is formed on their assessment of us. They look to this chair and see women of worth, and therefore the House is worthy of such women and the master is respected." She frowned. "You are here to observe how they regard me and how to frame your next venture, when I am not here to draw their respect. You will learn. I have sons and you shall not, but there is a reserve of respect for a ghost bride outside the bounds of the house. Your duty and obedience will reward us."

Chi Lin sat silently listening to Jasmine outline her own superiority. Not even the Old Lady of the House was as virulently specific on the matter. Still, her mother-in-law could hold to such ideas, because her position allowed it. Chi Lin could not understand why Jasmine needed to fortify her position. She had sons, after all — clear evidence of her status.

They turned off the main road near a larger house — a pavilion with a wide porch. It did not have crenulated tiles or an upturned roof because it did not have the proper permissions, but it was a large affair — large enough to hold dozens of tenants on the porch as the procession approached.

"What is this place?" Chi Lin asked.

"It is the *pao-t'ien* house."

Chi Lin understood. This is where the tenant families held congress to decide mutual issues before deferring to the *Ya-men* or the landlord. The *pao-t'ien* elder resided here when issues were rife for discussion. It was here also where the books were presented for inspection. It was here Chou Kuai-tze and Lin Wu-luo dismounted to be greeted with a bucket of wine and a host of reverential bows. The ladies were greeted by bows only. The elder appeared on the threshold and there was a convivial exchange with the journeyman and the proxy.

Chi Lin realized that she alone was new to this. These men were accustomed to the company and indeed the expectations. Whether the elder was Lu, or Wei (she doubted Wei), or Chou, Ch'u, Ch'ao or Li, Chi Lin could not guess. But the men greeted each other, presented growing sons to be admired, waved some cash strings about and made highly charged sexual comments to which she could not be a reflection, because Jasmine remained as frozen as an idol.

When these niceties were completed, Chou Kuai-tze turned to Jasmine, who arose. She looked to Chi Lin, who took her cue from her and also stood. Jasmine walked to the porch, Chi Lin following. It was a mystery to her. She had no idea what to expect inside except the overbearing smell of sweat and salt.

3

An observer. Chi Lin was an observer — demure and still and patiently so. The *pao-t'ien* house was plain inside, the walls unadorned and the floor bare. A table was center-room with two chairs, and, upon it, a bamboo book was opened to a place for convenience, Chi Lin was sure. To the side, a partitioning screen stood, two chairs behind it, and, to these chairs, Jasmine and Purple Sage were led. The screen was unadorned, thinly gauzed, and no impediment for observation or from being observed. But it served to phantomize the ladies of the Wu House, as was proper to the proceeding. Beside the screen was a shallow basket.

Once settled behind the screen, Chi Lin sat without a sense of action. However, she noticed Jasmine closing her eyes and thought to do so also. But her interest in the inspection was too intense to be shut out from what the screen failed to obscure, so she remained fully alert. Chou Kuai –tze sat in one chair, while Lin Wo-luo took to the other. They unfurled their brushes, wells, ink sticks, chop seals and lacquer pots. The elder bowed and presented them both with one purse each, of which both men seemed to ignore. The elder bowed and placed these purses to the side of the book, and then produced a small cache of silver coins. He looked to the screen, catching Chi Lin's eyes. She almost closed them, but curiosity kept them open. The elder bowed to the screen, and then tossed the coins into the shallow basket, and then bowed again. Jasmine grunted upon hearing the sound.

So that was it. Chi Lin watched now as the journeyman and Imperial proxy perused the bamboo slips, making a note here and a note there. They grinned and winked and finally looked up at the elder.

"Very good," Chou Kuai-tze said, dipping his seal in the lacquer pot and pressing it into the book.

"Very fine," Lin Wo-luo echoed, doing the same with his own seal and pot.

Chi Lin noticed that during the perusal, the two purses somehow disappeared. She knew where they went and guessed their purpose. She imagined that salt production could be high or low, the approval depended on those purses and their weight in the recipient's hands. She would later find out that the amount offered could be determined beyond weight by counting the number of silver coins in the shallow basket, each coin denoting an ingot in the purse. The one thing eluding Chi Lin was why the journeyman and proxy would cheat the monopoly beyond the certainty of greed. If the monopoly was short and the Imperial Certificate compromised, would not the House of Wu lose the award? Then again, if tenants like the Lu overproduced, it would even things out from tenants like the Wei who were nearly vagrant. There had to be a better way, but who was she to question it?

After the accounting and sealing, tea was served, followed by some small wine, not in buckets, but poured from leather flasks. Nothing was offered to the ladies, but during this post-inspection ritual, the small basket was retrieved by the elder and the silver coins wrapped in gauze. This was passed through the screen to Jasmine, whose eyes were wide open now.

The journey back was different, the roads veering to the Lu Family's silk *ji-tzao*. Chi Lin was conscious that the inspection of the silk works was a secondary act, one not accounted for in books and completely free of male intervention. In fact, when they approached the *ji-tzao*, Chou Kuai-tze and Lin Wo-luo held back at a distance, the Lu family women escorting the porters and chairs into a special space where three baskets of cocoons were ready for inspection, the best batches, no doubt.

Jasmine looked to Chi Lin as if this was her moment to shine.

"Never be pleased with the state of things, sister-in-law," she said as they approached. "To show favor breeds encouragement for lesser results. Always be critical."

The chairs were set in the middle of two dozen women, who curtsied. No bribery here, Chi Lin noted, but a sincere regard for Jasmine's opinion. A basket was lifted to her. She sniffed, and then poked her fingers into the cocoons. Her head cocked, and then she frowned.

"They could be brighter," she said. "But they will do."

The woman sighed as if the highest praise had been delivered. Chi Lin could see, even from her standpoint that these cocoons were perfect and would produce the finest thread. It was her turn to inspect. She followed Jasmine's lead, poking her finger into the basket.

"I agree," she said. "The color is off, but they are soft to the touch and should boil up fine."

Jasmine frowned. Too much praise, perhaps, but Chi Lin would perform the next inspection on her own and might revise the usual discouragement into something better suited to her temperament. Indeed, her comment pleased the women better.

Unlike the conclusion of the salt books, no tea or wine was offered. But Chi Lin sensed a happy mood among the women. She was sure that the tea would be poured shortly after their departure.

Chi Lin wondered how the First Wife could tell whether cocoons meant for the Wu House managed to slip away to direct weaving? There was no physical count of the harvest; no practical accounting for the worms. It was much the same for the salt, except the silk was not a monopoly and mostly the realm of women.

Chi Lin pondered as they traveled back to the *Ya-men*. She was disturbed at the state of the tenants. She had been brought up in a poor scholar's house, but it was never so distraught that food lacked or repairs neglected. However, the tenancies, even among the Lu, were rat holes, the men thin and wiry, their backs bent, and their skin blackened from charcoal. The women were old before their time having produced many children and tending the fields and the mulberry patches under the worst conditions. And the children . . . This distressed Chi Lin most of all. Their hungry faces looked up at her, happy to see the prosperity of her robes and the white sheen of her nape. It was as if they were treated to a special sight, beings from a different world. And yet they should yearn for a different prospect than the toil of salt pits and worm farming. They were children, after all, and had a spirit of play in their souls. There had to be something better for them than those bent backs and eternal pregnancies. This saddened Chi Lin greatly and she recalled that Gao Lin told her that *it was not an outing for pleasure*. Those faces confirmed it.

4

When they reached the *Ya-men*, Lin Wo-luo dismounted, approached Jasmine, and then bowed.

"I thank you, Lin Wu-Luo," Jasmine said. "Your service is to the Emperor, I know, but your credit to the House of Wu will be mentioned at our ancestral temple."

Chi Lin grinned. Yes, the proxy had been credited with a purse filled with silver ingots for his trouble, another drain on the tenants adding to their withering burden.

Lin Wu-luo approached Chi Lin, but as he stepped to her side, a voice came from the Ya-men Gate. A man stepped into the sunlight, a man Chi Lin recognized, because he had visited her father and taken dinner in her house. His name was Ai-lo Wun-kua.

"Wu-luo," he called

The proxy bowed quickly to Chi Lin, and then turned, going to the Commissioner (for Ai-lo Wun-kua was the Imperial Commissioner). They exchanged words, and then Wu-luo returned.

"His Honor Ai-lo Wun-kua pays his respects to honorable Chi Ming's daughter."

He bowed. Chi Lin looked to Jasmine, who appeared as ferocious as a tiger. But Chi Lin could not ignore such respect, especially from an imperial commissioner. She nodded.

"It is my honor," she said. "My honor that Ai-lo Wun-kua takes note of Chi Ming's daughter. But I am now the ghost bride of Wu Hung-lin, the fourth wife in Yan-cheng's most respected household. I cherish my father, but cannot take pride of place in his name."

"Just so," Lin Wo-luo snapped, coming to attention.

Chi Lin looked to the Commissioner, who lingered by the gate. She nodded subtly, but nothing beyond that.

Chou Kuai-tze commanded the porters to raise the chairs and the journey continued to the gates of the House of Wu.

Jasmine was silent for the balance of the trip. She did not admonish her sister-in-law for being free by accepting praise from the commissioner. She did not point out that the commissioner was a foreigner, a Mongol, who served the Yuan overlords in the same capacity. She did not express her loathing for these lingering officials, who fancied themselves native sons, learning the language and dressing the part, but were nothing more than steppe bastards raised on mare's milk and flannel. She said nothing more, even when they arrived in the courtyard of the Blue Heaven pavilion, where she opened the gauze purse she had kept clasped in her hand and gave Chi Lin two silver coins for her service. As it happened, silver secured silence on all levels.

Chapter Twelve

The Master Speaks

1

A woman's heart is sometimes plagued by things she knows and cannot address. Chi Lin thought for days after the tour of how it could be better engineered. This was her way, not that anyone would listen nor would she offer any alternative. Her thoughts were her own, but she suspected the First Wife had drawn some conclusions from their time together and formed an opinion that Chi Lin was a meddlesome woman, who would make trouble if she had the chance. Chi Lin would not call it trouble but a benefit to all. But her thinking, as organized as it was, was still scattered. So, she kept these thought to herself, except for one utterance to Gao Lin.

It was near nightfall and Gao Lin had been planting bushes near the courtyard wall. It was late for such activity. Chi Lin gently chided him for being too diligent.

"It is cooler now for such hot work," he replied. "I am practical."

"I am practical also," she said. "I have come to know which work to favor and at what times."

"Does that include the inspection of the *ji-tzao*?"

"That is not work, but folly." She caught herself, her hand going to her mouth. He laughed. "Please, Gao Lin, I did not mean to sound as if it is not important. It is. But I believe it could be improved."

"And in your seven tours you have formed a firm opinion of this?"

He knew she had been on one tour only, so she could do nothing but laugh, for indeed he was jesting.

"It takes only one time to see the tours of seven moons," she said, but then became more circumspect. "But it is not my place to do more than my duty as practically as I can."

"Just as I plant bushes at nightfall when it is cooler."

His voice was as soothing as nightfall, his hands patting the soil. He was skilled at every task he had undertaken. The roof was completed, or until the first rainfall proved the seal; and he had been working on the pool, the stone mountain emerging with miniature trees and wreathes of laurel. She bet if he was a journeyman on the tour, he would have denied the ingot purse. But could any industrious man do as much? She wondered.

"I should not speak to these things, Gao Lin."

"And yet you do. But keep it within these walls. The First Wife is keen to find fault with everyone and, although she is my better, she is not your better and would try to make you worse."

Chi Lin sighed. She would say no more. Jasmine had already frowned upon Gao Lin as a wandering *tea pot spout* among her maid servants. It was not necessarily an insult in Chi Lin's eyes, but definitely meant as detraction on Jasmine's part. So Chi Lin retreated to the pavilion to await Mo Li's coming with the evening meal and Lao Lao's chatter, which like having a caged bird complaining about a cuttlefish bone.

"My old woman stays in bed all day," Lao Lao complained. "She does not even help this cook of yours."

"This is not my fault, Lao Lao."

"It could never be your fault, mistress," he replied. "But she is different than usual."

"How so?"

"She weeps now. I am accustomed to her complaining and nagging. That she has done even before she had gray hairs. But now she just stays on the mat and weeps."

Chi Lin cocked her head, considering this. She remembered how her own mother retreated to weeping just before her death. Chi Lin wondered.

"I shall go to her, Lao Lao," she said.

"It is useless, mistress. She will not improve by the effort and you will only find it tiresome and distressing."

"Nonsense."

So Chi Lin put aside her pancakes with beef and went to the servant's hovel. She had never been inside, not wishing to shame them, but if Snapdragon refused to arise from her bed, what else could Purple Sage do?

The place was dark and fetid. Mo Li sat near the stove cleaning the cooking pan, the water falling to sizzle on the hot coals below. She was startled when the mistress arrived.

"Keep to your task, Mo Li," Chi Lin said. "I come to see . . ."

She spied the withered form of Lao Lao's old woman on the mat, a threadbare blanket covering her shoulders, but not her feet. The form trembled — clearing weeping. Chi Lin hunkered down beside her.

"Snapdragon," she whispered. No answer. She touched her shoulder, and then shook her. "Snapdragon," she repeated, louder.

The old lady turned, her eyes wet and her hair gnarled in the blanket.

"I know your voice," she said. "Is it death finally coming to me, because I am not ready?" Then she wept bitterly. "I will never be ready."

Chi Lin came closer.

"It is Purple Sage, the ghost bride."

"Mistress?" Snapdragon tried to raise herself, to no avail. "Why have come to witness my misery?"

"I have come to see why my faithful servant is so distressed?"

Snapdragon wiped her eyes.

"I am afraid, mistress. I am afraid that death will cross the threshold before I am prepared. I have nothing but these rags. How can I be buried in such things? And I shall be tossed in the ground to feed the beetles, no coffin to protect me, not even one of pinewood. I am afraid, mistress. I am afraid."

Chi Lin grasped the old woman. She felt her fear and also sensed what was true. She felt helpless and knew no remedy at hand. A woman's heart is sometimes plagued by things she knows and cannot address. Still, she had come to give comfort, so she rocked Snapdragon in her arms and smoothed her knotted hair.

"Be at rest," she said. "You may remain at your ease here. Mo Li will undertake all the cooking and we shall manage the remainder. I shall have Gao Lin raise the threshold to delay death's entry and . . . I shall place a mirror at the door with demon catching daggers. That should give you some peace."

"Yes, mistress. Yes, yes it would. You are too good."

Chi Lin hushed her, and then laid her down. Snapdragon wept still, watched by Mo Li who was useless at consoling. But that was not her job. When Chi Lin left the hovel, she spotted Lao Lao pacing outside.

"She would not speak to you, mistress," he said. "Am I not correct?"

"You are correct, Lao Lao," she said. "We must do our best and humor her until . . . until the remedy appears."

Lao Lao continued his pacing.

2

Chi Lin went the next morning to the shrine to perform her daily duty. However, as she approached she was surprised to see Willow and the Old Lady of the House before the temple. She was unsure whether to proceed because she had never witnessed her mother-in-law at the shrine. But to wait would fail her duty, so she quietly approached, and then knelt before her husband's effigy.

"I am here, Wu Hung-lin," she said. "I come to ease your spirit and be guided by your husbandly example."

She bowed, clapped three times and lit an incense stick, poking it into the sand pot. The Old Lady of the House burned red paper prayers, and then turned to Willow.

"See that Purple Sage comes to me before she sees him," she said. "Help me to stand."

Willow gave the old woman a boost. Once balanced, the Old Lady of the House shuffled out of the temple courtyard leaving Chi Lin alone with Willow.

"What did she mean?" Chi Lin asked. "Who am I to see?"

"The Master of the House has asked to speak with you, Purple Sage. That is all."

"Have I caused offense?"

"That is not for me to say," Willow replied. Then she came close to Chi Lin's ear. "The Autumn Festival approaches. It is the Master's custom to visit each wife in her quarters."

"But I am to see him in his," Chi Lin said. "Surely this is not the same thing."

"Surely, it is," Willow replied. "The Master is troubled still to enter the Silver Silence Pavilion. The remembrance of the Second Wife weighs heavy upon his heart. Yet, he will most likely ask you about your progress toward your hall's repair."

Chi Lin sighed. Was she always to be the outsider in the general order of things? Still, if the Master wanted to see her, she could not refuse. It was a fearful prospect. She had only seen him at her wedding and heard him entertaining guests in the *ke-ting* at the Jade Heart Pavilion. At most times he kept his own society.

Chi Lin cut short her morning prayers. She stood.

"I am ready, then."

Willow, as friendly as ever, walked beside her to the Jade Heart Pavilion, where they crossed the Old Lady of the House's threshold. Chi Lin's mother-in-law was the same as she had seen her at the shrine, but instead of her usual sewing circle of women, she sat alone near the latticework that divided her residence from her husband's. She beckoned Chi Lin to approach.

"Purple Sage," she said. "Has Willow told you?"

"She has, mother-in-law."

"Good. Now *I* shall tell you." She pointed through the latticework. "My lord is a great man with many responsibilities. We all support his efforts to rule here. He is fond of his household and we all know and keep our places. It is Autumn Festival. The family shall be in residence. We shall eat well and play well. Children will be under foot, and more wives than I can stand at any time will crave my attention. But such is the way of great houses. Do you understand?"

"I am happy to be part of the House of Wu, mother-in-law."

"You are lucky to be part of it. But part of it, you are. So the Master will offer you a gift of your choosing and will also ask you about your progress here. Remember, what a man asks, a woman should be careful to answer. He wants to hear his own voice ask, but rarely will listen to what you say in response." She twitched. "He comes. I will be here by the partition. I will hear your every word. Please do not give me cause for sorrow."

"No, mother-in-law."

The Old Lady of the House watched her husband enter, and then sit in his favorite chair. She nodded to Chi Lin.

"Go slowly and with the deepest respect."

3

Chi Lin entered the Master's presence. She went slowly and also quietly, her purple robes hardly whisking the floor. She curtsied and knelt. Her father-in-law had been perusing a document and did not acknowledge her. In fact, he waited so long, she worried that he was somehow offended by her presence. Perhaps he had forgotten that he had summoned her and would be cross when he discovered her presence. Still he perused his business.

"You are here," he said, flatly, without looking at her.

"As you have called for me, father-in-law, I have appeared."

He snorted, and continued to read. Chi Lin observed the man — old, to be sure, but still endowed with his full faculties. His teeth were broken, but his eyes seemed clear. He wore a sky blue robe with gold and black trim, pearls dotting the hem line and the robe sleeves. He sported a crimson satin turban with spatulated scholar flaps and a silver spike drawing the tie knots into a tiger's eye. Studying his face, she saw her own husband crenulated with the features. She was accustomed to address her ghost lord now, so she need not have been frightened at the living version of Wu Hung-lin. In fact, Wu T'ai-po had a gentle countenance redolent of a fragrant life.

"Good," he said, and finally putting aside the document. "I am much occupied and more so now that Autumn Festival is upon us. My sons will be presenting their wives and children to me and we shall all have a grand time — a family time. I know you must miss your father. I have seen him and he is well."

"Good of you to say, father-in-law."

"Do not mention it. I have heard from my old lady that you have been diligent with your chores and industrious within your own pavilion."

"It is my honor to serve."

"So it is. So it is." He leaned forward. "Take a seat beside me."

Chi Lin gazed at the latticework. She saw the Old Lady of the House's eyes batting through the design. Chi Lin awaited a sign, but none came, so she took a seat beside her father-in-law hoping that she had not offended her mother-in-law in the act.

"Be comforted," Wu T'ai-po said. "I know you are the least of wives — a ghost bride, but you also have honored us by being so. I have not forgotten." He sighed. "Tell me. Have you begun repairs on the Silver Silence . . . I mean, is some work going apace. My son wanted to have it completed before your wedding day, but alas, Heaven saw otherwise. You know the Silver Silence has a special place in my heart."

Chi Lin nodded, daring not to say that she did know about Peony and wore her clothes and slept in her bed.

"The roof has been retiled," she said, sharply in an attempt to move away from Wu T'ai-po's maudlin tone. "Much progress has been made on restoring the lotus pool and bushes have been planted — trees are planned, and autumn flowers are being fetched."

"Good. Good," he said. "Have you made improvements to the hall?"

"I plan some," Chi Lin said. "I am in no need for opulence, but I plan to find a scroll or three to hang and to renew the beadwork near my bed. I can sew and patch the carpeting, and I have my eye on a repaired table and three chairs in the wood shop."

"My old lady has told me that you were good with the sewing . . . and the worms too. And you have been on an inspection tour."

"Yes, father-in-law, I have been on one tour. Only one."

"And what did you think of that?"

Chi Lin's breath caught her tongue. *Remember, what a man asks, a woman should be careful to answer. He wants to hear his own voice ask, but rarely will listen to what you say in response.* She did not answer.

"Please, Purple Sage. Tell me your thoughts on the inspection. You are an outsider and perhaps have a suggestion that might improve things."

"I dare not say," Chi Lin said.

She heard her mother-in-law's warning cough. *You must not say.*

"If I did not want to hear you, I would not have asked," Wu T'ai-po said.

Chi Lin took a deep breath, and then spoke.

"The journeyman and the *Ya-men* authority were impressive, my lord," she said. "Our presence was respected and received by the tenants as such. I truly believe there is high regard for the House of Wu."

"I am glad to hear you say so."

"It is true. But . . . but, I would think in an inspection . . ."

"Yes?"

"In an inspection, things would be inspected."

Chi Lin heard her mother-in-law's nearby grunt.

"The tour is mostly ceremonial," Wu T'ai-po said, curtly. "It is detailed by law and I shall not apologize to a woman for her perceptions."

"Forgive me, father-in-law. I meant no disrespect. You asked me for my observations, and I have said too much already." She paused. "Only . . ."

"Only?"

"The elder prepares the books for inspection. He is a tenant and could perhaps misjudge the weights and measures. The commissioner's proxy and your journeyman merely inspect the written characters and validate them. And when inspecting the silk *ji-tzao* . . ."

"The silk is not my concern," he said, coolly. "That is for a woman's eye. You must know, Purple Sage, we must trust the elder to record correctly."

"Even if . . ."

He raised his hand. She looked to her hands.

"And how would *you* redesign the universe?" He grinned. "I am anxious to know."

Chi Lin gazed now at the carpet. The repeated designs, circles, drew her attention into desperate focus.

"I would not change the way of law, but I would add a refinement."

"A refinement?"

"I would ask for an accounting beyond the tenants and the *Yamen*. And I would have it supervised by men paid for their loyalty to make accurate measurements."

"You mean those uncorrupted by the lure of bribes? Where are such men?"

"I have a brother, father-in-law. His name is Chi Sheng. He excels in accounts, but he is lame and would tarnish the House of Wu's name. But . . ."

"I am listening."

Was he? Chi Lin recalled her mother-in-law's words. *What a man asks, a woman should be careful to answer. He wants to hear his own voice ask, but rarely will listen to what you say in response.* She continued with care.

"He could review the accounts out of sight, while others supervise the weights and measures."

"Others?"

"My father's brother has a large family. They are weavers and farmers and assume no man's tenancy. My cousins could be employed to oversee the weighing and the measuring. This would benefit the House of Wu and also show my gratitude as a ghost bride."

Wu T'ai-po scratched his chin, his eyes squinting.

"Let us not speak of this," he said. "You must not bother your head about matters of the monopoly except to play your part in the tour. Now, I have called you here to greet you for the Autumn Festival, a time of great joy in our household. These walls shall embrace my sons and their family. There shall be much revelry — games and feasting. You will be busier than usual and I recognize this by giving a gift to all the resident wives."

Chi Lin arose, curtsied, and then bowed. It seemed appropriate, especially after the embarrassment of voicing her thoughts.

"Thank you, father-in-law."

"So, what would you like to add to the peace and tranquility of the Silver Silence Pavilion?"

Chi Lin remained silent for some time, pressing her lord's patience, but then decided.

"It is a costly need, father-in-law."

"It always is," he said laughing. "But say it and I shall make it so."

She bowed, her words caught in her throat. Then she faced him squarely.

"I would like a silk funeral shroud and an ironwood coffin."

Wu T'ai-po baulked. He stood, and then sat again. Chi Lin heard the Old Lady of the House rapping on the latticework.

"You are young, Purple Sage," Wu T'ai-po said. "What use would such things be in restoring the hall?"

"Pardon, my lord," she said. "They are not for me, but for Lao Lao's old lady, Snapdragon. Death approaches my household and such things are needed for peace and tranquility."

It was Wu T'ai-po's time for silence. Then he nodded to his daughter-in-law.

"It shall be so. I had quite forgotten those loyal servants at the Silver Silence. Indeed, they are faithful and deserving. It shall be so."

He picked up his document again, but Chi Lin knew he only pretended to read it. He was far away in the arms of his Second Wife and perhaps recalling her faithful servants. Chi Lin bowed herself out. When she passed the latticework, she caught the eye of the Old Lady of the House. She expected a resumption of criticism concerning the boldness of tongue and uselessness in advising men on business. She expected more than a lecture. Perhaps a beating.

But her mother-in-law was demure, watching as her daughter-in-law passed her.

"I shall feed the worms, mother-in-law," Chi Lin said.

The old lady said nothing — no lecture, admonishment or promise for pain. Perhaps she had heard the words truly and was impressed. More likely, she recalled her our need for a shroud and coffin and would find Purple Sage a great ally in the end, the ghost bride being more like her than not. In the end, a woman's heart is sometimes plagued by things she knows and cannot address — and the words of men lived in beehives gathering honey and doling out stings.

Chapter Thirteen

Gentle Rain and Lanterns

1

Wu T'ai-po was good on his word. Within a week, an ironwood coffin and a fine white funeral shroud was drawn on a donkey cart into the Silver Silence courtyard. Snapdragon, who expected them, stood in the threshold watching as the porters unloaded the cart and flopped the shroud loosely over the dark wood. Snapdragon's blindness kept her from fully seeing her burial furniture, but when the cart departed, Lao Lao led her to it, her hand running across the handles and latch. A grin overcame her as she touched the shroud, bringing it to her nose. She pulled it from the coffin and draped it over her shoulders, and then clapped.

Chi Lin watched from afar, but soon the old woman shuffled to the hall looking for her benefactress.

"Mistress," she called. "Heaven had sent me a living saint on the day you came into this courtyard."

"You deserve no less," Chi Lin said.

Snapdragon went to her knees and touched her mistress' feet, wiping the toes with the silk shroud. In fact, Snapdragon would come into the hall daily to help with hair and wardrobe. She fumbled most of the time, but Chi Lin allowed her to manage the first steps, only to correct them herself when the old woman left. Always Snapdragon wore the white shroud, and the coffin was moved into the servant's hovel sitting beside the bed mat. Chi Lin supposed Snapdragon tried the coffin out in the evening, but it was no great matter. Peace and tranquility descended over Lao Lao and his old lady. In fact, it descended over the entire Hall of Silver Silence as the Autumn Festival approached.

There was much to do in preparation for the festival, especially making lanterns of various types. The general sort would swag from rope lines along the pathways, but the more elaborate would be hoisted on tall poles reflecting the reason for the festival — the moon in all her radiant glory. Others were prepared to fly skyward, flights of illuminated prayers to the Lady in the Moon. Chi Lin's tasks evolved around lantern construction, both cloth and paper – preparing surfaces so the men could brush poetry and prayers in their most stylish hand. Even Lin-kua and Chou-fa practiced making their mark upon the lanterns.

In addition to folding and shaping lanterns, Chi Lin had extra work with the shoes. There would be many more children in the house now that the brothers were coming. The Old Lady of the House would give each of her grandchildren shoes and slippers, and on the shoe faces would be tigers and lotuses and rabbits. Chi Lin was good at sewing rabbit ears on slippers and adept at embroidering tiger faces on shoes. Her fingers were more calloused now, so she could stay at it longer, her mother-in-law prizing her work.

The worms still needed attending. But the *ji-tzao* was filled with music now from the nearby Crimson Blossom and Golden Oak pavilions. The Second and Third wife excelled in song and playing, having been former pleasure girls. They now stepped away from their *ji-tzao* duties to practice for the approaching festivities. Lotus was expert on the *p'i-pa*, her fingers picking out sultry melodies from the strings.

Chi Lin visited Lotus during this time, even being offered a bowl of tea and a slice of melon. Crimson Blossom Hall was elegant, covered in gold and silver beadwork and festooned with silk pillows. Centered on a teakwood chair, Lotus played and sang sweet songs of the pleasure house; only the words were altered for family listening. She was poised over her tiny feet, a pink robe cascading just high enough to leave them exposed. Her hair was triple coifed with ebony pins, jade clusters dangling from the ends. Her face paint was as near to death white as death itself, except Chi Lin had learned that, despite the moribund references, men liked pale faced women. She wondered why she, as the ghost wife, could not blanch her face instead of remaining in her purple robe. As she sat listening, Pearl and Jade emerged with their *amah*. They winked at Purple Sage, the auntie who had brought them moon cakes. Chi Lin smiled in return, but the *amah* brought the girls harshly to attention, their mother's playing to be accounted as the important event.

Chi Lin admired Lotus' talent. She also played the *p'i-pa* – mother taught and guided. But playing to while away the time in the silence of your house and playing to wile men in a pleasure pavilion were different applications. So Chi Lin accepted the Second Wife's special place for what it was – Wu Hung-lin's homage to a night of sweet dreams and his attempt to capture it for all times.

Orchid was a different flavor. Chi Lin visited while Orchid practiced on the *ehr-hu*. Her pavilion – The Golden Oak was less ornate, pastel in effect, draped with silk gauze and decorated with pearl strands. Orchid's temperament was different. She neither offered Chi Lin a tea bowl or melon – not even the rind. But she did nod her welcome and began to play a melancholy song, the bow arching the single string, catching it front and back as the hand decided. The melody was mournful, Chi Lin depressed after hearing it. It sought a place far from here – a solitary rock in a barren land. As Orchid played, her daughter, Sapphire peeked around a partition. She grinned at Auntie Purple Sage, but was immediate poked by her *amah*. Sapphire pouted, a face that mimicked her mother's demure, melancholy look. The Golden Oak was a morose place. Chi Lin wondered if Orchid was more prisoner than wife. Chi Lin was glad to leave this sad place. Despite this, Orchid was an expert player, but she had ceased singing. If she had sung, Chi Lin supposed it would have been a lament.

2

Chi Lin enjoyed preparing for the Autumn Festival. She saw cheery faces on the servants as they anticipated the extra rations of food and the sparkle of entertainment approaching. New work made the time pass quicker. Still, when she retuned to her pavilion, she was tired. She would eat her repast in the quiet of her *ke-ting* and imagine how she could improve the place – a new wall hanging *here* and a set of chairs *there*. As she mused, she could hear Mo Li complaining about new dents in her old *wok* and Lao Lao laughing about old days before he came to the House of Wu. And there was always Snapdragon talking about how lucky she was to have her shroud and coffin – no fear now for the trip to *the Yellow Springs*. Then Gao Lin, who worked until moonrise, sang a fascinating song about a cricket in a cage:

> *"Old Man cricket sings his song*
> *Caring not for the beetles at play.*
> *He knows he can beat them at their dance*
> *And taunts them to fight him as they may.*

They laugh at his mocking
They joke at his sneers
But they keep their distance with their fears,
For Old Man Cricket is a crafty one,
There is no one like him under the sun."

Chi Lin leaned out the window.

"That is a fine song, Gao Lin," she called. "Is that from your native village?"

"No, mistress," he said, waving to her. "I wrote it myself."

"Truly?"

"It is a brash verse and stands on its own. I would think it would make a nice wall hanging and would do it myself . . . if I could write."

Chi Lin laughed and asked for another verse, but he sang the same one.

"It would be nice if I knew someone who could write it down," he said, whistling.

Suddenly, Chi Lin shivered. The *man* knew she was schooled. *How did he know?* She had taken a book from the schoolroom when master P'ing Chin was not looking and she read it by dimmed light after Gao Lin was asleep. He must have seen this. He must have seen her practicing her brush strokes too, something she never did when he was in the hall. But he was a keen observer and ink stained fingers.

She grinned, and then peeked out the window again. He sang the song louder still. She quickly retrieved her brush, well and ink stick – only one so as not to make much mess. She kept her rice paper in the cache beneath her bed. She would not have time to prepare it properly, now tacking it roughly to the floor with her tea bowl and her shoe. She used tea water in the well, pressing the stick lightly into the wet, and then rubbing it on the stone. Dipping her brush into the water, and then slathering it against the stone, she tested for consistency on a remote edge. A few tries achieved success, and then she held the instrument in her fist and began to write, hoping she recalled the poems.

"Sing it again," she called, and he complied, laughing between strophes.

Chi Lin hesitated, trying to remember the character for *cricket*, but then happily recalled it. The brush flew perfectly down the sheet, breaking to the right for each measure. *Dancing* and *fighting* and *joking* and *mocking*, all came forth in lyrical arrays until *there was nothing like him under the sun.* At this Chi Lin mused.

"Indeed, there is no one like him under the sun," she whispered.

With a few flicks of the brush tip she created a small cricket creature escaping from a cage. She wished she had a chop seal to make the work official. She dared not put her name to it, but since Gao Lin claimed authorship, she scrawled his name, or how she supposed his name should be presented, at the lower left side. She used the characters *Gao Lin*, which, in his case meant *tall forest*. She removed the bowl and her shoe, assuring the ink was set. It was. So she rolled it loosely, went to the window and threw it at him, ducking quickly back into the hall, laughing like a silly girl.

"What is this?" he asked. "I wish I could I read it."

"It is your poem," she shouted from out of sight.

"What scholar god has visited us?" he laughed.

Soon he came inside, the scroll grasped in his fist. Chi Lin sat on the floor examining her big feet by candlelight.

"Mistress," he said. "Look what fell from Heaven while I worked."

She gazed at the scroll.

"You are fortunate, Gao Lin. Your words flew to the Jade Emperor, who, liking your song, preserved it for you."

"I think it should hang in the hall, behind my screen, so I can admire it when I wake in the morning. And it will be the last thing I see at night. I would show it to you, but alas you cannot read it either, so it will be a glorious mystery for the Hall of Silver Silence."

He laughed, and then disappeared into the shadows. Chi Lin smiled, but then sighed. She heard him tacking the scroll to his partition and whistling his song. Her hands trembled, and her heart leapt just a little. She knew she needed to climb into her bed and draw the bed clothing very high – up to her shoulders if need be. She was unsure of her desires, but she felt it would insult Wu Hung-lin if she pursued them.

Gao Lin was called away from the hall the next morning. The sky portended rain and the worms needed protection. Every man who was skilled in construction was ordered to build tents over the mulberry grove. When the winds picked up, the challenge increased. Gao Lin was absent for a week tending to the *ji-tzao*.

Chi Lin attended the shrine, assuring, when the rain began, her husband's effigy would stay dry and the incense would remain burning. The new lanterns were stored in a dry place, those that had been hung already or bolted to the towers, were retrieved and secured. The Old Lady of the House was sterner than usual, fearing the Autumn Festival preparations would have a set back. A little rain would not matter and could be welcomed to clear the air of bad smells, but if the lanterns were ruined, there would not be much point in celebrating. So she barked orders to everyone to secure *this* and stow *that*, threatening that any damage would be taken out in promised beatings and diminished rewards.

Chi Lin had two concerns. The first was Snapdragon's health and the second, the condition of the Hall's roof. To the first, she visited the old lady to set aside her concerns. She found Lao Lao's old lady sitting inside her coffin draped in her shroud. Lao Lao sat at one end, shaking his head.

"She is still grateful for this, mistress," he said.

"I can see," Chi Lin replied.

Snapdragon upon hearing the mistress' voice, rocked back and forth.

"Death did not get me last night, mistress," she said. "And if he had showed up, I would only need to lay back and welcome him, thanks to you." Then she pouted. "I am sorry I did not come to you this morning, but I was feeling poorly. Waiting for death is very wearisome, you know."

"When he comes," Mo Li said, looking up from her rolling pins, "tell him to leave his hands off my pastries. They are all accounted for."

"You jest," Snapdragon says. "But you do not have a coffin or a fine funeral shroud. You will need to fall into your stew to save your silly tongue."

"At least I have a stew to escape him."

Chi Lin did not referee this verbal combat, such as it was. It proved that all was normal in the hovel and might be for some time to come.

The other concern was proving the roof. The new tiles and repaired portions appeared fine, but Gao Lin had said repeatedly that a roof cannot be deemed worthy until proved, and that could not happen until the first rainfall after the repairs. He also stated that, despite his fine workmanship, there would be leaks and more work. More work would mean more cost, so Chi Lin hoped there would only be a trickle here and there – nothing more than a patch needed to stop a runnel. So when the rain finally came, Chi Lin's mind was set on capturing every little drip. She had five buckets at the ready at the hall's far end.

3

Distant thunder and gentle rain. The thunder awoke Chi Lin, but the rain kept her in bed. She had goose bumps, a pleasant, soothing feeling, lulling her into a need to remain warm and comfortable under her bed clothing. Then she suddenly remembered the roof. She sat quickly at the edge, her feet bouncing to the carpet. Once in her shift, she listened for signed of dripping. She thought she heard a metallic sound from one of the buckets. Gao Lin must have preceded her and located seepage, setting the pail beneath the leak.

Chi Lin found the spot, looking to the eaves. It was not severe, but it was seepage nonetheless. She heard knocking on the roof. Gao Lin was already mending the spot. A quick walk about the hall assessed the rest as dry. She grinned. The roof was proved. She was suddenly hungry, but the table was bare, Mo Li not having stirred yet. She could not blame her. Chi Lin would forgo her own chores this morning.

As she gazed out the window, she spotted Lao Lao dancing in the rain. The old man whipped off his clothing and embraced the downpour, light as it was, for a gentle bathe. The act made her jealous. It would be a fine thing to emerge into the courtyard and let the cool drops kiss her body. Just the thought of it assuaged her hunger.

Lao Lao was splashing about near the pool, his hair matted to his forehead. He closed his eyes, perhaps to ignore that he was being watched. But he showed no signs of embarrassment or remorse. Then Gao Lin climbed from the roof and applauded him. At first, Lao Lao stopped, looked to the young man, but then threw him a hand gesture and continued his lark. Gao Lin laughed, and then began to peel his own garments away. His dance was not as silly or rollicking as Lao Lao's, but it was a sight to see.

Chi Lin was caught by the image. She had spied this man when he washed, admiring his fine form — his glistening buttocks and his hedgerow groin. But it was always a quick flash, passing as fast as the water source. But now, with a steady cascade from Heaven, the sight was delectably slow and fully drawn. There was no peeking now, but a full stare at the wonders of a horse washed under a fountain — a fine specimen sparkling beneath the flow. She could not free her eyes from him, her own body tensing with delight. But then he threw his shambled clothing over his shoulders and headed for the hall. The display was over and she wanted it still.

Gao Lin stood on the threshold drying his chest with his wet robes. He was covered now after a fashion, the former spectacle only guessed at in quick jerks below his hemline. Chi Lin came to him.

"The roof is proved," she said.

"It is so," he replied. "One spot had a cracked tile, but it is temporarily repaired. When the sun shines again, I shall make it permanent." He stopped drying himself, a useless attempt with wet clothing. "I am afraid I found inspiration in the old man's lark."

"All men are children," she said. "You have earned your bath, Gao Lin."

"Have I?" he asked, letting the sopping robe fall, revealing himself again, this time brashly and without apology. "I would do better with a dry rag."

Chi Lin took a step toward him, her eyes coursing his entire body from shoulder to knee. She sighed, and yet trembled. It was not proper for her to enjoy such a sight, and yet it was not proper for him to stand naked before her. If the servants discovered them, she would be the talk of the house. But Lao Lao, the crazy old fool was like *Old Man Cricket* caring not for the beetles at play. It was but a little step for Chi Lin to undo her shift letting it fall beside his wet robes. She took that step. Her ghost husband might see her, but she would ask forgiveness later at the shrine. It was just clothing, was it not?

"I shall not leave the hall today," she whispered, grasping his hand.

"No need," he replied. "The roof is proved and *Old Man Cricket* seeks his cage."

She smiled and pulled him forward.

And thus Chi Lin took Gao Lin to her bed with the soft sighs of the gentle rain in her mind. The wind lacking in the rain, now swept the sheets, as his passion, pent up, and then let loose as she let him find his way as he wanted and as she would have it. Nothing harnessed time, which was overdue in this case. Nothing made less of the fullness of the horse that washed under the fountain, sparkling to put the fires out. The partition that kept them apart — mistress and servant, came down in this moment, if only for a moment, and they would burn the evidence, near the far wall later. To do otherwise would have caused the servants to tell laundry tales, fleshing out the passionate moments that they could only have surmised if they had witnessed the stain.

Distant thunder.

Chapter Fourteen

Reunion

1

The rain days were long and blissful, keeping Chi Lin away from her chores and Gao Lin off the roof. That they found each other fascinating was a secret joy to Chi Lin, but they both knew the boundary crossed was merely a foray. Care was taken, because Lao Lao lurked and Snapdragon showed up daily to untangle her mistress's hair. Mo Li darted in and out with meals and wondered perhaps why it sometimes remained untouched, having, in truth, gone cold while Purple Sage whiled away her time in her bed and not necessarily alone.

"None of this is proper," she whispered to Gao Lin during an interval.

"Life is not proper, mistress," Gao Lin replied. "We maintain our faces to the world as the world expects, but the world also expects a secret behind every moonrise."

Chi Lin supposed he was correct, although she had never had many secrets herself, except that she could read and write. This liaison must remain a secret, for both their sakes. She was already the lowest wife on the ladder and could not imagine anything lower except to be chastised and thrown out to fend for herself in the town gutters. If that became the case, she would just swallow her earrings and be done with it. As for Gao Lin, he would be beaten with the bamboo pole until he could never be able to climb a roof again. So after a week of happy congress, it ended. There was no pleading or weeping. It had been what it had been and no more. Chi Lin thought it was perhaps a little more, for her at least. Gao Lin had a reputation for being free with his *tea spout* in other quarters of the house. Chi Lin was sure that she was no more than a release or perhaps a reward for good work completed. But he was a tender man — filled with humorous quips. Yet he knew his place and never made bold in his privileged position.

The rain still accompanied the mornings when Gao Lin returned to his duties. Chi Lin, as a dutiful wife, called for a *san-tze* and went to the shrine. Mo Li was the only one available for this task and she made it clear that she was a cook and not a maid servant. Still, she held the *san-tze* high, keeping her mistress dry. The incense was hard to fire, but once lit, Chi Lin stared at Wu Hung-lin's effigy.

"Husband," she said. She wanted to say: "I cannot hide the truth from you because you see what others cannot see. But if you disapproved you would have shaken me out of bed and driven Gao Lin mad by degrees." But Mo Li was present, so the truth would needed veiling. "Husband," she said (instead). "Forgive my delay in coming to your shrine, but the dragon spits and would have us huddle beneath our counterpanes for warmth. But you can see me, I can tell, and if my conduct has offended you, you would not have drawn me out of my bed to your temple this day."

She waited. Mo Li yawned — a good sign that she had no notion of her mistress' palaver. Chi Lin then reached for the red paper prayers and began burning them one by one.

"Your touch," she said, "your gentle hand upon my breast would be a thrill awaited by a bride of seventeen from her wise lord. Your caresses in the depths of night would be the fire needed to make a wife fulfill her duties. Your subtle sigh through my hair would be like the winds of the *xien* from the isles of the blessed, to cradle my thigh about your loins." She sighed. "What your ghost bride lacks, she can imagine now and know the kernel meant to bloom in the barren garden."

She looked to Mo Li again. The words were too arcane for the cook, who shifted the *san-tze* about as if it had grown heavy. Chi Lin was satisfied. Wu Hung-lin was not a cook. He was a ghost of quality and would know what his wife imparted over the burning red paper prayers.

Chi Lin waited for a wind gust or an errant spark — anything to chastise her for her nights of passion with Gao Lin. None came, so she bowed to her husband and clapped three times. She glanced at *Guan-yin* and thought she saw a smile on the goddess' lips. *What did it mean? Was this supreme approval?* Or was the fertile goddess clarifying the morning prayers with fecundity. Chi Lin was uneasy, but was filled also with a sense of well-being — a sugary charge from *Guan-yin* that something was apace, here in the presence of the Wu family ancestors and her ghost husband above all.

Chi Lin stood, almost hitting her head on the *san-tze*.

"You are correct, Mo Li. You are a cook and no hand maiden."

"A tree limb could hold this *san-tze* and needs no recipe to do it," Mo Li grumbled. "I would like to see a tree limb cook the morning congee or steam buns."

Chi Lin grasped the *san-tze*, Mo Li relinquishing it happily.

"Moon Cakes," Chi Lin said. "It is the time for Moon Cakes. Go ahead and make your pastries. I will be the tree limb and keep myself dry."

Mo Li did not stand on ceremony, but bounced toward the courtyard gate. Chi Lin turned to the shrine, staring at the effigy.

"Is there anything to forgive?" she asked her husband.

Silence. She nodded to *Guan-yin*.

"Is there anything to expect?"

The incense sticks in the sand pot suddenly glowed. Chi Lin touched her belly. It was then that she knew. By the week's end, Chi Lin would do more than guess. She would feel physically different, but would not voice the matter, because the rain had ceased and the Autumn Festival was upon the house.

2

The Second Son, Wu Liang-tze arrived on the first day after the rain. He sat astride his horse nearly tottering from the saddle. Chi Lin espied him from the Jade Heart Pavilion and, from his appearance, he had been drinking plum and rice wine on the short journey between his estate and his father's. He needed considerable help to dismount, boisterously greeting his father, who accepted the jollity, it being the Autumn Festival. Three carry-chairs transported his wives, each surrounded by their children — so many that Chi Lin did not think to count them. They were noisy and scrappy, unruly even before their grandfather. Their *amahs* chastised them into a civilized bow to the head of the house, who raised his arms to gather them under his robes. As for the wives, they were a sour lot. Chi Lin pitied them being married to Wu Liang-tze, exposed to his wanton ways. When the Second Son finished his greeting to his father, he turned to the Old Lady of the House, bowing demurely as if she was the only chastisement in his life. She scarcely returned the compliment. Once Liang-tze disappeared into the *ke-ting*, seeking more plum wine, no doubt, the carry-chairs moved through the courtyard toward the guest pavilions — kept for such occasions. The children skipped behind them. Once the noise trailed away, Chi Lin found Willow.

"Is it always so?" she asked.

"Always." Willow looked about assuring no one listened. "The Second Son will rove, so beware."

"He does not like me," Chi Lin said. "He thinks me plain and has said so to my face."

"You should pray you stay ugly, because the more he drinks the prettier you may become."

Chi Lin laughed. Willow did not.

"Orchid and Lotus would be more the draw,"

"You would think it, but they are much like his own wives." Willow looked again. "His wives are much put upon and he tires of them quickly. He has more than three, but nobody is sure just how many, the weddings happening at all times and in all seasons. But these three are the principle ones and the only ones arranged by the family. The Second Son spends much time at the pleasure house, or so I have been told."

Who told her that could be of little doubt. This would be the plain talk of the Old Lady of the House. A mother knows her own. Chi Lin caught the cold greeting between mother and son. Despite Willow's warning, Chi Lin dismissed the threat. She was more concerned about lingering thoughts of her possible condition, which she almost broached with Willow, but decided it spoke to directly to family honor. Willow had become a friend, but not so close that she would not hint of things to her mistress.

Three days after Wu Liang-tze's arrival, Wu San-ehr arrived. The Third Son was taller than his brother and sat astride a war horse. He was accompanied by a retinue of aides — soldiers wearing the Imperial insignia, carrying the banner of Prince Chu Di, the Emperor's fourth son. Wu San-ehr was a Lieutenant, directly attending the Prince and the strongest link the Wu family had to Imperial favor. San-ehr was broad in shoulder and stood proudly — almost imperially, a trait prized by his lord. There was no sign of drink about him, or so Chi Lin thought. His hands gripped the reins tightly. He needed no help to dismount.

Wu San-ehr had two wives, both carried behind him, each smiling to the journeymen and servants in welcome. Four children abided, quietly and reverentially beside their *amahs*. They were sons — four wonderful contributions to the Wu legacy. While Wu Liang-tze had a distant resemblance to his brother, Wu Hung-lin, Wu San-ehr was a younger copy. It took Chi Lin's breath away. It was the closest she had been to seeing her own husband apart from the effigy.

The Master of the House strode into the courtyard, Liang-tze beside him.

"Is this my son, Wu San-ehr, before me?" he asked. "Is this the boy who left my gates in service to His Majesty, may He live ten thousand years."

Wu San-ehr grinned, and then took a knee.

"Father," he said, choked. "I have returned to this house as your humble child, bringing you daughters-in-law who serve you well. Sons! Behold my sons."

Before Wu T'ai-po could acknowledge them, the Old Lady of the House emerged, raising her arms.

"Come to your grandmother, sons of Wu San-ehr," she said.

The boys came forward, taking a knee beside their father.

"Indeed, they are well disciplined," T'ai-po said approvingly, looking askance at Wu Liang-tze, who grunted.

"My children are the sons of a warrior, who finds discipline the only way to show respect in this world."

"Respect?" Liang-tze said. "Remember your place, little brother. There are warriors who see many battles and there are those who ride for the courtesy of princes."

"I know my place, brother," Wu San-ehr replied. "And it is here, standing before my betters, asking for courtesy at this reunion time that my place is known best."

"You have my respect," Wu T'ai-po said, raising his son to his feet and embracing him. "Come share a cup with me . . . and your brother, while your mother dotes on your sons. I am sure a little doting will not ruin their fine discipline. After all, there will be games later and they may find a way to play with their cousins."

"Surely," Wu San-ehr said. "Surely."

There was little more to be said. The brothers retreated into the *ke-ting*. The Old Lady of the House presented the sons with new shoes. And the retinue escorted the wives through the gateway to the guest quarters.

"He is so different," Chi Lin said to Willow.

"He is the favorite and, now that Hung-lin is at *the Yellow Springs*, the Third Son would abide here if it were not for his commitment to Prince Chu Di."

"It is a shame that he will leave. It is . . ."

Suddenly, she felt strange — a rumble in her head, and then her belly.

"What is the matter, mistress?" Willow asked.

Chi Lin was not sure, but still would not chance speculation.

"I felt a momentary qualm, that is all — one of Mo Li's ingredients, no doubt."

"Please take care. You would not wish to be ill for the festivities."

Chi Lin smiled wanly. Whatever it was, it had passed.

"I look forward to the festivities."

3

Fireworks. The Master of the House did not stint on the display. He hired the Yan-cheng town entertainers to put on a full display on the first evening for the family and invited guests, which included Superintendent Po T'ai-kuan and Commissioner Ai-lo Wun-kua and assorted Ya-men officials. Chi Lin marveled at their attire, especially Ai-lo Wun-kua in his steep turban, jade girdle and bright red robes. The wine flowed freely and Moon Cakes were in abundance almost in need of replenishment, which the cooks remedied early the next morning, because Moon Cakes, especially the ones stuffed with bean curd, were the principle essential for the second day.

Chi Lin roused early and, although she was particularly tired, she managed to wear her best purple robe and ascend the carry-chair sent for her, because today was the parade — when the House of Wu reached out to the community and tenants with gifts and spectacle. All the wives were seated in carry-chairs, their porters uniformed in bright green surcoats and red pantaloons. The wives — nine in all, were surrounded by their sons, if they had any, these sons on ponies draped in red and green finery. Leading the parade, on horseback, was Wu T'ai-po and his two sons, and behind them was an army of journeymen guiding carts of Moon Cakes and small paper lanterns. Chi Lin, the least wife, was the last wife, but she did not care because her heart was glad to be a part of this family, especially when they departed through the gates and were greeted by the citizens of Yan-cheng.

As the family marched along the course, they were met by the entertainers again — this time the dragon dancers, a long beast with a giant head and two dozen legs, which wended its way before them to the beat of a noisy gong and a thunderous drum. Horns and flutes joined in as the beast frightened the children and amused the adults. Fireworks blazed the morning air as the carts wheeled through well-wishers towards the tenancies.

Chi Lin laughed at the little children hiding their faces from the dragons with its black marble eyes and jaundiced wargles. As the parade wended its way through the tenancies, the salt workers and their families lined the road, cheering and bowing, waving little banners of coarse cloth. They wore their best attire, which was poor to say the least, but the effort was counted toward the respect they owed to the Wu family. Then, as the dragon dancers coursed through the crowd, the journeymen distributed the Moon Cakes and paper lanterns. Chi Lin was happy in this. She watched faces, some familiar from her tour, beam and grin, where once they had been grim and weary. Tomorrow they would be grim and weary again, but while the dragon danced and the family waved their greetings, lanterns would be embraced and faces stuffed with Moon Cake. Of course, some stole away with their prizes, perhaps to hide them for later. Perhaps to admire them for a week or more, the monkey faces on the cakes being too pretty to destroy. But hunger in the end would triumph over a need to horde. It was a fine day, indeed, but wearied Chi Lin. She was glad to see her bed at the end of it.

The festivities continued within the house, much dining and chatter. The wives gathered each night in the Old Lady of the House's *ke-ting* to exchange gossip and take tea. Chi Lin took her customary place apart on the first gathering, but on the second, the Old Lady of the House ordered her to sit beside Rutabaga, Liang-tze's third wife — a twittery woman, who spoke much but said nothing. Chi Lin just smiled and enjoyed the sound of her silvery voice. But for each gathering of the wives, Chi Lin said nothing, the conversation dominated by Jasmine and the Old Lady of the House.

The daughters had indulged in games — special Autumn Festival games, the lot of them standing in a row waiting for their mothers to hand them a sprig of wisteria. Then they drew a small silk sheet with a number written upon it. They may not have been able to read, but they knew the numbers. Then one of the wives would call out a number and that daughter would come forward before the company of silly twittering girls and *descend into the garden*. It was a make-believe garden, the branches waving over her head. But she was to tell all what her husband would be like and enumerate the items in her dowry. Then the wives would confer and announce how many children she would most likely have — how many boys and how many girls. It all seemed pointless to Chi Lin, but the girls enjoyed it, especially Pearl and Jade, which gladdened Chi Lin, because she was fond of Lotus' daughters. Sapphire, however, seemed glum at this game, which puzzled Chi Lin. Still, people were different, she supposed and not all children loved games.

The boys played a sillier game, or at least to Chi Lin's mind it was sillier, although it amused her. The men and their sons ran about the courtyard until one son was caught by one of their uncles. Just who was actually snared did not matter. In this case it was Wu Bo-fei, Wu San-ehr's second son. Then they everyone surrounded him and *encircled the toad*. This meant calling him frog names until he acted like a toad, hopping around ridiculously, spitting and croaking. Wu Bo-fei, like all of Wu San-ehr's sons, was a serious lad and not prone to acting like a toad. But there was no help for it. He went from belligerent to sulky to finally hopping around as a rather fierce toad indeed. He was given six Moon Cakes for his trouble.

4

One the fifth night, the family gathered to observe the *Ascent to Heaven*. As an honor to the Lady in the Moon, the goddess of the Autumn Festival, one wife was selected to perform this ritual. Chi Lin was glad she was not selected, but was eager to watch Lotus perform the rite. It was to this rite the Second Wife had been practicing on her *p'i-pa* for weeks. But for more than just her playing. Because her feet were bound into golden lily pad slippers, Lotus had a physical feat to overcome. The stairway was decorated with silk drapes and painted to represent the night sky. Lotus was lovelier than ever she had appeared to Chi Lin, her face painted white. She was draped in a long silver robe. Her handmaidens guided her to the first step, and then, with care, she ascended, the invested practice allowing her to achieve all ten steps, and then sit in a sky blue chair, where the *p'i-pa* awaited her.

Once perched, the family raised their voices, acclaiming her ascent. Then, she raised her instrument and sang to *Chang O*, the Lady in the Moon:

> *From silver throne, I rule the night,*
> *From Tai-yang Shen I borrow light*
> *And touch the stars with night bird song*
> *So they may move the dark along.*
>
> *And when the morning glows apace*
> *And washes clean my celestial face,*
> *I to the cock's crow wail and weep*
> *Until behind the hills I sleep.*

More acclaim — sighs and hearty cheers as Lotus beamed from her high seat, allowing the *p'i-pa* to rest near her feet. The Master of the House was upstanding. He raised a cup of cassia wine high and all who would and could drink, drank to the honor of *Chang O* and Lotus' fitting tribute. Chi Lin decided she would like to better know the Second Wife — although more subdued than Jasmine, Lotus was still ensconced in a tinsel realm of ornamentation and carefully detailed decorum. Yet, Chi Lin would like to know Lotus better.

On the sixth night, a great feast was spread in the White Heart Pavilion, a place for full family gatherings. Men, women and children were seated in family clusters with Wu T'ai-po and his wife at the head table, taking in the glories of the entire crew. Chi Lin sat alone, but prominently enough, although there were eight other tables, one for each wife and their children. Ceremony was loose at this meal, the younger children allowed to roam and visit with their cousins. The older ones adhered to protocols, but just.

Chi Lin was amazed at the quality of the cuisine — special dishes prepared by Wu T'ai-po's private cook and three specialists from Yan-cheng hired to prepare the Moon Fish and the steamed eels, T'ai-po's favorite dish. Chi Lin did not much care for it, but she tried it, and then smiled at her father-in-law who bubbled with questions as each wife and son sampled a menu item. *You cannot find crabs like these in the North,* he announced to Wu San-ehr. *This swan was captured on Tai-hu Lake yesterday,* he boasted to Wu Liang-tze, who was too drunk to know a swan from a goose.

The persimmon cake is a specialty of Pu-yen Village and they only make it for us at this time of year, he boasted waiting for a response from Orchid, who managed a smile above her usual mope. But to the eels he wanted Chi Lin's assessment. She thought they smelled like the inside of well-worn shoes as she raised a morsel to her lips. She braced to not disappoint, grinning as she sucked the eel into her mouth. Somehow she kept it there without spitting it across the hall.

"It is tender," she said. "I know no other word to describe it."

Wu T'ai-po was cheered and moved on to Lotus' reaction to the melon soup. Chi Lin was glad for that. She quietly pushed the eel dish aside in favor of a Moon Cake. But even that was bedeviled by the after taste of the eel, or so she thought. Or perhaps it was her growing distaste for the entire meal. She could only guess, so guess she did.

When the feast concluded, the children were set free to prepare the sky lanterns, while the adults solemnly retreated to the courtyard. There, on a long table, sat cups of cassia wine filled to the brim. Chi Lin knew this ceremony. Her mother had taught her and her family practiced it during every Autumn Festival. She approached the cup as did the sons and wives also. She trained her eye to the cup's surface — a reflective lake, a soft tan to match the cassia bark. The entire group stared at their cups for some time until *Chang O* arrived, rising high over the wall, her light moving across the table. Then, the moon appeared in the cups — a silver disk in a sweetly prepared drink. When she was centered in the Master of the House's cup, they would all drink, but not until then. Chi Lin watched as the Lady in the Moon moved across the surface of her wine. Then Wu T'ai-po's craggy voice broke the silence.

"She has come to give the House of Wu good luck and much fortune — many wives and many sons. I honor her."

He drank, and the others joined him, for such was the custom on the Autumn Festival.

5

The children broke the solemnity, cheering as a troupe of dancers entered the courtyard. It was time to send the sky lanterns aloft. The dancers were an expensive treat, six ladies dressed in blue moon gowns, with feather fans, their headdresses arrayed with fuzzy red pom-poms. They danced to a *chuan* and flute band, their movements graceful, yet poignant. Chi Lin enjoyed this, but also liked the bird call artist — an odd looking man dressed in tatters, who pranced among the children imitating ducks and chickens and geese. He finely imitated an owl, and then an Imperial crane, which garnered the most applause.

The sky lanterns were fetched, the children hopping about anxious to see them lit. Wu T'ai-po kindled the first one and it arose above his head and drifted toward the moon. *Cheering.* Then the others were lit and sent aloft, the sky filled with a host of disks, flickering across the outer walls. Chi Lin could see other lanterns in the distance — towns folk and tenants launching their own lanterns. The sight thrilled her. Then the children moved forward toward the gate. They wanted to see the water displays — the candle lamps which were floated down streams and across the salt flats. They wanted to see the distant ship lights as they joined the festivities at sea. But Chi Lin was suddenly weary. She saw Willow carrying a great red lantern.

"I will stay," Chi Lin said, not following the servant's beckon.

"Will you be fine?" Willow asked.

"I shall be. I am not accustomed to the late hour."

She was actually beginning to feel a wave of nausea and wondered if she could keep her dinner down, especially the eel. But if she was to spoil the jollity, it would be in silence and away from other eyes. She noticed the Lady of the House frowning. Chi Lin supposed her mother-in-law disapproved of any wife leaving the festivities, but it could not be helped. She nodded to the Lady, and then turned to the gate.

"Auntie," came a voice.

It was Wu Lin-kua.

"Go see the moon sky," she said to the boy.

"But I would like you to see it too."

"I have seen my share of moon skies," she said. "I have eaten too much and need to rest my head."

"But I want you to come, Auntie."

The boy looked so crestfallen, Chi Lin almost conceded. But then she thought better.

"You have many Aunties, Lin-kua."

"None like you."

Chi Lin grinned at the compliment, but knew it was a conceit not safely expressed with the relatives within earshot.

"Nonsense," she said. "Go watch the moon sky. I shall be fine."

Wu Lin-kua kicked the ground, but did her bidding. Chi Lin gazed to the sky — the wondrous proliferation of light, almost shaming *Chang O* herself. She briefly closed her eyes, seeing the sea and the salt flats and the streams and creeks laden with candled lanterns. She remembered them from home — a gentle blessing for good fortune and a pathway for the *ch'i* of those who roamed the night seeking their way toward rest. With that, she opened her eyes and turned toward the promenade. She would be alone, but at rest, the lanterns burning in her mind — no better place to be kindled.

Chapter Fifteen

Plum Wine

The Hall of Silver Silence was a welcomed refuge from the festival. Chi Lin was weary and suffered queasiness, the eels perhaps the culprit, although she suspected something else. She drifted alone into the hall. Despite the wake of a great feast, Mo Li had set the table with a steam bun, two Moon Cakes and a bowl of plum wine. Chi Lin shuddered and passed them by. She sat on an old chair, the new one of her dreams still beyond her means. She loosened her sash and opened her robe, the night air feeling good upon her belly. A soft breeze rattled the beads about the window. She could see the sky dotted with lanterns from where she sat, but only sleep would be a comfort now.

Suddenly, she realized that she might not be alone.

"Gao Lin?" she muttered.

No answer. Then she recalled he had been deep in his cups and playing tile games with the porters. She was glad he relaxed, and hoped he might win some cash, he being cleverer than any porter to her knowledge.

Chi Lin further opened her robe and lifted her shift, inspecting her flesh, which felt unusually warm. Her breasts were sore and her belly roiled, a kettle of eels inside wanting to get loose. She belched and felt better, but not so well as to change her plans for sleep. She meant to stand and approached her bed, but sitting seemed a better easement. So she delayed and delayed until rising was an effort. But rise she did. Her feet rebelled, swollen, so she sat again and untied her slippers, kicking them far from the seat. Now her head swam. She was sure she was going to swoon. But she fought it, pushing up from the chair, wobbling across to the bed cabinet, where she held onto the post.

"I will never eat eels again," she said.

Then she smiled. Nothing eaten could make her breasts tender or her feet swell to this extent. Nothing in the world's seas or lakes could do it. To bed she would go and worry about it in the morning. But then she heard a grunt from the courtyard. It was loud and boisterous and was followed by a hearty laugh. Someone was coming. She did not want company, especially now, but especially not *this* man, because she recognized the mumbling voice.

"This is it," the voice declared, slurred and sloppy. "And I see a light inside. I knew it, when I saw her leave."

Suddenly, on the threshold, holding onto the lintel was the man, Wu Liang-tze, tripping over the high step, but still managing to enter.

"Brother-in-law," Chi Lin gasped, closing her shift and clinging to the bed post. "Do not enter. I am alone and it is not proper."

"Ah, alone," he stammered, and then laughed. "You need my protection, then."

"I need only protection from intruders like you. Go, or I will sound an alarm."

"Go ahead. Scream, if you must. But they are all into their lanterns and Moon Cakes. You will be no more than a crane's call lost in the weeds and marshes."

He staggered further into the hall. Chi Lin gripped the side of the bed, but she would have done better to fall back into the chair because Liang-tze aimed directly for her, loosening his jade corset as he approached.

"I love a good feast followed by a good woman."

"I am ugly," she said. "You told me so yourself."

"Ah, in face you are plain, but I am not interested in your face, sister-in-law."

He laughed again and thrust forward, catching her arm and pushing her onto the bed. Chi Lin screamed, but her voice sounded weak and puny compared to the racing of her heart. Liang-tze was a heavy man, who knew his way about removing his clothes in any fashion while maintaining dominance over a woman. Chi Lin knew he was prolific at it. But now, with his jowls dripping with spit and his breath stinking of wine, she was more nauseous than ever.

"Be merciful," she stammered.

"You shall live," he said, ripping her shift open, while dipping his loin cloth beyond requisition. "I know you are new to this. So the pleasure will be mutual."

Chi Lin was flattened on bed, Liang-tze's weight extreme. She tried to push him off, but failed. She hit his shoulders, but he only laughed. She felt him groping under her, and knew he was succeeding, his worm growing as hard as ironwood and seeking to take the plunge. Suddenly, his weight eased off her, his face puckering in disgust. His head snapped back. He faltered, falling backwards. Chi Lin saw hands prying him off her. These were dainty hands, the hands of a woman, perhaps. But then she saw something astonishing. She saw Wu Lin-kua and Wu Chou-fa wrestling their uncle to the ground.

"Get off me," Liang-tze screamed at the boys, as they managed to roll him toward the table.

Liang-tze was up in a flash, but the boys jumped on him again, less successful this time, their uncle throwing them around haphazardly. Chi Lin screamed again. She managed to cover herself, but before she did, she quickly inspected to see if Liang-tze had completed the act. He had not. This gave her little consolation. Her arms were bruised and her shoulders were sore. She gasped, and then belched, surely about to vomit. Then a notion overtook her. She quickly staggered to the table, grabbed the bowl of plum wine and spilled it on the sheets. Then she tossed the bowl into the darkness.

"Mistress," came a voice.

It was Gao Lin. He ran to her, and then tried to help the boys, but Liang-tze was regaining his control. As he righted himself, he paused.

"Who is this who dares interrupt me," she shouted at Gao Lin.

Chi Lin was sure that Gao Lin would fight the Second son, an act that would bring untold punishments upon Gao Lin's head.

"No, Gao Lin, do not do it," she stammered.

It was then that the Third Son appeared at the door, with three journeymen, who clamped Liang-tze's arms in rope restraints. Liang-tze tried to push them away, but upon seeing his brother at the door and his father at a respectable distance behind him, Liang-tze spit at his two nephews.

"My brother's sons are meddlesome curs," he shouted as he was led away.

Chi Lin slumped to the bed. Willow entered, quietly slipping by Wu San-ehr and the two boys. She had never entered the Silver Silence before, but showed no hesitation now. Lao Lao and Snapdragon followed her, all three attending to Chi Lin's stress.

Wu Lin-kua and Wu Chou-fa bowed low to their uncle, the Third Son.

"How dare you," Wu San-ehr growled. "How dare you lay hands upon your elder, your Uncle Liang-tze?"

"But he was harming Auntie," Lin-kua wept.

"He had his thing between her legs," Chou-fa complained.

"That is not your concern," San-ehr shouted. "Those who show no respect for their elders shall be punished for it."

Both boys shivered, but then took off at a gallop, no doubt to seek their mother's council. Chi Lin knew there was no help for it. Liang-tze would be chastised, perhaps banned from the house, but the two boys would be whipped for their transgression. She supposed they were paying her back for the broken *Guan-yin*, but she would not wish a beating for them. Still, they had saved her from Liang-tze consummating the act. Would that they had saved her from a far worse terror he had inflicted.

"The sheets are wet," Snapdragon announced.

Willow immediately inspected them, and then yanked them from the bed. Now the Master of the House was on the threshold standing beside the Third Son. Neither man entered. Willow held the sheets up. Wu T'ai-po grunted in disgust, and then departed quickly. Wu San-ehr nodded to Chi Lin, and then stared at Gao Lin.

"Sir," he said. "I am glad you had the presence of mind to keep your place."

Gao Lin bowed. Wu San-ehr departed.

"Oh, my poor mistress," Snapdragon wailed.

"It is what it is," Lao Lao said. "The man has done this before."

Chi Lin was dizzy now. She wanted to be alone, but Willow was fetching clean bed clothing and Snapdragon was fussing over Chi Lin's hair. Gao Lin was like a dumb dog. It was then she realized he was drunk also, but had kept it under control during the havoc. She was glad of that, but now he offered her no consolation. She was glad of that also.

"I am so weary," she declared. She was shaken to the bone. She had been shaken, in all but the final act, and she was the only one who knew *that* truth, except Liang-tze himself, who might be too drunk to have remembered that he missed the final point or too proud to admit the failure. But what was the act compared with the brutality of the attempt. "I am so very, very weary and would like to sleep."

Willow ordered everyone out before helping Chi Lin into bed, and then departed. Gao Lin retreated to his corner, but even if he was amorous tonight, his touch would have been as hideous as any man's. When the light faded, even from the panoply of the heavens, Chi Lin did not succumb to sleep. Her mind was crowded with spitting jowls and stale wine, and would be for some time to come.

Chapter Sixteen

Growing Pains

1

A sleepless night filled with ugly images plagued Purple Sage. Not even the consolation that she had the presence of mind to cause the Master of the House to believe that Liang-tze was guilty of the ultimate penetration did not give her solace. Every shadow made her blanch. The Second Son was now under restraint. What if he should become loose and try again or even try to make amends as men do, or so she was told? She could never forgive him the brutality of his actions and, for that, she could be chastised as an ungrateful woman — a meddlesome ghost bride bent on bringing shame upon the House of Wu.

At dawn, Gao Lin knelt beside her bed cabinet, his head bowed, the plum wine bowl held in both hands.

"I found this," he said.

"Hide it," she commanded, her voice weak but determined. "It is the evidence of my duplicity."

Chi Lin sat at the bed's edge. Her head swam, but she managed to touch her belly. Gao Lin caught her meaning.

"It has started," she said. "You are the man who has stung me with passion. But you know you can never be its father."

"I know," Gao Lin said, his voice choking. "I am sorry for it, but I know it could never be. Do they believe it is the Second Son's?"

"They do not know yet, because I have been careful. It is too soon to show the world. But when my changes become more evident, they will know and I believe they will remember last night and the Second Son's attack."

"And the stain on your sheets."

"It is a stain on my heart, but I think well of you, Gao Lin. If they should know, it would be my ruin and the end of your tether here."

"My tether is broken now," he said, standing. "I shall depart the house."

Chi Lin stirred.

"Yes," she said. "You must, but not yet. To go now would be suspicious."

He bowed.

"I shall complete my tasks. I shall finish the pool and restore the servant's quarters."

"And you shall abandon your corner of this hall. But say no more. Mo Li will be bringing the meal. No one must suspect."

When he departed to his tasks, Chi Lin sighed. Her passion for the man waned. Perhaps her passion for all men waned, but she would miss his company — his bantering and his singing. She would need to reveal her secret carefully and indirectly. She knew how.

Because she was bruised and ached, she did not attend the temple shrine or the Jade Heart Pavilion that day. Such absence brought Willow to her side. She now viewed Willow as a friend and an unwitting accomplice to the events. Over the next week, Chi Lin needed to know the gossip of the house and, through Willow, she learned that the Second Son was sent packing — his wives and children with him. He received a severe scolding from his mother and silence from his father. Two days after his departure, the gifts began to come through the main gate — a fine black stallion, two carts of the finest woven silk, three baskets of *ju-tzi*, their orange skins brightly shining and three baskets of *tao-tzi*, golden and fuzzy with emerald leaves still on the stems. Finally, an order was read to the Master of the House, asking forgiveness for insulting *Chang O* on her festival and, as an apology to his brother, Wu Hung-lin, Liang-tze donated a gilded Buddha for the shrine. Chi Lin was sure that these gifts would grant Wu Liang-tze pardon, but not so far as to allow him entry into the family house any time soon. She was more concerned for Wu Lin-kua and Wu Chou-fa. Willow said that the boys each received five strokes with the bamboo pole until blood was drawn. Their uncle, Wu San-ehr gave them a lecture on filial piety and to be more upstanding and respectful in the future.

"Neither boy so much as whimpered," Willow said, "even when the blood was drawn."

"I am sorrowful that they had to suffer on my behalf," Chi Lin said. "I will never forget their sacrifice."

"You cannot thank them," Willow cautioned. "To do so would condone their actions."

Chi Lin was well aware of that. She would need to keep her nephews' courageous act close to her heart, out of sight of the family.

2

Chi Lin resumed her tasks, but did so haltingly. She walked with a slight hop, because she knew that if she had been taken during the rape, she would walk thus. This was a small accommodation to a calculated fiction. Her mother-in-law said nothing about the incident, but scrutinized her when she showed up to sew shoes. The Second and Third wives also observed her keenly when Chi Lin undertook to feed the worms. These were easy tasks for her now, but still, as the weeks progressed, she tired readily and began to sicken, especially in the morning when in her own pavilion and out of sight. Her muscles ached and her breasts began to swell. There was no doubt of her condition now, the household whispering about it.

"Ji Ji-bang is here," Willow said to Chi Lin one morning when she was particularly beset with symptoms.

Ji Ji-bang, the third attending doctor from the Ya-men staff, would never be bothered with such incidentals as a pregnancy, but Chi Lin was feverish and Willow told the Old Lady of the House that she feared that a malady had crossed over the Silver Silence's threshold and had taken root. So Ji Ji-bang was summoned.

"It is not necessary," Chi Lin complained. "I am with child, that is all. Such sickness attends my condition."

"Mistress," Willow replied. "Your head is hot and your hands are sweaty. Such things are not unknown to child bearing, but they can also be most worrisome. The Lady of the House insists."

Chi Lin, who was sitting in her chair, a bucket nearby, resigned to her mother-in-law's wishes and allowed Ji Ji-bang to examine her. He took her pulse and smelled her breath, his young head bobbing as he thought. He was an apprentice physician, but still was well regarded in the House of Wu. He felt her ankles and peered into her eyes. Silently, he arose, opening his doctor's bag on the table, handling three jars and combining their contents in a bowl. He returned, raising the concoction to Chi Lin's nose.

"Drink it."

"It smells vile," she replied. "I cannot."

"It will settle your stomach and extinguish the head fires." She took it, and sipped. "Drink it down. Drink it all." She did so, and then choked. "Good. You are with child, that is all."

"It is definite?" Willow asked.

Ji Ji-bang grimaced.

"Did you think otherwise?" he quipped. "This is not illness. It is the natural function of the body, like defecation and expectoration. Babies are conceived every day. But it is a discomfiture to be borne and those things *do* come under my jurisdiction. I will leave you some more elixir and you will thank me by telling Wu T'ai-po that I deserve a premium above my contract. Small price, because, if I subscribe to rumor, he is to become a grandfather again."

Willow glanced at Chi Lin, who choked again but did feel the vile smelling drink easing her need to vomit. That was something, at least. As to rumor, she would let that grow to her advantage.

Two days after Ji Ji-bang's visit, Chi Lin had another visitation — three Taoist priests lead by Kan Fu-lai, Yan-cheng's chief *fa-shr*. He startled her with his humming and chanting, the others beating drums. Willow came to her side, while Lao Lao, Snapdragon and Mo Li drifted to the shadows. Even Gao Lin peeked in through the window. This was a trial, because Kan Fu-lai ordered Chi Lin to lay on the bed, and then he set a burning taper on her belly. With that the other two priests danced about the room, while the *fa-shr* touched Chi Lin from head to toe. As the *fa-shr* was a man, she cringed, the touch reminding her of Liang-tze. But this was a priest — a holy man who had no appetite for manly indulgences. His touch was an exercise in Taoist determination. Then he removed the taper and laughed.

"It is true," he chanted. "It will be a man child and Wu Hung-lin is his father."

The trio hopped about the room, laughing and banging the drums. Snapdragon was giddy and Willow delighted. Gao Lin shrugged his shoulders and disappeared from sight. His presence in the window was replaced by three little heads — the girls, Pearl, Jade and Sapphire.

"It is true," Jade sang. "Auntie is having a ghost baby."

"He will be a pretty brother," Pearl added.

"Another boy," Sapphire concluded, exasperation in her voice.

Chi Lin leaned back to see the children, but they were gone before she could spy them. The priests left, but their singing and drumming echoed through the courtyard, and then through the rest of the house.

"What has happened?" Chi Lin said to Willow.

Before she could explain, Snapdragon was by Chi Lin's side, pawing her mistress's hair.

"Your husband returned to give you a son," she babbled. "I knew my master had returned. I saw him one night as I lay in my coffin and watched the sky through the hole in the roof. I saw his face and he stopped and said *Snapdragon, how are you, you old lady. I see you have an Ironwood Coffin and a fine white silk shroud. Good for you. I will save you a place beside the Yellow Springs.* He was a beautiful sight, mistress, and it must have been that night he came and made a baby with you. I am so happy. I am so happy."

Snapdragon's teary clutch gave Chi Lin the hope that the household eschewed the nonsense that Liang-tze was the father, although in fact no one could deny it. It would take the consecration of the city *fa-shr* and perhaps several silver ingots to declare Wu Hung-lin a ghost lover elevating Chi Lin in status because she carried a Wu family son. She looked to Willow, who smiled dimly. Who would challenge the pronouncement of the *fa-shr*? Certainly not Chi Lin, although she felt disconcerted as the lies piled up.

3

A week later, on a chilly morning, Mi Tso-tze arrived. Willow led her into the Silver Silence courtyard, leaving her standing by the nearly finished pool. Chi Lin was feeling well that day, although was too tired to do her chores, her mother-in-law being lenient since her pregnancy became evident. Chi Lin had been gazing out the window at Gao Lin working on the servant's quarters when she noticed the young woman by the pool. She was nearly Chi Lin's age, perhaps, wore a fine blue tunic and pants underneath, and a gray shawl to ward off chill. She was unadorned. Chi Lin wondered until Willow came to her.

"Purple Sage," she said. "The Lady of the House has deemed fit to give you a new maid servant since Snapdragon has become feeble. She is of good stock and schooled in dressing ladies. Her voice is gentle."

"Who is she?" Chi Lin asked.

"Her name does not matter, just as mine does not. Although my name is Bo La-tso, the mistress chose to call me Willow, so Willow I am."

"What is her name, Willow?"

"Whatever name you choose."

Chi Lin thought this odd. But she was glad to have her household increased.

"Who did she serve before me?"

Willow was silent, her eyes downcast.

"It will not please you, but it is so. She served Wisteria, Wu Liang-tze's second wife." Chi Lin grunted. "But it is my mistress' will that you shall have her."

"Is this a gift from the Second Son?"

"No. That would insult his brother's name. The Master of the House selected four candidates, and the mistress thought this one suited best."

Chi Lin sighed. Women from the Second Son's house were susceptible to Liang-tze sexual prowling. Two damaged women beneath one roof would not bode well. But she decided to obey her mother-in-law.

"Send her to me, if you would," she asked Willow.

The young woman entered softly. On closer inspection, she was the same age as her new mistress. Her face was clear and pleasant. It would be a change from having old Snapdragon molesting her each morning. She was sturdy, a good sign that she could undertake heavy work and yet she seemed bright. She bowed before her new mistress.

"What is your name, child?" Chi Lin asked, conscious that the title *child* was unctuous.

"Mi Tso-tze, mistress."

"And what did your last mistress call you?"

"Thujaberry, mistress."

Chi Lin grinned.

"Did you like that name?"

"Not very much."

"I do not like it either. I will name you Juniper. Does that suit you?"

"Thank you, mistress."

Mi Tso-tze smiled, a bright and beautiful smile, her temperament captured over her lips.

"But that name is given because it is the custom. If you are not uncomfortable, I will call you Tso-tze."

Mi Tso-tze went to her knees.

"You are most kind, mistress. My father would be honored."

"We must always honor our fathers."

Chi Lin found Tso-tze an excellent choice, quiet at first and most respectful, but she began her duties at once by dressing her mistress appropriately to the chilly weather and accompanied her to the shrine, where she was introduced to Wu Hung-lin. Tso-tze held the *san-tze* steady to shade the sun from her mistress' head, and also helped gather the red paper prayers. In the weeks to come she was punctual and protective of Chi Lin's toilet, which at first brought her into conflict with Snapdragon, but not permanently.

"Old Snapdragon must be respected," Chi Lin told Tso-tze. "She will want to arrange my hair and will do it poorly, but we must compliment her on the task and wait until she is away before we rearrange it. She will not notice, being nearly blind."

"She spits at me," Tso-tze said, not too unkindly.

"She is not expected to like you. You are new. She once attended the Master of the House's second wife. Snapdragon was honored in her place. Now that she is on the wane we must forbear and keep her happy. Try to find honor in the spit of one who has served long and hard. Besides, she has an ironwood coffin and a fine white silk shroud."

Tso-tze smiled, because she had heard as much from Snapdragon and several times a day. Chi Lin liked her new maid servant, especially as the pregnancy grew. Nausea came and went, and she began to feel like a field buffalo, her chores becoming heavier to bear. Tso-tze attended to her every need. The only regret Chi Lin had was that Willow came to visit less.

4

"It is finished," Gao Lin announced one afternoon.

Chi Lin had returned from feeding the worms and, beyond weary, Tso-tze helping her through the gate toward the house. Gao Lin, hat in hand, greeted her; Lao Lao, Mo Li and Snapdragon standing behind him. Chi Lin looked toward the servant's quarters to understand what he meant by *it is finished.*

"So it is, Gao Lin," Chi Lin said. "Tso-tze, help me."

Purple Sage managed to come before the quarters. From the outside it looked the same, but the changes were made to the back, an extension added to accommodate Tso-tze and the roof repaired.

"Very fine," she said.

"Indeed," Snapdragon said. "The builder has sealed up where the wind blew me cold. He is a skilled builder, indeed."

"If my old lady is happy," Lao Lao said, "I am content, because she will nag me less and speak little."

Chi Lin doubted that. Mo Li was quiet on the issue, her kitchen needing the least repairs.

"There is a new room for your new hand maiden," Gao Lin said, "since I will depart now, my work completed."

Chi Lin felt a sudden pang. At first she thought it was the baby, but then realized that Gao Lin would be leaving and the days of his happy presence in the Silver Silence would come to an end.

"Will you leave today?"

"I leave now," he said, bowing.

She noticed his tools in a basket and a carry pole nearby.

"Where will you go?"

"There is a corvee order in town for shipbuilding at the port."

"What do you know about building ships?"

Chi Lin was uncustomarily stern as if she was about to talk Gao Lin out of the decision to leave. But she knew he must go before she grew more attached to him, and certainly before their child was born. Such temptations needed distance.

"I climb trees and scale roofs," he replied. "I know silk cloth and how to tie knots. What I lack I will learn. It is better than digging a ditch or clearing a road."

"Then if you must leave," she said, "it is *best* you leave now."

She turned away. If she had remained constant she would have seen the pain on his face and the near tear in his eye. She might have succumbed to the urge to embrace him one last time. But she kept her back to him until she reached the Hall. When she turned, he was gone.

"Let me help you," Tso-tze said.

"I need solitude, Tso-tze, if you please."

"Have I offended you, mistress?"

"Not in the least."

Chi Lin crossed the threshold walking slowly to the chair, where she slumped like a sack of rice. There she sat in silence, sad and sorry. She needed Tso-tze to prepare her for bed, but decided that for this evening the chair would do. There, as darkness spread its pall, she wept, her nose filling up and her head swimming. Through the night she shed tears for the man — her first man and father to this child, because she would never see him again and would never be permitted to tell the child about his father. His father would be a fairy tale ghost because the family was proud and the *fa-shr* was rich. She could never reveal this beautiful truth. A woman's heart is sometimes plagued by things she knows and cannot address. This was the heavy burden of the ghost bride.

Chapter Seventeen

Winter Measures

1

Chi Lin greeted the gray skies of the colder season as best she could. She was growing larger, her legs aching and her back strained. But Mi Tso-tze proved a mighty help, responding to her mistress' needs, assuring the garments were loose and the robe sash longer to accommodate new girth. Chi Lin spent another silver ingot on a fur shawl, nothing elaborate – a fox fur garment, although Tso-tze insisted on ermine. She lost that argument, because the remaining cash from the ingot went to hang a leather drape over the hall's doorway and another to block drafts through the window. The partition at the end of the hall was repaired with brocade remnants and became a place for Mi Tso-tze to reside, because Chi Lin needed her nearby now. New sleeping cushions were bought and a duck feather quilt for Chi Lin's bed.

Chi Lin moved slower to her tasks and, on some days, delayed at the shrine, the incense brazier warming her. She also took side trips to Crimson Blossom and Golden Oak Halls to watch the girls learning to sew. Mostly she enjoyed their childish prattle. Pearl and Jade reminded her of herself and her sister when their mother was not teaching them some new art or craft. They would make-believe they were grown married women discussing the business of the house.

"I believe we need to buy new tables and chairs," Pearl said to her sister.

"Only if you can find sweet sandalwood," Jade replied. "It would smell ever so fresh in the morning with our tea."

Then they would giggle and cover their faces until the *amah* would sweep by and reset their learning attitude. Their mother was aloof, always relaxing on her golden chair, tasting sweet fruit and steam buns. When she was not spooling the silk, Lotus played her *p'i-p'a* and sang. It was a lonely existence, but Chi Lin thought it was as lonely as her own. She was glad that her feet were unbound. She could not imagine depending upon two servants to guide her about. Although now that the pregnancy advanced, she wished she had two servants to help her.

When she visited Crimson Blossom Hall, the girls would stir and dance about her. They would cautiously wink at her belly, until Auntie Purple Sage allowed them to touch it.

"It is life," Chi Lin said. "It grows."

"Like the worms in the cocoons?" Pearl asked.

She was the clever one.

"Yes, indeed," Chi Lin replied. "Only it is not a worm."

"And we will not boil you and spin you into cloth," Jade quipped.

She was the silly one.

Visits to Golden Oak Hall were less happy. Not that the hall was poor, but its drapes were maudlin, reflecting Orchid's morose mood. Chi Lin rarely saw her sister-in-law, because she slept most days, and when she was seen in the *ji-tzao*, she kept to her place silently. Sapphire was always in the hall, when she was not playing with her sisters. She was a child apart, a mirror of her mother in many ways. Chi Lin wondered about this sadness. Willow told her that Orchid was accosted by Liang-tze when she first arrived as Third Wife. She was lucky not to have been raped, but his threats made her nervous and caused a rift between the two brothers, one that became violent one night. That night, Liang-tze was expelled from the house. That night upset mother and child so much that both shook in terror. After that, Wu Hung-lin stopped visiting Orchid and neglected Sapphire. Sad to say and sadder to hear, the household came to regard the Golden Oak more asylum than residence.

Sapphire would approach Chi Lin quietly, smiling sourly.

"Child," Chi Lin would say, "do you have enough to eat?" Chi Lin feared that her diet was amiss, pale and thin as she was. "Is your *amah* giving you melon?"

"I do not like melon, Auntie. It makes my tummy bubble. I do like tea, but they say it will make my skin tough too soon."

Chi Lin always brought a Moon Cake for each girl, but she brought two for Sapphire when they met apart from the others. The sight of a Moon Cake always made the little girl weep for joy and the *amah* pout. Chi Lin did not care for any of the *amahs* and wondered why the Old Lady of the House chose such cold sorts to wean these children. But Chi Lin's concern was who would be sent to wean *her* son when the time came. In any event, all three daughters were spared the foot binding – a blessing from her mother-in-law who despised the new custom despite leaving feet full-sized might limit future matrimonial matches, men such as they are.

The other detour Chi Lin took would put her at odds with the First Wife.

2

Chi Lin often passed the school room as she went to and from her chores. Always she would pause and watch Wu Lin-kua and Wu Chou-fa at their studies. Sometimes they would look up and nod to her when in view. So would the scholar P'ing Chin. On one chilly day, as Chi Lin walked from her sewing chores to her worm feeding tasks, she paused longer than usual before the schoolroom door. She was out of breath and a cold wind penetrated her fox collar. The door was cloaked in heavy leather and beyond the door, inside, would be warm. So she move to the edge and peered in.

"Purple Sage," P'ing Chin said, looking up from his writing desk. "You look pale. Come into the warmth."

"I dare not, Master P'ing."

"Oh, but you must. As you can see, we are not alone."

The boys looked up from their writing, their brushes suspended over the page. Chi Lin was drawn by the warmth in their eyes as much as the warmth from the room. She entered, shivering and sought a chair between them.

"We work, Auntie," Lin-kua said.

"We are good at it," Chou-fa added.

"They think they are proficient," P'ing Chin commented, "but as you can see, the character *shen* is poorly derived, the brush stroke order incorrect and thus too loose to be anything but sloppy."

"It is my way," Lin-kua said.

"When you brush in the correct order and emulate the master brushwork of Su Tung-po and Li K'ai-men, then you can adopt your own order and call it *your way*. Until then, do it correctly or your mother shall know of it." P'ing Chin grinned and looked to Chi Lin. "Am I not correct, mistress?"

"How would I know?" Chi Lin said nervously, clearly seeing Lin-kua's error and knowing how to right it.

"You know," P'ing Chin said. "Your father would have slapped the hand for such poor scholarship."

"Auntie," Chou-fa asked. "You know the characters?"

"You can use the brush?" Lin-kua added.

"Only as a foolish child in a scholar's household," she replied, softly.

This was a secret best left undiscussed, but the boys were only too eager, having been taught that women knew no such things. They seemed pleased.

"Mother does not know," Lin-kua said.

Chi Lin mistook the meaning that Jasmine was ignorant of her secret.

"Nor should we tell her," she replied.

"No, Auntie. Mother does not know how to read and write."

"What use would she have for it?" P'ing Chin said, perhaps realizing he had breached a forbidden topic. "If she needs a letter written, she can ask you, after you are a master of the brush. And if she receives a letter, she can have it read to her."

The boys fell silent. They surely sensed an issue. Then, Wu Lin-kua sighed.

"I am sorrowful, Auntie, that our uncle misused you," he said.

"You must not say that," Chi Lin snapped. "You laid hands on the man and have paid for your lack of respect. Is that not so, Master P'ing?"

Master P'ing was silent. Surely he agreed with the punishment levied on unfilial children. But in his silence, Chi Lin reaped his true feelings. And so did the boys. Suddenly there was a sound at the door, the leather shifting.

"Who is there?" P'ing Chin asked, arising and parting the drape.

He peered outside, and then grunted.

"Do we have a visitor, master?" Chou-fa asked.

"Is it Ma Mai-to with our tea?"

"No," P'ing Chin said, resignedly. "It was your mother. But she is gone now."

Chi Lin moved quickly to the leather windbreak, parting it. She saw in the distance Jasmine's long coat in the wind, her sister-in-law clearly departing in a huff.

"I must go," Chi Lin said, turning to the company. "You must study. You must teach. I must make amends, because your mother does not seem happy with my visit here."

The chill clipped her nose as she returned to the path and did her best to keep a true course to Blue Heaven Hall.

3

Jasmine would not see her, at first. The maid servant, Ma Mai-to, was poor company indeed. Unlike Willow, she was reticent and churlish. No tea was offered. No chair either, although after a long while Chi Lin made bold to sit on the second quality chair in the *ke-ting*. Ma Mai-to was still surly and did not even object to this, but disappeared from the room altogether.

Chi Lin pondered any offense she may have committed against her sister-in-law. She knew what it was, but felt it was not just. Chi Lin could speak up to the First Wife, who was not the Old Lady of the House . . . yet. But she needed to be circumspect. When Chi Lin's baby came, Jasmine would become its mother. Angering the First Wife could have undue consequences for her son. So she sat in the *keting* thankful to be off her feet and out of the wind.

After a while, Jasmine appeared, mounting the first quality chair, and sitting like an Empress before a full court.

"I see you have come, Purple Sage," she said.

"I have not been summoned and come freely," Chi Lin answered; however, she neglected to bow.

"What business do you have with me?" Jasmine snapped. "You should be feeding the worms."

"I should, but I have come to assure that you have not been offended because I took shelter in the school."

"That you speak to my sons is no hardship for me," she said. "But it reminded me that they were punished because of you, and that is difficult for a mother to overcome."

"I am sorry for that," Chi Lin said. "But as you see, I am growing big with my son."

"Your son?"

"Our son."

"You are the child's aunt," Jasmine sneered. "You know as well as I do, the boy will be an honored member of this household under my jurisdiction."

Now Chi Lin bowed.

"I wish you the best. May you proper, sister-in-law."

Chi Lin arose to leave.

"I believe it is time for a tour of the *ji-tzao*," Jasmine proposed. "It is time for you to undertake the task on your own."

Chi Lin's marrow froze. She was having more and more difficulty walking from one pavilion to another, yet Jasmine wanted her to venture out to the tenancies and validate the *ji-tzao*. This had to be revenge for the visit to the school room. This had to be revenge for having the audacity of carrying a son. She turned to Jasmine.

"Reconsider, sister-in-law," she said.

"I have made up my mind."

"But I am in a tender way."

"All the more important to impress the tenants with their great fortune to witness the ghost bride and her ghost child. It will honor the household three-fold."

"But . . ."

"Expect the porters tomorrow." Jasmine arose. She clapped and Ma Mai-to came. "Assure Purple Sage overtakes the path safely."

Jasmine was gone. Chi Lin was stunned. The maid servant marched ahead of her to the path, waiting there until Chi Lin stepped on the first cobblestone. Then, the maid disappeared as fast as she had appeared. The porters would arrive early the next morning.

4

"But mistress," Mi Tso-tze pleaded. "You cannot go. It is dangerous. You must ask Willow to speak to the Old Lady."

These words were the most Tso-tze had spoken in one go since her arrival, and she spoke them over and over again. But Chi Lin was resigned to do her sister-in-law's bidding. The morning sickness was minimal this day, but her legs were sore and she had a headache. If the porters held the chair steady, she would survive. Besides, the journeyman Chou Kuai-tze would assure her safety.

"But mistress."

"No, Tso-tze. When they come, I shall go."

"Lao Lao," Tso-tze said to the ever lurking custodian. "Tell her she must stay."

"It is not my place to tell the mistress what she can do and cannot do," Lao Lao said. "She is strong-willed. Might I suggest you finish her toilet, bow your head obediently and retire to your corner."

"I shall not," Tso-tze snapped. "The mistress needs to hear reason."

"I hear you, Tso-tze," Chi Lin said. "Your words are generous today. Perhaps, too generous, but there are things a wife must do for the good of the household."

"Then why not just climb the roof and jump off it."

After saying these words, Tso-tze went to her knees and coiled into a pathetic, but apologetic ball. She rocked and wept.

"Be of better cheer, Tso-tze," Chi Lin said. "That you think I should jump off the roof is a testament to your loyalty, because if I did so, I know you would follow me."

"I would, mistress, I would."

The sound of clopping came from the courtyard. Chou Kuai-tze had arrived with a two-porter carry-chair.

"They brought the small chair," Lao Lao remarked. "You should head for the roof."

Chi Lin found his remark humorous, but did not laugh, because the small chair with only two porters would be quite a wobbly affair. Mi Tso-tze arose and finished wrapping her mistress in a double layer of undergarments and a stiff brocaded robe. She covered her head with a fur cap, the fox scarf drawn up over her nape.

"I shall go with you," she said.

"There is only one chair, Tso-tze."

"No matter. I will walk beside you."

"It is not the custom. Wait here. I shall return intact. It is better than if I jumped off the roof."

Chi Lin graciously held her aching body erect and walked proudly to the chair, nodding to Chou Kuai-tze. When he saw her, he cocked his head. Perhaps this was the first time he realized that his cargo was a pregnant women. Surely that was not the case. But perhaps he had underestimated her condition. He dismounted and, quite beyond convention, helped her into the chair.

"Steady," he snapped at the porters. "If you drop her, you shall be digging ditches in *Yuan-ch'i-fu*."

The porters lifted their cargo as steady as they could, but Chi Lin saw that they were scantily dressed for the weather – a gray steely morning with no sun on the horizon. They were barefoot and bare-shinned up past their calves. It was to be as miserable for them as it would be for her. Still, everyone under Heaven had their duty and ordeal to perform. They were to keep her *steady* or face a worse fate.

Chou Kuai-tze remounted, straightened his Salt Monopoly badge and rode to the fore. The porters were quick about their work, the chill propelling them over the cold ground as fast as they could. Chi Lin was immediately ill. By the time she reached the outer gate, she was wishing for her morning bucket. The main road was devoid of people, business on such a gray day at a minimum, so only this small parade raced through the town to the Ya-men.

The porters slogged the chair from side to side, Chi Lin holding firmly to the arm rests. The breeze bit her nose, not helping her aching head. She supposed this was the feeling one had at sea, if she had ever been to sea. Added to that, Chou Kuai-tze's horse was no better this day than on the first tour, the stench wafting over Chi Lin, her gorges rising. Suddenly, she choked, her morning congee coming up.

The porters halted when they heard her. She leaned over the side and vomited, the tears welling and her nose clogged. Chou Kuai-tze heard the choking and turned about. He was out of the saddle and over to the chair.

"Set her down," he shouted.

The porters dropped the chair, Chi Lin nearly falling out. Chou Kuai-tze struck the lead porter, while the second one cowered.

"Do not blame them, Chou Kuai-tze," Chi Lin muttered. "They are not at fault. It is my condition."

Kuai-tze came to her, nodding respectfully, but clearly at a loss. Chi Lin continued to heave, when a second horse arrived – Lin Wu-luo, the Imperial Commissioner's proxy. He remained on horseback, leering at the scene.

"Is all correct?" he asked.

"Not so," Chou Kuai-tze snapped. "The ghost bride is ill."

"She is pregnant, that is all," Lin said, drawing an unkind glare from the journeyman.

"What is happening?" came a sterner voice.

A man approached on foot. Lin dismounted and bowed. Kuai-tze also bowed, but the man ignored them, coming to Chi Lin. It was the Imperial Commissioner himself – Ai-lo Wun-kua.

"What do I see?" he said, touching Chi Lin's shoulder. "Is this Master Wu Hung-lin's wife abroad in such a condition? Shameful."

"I am sorry for it, my lord," Chi Lin whimpered.

"It is not your fault that such errands send you forth in such a state. Not your fault." He turned to the porters, who trembled in his presence. "Take her inside the Ya-men at once. Take her to my residence."

The porters nodded, and then raised the chair, Chi Lin still miraculously intact. They raced to the Ya-men gate. Chi Lin was near to fainting.

5

Chi Lin had never entered the Ya-men before and scarcely noted it now, except her entrance caused a stir, the guards and clerks mumbling indignantly as she passed. It was an uncommon event. She did note the large courtyard and an array of offices and residences inside the governmental hive. She recognized the Superintendent, Po T'ai-kuan racing toward her, objections on his lips until he espied Ai-lo Wun-kua marching behind her like an angry prince.

"They sent her out to tour the *ji-tzao*," he shouted at Po T'ai-kuan. "In her condition. What were they thinking?"

Superintendent Po shrugged, and then shook his head in agreement.

"I shall send for Ji Ji-bang," he said.

"Send him to my residence. My wife will tend to her until then."

"Just so, my lord," Po T'ai-kuan replied. "Just so."

"Tell Chou Kuai-tze and my proxy to do their inspection without the woman. I do not know what they were thinking."

"Just so, my lord. Just so."

The porters carried Chi Lin through a triple tiered gateway into a wide courtyard. She felt slightly better. Perhaps the curtailment of her part in the tour made her rally. Still, the chastisement Ai-lo Wu-kua might have for the House of Wu would be a heavy burden to bear. She fretted to be the cause of such calamity.

When they reached the Commissioner's residence, a woman rushed to the chair – a tall woman with her hair in a high headdress topped with a red beaded bonnet. Chi Lin had never seen the likes of this before. The woman was wrapped in fur and spoke to two servants in a language unknown to Chi Lin. Then she helped Chi Lin out of the chair.

"Come and sit by our hearth. Warm yourself."

"Ji Ji-bang comes," Ai-lo Wun-kua said to his wife. "This is Chi Ming's daughter, who now lives in the house of Wu."

"The ghost bride?" the wife said. "I am honored. Come, come."

Chi Lin was overwhelmed by the good nature of the woman and encouraged by the Commissioner's acknowledgment of her father. The fact that Ji Ji-bang was coming with one of his smelly, but restoring potions was also sweet to hear. Once settled by the fire, a bucket was brought.

"Do not be ashamed if you need to use it," the wife said. "I have six children and have filled many buckets of my own."

Chi Lin embraced the device, but her vomit was spent. She feared retching with nothing left to deliver. She knew that to be worse than a steady stream. Instead, she bowed to the woman and sighed.

"You are kind," Chi Lin said. She then turned to Ai-lo Wun-kua. "I am sorry for violating the Ya-men. I am sure the place will need purification."

"Nonsense," he snapped. "I embrace the ways of the Han people. I was born and raised south of the Wall. But when it comes to practical measures, Mongols set aside nonsense and do what is necessary to get the job done."

"Please do not be angry with the House of Wu," she pleaded.

"Why not? Who sends a pregnant woman out in bad weather to sit behind a screen and watch men bribe each other with ingots and wine?"

He sat sternly, his arms crossed. He wore a thick black robe with silver trim, and an oversized fur hat, even indoors. His mustache was long and thin. He wore his commissioner's badge, a red metal plate on his left shoulder. It caught the shimmering light of the hearth.

"I am grateful for the fire," Chi Lin said, "but if you insist on punishing my master for not halting my household duty, I will need to return to the chair and catch up to Chou Kuai-tze."

Slowly, Ai-lo Wun-kua grinned, and then turned to his wife.

"Surely, this is Chi Ming's daughter."

He wife grinned also, and then arose to greet the doctor.

6

Ji Ji-bang was curt, giving Chi Lin a cursory glance, and then prepared the stomach-settling potion.

"You are lucky I am here," he said the Chi Lin. "I have a portion to help you before the Commissioner prays to his god and waves the cross talisman over your head."

Chi Lin did not understand the man. She felt relieved with the potion.

"I am grateful," she said.

"Grateful for my brew or grateful that he does not cast a spell upon you?'

"This doctor believes in fewer things than any of us," Ai-lo Wun-kua said, laughing. "My God would find him annoying if ever he had a chance encounter with him."

"Which I shall not," Ji Ji-bang said, wrapping his bottles in a leather roll. "Now, good lady, listen to me. Do not over do things. Your time is not near yet, but you must not compromise nature by heavy lifting or unwarranted travel. If you cannot tell Wu T'ai-po such things, I will do it. He pays me well, as the Commissioner can attest."

Ji Ji-bang bowed to the Commissioner, the first time he did so because his fee was near at hand. Of course, the Commissioner did not pay him directly, so the bow was short and the physician disappeared in short order.

"I am in debt to you, my lord," Chi Lin said to Ai-lo Wun-kua.

"Fret not," he said. "Rest here and speak to me."

"Would that be proper?"

"Tush. I am a Mongol and do not subscribe to Han proscriptions." He leaned toward her. "I am a believer in the one God and follow the teachings of the prophet *Ye-su*. Do you know of what I speak?"

"I have heard of this."

"From your father, no doubt. I am an *Arka-'un*, guided by the ways of the *Ne-tze-ehr*. So when I heard the tale of your pregnancy by your dead husband, I shrugged my shoulders and looked to my God and thought of the many fairy stories told by my Han brethren."

Chi Lin glanced to the ceiling.

"Please, my lord, *Heaven* will hear you."

"*Heaven* always hears me, but not a celestial court or the souls of the many who have gone before, but a single spirit who sees all and knows all."

Chi Lin drew her eyes away, afraid that such talk would compromise her state, perhaps more than the weather could.

"I am sorry for you," she muttered.

"I know you are," Ai-lo Wun-kua said. "You could not understand these things. Your father chastised me for the heresy, but he is a man of virtue and would not compromise me or my household beyond a head nod and a finger wag." He laughed. "You father is well."

"You have seen him?"

"I have. I visited him three moons ago. He complained of gas and the usual joint aches, but otherwise he appeared spry enough. I wish that I could bring him to the Ya-men and set him to best use, but nothing escapes his Majesty's eye. I would not set your father up for a fall."

"You are kind, sir."

"I am as I am. I send him copy work . . . for your father and your brother."

Chi Lin brightened. It was clear that this man was a friend of the family, and yet she never recalled seeing him. She had known the Superintendent, but the Commission was always no more than a name on the wind.

"And are you allowed to study in the House of Wu?" he asked.

Chi Lin feared to reply, but did not need to reply because, by Ai-lo Wun-kua's facial expression, the question was a tease. Surely he knew the answer.

"I am a ghost bride, my lord."

"Yes, and you carry a ghost child." He winked. "But I know better. And when you have given birth and return to your tour inspections, you must always come to the Ya-men and sit with me. We can discuss the classics, if you wish and I will tell you the latest gossip from court."

Chi Lin smiled, the prospect of such stimuli tempting.

"I am a mere woman, my lord. Pursuit of scholarship is forbidden."

"Not under my roof. My wife reads and writes, but . . ." He leaned forward and whispered. "She has a poor head for philosophy and poetry. She can discuss flower arrangement and basket weaving, which is interesting for a moment or two, but does not keep my attention fixed."

Chi Lin bowed again, and then silence prevailed.

The Commission napped by the fire.

7

Chou Kuai-tze returned, the inspection completed. Chi Lin felt restored and, although the chair was as rocky as ever, the porters had been rested and fed and were more inclined to keep her steady. The Commissioner's wife said her goodbyes, Ai-lo Wun-kua allowed to sleep by the hearth. Chi Lin found the woman most accommodating and sensed a secret kinship to her — reading and writing.

One thing had changed on the return trip. The sky was dark gray and it began to snow — a light flurry and rare for the region. Chi Lin's spirits raised as the flakes coated her lap and cap. She had remembered snow before, but it was many years ago when she was a child. The porters managed through the small accumulation, their feet bare and their skin bluish. More townsfolk were abroad now, the snow drawing their attention and wonder. By the time Chou Kuai-tze's horse crossed beneath the outer gate to the Wu Homestead, the ground was covered entirely with white.

The entourage, such as it was, halted before the Jade Heart Pavilion. The Old Lady of the House stood on the porch clad in heavy fur and an ermine scarf. The flakes were sticking to her eyelashes underscoring the dissatisfaction she felt. Willow stood beside her with a furled *san-tze*. Upon seeing the Old Lady, Chou Kuai-tze dismounted, bowed and then escorted his horse toward the stable. The porters were at a loss at their next steps, so they stood shivering before the Old Lady of the House.

"Purple Sage," the Old Lady snapped. "Why have you chanced it? Why?"

Chi Lin was downcast, but could do nothing more than apologize and explain, curtly.

"I am sorry, mother-in-law. I was ordered to do so."

"Ordered?"

"Jasmine said it would bring glory and honor to the House of Wu."

The Old Lady's bottom lip curled. She looked beyond Chi Lin to the Blue Heaven Pavilion. She marched off toward the slick wooden boardwalk.

"My lady," Willow said. "You will slip and fall."

"Then you will pick me up and brush me off."

The Old Lady marched beyond the chair, a trail formed by the sweep of her robe. Chi Lin grinned secretly. The First Wife would be berated, to be sure, and with good reason. Then, Chi Lin looked beyond the courtyard. Standing at a distance through the curtain of snow was Mi Tso-tze waving to the porters to come. They took her cue, lifted the chair and completed the journey.

Chi Lin would sleep deeply that night and not emerge from the Silver Silence Hall for three days.

Chapter Eighteen

Full Blossoming

1

A basket of *Cheng-tze* arrived at the Silver Silence Hall much to the delight of Mo Li, who said she could steam a delicious basket of buns from the orange fruit, and even could use the peel in her ingredient cupboard. Chi Lin was happier for the sight of the fruit than the promised taste. This was a gift from the First Wife — a sign that she had been chastised by the Old Lady of the House and wanted to make amends. Although, there was no word of regret from Ma Mai-to, who delivered them.

"These are hearty delicacies, my lady," Mi Tso-tze said, peeling one for her mistress. "I have only tasted them once, but I know they will soothe your tummy and raise a smile to your lips."

Chi Lin listened. She had had *Cheng-tze* before, her father being partial to them and also had some at the wives' table in the Jade Heart Hall when Liang-tze sent baskets in filial respect to his father. On this occasion, Wu T'ai-po had taken three fruit, separated them into the sections and sent these to the women on silver plates. The fruit was delectable. But Chi Lin thought, as sweet as these might have been, Jasmine's gift might prove bitter.

Chi Lin took a slice and brought it to her lips. She had not been outside in a week and requested that work be brought to her in the Silver Silence. Sitting on the chair and staring at the walls did not suit her and, although Mo Li kept a steady stream of buns and rice balls coming into the hall, Chi Lin feared overeating them, only to bring them up. Her morning sickness was slackening, but any untoward push might bring it on again. So now she ate this sweet fruit slice.

The bitterness not in the taste, but in the prospect. Chi Lin's son, if the *fa-shr* was correct and her baby would be a man-child, would leave the Silver Silence Hall immediately to be weaned by an *amah* and taught to regard Jasmine as his mother and Purple Sage as his Auntie, much like Lotus and Orchid's daughters. In this, Chi Lin had a sorrowful pang, her heart filled with regrets even before the child was born. If she was in another household, her children would be her own. But here she was just the Fourth

Wife, and the ghost bride. She could prevent this by declaring the real father, but that would only bring dishonor to the house, herself and her unborn son. She would be able to keep him and be his mother, but she would be forced to fend from the roadside, and he would have no advantage of his adopted blood line.

Chi Lin swallowed the fruit, and then took another slice. She knew Jasmine had been berated by the Old Lady. She had not heard this from Willow, who only nodded and kept silent when asked, as was proper, but from Wu Chou-fa. The boys would drift over to Chi Lin's window on occasion and greet her. On one visit, both brothers were contrite that their auntie was forced to *ride the chair*. But the younger son spit on the ground, and then laughed.

"Grandmother was extremely cross with mother," he said.

"You should not say so," Chi Lin protested, but not too insistently.

"You should not tell her such things," Lin-kua said. "It is not for her ears."

"But it was for our ears, brother," Chou-fa said. "That was how loud grandmother shouted. So loud the worms stopped their eating and listened. So loud the servants were abuzz for days."

"Really so loud?" Chi Lin said, secretly glad.

"He stretches the truth," Lin-kua said. "He always makes more of nothing."

At that point they began to slap each other until they raced away, no doubt to convert such energy into play. But Chi Lin was happy that Jasmine was chastised. That the First Wife could still lash out at her was a possibility, but it was a sign that Purple Sage's unborn son stood well in the eyes of the Old Lady of the House. It was a warm sign — one of endearment.

Chi Lin took another slice, and then paused.

"Tso-tze."

"Yes, my lady."

"Take this and enjoy it."

Mi Tso-tze did not protest, but embraced the fruit slice greedily. She had been licking her fingers after she completed the peeling, but the slice would be better indeed. As she sniffed the fragrance of the slice and let the pulp linger in her mouth, the world seemed to slip away.

Chi Lin heard a child-like song from the courtyard.

> *"The Monkey King outfoxed Prince Demon Pig*
> *Ho ho he and a wo wo wei,*
> *Then he drank the Heavens in one happy swig,*
> *Wo wo ho ho he, wo wei."*

"He is here," Chi Lin said, attempting to rise.

"Let me help you," Tso-tze said, swallowing the slice.

Chi Lin wobbled to the window where she saw the source of the song, and heard another verse.

> *"Lord Buddha danced a jig to see it so*
> *Wo wo wei and a he he ho,*
> *And he struck the demon with his lightning bow,*
> *Ho ho ho he, wei, wei, wo."*

The boy, Po Bo, who everyone called little Monkey, carried two baskets slung on the end of his carry pole. He was a slight child of ten *sui*, but the cargo was light and easily handled. Chi Lin looked forward to the cargo, because it was her sewing work — shoes and linen and clothing for repair and embroidery. She would not need to stare at the walls for the next week. She was grateful to her mother-in-law for allowing her to work from the hall.

Po Bo came near the window, and bowed.

"Mistress Purple Sage, I am sorry. I bring you more than usual."

"Do not be sorry," Chi Lin replied. "I am happy for it."

Lao Lao appeared, hopping to the boy, who let the baskets fall.

"Rascal Monkey," Lao Lao said. "You are letting the work touch the ground. Will you scrub the soil away?"

"Old Lao Lao," the boy laughed. "I am not an old woman, like you."

He giggled, while Lao Lao righted one basket.

"Tso-tze," Chi Lin said. "Please help Lao Lao and . . . bring little Monkey three *Cheng-tze* slices."

"Three slices, mistress? He will sing his song all day."

"It is much, I know, but *you* must take and eat the remaining slices."

Mi Tso-tze grinned, the sweet remembrance of the last slice still lingering, no doubt. She hastened outside and helped Lao Lao gather the baskets. Then she turned to Po Bo extending the fruit slices. The boy's lips trembled. Chi Lin thought he would cry. Mi Tso-tze indicated the window, and Po Bo bowed low. He did not eat the fruit, but carefully placed them into his sash purse, which was otherwise empty, Chi Lin was sure. He would find a secret place and eat the slices like Prince Demon Pig. As he hoisted his empty carry pole and departed, he hummed his song. Chi Lin thought he was a fine lad — useful and bubbling with life. She sighed, because she was bubbling with life now, as her aching back and swollen belly told her.

2

Chi Lin often thought of her visit to the Ya-men and Ai-lo Wun-kua. She would have liked to visit there now, except it would mean a trip in the unsteady chair. Besides, she would not attempt a tour now after Jasmine had been chastised. Still, she needed company. Mi Tso-tze was fine as far as it went. Chi Lin knew little about her, but was afraid to pursue it since Tso-tze had been in service in the Second Son's household. Such conversation would be a last resort. She had to settle with the occasional visit from Willow, and Snapdragon's inevitable morning hair comb, and Lao Lao's nonsensical chatter. The children made their appearance more often. She guessed they liked her company as much as she liked theirs.

Winter had closed in, and the sun shone lower in the sky. The wind whistled through the eaves and fog sometimes swept in from the coast. Despite her growth and discomfort, Chi Lin still managed to go to the shrine and visit with her husband – less frequently, true, but she feared that *Heaven* might be angered by any lapse. Mi Tso-tze was more than helpful, guiding her mistress over the cobblestones and into the alcove, sheltering her with the *san-tze* from the dim sun on clear days and from mists, drizzle and flurries on moist days. She would hand Chi Lin the incense sticks and the red paper. If the girls should show up, she would keep them silent while Chi Lin prayed. The girls seemed to like Mi Tso-tze, but wanted to chatter about Auntie Purple Sage's big belly and *when will the baby come* and *can we play with him when he is old enough*. Chi Lin just grinned and nodded, while Tso-tze replied with pat answers – noncommittal and sweetly vague.

Mostly Chi Lin wanted to talk with her husband, so Mi Tso-tze would tend to *Guan-yin's* alter while her mistress conversed.

"The *fa-shr* says it is a boy and you will have a third son. Just think of that, husband. Your ghost has been busy, they say, and I am glad for it. *Heaven* is gracious that I am big with child and you are content within your tablet."

It was much the same on all visitation days, Chi Lin glad to rest before Wu Hung-lin's effigy, choking a little on the incense and rejoicing when a chilly breeze blew it away in a different direction. She also reckoned that the exercise between the Silver Silence and the shrine was good. It eased the boredom, at least, and reminded her how lucky she was to have big feet, at best. And then there were the girls and their chatter. One day she turned to them.

"How goes your sewing lessons?" she asked.

"I do not like to sew," Jade said. "It bites my fingers."

"The *amah* is mean," Pearl added. "She says I will never be good at it."

"I can sew a tiger's face," Sapphire said, bragging at first, but then frowning when her sisters gave her a sharp glance. "Well, I can. My *amah* does not scold me for it."

"Because she does not care," Jade said.

"She does so," Sapphire complained.

"You could stitch a loopy mess," Pearl added, "and Day Lily would not know it."

Chi Lin looked to Mi Tso-tze. It was the time to help her stand and return. Once on her feet, the girls turned their attention to the big belly, reaching out to touch it, but waiting for permission."

"You may do so," Chi Lin said.

"But gently," Mi Tso-tze added. "You must not harm your brother."

While the girls patted Chi Lin's tummy in wonder, Tso-tze opened the *san-tze*, the day being particularly bright.

"How would you like to sew flowers and faces on shoes?" Chi Li asked them.

"We can already do it," Jade replied.

"But you do not like it. I can show you how to do it so it is easy, beautiful and fun."

The girls responded. So they followed Auntie Purple Sage and her handmaiden to the Silver Silence, where Chi Lin taught them how – simple floral stitches at first, but with care and a compelling voice. Now she would have company through the balance of the winter, at least two girls showing up a few days a week to learn and chatter. Sapphire did not always come, but she was a moody child and Chi Lin understood. Purple Sage had visited the Golden Oak Pavilion enough to know an ill spirit dwelt there. Still, to guide little fingers making lilies and cherry blossoms, and soon tiger faces and monkey maws, delighted Purple Sage and filled the hall with laughter. Boredom came and went, but was less so now with this little sewing circle of silly girls, not all of whom were children.

"She scares me," Jade said.

"Who?"

"The old blind one," Jade admitted.

"Snapdragon?" Chi Lin replied. "You must not be afraid of her. She is a kind soul inside."

"She is always telling us to go away and not bother her, because she has a coffin and a shroud," Pearl said.

"But she does," Chi Lin explained. "You will understand one day when you have a household of your own and appreciate the people who do you service. When you honor them with kindness and consideration, you will know."

"But a coffin is not a kindness," Jade stated. "It is an old box where people go when their *ch'i* escapes their bodies."

Chi Lin sighed. How was a young girl to grasp the kindness within death? It was a far away notion. Yet Chi Lin had learned that children see more plainly than adults and latch on more simply to the more complicated concepts of the world.

"That the *ch'i* escapes, it is true," Chi Lin said. "But our bodies are a gift from our parents. If we have no place to store it away, how will the *ch'i* know where to go when it returns?"

"As a ghost?" Pearl asked, chillingly.

"No. To rest and carry on with the business of our ancestors. How can those who are gone look after us if they have no place to keep their body or their *ch'i*? So it is a kindness that Snapdragon has a place and knows about it now while she still breathes."

"Now I see," Jade said. "So she is worried we will steal her coffin and her shroud."

"No fear," Pearl said. "I am sure we will have our own coffin and shroud when the time comes. And I would not know where to put it now anyway."

"That is so," Chi Lin said. "I am glad you understand. Do not fear the old ones. They have much on their minds and you must let them finish out their lives in peace."

This said, the girls went about their sewing as if the subject had never been broached; so much like children solving life's complicated knots.

3

As winter waned and spring dawned, the girls came less often. Chi Lin wearied more easily, moved about less and embraced sleep more often to ward off the boredom. There was a bit of cheer at New Year – a week of noise makers and celebration, but Chi Lin remained confined. Mo Li brought her confections from the Jade Heart's kitchen and Wu T'ai-po sent around fresh red paper for the outside wall of the Silver Silence – *Prosperity* characters and a portrait of the K'ai Chiao, Yan-cheng's city wall god. The children visited to rub Purple Sage's belly for good luck. But New Years whirled by Chi Lin leaving scant impression upon her. She secretly wished it would be spent fast so the world could return to silence and her courtyard could be at peace.

It was on the last day of the Lantern Festival, when the girls paraded to her door in rabbit costumes that she finally emerged to enjoy the sun's warmth. She sat on the porch and listened to household chatter, nodding when complimented. She laughed at Po Bo's antics and watched Wu Lin-kua and Wu Chou-fa chase after him with a long pole. Lao Lao thought it delicious, rolling around on the cobblestones while Mo Li was upset at a rat she had found in her kitchen. She chased it almost as heartily as the boys chased little Monkey, only she was intent on killing it. Chi Lin hoped the rat got away, not wanting it served up inside a bun.

As the sun set, she sat outside until no one remained except Mi Tso-tze who waved a fan to assure her mistress was not overheated. The sun was not very hot yet, but still, in Chi Lin's condition, Tso-tze chanced nothing. Chi Lin regarded her handmaiden – an essential in her life now. She often wondered what Tso-tze's life was before she came here, but feared to ask because she had come from the Second Son's household. But in the falling shade of this evening, she asked.

"Are you content here, Tso-tze?" Chi Lin asked.

Mi Tso-tze did not answer at first, which concerned Chi Lin.

"I am content, mistress."

"I ask because if you were not I would allow you to return to the Second Son's House."

Mi Tso-tze trembled.

"Please, mistress. Do not send me away. I meant not to give offense."

"You have not given offense. In fact, I am pleased with you. So much so I give you leave to go if you wish it."

"No. No. The Second Son's House is . . . I cannot say."

"Please me and do say."

Mi Tso-tze cocked her head, and then looked to the ground.

"My life has not been happy until now, mistress. The Mi clan are rice growers in *Tua-ching-xien* where the ground is not competent for many good seasons. So a girl child is not a blessing. When my father had a chance to sell his daughters to rich neighbors, he did so. And who can blame ones father?................."

"No one," Chi Lin said touching Tso-tze shoulder. "My father has two daughters and, although he did not sell us, we were both unfortunate to his household."

"You have a sister, mistress?"

"I do. And she, like me was set to marry, but into the Guo clan. Like me, her groom died before the ceremony. But unlike me, she chose to remain aloof. It saddened her and would have dishonored our household had she not decided to enter a nunnery."

"That is an unfortunate life," Tso-tze mused.

"She will go there when she reaches her twentieth summer. But I decided to be a ghost bride."

"That was fortunate for me, mistress." She bowed. "I was sold to Wu Liang-tze to serve his Second Wife. She is a pleasure house woman demanding much attention. I was one of six handmaidens and not the favorite. There was much squabbling over who was closest to the mistress. But our fear was from the Second Son, because, despite his many wives and his nightly trips to the town for pleasure, he insisted on having every woman in his household at least once."

"It is as I feared," Chi Lin said.

"No, mistress. It would have been improper for me to come serve you if I had been so sullied. You are big from the ghost, I know, but . . ." She sighed. "I shall say no more."

"It is best you do not. But I am surprised you escaped his attention."

"I did not escape his attention or his entreaties. If it were his decision, I would not have come here. But I was selected by the Old Lady of the House, and perhaps because I was, I am still unsullied."

"Blameless."

"I yearn like any woman, mistress. I should not say it. I have seen many attractive men much above my station, but not above my inclinations. Such is the trap."

"Such is the trap."

They fell silent as if the truth of the moment engulfed them as the shadows fell.

Chapter Nineteen

Springing Toward Summer

1

As the purple *zi ding-xiang* and *zi-teng* began their first bloom near the porch and over the eaves, Chi Lin came full term. Mi Tso-tze brought buckets of ornamental cabbage to be secured along the courtyard path, while Mo Li nurtured a crop of *pen-tsao* for their yellow hearts — good for both cooking and as an herb. The Old Lady of the House sent Po Bo to all the pavilions with bowls of fresh honey. But the best comb was reserved for Purple Sage, honey being particularly good for the unborn child, or so it was said. The girls came with nosegays of red *mei-gui*, the thorns removed, and with fistfuls of cheerful yellow *chu-ju* and played the petal picking game with their auntie Purple Sage. Chi Lin enjoyed the game and the fragrance of the deep red *mei-gui*, but the sprigs of *zi ding-xiang* — purple beards gathering like grapes beneath the boughs trumped all the fragrances save one — the renewed nip of salt from the *ji-tzao*. In fact, mixed with the filtered salt came briny aromas from the sea as it awoke to spring, anticipating summer. Chi Lin had only seen the sea from afar, but she respected those men who sailed on it, hunting for the monsters of the deep. The port was small, but rumors came that it was being expanded, the Imperial interest in trading missions on the cusp.

Generally, Chi Lin tried to work on the porch, but when the sun was high, she would squint and made no progress. So in the afternoons, she moved inside where it was less bright and cooler. One day while she busied her fingers on a tablecloth, the fabric on a flat stretcher, she heard someone at the window. She supposed it was one of the girls, particularly Sapphire, who would always peek in before coming to the door. But when Chi Lin looked up, she was startled.

"Wu Lin-kua," she said. "You have given me a fright."

Mi Tso-tze was on the spot, emerging from behind her partition.

"Young master," she snapped. "You should not be here."

Lin-kua nodded, and then leaned into the room

"But I have come to give Auntie Purple Sage a gift."

"It is not proper," Tso-tze said.

"And why not?"

Chi Lin set aside her needle, lodging it into the tablecloth. She looked kindly to Lin-kua.

"I appreciate the gesture, Master Lin-kua, but a man does not present gifts to their Auntie. Gifts are reserved for the women of the pleasure houses. When you are older you will know what I mean."

"I know now," he replied. "I know about the pleasure houses and what happens there. Uncle Liang-tze has told me many times. He goes there often."

"You must not say such things," Tso-tze scolded.

"You must not be so abrupt with me," Lin-kua said.

Mi Tso-tze pouted, but returned to her place.

"She *may* not, but I must," Chi Lin said.

"Father had two wives from the pleasure house," Lin-kua said, swagger in his voice. "When I am the Master of the House, I will have sixteen wives, and ten will come from the pleasure house."

Chi Lin chuckled.

"When you are Master of the House, you may do whatever you please. I must caution you, as your auntie, having many wives might make you old fast. Wives from the pleasure house are expensive to acquire, so you must adhere to your studies and come to know the business of salt, so you can afford such opulence as sixteen wives."

Lin-kua appeared crestfallen.

"That is what I want to do," he said. "But for now I want to give you a gift, because you are my auntie and I think you will like the gift. It is not a gift for a woman in the pleasure house. It is a gift worthy of a nephew to his auntie. But if you think it not proper, you can return it. I will leave it at the door."

He disappeared, leaving Chi Lin a bit concerned that she may have insulted him. Young men always think more of themselves without considering matters completely. There was no reason for this gift except that Lin-kua strove to be a man and knew no women except those in the household.

"Tso-tze," she said. "See what he has brought."

Mi Tso-tze hurried to the threshold, returning with an oblong parcel wrapped in silk. She cocked her head as she observed it, perhaps trying to determine its nature.

"What is it?" Chi Lin asked.

"It is an odd thing, mistress. It appears to be a book. What use do you have for such a thing?"

Chi Lin grinned, thrusting her hands out above her belly, awaiting the gift. Tso-tze bowed and handed it to her.

"Sit beside me, Tso-tze, and I will tell you a secret."

Tso-tze seemed uneasy, but obeyed. Chi Lin unwrapped the book, glancing at its cover — a creamy board edged in gold. She opened it, and then sighed.

"It is the *Shr Jing*," she said. *"The Classic of Odes."*

"How can you tell, mistress?"

"Hush, and listen."

Chi Lin touched the first column with her index finger and grinned as if she had found a long lost friend. She read:

> *"Guan-guan go the ospreys,*
> *On the islet in the river.*
> *The modest, retiring, virtuous, young lady:*
> *For our prince a good mate she."*

"Who would have thought?" Tso-tze said. "You can speak the characters."

"They are more than characters, Tso-tze. They are beautiful thoughts. Indeed, Wu Lin-kua has given me a mighty gift, one that shall be my companion as much as you are. I am a scholar's daughter, Tso-tze. All my father's children know the Classics."

"But does it not offend *Heaven*?"

"How so? I know it is not looked upon with favor, so I have been circumspect, but perhaps not circumspect enough, because the boys have gone beyond guessing. This is a gift a nephew might give his auntie, because no pleasure house woman would know the use of it."

She returned to the next ode.

> *"Here long, there short, is the duckweed,*
> *To the left, to the right, borne about by the current.*
> *The modest, retiring, virtuous, young lady:*
> *Waking and sleeping, he sought her.*
> *He sought her and found her not,*

*And waking and sleeping he thought about her.
Long he thought; oh! long and anxiously;
On his side, on his back, he turned, and back
again."*

"It is beautiful," Tso-tze said, "although I do not quite follow its meaning. Is it about love?"

"The *Shr Jing* abounds in love poetry and also songs of the seasons and war and statecraft." She nestled the book upon her womb. "Wu Lin-kua is not to be mocked again."

And she read some more, and for hours. Each day was now filled with less work and more reading. Mi Tso-tze sometimes listened and sometimes slept. When Lao Lao first saw this, he shuddered.

"The sky shall fall upon us, mistress," he said. "We are doomed if you keep on with this."

"You best get indoors then, Lao Lao," she said.

Lao Lao moaned and ran away. But in time, he came to ignore the fact that his mistress had learned what only men should know, although *he* could not read or write a single character. Snapdragon did not make any fuss. Certainly, Lao Lao had told her, but she could not see it for herself. Mo Li made it a point to close her eyes to it, although she probably gossiped in the Jade Heart kitchen. Chi Lin did not care who knew now. She was about to give the household a man child and, if that did not give her easement to read harmlessly, she had underestimated her growing status.

2

Summer made bolder still with high heat and stickiness. Rain came more frequently, a welcome to cool off the day. But Chi Lin worried that she was past her time, because the child did not come. Perhaps *Heaven* was peeved by her reading and Lao Lao was correct. She could not tell. But in the last days, she read less as an appeasement, just in case. One afternoon, after a cleansing morning rain, porters arrived in the courtyard with a chair. Willow stood nearby.

"Willow is here, mistress."

"Willow?"

Chi Lin managed to get to the porch, where she received the handmaiden fondly. Willow had not been around to see her in at least a moon — perhaps two.

"Why has a chair be brought?" Chi Lin asked. "I am not to tour again, am I?"

"No, mistress," Willow replied. "The Master of the House has visitors who have expressed a desire to visit with you."

Chi Lin wondered. Was it her father? Perhaps her sister bound for the nunnery. Certainly not her crippled brother.

"Who is it, Willow? I am too tender to be left to guessing."

"It is Commissioner Ai-lo Wun-kua and his wife."

"Ah."

This pleased Chi Lin, so much so, she groped for Tso-tze to help her to the chair. But after two steps, she halted.

"I would be pleased to see them," she said. "The commissioner is a kind man."

"But she will not be able to walk there and the chair will be a challenge," Tso-tze snapped, quite put out that anyone would suggest such a thing.

"Please tell the Commissioner that I am well enough, but near to full term."

"Past full term," Tso-tze added.

"He will be disappointed," Willow said. "But he cannot come here, surely."

"Surely not," Tso-tze snapped.

Chi Lin was disappointed. A conversation with Ai-lo Wun-kua would be stimulating indeed. What a disappointment that he could not enter the Silver Silence while she was in her condition. Chi Lin made it to the seat on the porch, and then watched the porters take away the chair, Willow in tow.

"It is for the best, mistress," Tso-tze said.

"Perhaps."

Less than an hour passed and the chair returned, this time filled with the Commissioner's wife. Chi Lin was glad to see her. The woman wobbled in the chair, the porters having difficulty because she was a tall woman. But once the chair settled to the cobblestones, the Commissioner's wife was out of the chair and approaching Chi Lin, hands outstretched.

"Child," she said. "My husband is disappointed that you could not come see him in your father-in-law's *ke-ting*, but I have come to you, as it is more appropriate."

"Welcome, madam," Chi Lin said, standing unsteadily with Mi Tso-tze help.

"My husband has brought you a gift, which perhaps is more proper to present to you here, in the quiet of your own pavilion." She turned back to the chair and grabbed a thick bamboo scroll. "And here it is."

Chi Lin squinted. Her father had many books in bamboo rolls, but the style of this one was older, paper and silk rag being more the fashion.

"Tso-tze," Chi Lin said, and the maid fetched the roll, bowing to the Commissioner's wife as she took it.

Chi Lin looked at the work, but could not discern which one it was.

"It is a fine rendition of the *Chun-chiu*," the wife said.

"The *Spring and Autumn Annals*," Chi Lin replied, gasping with joy. "This is too kind of your husband."

"Not so," the woman said, now on the porch. "It is an essential work. I have read it through and find it most engrossing."

Mi Tso-tze gazed at the woman as if she was some new species of water buffalo. Chi Lin touched the book and began to take it into her own hands, when she experienced a sharp pain, sharper than anything so far in her blossoming. Then a warm wetness cascaded from beneath.

"What is happening?" she asked, alarmed.

The Commissioner's wife stared at the ground.

"You have let your water go," she said, laughing. "It has started, and almost your time." She looked to Tso-tze. "Take your mistress inside." She yelled to the porters. "Return your chair and tell the Jade Heart hall that the baby comes."

"Will they send someone?" Chi Lin asked.

"For what reason?" the wife asked. "Are you the Emperor's wife?"

"But what shall I do?"

"What is natural? But have no fear. I have done this six times myself and can advise you as you go."

Chi Lin suddenly experienced a horrific pain and felt the baby stir.

"He wants to come out," the wife said. "That is all." She turned to Tso-tze. "Do not stand there like sleeping ox. Get her inside, and then fetch clean rags and a knife."

"A knife?" Chi Lin asked.

"You will see. Did not your mother teach you anything?"

Chi Lin shook her head, and then winced with pain. Tso-tze guided her inside.

3

In her lifetime, Chi Lin had been stung by a bee, scraped in a fall and even had had a stomach distemper, all of which were painful. But she had never been so overcome with pain as she was now. It came in spurts, not all at once — a pulsating fire that made her wish she never had seen Gao Lin and his manhood. Although she was inclined to sit on the chair or climb into bed, the Commissioner's wife told her to squat near the table and hold briskly to its edge. Then she offered her own hand. With each wave of pain, Chi Lin saw red and gripped first the Commissioner's wife's hand, and then Tso-tze, who wept, for all it was worth.

When Lao Lao showed up, he was immediately chastised.

"Who is this?" the Commissioner's wife shouted.

"It is the custodian of the hall," Tso-tze replied.

"Leave, man. This is no place for you. Leave at once or *Heaven* will pollute your heart and the birth shall go awry."

Lao Lao shook his hands and ran like lightning after thunder. Snapdragon, however, laughed and approached the table.

"The ghost baby will be born," she said, and then began to dance. No one shooed her away, because her voice was overpowered by Chi Lin's screams.

As the pain became ever-present, Chi Lin pushed as best she could, the Commissioner's wife doing nothing more than allowing her wrists to be bruised, and occasionally looking underneath the squatting woman.

"You are doing well, Purple Sage," she said. "You are lucky I am here to give you company. My six were born alone and I could not scream. It would have disturbed my lord. You can scream all you want. Your lord is far away at the *Yellow Springs* — if we are to subscribe to the current fiction."

Chi Lin found the wife's voice mere patter — no meaning and far from soothing, but she did note between pains that she was encouraged to continue and that there was progress. However, it seemed as if the baby would never come, that he liked his warm home inside her.

"It is time to leave," she huffed. "You must leave me and take up your place."

Then, one last excruciating bolt and the baby dropped free. Chi Lin felt the Commissioner's wife groping beneath her, and then she heard Mi Tso-tze say *what are you doing with the knife* and the wife replying *Does not any mother tell their daughters of these things?* Then it was over. The baby cried, and Chi Lin was helped into bed.

4

Purple Sage was exhausted, a strange haze clouding her mind. She wanted to sleep, but instead she drifted in a dream world partially awake. Then she was astounded, because her son was thrust into her arms. She peered at him — his black eyes seeming to see her, but she knew better. His creamy skin was soft to her touch.

"He is fine," she whispered.

"Yes, mistress. He will be a credit to the household."

Then the truth rushed upon her. This little button who wiggled gently in her arms would find himself elsewhere. She wanted to lock him in her arms forever. Gently, she kissed his forehead, and then wept. She felt him released from her arms as the dream returned — the haze overcoming her. When she woke again, her son was no longer with her.

Chi Lin heard voices at the far end of the hall. She tried to see and, at first, could only discern a cluster of women dressed in bright red robes — all but one, who wore a lilac tunic. She recognized her mother-in-law's voice, gravelly and doting. Then there was Jasmine's, proud and supercilious. Then came a soft voice. *I shall regard your son as my son*, it said. Chi Lin knew. This was the *amah* ceremony. Her brightest joy was being given over to the *amah's* care. But the address of motherhood was directed at Jasmine not her. Chi Lin gasped, suppressed a tear and rolled over to hide the sight.

In her misty eyes, she awoke to see the Old Lady of the House standing over her. It was the first time this woman had set foot in the Silver Silence. Her mother-in-law smiled wanly. Beside her stood the Commissioner's wife. Both women were gentle.

"Purple Sage," the Old Lady said. "You have done well."

"He is my child," she whispered.

"In your heart," her mother-in-law replied. "You will see him always, and you have earned the right to name him."

"Ming-kuan," Chi Lin said, without hesitation. She had considered this name for weeks. "Ming-kuan."

"We shall see," the Old Lady replied. "Rest now. You must become strong for the work. You are an honorable Auntie and all the children of the house look upon you as a blessing. You have done well. Very well, indeed."

Chi Lin knew that now she would gain further status. But this was not what she wanted. She wanted her baby, to love and caress. She wanted to play with his little fingers as they budded and to see him crawl and walk and run. She knew she would, but as a household fixture not as an adoring mother. He would bow to her and call her Auntie, much like his brothers and sisters did.

She drifted into the haze again. She stirred. The hall was dark. She was alone.

"Mi Tso-tze."

"Yes, mistress."

Not alone. Her faithful maid servant had fallen asleep near the bed and stirred now. When her shadowy form loomed, Chi Lin grasped her wrist.

"I am sore, mistress," Tso-tze said.

"How so?"

"You gripped me during your time. You do not recall it?"

Chi Lin recalled it. She released Tso-tze's arm.

"I do recall it. I do. But what am I to do now? They have taken him away."

Tso-tze remained silent. She stroked her mistresses' shoulder. Chi Lin had nothing more to recall. So she returned to slumber in this Hall of Silver Silence.

Chapter Twenty

Mistress Purple Sage

1

Work can be a savior in times of stress and disappointment. It can distract and concentrate attention to details other than those of the heart. When the mind and fingers are engaged, striving for perfection, the heart can bear most anything. Thus, Chi Lin managed to bury her grief at losing her son to the First Wife through sewing and mending and feeding the worms. At first she took no notice of the improvement of her status in the house. The work was much the same as it was before, but she was no longer summoned and told where to report. When she appeared for the sewing, her mother-in-law was surprised to see her, but welcomed her nonetheless. The only formal task subject to a schedule was the tour of the *ji-tzao*, and that was under the First Wife's jurisdiction.

As the seasons progressed, Chi Lin *did* notice changes. Her advice was sought by the servants about particular stitches which she had mastered. In the silk *ji-tzao*, the workers turned to her to direct their duties. She had become a driving force and supervised the business of the cocoons. On some days, when she thought of her child, she would think to remain in the Silver Silence and read or attend her personal sewing. But then she would always change her mind and head to the shrine, and then to her chores.

At the shrine she would linger, sometimes with Mi Tso-tze holding the *san-tze*, sometimes not, her maid having her own chores to attend to in her mistress' absence. Chi Lin's routine before Wu Hung-lin's effigy was standard, but her words were not. She offered up prayers to him and asked advice, always awaiting an answer, but never to hear one. But she came to love the man, perhaps because he did not intrude upon her daily life and he never had befouled her flesh.

"We have added five golden *koi* to the pond today," she told him. "The *yuan-wei* flowers are happy there. They are as purple as I am, although they have golden beards, which I have not."

Chi Lin loved the pool and would sit there with her hand caressing the surface, all the while drifting back to her childhood and her days sitting beside the pond at home. She thought of her mother more and sometimes her poor sister, lost now to the nunnery.

Chi Lin rarely mentioned her son at the shrine until one morning when she made a full accounting to Wu Hung-lin of all his children.

"Wu Lin-kua is becoming a fine scholar," she said. "I have seen him improve steadily. It would be better if Chou-fa excelled at it, because the scholar's lot will fall to him when *Heaven* sees fit to make your first son the Master of the House. As for Wu Ming-kuan, he took his first step last week. I was not there to see it, but I have watched him crawl and waddle in Jasmine's *ke-ting*, a miracle of nature, which he has become."

She grinned, but would speak no more of it because Tso-tze was there this day and Chi Lin feared to weep before her handmaiden, because Tso-tze would join her – most improper conduct at the shrine.

"The girls are well," she continued and said no more on that score, because she worried about Sapphire, who was *not* well — shy and slow-witted, morose at times and, at other times, argumentative.

As another year drew to a close, Chi Lin was a constant figure in the household — a welcome sight to both servant and relative. She often conversed with Pearl and Jade, who were learning a range of useful pursuits for young ladies beyond their sewing. They applied themselves to painting and singing acquired from their mother. Their *p'i-p'a* playing skills were rudimentary, befitting their small and dainty hands, but it would come in time. Sapphire, on the other hand, spent her hours sitting alone in her mother's unkempt *ke-ting*, playing with her dolls and occasionally wandering to the Jade Heart kitchen for a sweet bun, always getting under the kitchen staff's feet. Chi Lin tried to take her in hand, engaging her in some sewing or even telling her a story. She suggested that she learn the *ehr-hu* like her mother. But Orchid, languid and silent, rarely noticed her daughter, leaving her care to the *amah*, who detested her duties and, when no one was looking, pinched the child. But Chi Lin was looking and took the *amah* to task several times until Jasmine scolded Purple Sage for interfering with affairs which did not concern her. Chi Lin desisted, not wishing to anger the First Wife.

Chi Lin liked both boys, but not equally. She found Wu Chou-fa to have a jealous streak, complaining whenever he felt his brother received more attention — a gift from Wu T'ai-po or an extra bun at dinnertime. He tended to pout and kick the cat, when he thought no one was looking. Of course, Chi Lin was looking. She would shake her head, which Chou-fa respected, bowing and running away.

Wu Lin-kua was a brilliant boy, refined in his ways and superior to his brother in reading and writing, but he was not modest about it. He crowed often. But Chi Lin thought it appropriate for the future Master of the Wu House, who had sixteen wives as a marital goal. She also could not forget the gifts. Besides the *Shr-ching*, which was the first book she had acquired, once per moon a new book would show up on her doorstep. Where Lin-kua obtained these books, she knew not, but guessed that Master P'ing Chin had supplied them for favors or cash. It was common knowledge that Chi Lin was literate, but her value exceeded such disgrace. Everyone looked askance at the fault. What she did in the Silver Silence was her own business. However it did increase her respect from the Master of the House, who always nodded to her when she came into his view. In fact, besides books, there were other gifts — fruit, wall hangings, odd rocks for the poolscape and a *Zhang* puppy, which Lao Lao complained barked too much and Snapdragon complained because it defecated in places she managed to step into, blind as she was. Po Bo carried many gracious items in his carry pole into the Hall of Silver Silence. But, for Chi Lin, the greatest gift of all was the sight of Ming-kuan.

2

When Ming-kuan began to suckle on the *amah's* breasts, Chi Lin sought to supervise. This she was denied, although it was appropriate, given her status as Auntie. But the First Wife frowned upon it. Chi Lin understood that it could mislead the household and eventually Ming-kuan on the relationship between Jasmine and Wu Hung-lin's Third Son. So Chi Lin watched him from afar. Once a moon Jasmine permitted her to visit at the Blue Heaven Hall, where the *amah* would bring Ming-kuan, lift him in presentation and gave him up to the First Wife to cradle him. Chi Lin would then bow and say as she was instructed to say. *What a fine son you have, Mei Lo. He is a credit to the household and to our husband.* She was then allowed an approach, where she came within touching distance, but not allowed to touch. *I am your Auntie Chi Lin, who will be at hand to serve you.* Jasmine would smile, nod to the *amah*, who would quickly gather Ming-kuan back to her care and disappear from the hall. Chi Lin would then bow and thank Jasmine for her kindness, and then depart.

But this was not the only time Chi Lin saw Ming-kuan. She would spy through the window at him sleeping when no one could see her. When he began to crawl and walk, she made a point to pass by the nursery gate to catch a glimpse. She knew that if Jasmine found her out, there would be sour faces and wagging fingers, but Chi Lin would not be denied. She had a presence with her mother-in-law now. Surely the Lady of the House guessed at these lapses, but said nothing. The Old Lady knew that Purple Sage had well-managed her place as an Auntie to all the children. *How was this different?*

When spring passed again and summer crept on dog's hind quarters, Chi Lin had found her life routinely uneventful. There was always the sewing, the mending, the worms, the touring and a steady improvement to the Hall. Then one day Mi Tso-tze roused her mistress earlier than usual.

"Mistress, please come."

"Why so early, Tso-tze? Surely the world will wait upon my coming."

"Surely not."

Chi Lin arose from her meal, the tea having gone cold anyway. She followed her handmaiden to the door, over the high threshold and onto the porch. There she gasped. Standing before her were Wu Lin-kua and Wu Chou-fa. Between them stood, short and fidgeting, but on his own two legs, Wu Ming-kuan. The older boys bowed, and then forced the baby into a little bow. He did so, his blue robe flopping before him, his small top knot facing Chi Lin.

"You must pay respects to Auntie," Wu Lin-kua said.

The First Son had sprouted in the last year and was a full head taller than Chou-fa.

Chi Lin trembled. She felt weak and reached tentatively for Mi Tso-tze, who grasped her arm. How beautiful was her child, astounding in the morning light. How did he get free of his *amah*? Chi Lin did not care. She wanted to rush to him, lift him to the sun and shout to the world, *this is my creation. This is Ming-kuan, the wonderful.* But she knew this would bring dishonor and certainly confuse the child, who was ignorant of the circumstances and must remain so. She bowed to her three nephews.

"Welcome to the Silver Silence Hall," she said.

The boys bowed again.

"We thought it was time that our little brother sees his auntie in her own place," Lin-kua said. "We cannot stay. The *amah* will notice he is gone and perhaps will sound the alarm."

"She does not know?"

"She is a child herself," Lin-kua replied. "She sleeps too often than it is good for her."

"But indeed to our advantage," Chou-fa added, slyly winking. He turned to Ming-kuan. "Say Hello to Auntie Purple Sage."

Ming-kuan shook his head. *No,* it said. But Lin-kua frowned, and the little boy pouted, stamping his foot.

"You are my Auntie," he snapped. "You are my Auntie."

The words cut Chi Lin, but at the same time it was the first words she had heard from him. They were precious, despite their brutality. She bowed.

"I have seen you with your mother," she said. "You are a growing boy and soon will learn your brush strokes."

Ming-kuan shook his head again, and then hopped about, his attention gone from the moment.

"It will be a long time before that," Lin-kua said. "We must go now, Auntie." The two boys turned, loosely controlling their brother. They walked ceremoniously away, but near the gate Lin-kua turned.

"Are you pleased, Auntie?"

Chi Lin held onto Tso-tze.

"Very much, so."

These visits would repeat over the next few moons until Chi Lin came to expect them, awaiting patiently for the day that Ming-kuan spoke better, fidgeted less and approached her closer. It was well and by far an improvement over the official visits to Blue Heaven Hall, which soon were curtailed, and then ceased altogether.

3

Chi Lin toured as a matter of course now, an expert at the form. The First Wife never accompanied her, although Purple Sage was viewed as Jasmine's proxy. But as one year progressed into another year and yet another, the tenants forgot Jasmine except for the formality of her name. It was Mistress Purple Sage who came to represent the Wu House in the inspection tours. As Chi Li was pleasant and sometimes brought simple gifts – paper dolls and dried fruit for the children, her visits were esteemed and, at times, even cheered. While the Imperial Commissioner's proxy, Lin Wu-luo, remained a constant fixture, the journeymen varied. Chou Kuai-tze was the most familiar, but Fu Chia-min, Pa Li-tze and Pang Guo-ta were sometimes assigned. They were always formal, except Pang Guo-ta, who kept a cleaner horse and whistled as he rode. He also joked with the elder of the *Pao-t'ien* during the exchange of silver and the reckoning of the books. So it was one such tour under Pang Guo-ta that Chi Lin decided to take a detour.

The tour was approaching the road to the *ji-tzao*, when Chi Lin struck the side of the chair with her fan.

"Pang Guo-ta," she called.

The journeyman turned, stopped his whistling and nodded. The porters set the chair down.

"Mistress Purple Sage," he inquired. "Do you need to make water? The culvert is deepest here and can accommodate your need."

"No, Pang Guo-ta," she said. "I have business in the market."

"Business?"

"I wish to be taken there before we inspect the *ji-tzao*."

Pang Guo-ta looked to Lin Wu-luo, who shrugged. This was highly unusual, but also problematic. How could they chastise the fourth wife?

"Mistress," Guo-ta said. "Could not your maid servant run errands to the marketplace so as to not interfere with business?"

"No, Guo-ta. This business is too important, even for Mi Tso-tze."

Pang Guo-ta sighed, but bowed from his horse. He then pointed the way toward the market. The porters obeyed.

Chi Lin was anxious. What would Jasmine say when this detour was reported to her? But Chi Lin could justify it. After all, every tour ended at the Ya-men and, each time, she was invited in to see Ai-lo Wun-kua. Each time, she had declined, because it was not part of the business. But she knew she could visit with the Commissioner as the invitation came from him. So, in her defense, she could say that her conduct on the tours had been exemplary. A trip to the market to fulfill a family need could not be denied.

The marketplace was not accustomed to seeing a wife from the House of Wu mingling in the common stalls. Despite the activity, merchants and shoppers stopped, bowed and then whispered as Chi Lin's chair passed fruit stalls, vegetable racks and fish barrels. But her destination was not here. Since she had never been in the market, she was at a loss until she saw the dizzy array of silk bolts in the cloth shop. She called for the chair to halt.

"Guo-ta," she called.

"Yes, mistress.

"This is the place I seek. Stay here. I shall not be long."

"Yes, mistress."

Pang Guo-ta had ceased his whistling.

Amazed, the silk merchant greeted Purple Sage as if she were the Empress come for a fitting. He waved to his assistants to present the finest weaves and the brightest colors. But Chi Lin raised her hands.

"I want your best," she said. "Shimmering blue, rosal pink, deep green, acceptable yellow, gentle fawn and melon."

She said this with such resolve and specification, the merchant set his assistants to the task, bringing an array of each color for Chi Lin to inspect. In this she was careful, because she meant to sew robes for the children – acceptable yellow for Lin-kua, gentle fawn for Chou-fa and melon for her . . . well, for Ming-kuan. For the girls, shimmering blue for Sapphire, rosal pink for Pearl and deep green for Jade. She wanted enough to embroider sashes and shoes for the girls and little Ming-kuan, and sashes and caps for the boys, they already being in their leathers. She reviewed each bolt for sheen, matching the color to her imagination until she had her choices and spent a mighty sum.

"Have these brought to the Hall of Silver Silence in two days time," she said to the merchant. "I will trust to you the choice of buttons and hem tats."

He bowed, and she returned the bow, while the assistants rushed about as if the order necessitated immediate delivery, which it did not. Chi Lin was content. It would be her New Year gift to the children and would cost her one of her two remaining silver ingots. She could already see the beaming faces standing in a row as they accepted the robes from her hands. She envisioned Ming-kuan taking his tan robe into his baby arms and dancing between his brothers. Chi Lin was content at the thought, and returned to Pang Guo-ta.

"Is it finished, mistress?" he asked.

"Most decidedly," she replied, climbing into the chair.

The cloth merchant came to the door and bowed deeply. Pang Guo-ta looked to Lin Wu-luo, who shrugged.

"Then it was house business, mistress?"

"Most decidedly," she replied again.

Pang Guo-ta resumed his whistling. Chi Lin was glad that the journeyman would never mention the side trip to Jasmine because it was house business and, as such, none of his business.

4

Chi Lin worked diligently on the robes, secretly, except for Mi Tso-tze's help. When the children appeared in the courtyard on occasion, the works in progress were shuffled into a large bamboo basket, which the cloth merchant had provided at no extra cost. Only once was the secret project almost revealed, and then the circumstances trumped any secret gift.

Chi Lin had returned from the *ji-tzao* after supervising the restringing of several mulberry bushes. She set her attentions to the robes and, being a warm day, she had Po Bo lug the basket to the edge of the pool, where she proceeded to embroider a fierce lion's head on the acceptable yellow fabric destined for Wu Lin-kua, when Wu Lin-kua raced through the gate as if he was chased by a dog. In fact, Chi Lin's *Zhang* dog, which she had named *Raisin Cake* because his eyes were as purple as his tongue, barked and nipped at Lin-kua's heels.

"Go away," Lin-kua shouted at the dog.

Chi Lin quickly slipped the embroidery under her robes. The barking had brought Lao Lao out of the hut.

"You are running, Master Lin-kua," Lao Lao said. "If you run, he will nip. I have the scars to prove it."

Lin-kua halted, and then pushed *Raisin Cake* away.

"Come here, little one," Chi Lin said to her pet, and the dog padded over to her, panting beside the bamboo basket. "He was just startled, Master Lin-kua."

"It is fine," Lin-kua replied, frowning at *Raisin Cake,* who whined, and then took a run at Lao Lao.

"There he goes now," Lao Lao said. "He wants Mo Li to give him some pig rind."

Lao Lao moved toward the kitchen, *Raisin Cake* following in anticipation. Chi Lin looked to Lin-kua.

"You are excited, Lin-kua. Is there a reason?"

"Yes," Lin-kua said, panting as hard as the dog had. He looked around, obviously checking to see if anyone was about and listening. "Where is your handmaiden?"

"Tso-tze is fetching wood. What is so important? Tell me."

Lin-kua went to one knee.

"Auntie," he said. "You should know. My uncle is dead."

Chi Lin dropped her hands to her side.

"Which one?"

"Uncle Liang-tze."

Chi Lin trembled. She was relieved that it was not Wu San-ehr. Despite being a rigid disciplinarian, the Third Son was honorable and served the dynasty. But Liang-tze brought no honor to the house.

"How?"

"I cannot say."

"It is not proper, I agree."

"No. I cannot say, because it has not been said. There is whispering and grandfather seems sad, but not mournful." He paused. "I do not think Uncle Liang-tze will be accorded the wearing of the white."

"How can that be?"

"I cannot say, but I can guess . . . as you can guess."

"That is a sharp remark, young sir."

"Sharp, but true. That is why I tell you, because otherwise you might not come to know it."

Chi Lin felt the pain in this remark. The future Master of the House was astute. He knew about the rape first hand. He had latched his arms about his uncle's throat and saved his Auntie. Of course, he could no more guess the truth than know it, but his mission here was clear. He wanted to lay news of retribution at Chi Lin's feet. The monster who injured her was dead and it did not matter how or why. Liang-tze's demise would be satisfaction enough. Chi Lin was again beholden to Wu Lin-kua. Indeed, the embroidered Lion's head hidden on her lap befitted this young man.

Chi Lin looked for signs during the next few days – changes in the other wives and a sign in her mother-in-law's mood, but she could not detect a thing. Was Wu Lin-kua's news incorrect? Then, she made bold to ask Willow. It was inappropriate to do so, but she found the handmaiden cleaning her mistress' jewelry and approached her with small talk – remarks on the weather, on health and telling her about the secret robes she was creating for the children. Then, during a silence, which felt final, she asked.

"Forgive me, Willow, but I must ask."

"You may ask anything you wish, mistress," Willow replied. "I may not be able to answer, but I certainly will listen."

Chi Lin expected no less.

"I have heard something spoken on the wind and am curious to know the truth."

"Much comes on the wind. Much is untrue."

"I sense you are correct. But I must know." She paused, cocking her head as if to listen better. "The wind says that the Second Son has gone to the *Yellow Springs*."

Willow stopped cleaning earrings and hairpins. She looked away, her breath hitching.

"I cannot say," she said.

"You may not say or you will not say?"

"I cannot say, but . . . it is true. The wind who told you this should have been stopped in the eaves."

"That wind said that the House would not be donning the white."

"The wind speaks ill then, because it speaks true."

"But the wind does not say why. Nor does it settle the details upon my ears."

Willow set her work aside. She stood, and then bowed low to Chi Lin.

"I wish you a good day," she said, and entered the Jade Heart Hall leaving Mistress Purple Sage with no more detail than she had at the start.

"This is worrisome," Chi Lin muttered.

Although the wind may have been mysterious and Willow may have been curt, Chi Lin knew where she could settle this issue. She would tour again and, this time, accept a certain invitation long declined by decorum, but now considered a ripe opportunity to settle what the wind could not.

Chapter Twenty-One

Dismising the Shadows

1

"Pang Guo-ta," Chi Lin said at the end of the tour.

"Yes, mistress."

"Today I go see the Commissioner."

Pang Guo-ta, who had been whistling on his fine white and grey, nearly fell from the saddle. He looked to Lin Wu-luo, who also seemed surprised.

"You shall enter the Ya-men, mistress?"

"I shall enter. I have done so before, and shall do so now." She looked toward the proxy. "Lin Wu-luo, please announce me to your lord."

Lin Wu-luo, at first, hesitated, but then rode ahead to the Ya-men gate.

"But mistress," Guo-ta stammered. "Can we visit with the Commissioner without an invitation?"

"I have an invitation, Guo-ta. I have had it for some time but have declined it because there was no business to discuss. Now I have business."

"Business with the Commissioner that has not been discussed with me?"

"Why should it be discussed with you, Guo-ta?"

"*Ji-tzao* business is Master Wu's business, which I am a party to when we tour and inspect."

"We have toured and inspected, Guo-ta. The business I have with the Commissioner is not *ji-tzao* business, but business of the house nonetheless." She tapped her fan on the chair and the porters lifted her. "To the Ya-men gate," she commanded them.

Guo-ta sat on his fine horse like a memorial statue to some fallen hero. When he recovered, he moved forward at an awkward pace.

"You are set on doing this, mistress?" he asked.

"It does not dishonor us, Guo-ta, and you can sip wine and eat pork with the Superintendent's men while you wait for me. You deserve it."

Guo-ta overtook her, grinned, and then headed to the gate. He *did* deserve it. It was the business of the house, after all.

Chi Lin caused a stir when she entered the Ya-men, but not as much as the first time when she was big with child and brimming with vomit. This time the clerks grumbled, but they bowed. One time is precedent, but twice is a common annoyance. Lin Wu-luo had announced her, had he not? So there was a stir, but no surprise. Chi Lin expected Superintendent Po T'ai-kuan to emerge and frown, perhaps chastising her for impudence and inappropriate behavior, but he did not come. Instead, a young man, perhaps older than Lin-kua approached her, bowed and raised his hands in a ceremonious welcome.

"I welcome the ghost bride on behalf of my father," said the young man, his voice cracking. "I am Ai-lo Tu-fan, the First Son of Ai-lo Wun-kua."

Chi Lin nodded respectfully, and then disengaged the chair.

"I have come at your father's invitation."

"This is known. Follow me."

Chi Lin already knew the way, but dutifully followed Ai-lo Tu-fan into the Commissioner's courtyard. His hall, which was called The Pavilion of Pious Meditation, seemed hardly *pious* and scarcely *meditative*, his other children racing about, and their *amahs* trying to keep them in order. The sight delighted Chi Lin.

The First Son led her beyond this spot and into a willowy garden, where he crossed a decorative stream on a bow-arched bridge. On the other side, his father sat, a table spread with tea and red sugar buns.

Ai-lo Wun-kua stood upon seeing Purple Sage, she curtsying to him.

"Welcome, wife of Wu Hung-lin," the Commissioner boomed. "Long have I waited for a visit from you. But I know the protocols can be strict. Han ways are a mystery to me still although I have lived here all my life."

Chi Lin did not engage with these thoughts, but took a seat, bowing to the First Son as he drifted back across the bridge.

"Try this tea," Ai-lo Wun-kua said, pouring. "It is from the high mountains of Shu where the best green *ch'a* is harvested and prepared to the good effect."

Chi Lin nodded, took the bowl from his hands, and then sipped. It was true. Even the leaves whisked clean of her teeth. A red bun was offered, which she took but set aside.

"I do not have much time, my lord," she said.

"I know," Ai-lo Wun-kua agreed looking to the sky. "It looks like rain and you still have a journey home. But we can at least exchange the news of the day." He winked. "I am sure you have come to feel the pulse of the times."

"There are things I would know."

"I surely may guess them. And I am happy to be the pretext for such an inquiry."

Chi Lin eased her heart. Somehow the Commissioner knew why she was here. It would make her probe easier. She would not need to fill her belly with red buns and tea, and discuss the *Spring and Autumn Annals*, although that would please her and she was prepared to do it. She set the bowl aside.

"I am glad you know. There has been talk in the household about the Second Son."

Suddenly, Ai-lo Wun-kua frowned.

"So *that* is why you have come. You wish to know the town gossip."

"Not gossip, my lord." She was suddenly unsure. Had she misread him? "I do not mean to stir your head against me. I am not a woman who thrives on whispers. But there is an interest between me and . . ."

"Say no more," Ai-lo Wun-kua said abruptly. "Wu Liang-tze has been a source of gossip before. Indeed much is said now. I am privy to the inquest and will tell you plainly." He took a deep sigh, and then downed his precious tea in one gulp. "I know the man has caused much consternation to the women of Yan-cheng. I know he has misused you, shame on me to mention it, but you have asked and so you must hear."

"My lord," Chi Lin said anxiously. As much as she wanted to hear, she felt she had provoked his anger. Perhaps there were some discussions which must never occur between men and women. "If I have offended you, I must thank you for your hospitality and depart."

"I will not hear of it," Ai-lo Wun-kua said, softer. "I am distressed by Wu Liang-tze's conduct and the dishonor he has brought to his family. I will be as delicate as I can." He stood, walking to the foot of the bridge. He did not face her, but spoke in muffled tones. Chi Lin pitched forward to hear him. "Your brother-in-law had breached the code of decency many times with many women. His conduct with his own wives had been rumored, but that is a man's business within the hallows of his own hall. He also frequented the pleasure houses and liked The Sojourn of Heaven's Eye best. I need not tell you the attractions cuffed between its walls. Such places must be tolerated, business being business. But your brother-in-law strayed further." He turned abruptly. "He breached the House of Gui."

Chi Lin gasped. The Gui family was Yan-cheng's second richest household. It was to that house her sister was to be a ghost bride but had refused. They were a respectable clan, owned many fields on the periphery of the salt *ji-tzao,* and maintained orchards and a fish hatchery.

Ai-lo Wun-kua scowled. Chi Lin thought he would spit.

"Wu Liang-tze had his way with Gui Nung-xin's wife and she, too afraid to tell, kept the secret. But Liang-tze was not a quiet man as you well know. One night he had too much to drink at the Sojourn of Heaven's Eye and boasted of his Gui conquest."

"You need not tell me more," Chi Lin said, lowering her head to the table.

"I would not, except to say that word travels fast and far. The Gui clan waited outside the Sojourn. At the inquest it was difficult to recognize Wu Liang-tze from his many pieces."

Chi Lin choked. She would not have wished this upon anyone, even Wu Liang-tze, but it explained many things. It explained why the House of Wu did not speak of it. It explained the eschewing of the white and any signs of respect for the Second Son. To do so would compound the dishonor to the House of Gui. She suspected quiet compensation was sent to Gui Chou-ping, the Master of the Gui household. Wu Liang-tze's household was now at the mercy of Wu T'ai-po.

Ai-lo Wun-kua returned to the table. He poured more tea for his guest, and then some for himself.

"Do not be sad, Purple Sage," he said. "The man has descended to the pit of the seventh hell and will not disturb you again, even when you reach the *Yellow Springs.*"

"I am sorry I pressed for this news."

"I understand. I thought you had come on another matter."

Chi Lin sighed. What other matter would bring her here?

"I enjoyed the book, my lord," she said, guessing, "and would love to discuss it."

"I would love to hear your views. No women in my acquaintance, except my wife, can rise to that occasion, and she finds it a tedious effort. But I thought you came to see your father."

Chi Lin tensed.

"My father?"

"Yes. He is here today."

Chi Lin stood. She was confused, but excited. She had not seen her father in four years.

"Where is he, my lord?"

"With the superintendent. We should go at once." He looked to the sky. "The sky is turning nasty and would blow away your chances if you do not hasten."

Tea was over. Chi Lin followed Ai-lo Wun-kua back over the bridge and to her awaiting chair.

2

Whatever horror racing through Chi Lin's mind concerning the Second Son's demise was chastened by thoughts of seeing her father. She wondered why he was at the Ya-men. Chi Ming had not visited here since the Emperor's purge, which spared him his life, but not his job. Perhaps he was pardoned or perhaps the Emperor had a change in heart and decided he needed another head for the pyramid. Perhaps Chi Ming had resumed business with the Ya-men. How would Chi Lin know, after all? In either event, she swallowed hard as the chair entered the Hall of Presiding Solace, where Superintendent Po T'ai-kuan resided as Yan-cheng's Magistrate.

Chi Lin was sure her presence here would cause more than a stir if it had not been for Ai-lo Wun-kua who met the various clerks by spreading his arms to their insipient bows. The hall was honeycombed with partitions and offices, but at its end, on a covered verandah, which would have been a bright spot on any other day but this one, sat Po T'ai-kuan and his visitor. Upon seeing Ai-lo Wun-kua, the Superintendent was upstanding, his hands waving.

"Why is this woman here?" he snapped.

Chi Ming stood also, but was grinning broadly. Chi Lin thought he would jump about and dance the *jia-ju*.

"Forgive me, Magistrate Po," Ai-lo Wun-kua said. "My guest came on other business. I determined that it would not be adverse to *Heaven* if she were to pay a visit to her most esteemed father."

"But is it proper?" Po T'ai-kuan stated.

This was a rhetorical question, but Ai-lo Wun-kua took advantage of the slip.

"You know that it is, Magistrate Po. It is like the dutiful daughters of Chou, who were as steadfast in battle as the sons.

> *"I walk the land of my fathers,*
> *The wheat fields are green and wide.*
> *I'll tell the world of my sorrow,*
> *All friends will be at our side.*
> *O listen, ye lords and nobles,*
> *Blame not my stubbornness so!*
> *A hundred schemes you may conjure,*
> *None match this course that I know.*

"Come, I will recite some more while we walk." He cuffed Po T'ai-kuan's shoulder and led him away. "Do you know the verses of Xu Mu of Chou? They are indeed rich in sound as well as meaning. Let me regale you with them, while this dutiful daughter pays homage to her noble sire."

Po T'ai-kuan had no choice. Chi Lin left the chair approaching her father, who did not stand on ceremony.

"*Heaven* is good to me, my daughter," he said. "I never would have thought to see you again, even as this sky grows dark and my life reaches the edge of the forest."

Chi Lin trembled. She went to her father, kneeling at his feet, but he raised her up as best he could. She looked into his dim eyes and saw what she loved most in this world – the eyes of her son, Ming-kuan – the sparkling parts, the gray excluded.

"Tell me father," she whispered. "Tell me that you have not been summoned here on some fault."

"Who is not without fault, daughter?" he said. "Past or present, a man cannot wake without tripping over his sandals. But I come here once a moon to take the pulse of things. Po T'ai-kuan owes me that much, although he is good to accommodate my curiosity. But come, sit with me."

Chi Lin, relieved that her father's visit was routine, sat more comfortably.

"To set eyes on you again," she said. "Is my brother well?"

"As always. And your sister has retired as planned to *Chang-tzu* Temple. Through her our family will received many blessings from Lord Buddha."

"I am happy to hear it." She nodded. "I am settled in the Wu Household."

"Settled?" Chi Ming laughed. "I should say more than settled. You have added to their number and have become an important Auntie to your husband's children,"

Hearing this did not ease her mind. Her father knew then that she had given birth and had reconciled it to his mind like the rest of the world — a ghost child from the spirit of the house. She could embrace this fiction to cover her shame, but to hear her father embrace it unsettled her.

"You do know that . . ."

"I am no fool, daughter," he said, first frowning, and then puckering. "I know you do not water the flowers to make children sprout. I know how it is done and I know when it is best to not question tales from the *fa-shr*." He winked. "Besides, when the little one was born, your father-in-law sent me a fine new robe and five new brushes. Such brushes you have never seen — supple, commanding the strokes as if I had never practiced the art." He laughed. "Wu T'ai-po has even sent your brother work — several contracts to copy and a dozen tally sheets. I would say he is pleased with you, daughter. That brings me great honor."

Chi Lin nodded again.

"He is a good man," she said. "Even the Old Lady of the House is kind in her way. The other wives are tolerable and I have my own place with servants and a cook."

"A cook? And yet you are not fat."

"I was fat for nine moons and do not like the feeling." She grinned. "I did not cope with the chair then and my feet were swollen and tripsy."

"Good to stay as you are, Chi Lin," he said.

"I am the least in the house — just above the servants."

"And yet you are visiting the Imperial Commissioner in the Ya-men. I would say your betters sit at the foot of the Jade Emperor."

Chi Lin did not mean to boast. It was not in her nature, but it was a fine thing to hear her father praise her so.

"I do not come to the Ya-men often," she said. "The Commissioner is a different sort."

"A Mongol, to be sure, with different views, which are regarded as strange by some. But he has princely blood in his veins and has served the dynasty well. But the Emperor can be fickle, as well I know, and Ai-lo Wun-kua should keep an owl on his shoulder."

"Is that the pulse in the court?" she asked.

Her father did not answer. Instead, he took her hands in his and caressed them

"These are so like your mother's," he remarked. "You have her spirit. Remember your place in the House of Wu — keep to it, but know your influence."

"I suspect I already know."

"You can be content at being the least," he said. "Content and fed, industrious and a helpmate. But if you allow your mother to rule your steps, you will rise in influence. Do you know why?"

Chi Lin heard a whisper in her mind — her mother's voice. It said a woman finds influence only through her children. They carry her to the summit of respect.

"The children," she said. "I am the Auntie to six children."

"Your way is clear of a mother's place," her father said. "When an Auntie has the respect of the children, they become *her* children and she garners the highest respect. Remember that, Chi Lin. Only one child may be your flesh, but your husband's legacy belongs to you also." He stared at her, hooking her eyes with his. "And . . . children . . . grow. They need a champion to assure they are not weeds. That is the garden you keep, my daughter. That is your garden."

"Your journeyman is prepared to leave, Mistress Purple Sage," came a voice — Po T'ai-kuan's, now alone and returned to the verandah. "The sky is menacing. You should return home before the rain comes."

Chi Lin stood, curtsied to her father, and then bowed to the Superintendent. She knew this was the last time she would see Chi

Ming, but she was happy for the encounter — one that would linger even to the edge of the grave. Ai-lo Wun-kua was gone, so Chi Lin strode through the Hall of Presiding Solace, and then out to her awaiting chair.

3

On the road, Chi Lin noticed two things. The porters walked twice as fast as they had before and the sky was beyond menacing — a sooty morass drifting quickly as if pushed by a dragon. Other things were pushed also — bits of bamboo, dust and dirt, a renegade lantern. Town folk, some with carry poles, others holding their hats, ran against the grain toward the village. Then a gust took her fan, blasting it out of her hand.

"Pang Guo-ta," she said, the wind howling now. "What is happening?"

Guo-ta slowed his steed, who was unsettled.

"It is a big storm, mistress."

"Have you even seen one like this?"

"No."

Then the front porter whined. He was hit with something. He tottered, wobbling the chair. Chi Lin held fast, but then the conveyance tossed her to the ground. Guo-ta rode back, screaming at the porter, threatening him with his crop.

Chi Lin was stunned. She pushed up from the road, brushing the dust from her robe. Then she saw what had struck the porter. A bird — a sea bird. It was bloodied, its wings limp. She looked up, just as the rain began — a heavy downpour which washed the dust to mud and filled the road trench fast — a gully, swollen and rushing. She looked to the porters.

"Run back to the house," she shouted. "Leave the chair. It is useless. Run."

The porters looked to Guo-ta, who raised his crop. The porters ran.

Chi Lin, drenched now, staggered to the horse. She reached up.

"Lift me up. I will ride with you. We must warn the household."

"I am sure they know, mistress."

"Lift me up."

Pang Guo-ta reached down and pulled Chi Lin into the scant space before him. He clutched her firmly and cuffed the horse to a gallop. They passed the porters, who slipped and slid.

Chi Lin looked at the sky again just before they reached the gate. It was yellow now, with black streaks. She heard a howling wind and a strange vibration coming from the sea. She wondered whether this was Wu Liang-tze's revenge on the world — a world that sliced him up and spit him into the seventh circle of hell. No matter what the cause, Chi Lin was happy to reach the gate. She worried about her household and the children. She wondered whether the roof on the Hall of Silver Silence would hold, whether Gao Lin's work would continue to shelter her soul.

Through the gate they rode just as the first lightning bolt struck the Thuja tree nearest to the silk *ji-tzao*. The tenting caught fire. Chi Lin thought of her other babies – the worms.

Chapter Twenty-Two

Tai-feng

1

As the wind roared through the courtyard trees and the rain swept the already puddle dotted ground, Chi Lin had only one thought. *Safety*. Not her own, but her son's. Although Pang Guo-ta directed her into the Jade Heart Pavilion instructing her to take shelter in the root cellar, her feet went in a different direction — toward the nursery. When she reached the wooden walkway, which shook terrifically, she could see the residents of the eastern halls coming. On minced steps and supported by her two hand maidens, Lotus walked the course, babbling unintelligently to the wind. She was followed by the *amahs*, her two daughters and, to Chi Lin's delight (and relief), Ming-kuan, skipping as if it was a bright sunny day. He clutched his favorite toy — a miniature boat, which would have done finely in today's puddles.

"Ming-kuan," Chi Lin said, the boy ignoring her.

"Do not distract him," snapped an imperious voice.

Jasmine followed with her sons, P'ing Chin corralling them as if they were wayward sheep. Chi Lin stepped onto the causeway.

"I mean to help," she said.

"It is best you follow us to safety," Jasmine snapped. "The Third Son will be fine. You need not interfere in *my* business."

Chi Lin halted. This affront under such circumstances was unwarranted — mean-spirited and laced with impudence. However, what could she do? Ming-kuan was fine. Any untoward attention paid now would be out of place. So she turned away and set her sights on the Silver Silence Hall.

A stream rippled through her sandals, her *wai-tze* sopped. She had no *san-tze* and thought that it would not be useful in this wind. There was no help for it. She was drenched already and chanced being wet down to her *fu-chuang*. It was also difficult to see. As she came near the gate, a bough crashed at her feet.

"*Ai*," she cried, raising her hand.

The wind was strong enough to knock her down, but she managed to stay up. Then she saw two forms at the gate and heard diminutive barking.

"Mistress," Mi Tso-tze called.

Chi Lin hastened her pace. Mo Li was beside Tso-tze, toting her favoring *wok*. Mi Tso-tze clutched *Raisin Cake*, who wiggled free, running to his mistress. Chi Lin swooped him into her arms, the little beast licking her face.

"Calm. Calm," she said. "Tso-tze, where are Lao Lao and Snapdragon?"

"They would not come," Tso-tze replied. "You know they can be stubborn."

"The old woman hopped into her coffin," Mo Li added. "She wore her shroud and sang a death song."

"Nonsense," Chi Lin said. "I must persuade them."

"The Master of the House commands you to the Jade Heart Hall," came a booming voice.

Chi Lin thought it was the wind speaking to her. But it was Chou Kuai-tze on his steed, evidently corralling stragglers.

"But Kuai-tze, my custodian and his wife are still in the Silver Silence."

"It cannot be helped," Kuai-tze replied.

Chi Lin turned to Tso-tze, who followed the journeyman's orders. Mo Li took the *wok* and placed it on her head, the rain making a racket as she rushed along. Chi Lin hugged *Raisin Cake*, fearing to let him down again, the puddles rising.

"I guess it must be so," she said.

She went with a heavy heart.

2

Even inside the Jade Heart Hall, the wind could be heard rumbling across the land. The Master of the House sorted everyone for safety and yet keeping within the bounds of decorum and protocol. He ordered the children and wives into the cellar, the *amahs* and handmaidens allowed to go also. The servants were kept above ground, where they chattered and complained, but huddling made them safe enough, if the roof held. Servants could be replaced. The rest of the household needed to survive.

Chi Lin made her way with Tso-tze into the dark cellar, Mo Li sent to the kitchen for shelter. *Raisin Cake* fidgeted, but Chi Lin feared letting him loose under feet.

"Do not fall," Tso-tze said. "The lanterns are not lit."

But soon they were, revealing a shivering assembly of the family Wu. Chi Lin was fine above ground, but now her heart beat fast and her head pounded.

"I cannot stay here," she told Mi Tso-tze.

"But mistress, you must."

"Must I?"

Chi Lin thrust *Raisin Cake* into Tso-tze's arms, and turned back to the stairs.

"Mistress, I will come also."

"No. I need air."

"But the wind."

"I would be better outside wearing Mo Li's metal hat than under the ground."

Chi Lin ignored her handmaiden's pleas, and did not answer the journeymen's orders. She whisked by her father-in-law, who, perhaps knowing better, did not command her to return. The upper rooms were still dry, but crowded, the servants bustling for space. The wind pounded the walls and whistled through the eaves. Chi Lin thought that perhaps the wind would lift the roof away and there would be great damage to the hall. She went through the kitchen, and then to the edge of her mother-in-law's *ke-ting*. To her surprise, the Old Lady of the House sat sewing, perhaps to take her mind off the storm. When she saw Chi Lin, she said nothing, but pointed to a table.

"Under here," said a small voice.

It was Po Bo crouching under the table, tugging at Chi Lin's wet robe hem.

"What are doing down there?" Chi Lin asked.

"Hiding from the wind demons," Po Bo said. "They will never find me here."

Suddenly, the wind demons swept through the Jade Heart Hall. The windows had been blocked and the door sealed with leather, but that seal broke as two more servants entered. It was Orchid's handmaiden and Sapphire's *amah*. They whimpered, and immediately went to their knees to Wu T'ai-po.

"Where are they?" T'ai-po asked.

"She would not come," the handmaiden said. "I pleaded with her, but the hall was falling apart, and I feared for my life."

"You should still fear for your life," Wu T'ai-po shouted. "And my grand-daughter?"

"She would not leave her mother," the *amah* said. "You know how she is, my lord. You know how she is."

The Old Lady of the House threw her sewing aside and confronted these women.

"Why are you here?" she barked. "Why have you not stayed with your charges? If it is too late for them, it is certainly too late for you."

Then she did something Chi Lin had never witnessed before. The Old Lady grabbed a bamboo stick from the corner and beat the women. No one tried to stop her, not even her husband, who turned his back. Chi Lin knew these two deserved it. They should have forced Orchid to come — pulled her out of her chair and carried her. They could have brought Sapphire, kicking and screaming to be sure, but safe nonetheless. Chi Lin was overcome with outrage, not only for the lack of spirit from these women, but because no one in the Jade Heart Hall went out into the storm to rescue Orchid and her child.

"We must make an effort," she said, startling anyone who heard her.

The Old Lady stopped her beating.

"The time for that has passed," The Old Lady shouted, and then gave the miscreants two last strokes.

"But we must," Chi Lin cried. She looked the journeymen, and then to her father-in-law. "It is only wind and water."

"It might as well be on a vessel at sea," T'ai-po replied. "The power of the aroused dragon is not to be taken lightly."

Chi Lin bowed to Wu T'ai-po, and then, inexplicably, her eye caught the leather seal on the door. It was still broken. She clenched her fists, tensed her chest, and then pulled it open, charging outside to brave the *tai-feng*.

3

Chi Lin heard voices on the wind as she leaped puddles and hopped over fallen branches. Those voices called her name. She realized it came from the Jade Heart Hall, where her kin were calling back. But she saw no sturdy fellow stir out into the blast to help her or save her, if she needed saving. Respected as she was, she was the ghost bride — expendable among the wives.

She reached the wooden causeway, which shook severely, the wind trying to lift the roof off. It had given way in places. Then she heard footsteps padding behind her. It was little Monkey.

"Po Bo," she cried. "What are *you* doing here?"

"I come to help you, mistress."

"But you are afraid of the demon winds."

"Yes, and I am light enough to be blown away. But I like the daughter of the Golden Oak Hall and it would be a shame to see her gone."

"Just so. Give me your hand."

Po Bo grasped her hand just as a section of roof blew off. Chi Lin hopped off the causeway and onto the water soaked path. Other debris drifted by, including books and tables from the school. In fact, the school's walls had collapsed, the rain ruining precious classics and brushes. She thought of her own hall and the bamboo box with the gift robes for the children. She hoped they would survive, and then thought of Sapphire.

"Come," she said to Po Bo, "we must hurry."

Hurrying was not an option. The wind opposed them as they approached the remains of the Golden Oak Hall. Being on the east side, where the storm swept in from the sea, a floodtide had spilled through the *ji-tzao* and into the eastern halls. The Golden Oak Hall was the easternmost and, although the waters had abated, the initial rush had collapsed the outer wall and dashed the wooden barriers of the hall. It would be dangerous to enter the place.

"Mistress," Po Bo said. "I shall run ahead and see. If it is too late, I will call to you and you can turn around and be safe."

He did not wait for Chi Lin's agreement. Po Bo darted along the remaining causeway and into the wreckage. Chi Lin slipped on the boardwalk barely finding purchase to stay erect. Then she heard a voice on the wind.

"It is not too late."

She rushed now into the wreckage — the Golden Oak Hall. The silk drapes that had marked the place were sodden and plunged onto the furniture. The roof was gone. Although the pillars stood — a calamitous ruin, the ridgepole had fallen and crashed to the floor. She saw Po Bo pawing his way along the ridgepole. Under it was Orchid, her head bleeding and her face pale. Beside her, crying pathetically and clutching her dolly, was Sapphire.

Chi Lin tripped into this wreckage, her heart pounding. Orchid appeared beyond hope, but her daughter was alive. Then, as she reached the ridgepole, the journeymen finally arrived. Chi Lin did not care whether they had searched their souls or were shamed into coming, she was relieved to see them. They were her familiars — Chou Kuai-tze and Pang Guo-ta.

"You are meddlesome, Mistress Purple Sage," Kuai-tze said, working his way into the hall's remains.

"But you have come anyway," she remarked. "I do not think Orchid is well." When Pang Guo-ta reached her, she whispered. "Whatever the case, she must be taken from here, otherwise Sapphire will not come or, if she does, she will be distressed."

No further lecture was needed. Po Bo tried to help Sapphire, but the girl hit him with her dolly.

"I do not want to go.'

"But you must go," Po Bo said. "The wind is a demon and will steal you away."

Sapphire wept, choking in her fear.

"Come to me, child," Chi Lin said. "Come to Auntie."

"But *ma ma*."

"These men will help her."

Chou Kuai-tze had already given Pang Guo-ta the confirming look that Orchid had departed for *the Yellow Springs*, but at Chi Lin's coaxing, they began speaking to the Third Wife as if she were alive.

"You see. Come," Chi Lin said to Sapphire.

Sapphire *did* come, and Chi Lin lifted her, wondering whether she could bear the weight of the child along the damaged causeway.

4

Orchid's body was wrapped in gauze and silk and kept far from prying eyes. There was enough consternation in the Jade Heart Hall to raise despair. Sapphire, grasping her dolly and crying for her mother, was cuffed by the *amah*, but the Old Lady of the House pushed the servant aside and took charge of her granddaughter. The *amah* wept in despair probably knowing that she would live the remainder of her service in the cold harbor. Chi Lin was greeted by her father-in-law.

"You are a meddlesome woman," he said, not unkindly. "But a man cannot have so many grandchildren to expend even the least."

"You are cold," the Old Lady of the House said to Chi Lin, as she dried Sapphire. "Willow."

Willow disappeared into the *ke-ting*, returning with dry robes and a blanket. Mi Tso-tze was attending her mistress, but Willow ordered her to hold the blanket high, allowing Chi Lin to strip, dry off and don the dry robes in privacy.

"You are too kind," Chi Lin said to her mother-in-law.

"I cannot afford to lose the best stitches in the household," came the reply.

Chi Lin was chilled to the marrow, her teeth chattering. Her feet were soaked, even when bare, so once she had donned the fresh robe, she attacked her feet with the blanket, while Tso-tze attended to her hair. This took some time and she had an audience of servants. Even Lin-kua and Chou-fa came topside to watch. Chi Lin did not care. She was tired from the ordeal, sad that Orchid was dead, but glad that she had saved Sapphire. Suddenly, she had a thought.

"Po Bo," she said. "Where is he? He was so brave."

"He is in the kitchen," Wu T'ai-po said. "He is filling his jowls with the best buns we have. He shall soon have more belly ache than storm fever." He gazed at Chi Lin, she feeling his eyes in the softest way. "He is yours, Mistress Purple Sage. You need a servant and you might need a new custodian."

Chi Lin gasped. She had forgotten Lao Lao and Snapdragon, but she was not up to another rescue. What would be, would be.

"I thank you, father-in-law," she said.

Chi Lin felt warm, wrapped in robe and blanket, her hair wedged with paper, her feet dry now. The wind still howled and the timbers still shook, but if they fell on her now, she would be too tired to do more than pray for safe passage to *the Yellow Springs*. She closed her eyes. Then she felt a hand on hers and stirred.

"See my boat, Auntie?" came a wee voice.

She opened her eyes. Ming-kuan stood before her, touching her hand and waving his toy. Chi Lin smiled, but was wary of responding, not wishing to anger Jasmine. She looked about for the First Wife and found her rousing to end this interview. But as she approached, the Old Lady of the House nodded.

"Wu Ming-kuan has asked you a question, Purple Sage," she said.

Jasmine stopped short. Chi Lin grinned and reached for the boat.

"It is a fine boat, Ming-kuan."

"I know," the child said. "It is mine. When I grow big like Lin-kua and Chou-fa, I will ride in a boat far out on the water."

"You will?"

"Yes, Auntie. It is a fine boat."

He crawled onto her lap. Chi Lin's entire being quaked with joy. She looked for frowns from those in authority, but nothing came beyond Jasmine's smirk. So Chi Lin tugged Ming-kuan onto her lap.

"You will need to learn how to steer a boat like that one."

"I can learn, Auntie. I am smart. Lin-kua said I could climb to the tippy-top and see the world from there." He laughed. "Do you know the world, Auntie?"

She wanted to say she did, and that world sat on her lap now. But she did not want to press this brief encounter and raise Jasmine's jealousy further. So she kissed Ming-kuan topknot.

"I do not, but I am sure when you return from the sea you will come to your Auntie and tell her all about it."

"I will, Auntie. I will."

He giggled, and in that giggle, the howling wind was silenced, because the storm had given her what no amount of patience could provide — a new friend.

Chapter Twenty-Three

Assessment

1

Chi Lin's eyes were burning when she emerged from the Jade Heart Hall, The storm was diminished and the sky brightened, the sun glaring behind a grizzly halo. Chi Lin winced in order to see the wreckage of the courtyard. Trees lay crisscrossed and splintered over dashed benches and pots, partitions and statuary. Her mother-in-law's prized loft of miniature trees were uprooted, much to the Old Lady's chagrin. Family and servants lamented the damage and the loss, each looking at prized landmarks now fallen and smashed. The sons fled to the schoolhouse, or what remained of it, followed by Master P'ing Chin, who waved his hands and moaned at the loss of his books and brushes, not to mention the roof and walls. The *amahs* took charge of their children, except for Sapphire who remained in Willow's care until some arrangement could be made to care for the child. The kitchen staff tried to resuscitate soaked cabbages in the vegetable garden. Overall, a sense of loss and heavy weariness spread across the House of Wu.

Chi Lin had witnessed the worst of it at the height of the blow, so this aftermath was just a calmer version of what she had already embraced. She led her brood – Mi Tso-tze, carrying *Raisin Cake*, Mo Li, clutching her *wok*, and Po Bo, still eating buns, toward the Silver Silence. When she reached the family shrine, she paused, looking askance hoping the shrine still stood. It did. With that confirmation, she veered her troop to the incense pots. The sand was soaked, the incense not burning, but a single candle flickered in the interior – low, true, but burning nonetheless. The family plaques and epitaphs were intact, the statue of *Guan-yin* firmly planted, if not slightly askew and Wu Hung-lin's effigy stood proud and erect.

"See, Tso-tze," she said. "He has survived,"

"And out in the full force of it, mistress."

"Such is the man, my husband." She turned to Po Bo. "When we go to the hall, you must find dry incense and refill the pots with clean sand."

"Yes, mistress," little Monkey mumbled.

"Our husband still watches over us from his place in the Jade Emperor's court. And Mo Li, if the tinder is dry, you must start the stove and make Buddha Heart Buns to offer to our lord."

Mo Li tapped the *wok* (*clank, clank*), and then nodded.

Chi Lin was delighted by this good sign. Still, her heart sank when she thought of the possible fate of her custodian and his wife. *Why did they not come?* she thought, and then sighed.

The wall surrounding the Silver Silence's courtyard was breached and a Thuja tree compromised the gateway, but they were still able to pass under it. Then, to Chi Lin's great joy, she saw that the hall appeared intact.

"It may be well," Tso-tze said, letting *Raisin Cake* down.

"It is the proof of Gao Lin's work," Chi Lin replied. "The roof is strong and defied the demon wind." Then she looked to the servants' quarters, where the roof also survived, but one wall had collapsed. "Let us see how they have fared."

Nothing stirred outside except *Raisin Cake* finding his favorite spots. As Chi Lin passed the pool, she could see that the *koi* had survived and the landscaping was no less for wear. But the servant's quarter seemed a trap for anything within it, especially for two ancients.

Chi Lin crossed the remains of the threshold, the inside strewn with tables and chairs. The stove remained embedded in the remaining wall and the brick *kang*, although wet, still nabbed its linen. But the back quarters were as silent as the grave.

"*La la la la*," Chi Lin called. "Say something if you can."

No answer. She looked to Tso-tze, and then to Po Bo.

"Little Monkey," she said. "Poke about and see."

Po Bo lurched forward climbing over the overturned table, and then going into the next room.

"I see the old man here."

Chi Lin sighed, and then negotiated the broken furniture to see for herself. Lao Lao lay in a corner, his head against a box, that box being Snapdragon's coffin. He was motionless. His wind was gone and his eyes closed.

"The old lady must be in her coffin," Tso-tze said, tripping into the room.

"Help me," Chi Lin said to Po Bo. "Lift the cover."

Together they pushed aside the ironwood cover and peered in. There, in her fine white silk shroud, Snapdragon was laid to rest, her useless eyes shut, her lips closed and her hands lost beneath the coverlet.

"Poor lady," Chi Lin said. "She served me well."

Then suddenly, *Raisin Cake* scampered in, barking wildly, pouncing on Lao Lao's body. That body roused, pushing the dog away.

"Can I not sleep without that demon bark disturbing my rest?"

"Lao Lao."

"Mistress Purple Sage," Lao Lao said, trying to stand, but not quite making it. "You have survived the foul weather. I am glad of it."

"I am glad that you too are here and alive. I thought you were . . ."

"I may have almost reached *the Yellow Springs*. But as my boat came to shore, that damn dog brought me back."

Chi Lin laughed, but then frowned.

"Poor Snapdragon."

"Poor Snapdragon?" Lao Lao said. "Help me up, little Monkey. Give me your back." Lao Lao managed to stand and hover over the coffin. "Old woman," she shouted. "The storm is passed and our work is not done."

Snapdragon just lay there as dead as she was. Chi Lin patted Lao Lao's back.

"I am sorry, Lao Lao."

"Sorry?" He clapped over Snapdragon's body. "Wake up. You are blind, not deaf."

Suddenly, her eyes opened. Her shoulders wiggled. Her head shook.

"Snapdragon?" Chi Lin said, astounded.

"Is that you, death, come for me," the old lady croaked. "If so, your voice is sweet and much like my mistress'. It will be nice to have your company in the boat. But do take care not to spoil my fine white silk shroud."

"Silly old woman," Lao Lao snapped. "That *is* your mistress, Purple Sage."

"Death has not claimed me?"

"Not today," Chi Lin said.

"Up with you, old woman," Lao Lao commanded. "Help me get her out, Monkey."

Po Bo helped lift Snapdragon up and out of the coffin, where she sat beside it reaching for Chi Lin.

"That was a fierce storm, mistress," she said. "I remember one like that when I was a child. Took my brother, it did. I thought I would see him today, but now I must wait my turn. Everyone must wait their turn."

Lao Lao reached into the coffin.

"Help me, Monkey."

"But she is out."

"No. I mean, she is, but not these."

Chi Lin looked at the bottom of the coffin. There, in a neat stack and as dry as can be were the silk gift robes she was making for the children.

"I put them there for safety, mistress," Lao Lao said. "Such finery could not be chanced even under Gao-lin's fine roof. Under my old lady and her shroud and inside an ironwood coffin, they would brave the storm well."

Chi Lin grasped Lao Lao's hand.

"I am lucky to have such servants," she said. "And *Heaven* has granted that you and Snapdragon live. What better end to happenstance could there be?"

Lao Lao, flustered, turned away and hid his face. Then he became agitated.

"That damn dog should stop doing its business in the courtyard," he shouted. "I will get the broom."

He was gone. Chi Lin lifted the robes into her arms, and then sought the bamboo box.

2

The Silver Silence Hall was unscathed inside, only some damage to the outer porch, but nothing irreparable. The courtyard was strewn with debris and the decorative cabbage pots were smashed. Shrubbery was tumbled and the aforementioned Thuja tree was downed over the gate. But inside was as if nothing had happened. Chi Lin wondered whether the robes Lao Lao carefully stored in Snapdragon's coffin would have been just as safe, if not safer, left where they were. But it was the custodian's job to be vigilant. Nonetheless, Chi Lin checked the crack in the bedpost for the silver ingot just in case a squirrel might have sought safety there and decided the shiny thing was a good find. The last remaining ingot was still there.

In the morning, the Master of House arrived in Purple Sage's courtyard, an odd thing since he disliked coming to the Silver Silence for the memories it provoked. Four porters carried a chair, her mother-in-law's grand chair. Chi Lin at once made herself presentable and came out.

"My lord," she said curtsying. "Welcome over my threshold."

"Thank you, Purple Sage, but I shall not cross it." He dismounted, for he was astride his grand black stallion, a war horse gift from the Third Son,

"There has been much damage, but I see the Silver Silence has been spared." Lao Lao, Snapdragon, Mo Li and Po Bo stood by the servant's quarter, bowing reverentially. "I see the old ones have survived, a good omen for you, my daughter-in-law. But I need your presence on a tour."

"Yes, father-in-law."

"I know you just came from a tour, but this one is different."

"I understand, father-in-law."

Mi Tso-tze fetched a fan and a better robe – the purple one she used for touring, which had been carefully cleaned and dried.

"Wear black, my child," Wu T'ai-po said. "I dare not don the white yet, but since this storm came from the east, a good northern black is more appropriate than your ghostly purple."

Mi Tso-tze disappeared, returning with a silver trimmed black robe, which was perhaps too festive to the occasion, but fit the Master of the House's directive. Chi Lin donned it, gathered her fan and climbed into the chair, a larger chair for her. Wu T'ai-po returned to the saddle with some trouble, age having stolen his nimble mounting days.

Soon the chair joined the whole party – all the journeymen, mounted and arrayed by household rank. Chi Lin was glad that the horses had survived, the stables located in the western portion of the estate. Her contentment faded when they reached the main road, which was strewn with boughs, birds, people collecting their dead, furniture, and even boats blown ashore although the sea was twenty *li* away. She even noticed her touring chair, ripped apart and blown into the sewage ditch. The ground was a slippery screed, the horses managing, but the porters slipping, making the ride jittery. But Chi Lin managed to stay fast, the seat being cushioned and the arms being high.

Wu T'ai-po's procession rode past the Ya-men. The building had survived, only some roof tiles missing and the city god crashed and splintered across the gateway. Although that did not bode well, at least he did not injure anyone. Emerging as the procession passed, Ai-lo Wun-kua and Po T'ai-kuan came forward to greet Wu T'ai-po.

"How has the House of Wu fared?" Po T'ai-kuan called

"We shall be donning the white for Yu Lan-hua, my son's third wife, who has passed to *the Yellow Springs*."

"I am sorry to hear it," the superintendent replied.

"Otherwise we have repairs in the house to be made," Wu T'ai-po said. "But I fear my tenants and our monopoly have suffered worse. I go to inspect"

"Do you need my assistance?" Ai-lo Wun-kua asked. "I can be in the saddle immediately."

"No need, Commissioner," Wu replied. "Let me assess what is mine before I turn to the Emperor's good temper. I shall report well."

Ai-lo Wun-kua bowed, and then his eye caught Chi Lin's.

"I shall await the report. We have been most fortunate in the Ya-men. Everyone has weathered the storm." He looked directly at Chi Lin. "Everyone."

Chi Lin was gladdened to know that her father had not attempted to return home and was safe inside the Ya-men. She was also sure her father-in-law had caught the inference. But he did not protest.

"The marketplace," Po T'ai-kuan said. "There is much sorrow there. Collapsing stalls and gone roofs exposed many to the wind's terror. I suggest you stay clear of it in case the town's mood should shift."

Wu T'ai-po nodded his thanks for the warning and proceeded toward his monopoly holdings.

What Chi Lin saw plunged her heart into sorrow's depths. The tenancies were shorn of buildings, few walls standing and no roofs intact. The *ji-tzao* were inoperative, the filters blown apart, the evaporation towers fallen in heaps. Only one stood, and that one leaned at a precarious angle. The silk *ji-tzao* were in shambles also, mulberry trees crushed or naked, the tenting blown apart and the worms, no doubt, drowned. Chi Lin assumed they were much like the silk *ji-tzao* at home, except she could not bring herself to visit that one after the storm. Now she hoped it had fared better than these. But the worst sight were the children, many dead on the roadside, and others crawling about in the mud.

"Halt now," she said.

The porters obeyed, but hesitated. Then Wu T'ai-po turned, questioning their actions.

"What is this, now?" he asked.

"Halt and let me down," Chi Lin repeated.

Her father-in-law nodded in agreement and the chair was lowered. Chi Lin jumped into the mud, slogging to the nearest child, a girl it would appear, who could not find enough purchase to take more than a few steps before falling. Just beyond her were adults, not much better balanced and just as desperate.

Chi Lin reached the girl, clutched her, and then wiped her face.

"Do not be afraid," she said. "It is over."

"It is over," the girl murmured. "It is over, but my house is gone and my brother is dead."

Chi Lin clutched her to her chest, the black robe now sullied as if a dozen oxen had shat on her. The adults did not approach. They were in a haze as if they did not know where they were or what they did. Chi Lin thought that this must be the state of things throughout the tenancy. It broke her heart. Then her father-in-law was beside her.

"You are meddlesome again, daughter-in-law," he said.

"We must do something," she said.

"I am. I am assessing the situation."

"So am I," she muttered. "This child needs shelter and food and comfort. I know she is only a girl, but we cannot be so heartless as to let her die here by the roadside."

"She shall not die," her father-in-law said. "At least not today and not by the roadside." He hunkered down beside her. "I am responsible to the Emperor for his salt and to my family for the monopoly. Therefore I must assure the well-being of my tenants. But there is much work. We will take this girl back to the house. But no more waifs in the passage. No more. The others need to await my plan."

Chi Lin hugged the girl, but looked to her father-in-law. She knew that his kindness could only stretch so far before becoming empty words.

"You have a plan, father-in-law?" she prodded.

"Yes," He shook his head. "You are a meddlesome woman, Mistress Purple Sage. You once suggested that the monopoly could be served by better accounting and management. In fact, you proposed your own family as a good rallying point for such a change. I have considered it many times, but my old lady thought it a poor suggestion and did not wish to further extend our patronage to the Chi clan."

Chi Lin bowed her head. Of course her mother-in-law was correct. The monopoly must be jealously guarded from falling into the hands of other households.

"I understand, my lord. I am a mere woman and do not know about these things."

"That is correct. However, under these horrific circumstances, the Wu Household needs help. So, I will be calling on your brother to do an accounting of damage and extend a contract to your Chi cousins to manage the *ji-tzao* affairs with some gain to them, but much more for the Wu."

"Thank you, my lord."

"Do not thank me. Thank the *tai-feng*. But not too much because it might return the gratitude and I cannot afford that."

3

The little girl's name was Yu Li. Chi Lin brought her into the Silver Silence, turning her over to Mi Tso-tze for cleaning and dressing. The girl wept for her parents, perhaps, but Chi Lin thought not, because her parents were oblivious to her departure. It was more likely that she wailed for her brother. Still, once warmed, clothed and fed and put to bed near Tso-tze's partition, she quieted and even became curious. She struck up a playful liking for *Raisin Cake*. She did not talk much except to Po Bo, who, curious monkey that he was, asked her a dozen questions about her life, none of which she answered, but in turn she laughed at his jokes. Chi Lin thought that was something, at least. In time, Chi Lin named Yu Li little Butterfly and taught her to sew and help with Tso-tze's chores. As it turned out this little mud-packed waif never left the Silver Silence and never questioned it for the remainder of her life.

Purple Sage was weary after *tai-feng*. She was content that her brother, Chi Sheng, would handle the *ji-tzao* books and accounting, although he could never enter the Wu house in his crippled condition. But arrangements would be made to deliver the necessary materials to his brush. She was also delighted that her cousins would become foreman and work to restore the *ji-tzao* to full operation. Cousin Chi Fa was never her favorite, but he was industrious as were his brothers. It was a good match to her mind. They would energize the journeymen, the *pao-t'ien* and the tenant families to bury their dead, clean up the waste, restore the filters and flow and rebuild the evaporation towers. Yes, it was a good match to Chi Lin's mind.

After a week, it was announced that the family would don the white for three moons in mourning for Yu Lan-hua, Orchid. This meant a cessation of the New Year celebration, but it had to be done. It also meant that the New Year robes for the children would be set aside for a time after the Lantern Festival. But before Chi Lin packed them away, she asked Po Bo to carry the box to the family shrine. There she burned incense to her husband and to *Guan-yin*. She had already donned the white and the shrine was draped in white silk also.

"We are all sad at Orchid's departure," she told Wu Hung-lin. "Only you shall see her now at *the Yellow Springs*. May she delight you as even she did in life."

At this, she turned to Po Bo, who understood and departed. She carefully opened the bamboo box and withdrew the appropriate yellow robe.

"See what I have made for Wu Lin-kua, my lord. It shimmers in the sunlight as if made for an imperial prince. But I was careful to use appropriate yellow and not proscribed. I embroidered a tiger, because Lin-kua is fierce like one and will be a noble Master of the House in time."

She bowed and set it aside, and then withdrew the fawn robe.

"Wu Chou-fa shall have this one, the color of earth because his soul is practical and his mind is sharp. He does well with the brush and so I have embroidered a crane with a crimson comb. His voice is destined to be heard."

She bowed again, setting the fawn robe aside. Then withdrew three more robes from the box.

"And these are for your daughters, my lord. I have not completed the embroidery, but know this. Their beauty embarrasses the sun and they will cost you a mighty dowry. You should be pleased by this."

She set these aside also, and then slowly withdrew the last robe – a wee melon colored garment. She spread it before the effigy.

"And this robe is for Wu Ming-kuan. It is light like his smile and, as you can see, I have embroidered a sea-bird. It was not originally a sea-bird, but a woodland bird. But he has told me that he wants to go to sea and I think it is a fine thing and so I have changed it to a sea-bird, to fly away from here and be free over the open waters and above the horizon. Yes, my lord. He is the free spirit of my heart. He is . . . ." She bowed. "He is the child who fulfills your most humble servant's love for her most noble husband."

And she was Wu Ming-kuan's Auntie.

Part Two — The Crane Queen (1376 — 1405)

Chapter One

The Salt Goddess

1

Twenty-four summers had past, the passage of time having treated Chi Lin kindly. It was the second year of the Chien Wen Emperor's reign, the Hung Wu ruler having departed to *the Yellow Springs*. There were many who were glad to see his departure, but few who said so kept their heads. The Ming founder was a despot, without a doubt, his word law and his actions heavy on many households. He had built an edifice of rule, but upon his own shoulders, the council of state being relegated to a lesser role. One would think the Hung Wu Emperor would leave his empire to his sons, but he mistrusted his sons and designated his young grandson his successor – the Chien Wen Emperor. To such things Chi Lin paid no mind at first as they held little sway over her daily chores and her growing influence. But that would change.

Many changes had occurred in the household – many people passing including the Old lady of the House and the Master. Wu Lin-kua was Master now with his own Lady of the House. Wu Chou-kua was ensconced in Wu Liang-tze's old villa, his sisters both married and away. But the details of these events are at the heart of Chi Lin's influence and will make for a fine tale. Wu Ming-kuan was still on hand, but at school in nearby port of Lin-t'ao, where he studied ships and navigation. Lao Lao and Snapdragon had both passed to the *Yellow Springs*, Po Bo becoming the custodian of the Silver Silence. As for the Silver Silence, it had emerged as the center of the House – Chi Lin's pulse being the heart. Yes, much had changed, but Chi Lin was steady and predictable, never surprising anyone with her resourcefulness or her allegiance to family matters. There may have been many more servants in the Silver Silence, but it was still common to see Chi Lin on the verandah sewing shoes or walking with Mi Tso-tze to inspect the silk *ji-tzao*. Chi Lin still paid her respects to the First and Second Wives, and was diligent at the family shine; and she went to the Jade Heart Hall when summoned by the new Master, but more than likely, Wu Lin-kua paid his Auntie visits for advice. There were new wives and young children underfoot, but all respected Auntie Purple Sage. It was a wonder that this ghost bride had come full circle within the house despite resentment from Jasmine, which never had changed.

Purple Sage's anchor was set in the Chi family's new alliance with Wu, the Master of the House having taken Chi Lin's suggestion to employ her family as foremen for the salt *ji-tzao* to assure accurate accounting and increased production. But it went beyond that. After the *tai-feng* and the severe damage wrought by the catastrophic winds, the Chi undertook their commission as nothing short of a reestablishment of the monopoly. Chi Lin recalled the day.

The Master of the House had summoned her to attend on the Old Lady of the House in an unusual ceremony. Chi Lin met the First Wife before the Jade Heart Hall, Jasmine acknowledging her with a curt nod, but expecting a full curtsy in return, which Chi Lin bestowed. Together, led by Willow, they entered the Jade Heart Hall where their mother-in-law sat in a high backed chair flanked by two shorter chairs. The wives were instructed to take their places behind a screen. Wu T'ai-po, his journeymen and his two grandsons sat at the center of the hall. Once this arrangement conformed to the Master's liking, the visitor doors opened and, in addition to sunlight, in came three members of the Chi clan.

Chi Lin recognized her cousin Chi Fa immediately, but had only met the others, Chi Mu and Chi Ma once, but knew them by their sour faces. All three entered and bowed to Wu T'ai-po.

"We have come, Master Wu," Chi Fa said.

"So you have and promptly, I might add."

"We believe in keeping appointments in the House of Chi."

All three bowed again.

"Have you met with your venerable father, sir?" Wu T'ai-po asked.

"We have."

"Has he met with his venerable brother and your talented cousin?"

"He has."

"Then you know what we are about."

Chi Fa approached closer. Chi Lin saw his eyes and knew he could see her through the screen.

"Our household owes much to yours as does the county," Chi Fa said. "We are about industry. The winds have done their worst, but we shall do our best."

"And quickly too," Wu Lin-kua added, quite unexpectedly. But the aside pleased his grandfather. "Time is costly."

"It shall be done," Chi Fa said, bowing to . . . he was not sure who now, so it was more gesture than bow. "And will a timely restoration be met with a commensurate premium?"

"It surely shall," Wu T'ai-po said. "But do not expect a king's reward because I am no king. I hold the monopoly rights, which could very well drift if His Majesty, may He live ten-thousand years, is not pleased. So you will regard compensation as a rolling thing from on high to the good earth. We need the *ji-tzao* restored to operation."

"It shall be done."

"And once completed, the *ji-tzao* inspections shall precede on a different footing."

"I understand."

With this statement, Jasmine fidgeted and scowled at Chi Lin. Chi Lin had never consulted with Jasmine on these arrangements. The restoration of the salt *ji-tzao* could be expected to be outsourced, but then the tours would continue as they always had under Jasmine's proxy. But to hear of *a different footing* now and here, behind the screen, in a place where she could not object or speak her mind, was unforgivable. Chi Lin just shrugged as if she had nothing whatsoever to do with it. Their mother-in-law snapped her fan attempting to restore Jasmine's composure.

"Please present my chief journeyman, Chou Kuai-tze, with your plans," Wu T'ai-po said. "He shall oversee your progress."

"The plans are in the saddlebags, neighbor Wu."

"Very good."

And so it went. There was no further discussion. The council dispersed and the women returned to their places in their own halls. But Chi Lin knew Jasmine would find some way to upset these plans.

2

The Chi family had been an industrious clan for years, at least Chi Wan and his children were. Unlike brother Chi Ming, Chi Wan extended the family estate into rice production adapted to the marshlands and established looms at four locations taking in raw thread and weaving it into fine silk cloth. Some of this thread, he bought, but mostly he wove on consignment taking a percentage of the raw spools in to the finished bolts out. Chi Wan thought to expand into the trade itself, but a silk merchant was a low creature and the profit would not extend the family's position among the Yan-cheng gentry — a goal to be held as paramount. The major competition for the silk weaving business in Yan-cheng county was the Gui clan — a more rarified clan than the Chi being one of three original county families.

Chi Lin's brother, Chi Sheng, may have been crippled-born, but his mind was sharp and his brushwork keen. He created the plans to restore the *ji-tzao* with evaporation towers caissoned in stone to prevent them from being toppled again in a storm. He designed hoisting engines and cart wagons to transport stone from Ching-kua county. The traditional bamboo building materials were retained and the ability to assemble them rested squarely on the shoulders of tenant skill. The woman and children would be deployed to clean the pits and seek tinder for the charcoal fires. The marsh would provide the rest. Chi Lin showed an interest in tenant housing, which seemed to have missed the planning. She expressed this concern to her mother-in-law.

"Why not teach them to sew houses?" the Old Lady replied, grinning. "You are too focused on their welfare and not enough on ours. They have survived worse than this."

Chi Lin felt this to be an unfair assessment, but could not dispute it. She harbored Yu Li, whom she called little Butterfly, who now preferred to be a house servant than a tenant. In this Chi Lin's heart was shown to the world. So Chi Lin left the restoration to the men and concentrated on repairs to the folk silk *ji-tzao* and prepared for the first tour, which was still many moons off.

Jasmine found many ways to squeeze Purple Sage, but these attempts did not bother her. Any task the First Wife sent her way, she accomplished promptly and skillfully. Any attempt Jasmine made to highlight the fact that Chi Lin frittered away time on useless books or brushing poetry, had no effect, the Master of the House accepting it as much an asset as the dowry. Any reprisals through Lin-kua and Chou-fa were useless, because the boys sought out their Auntie for advice and enjoyed idle banter with her. Lin-kua continued to find books for Chi Lin's library and, when he asked her leading questions about the relationships between men and women, Chi Lin suggested to Pang Guo-ta that it might be time to take the young master to the Sojourn of Heaven's Eye to answer those questions. Chi Lin seemed impervious to the First Wife's abrasions except when it came to Wu Ming-kuan.

Ming-kuan came many times into his Auntie's courtyard with his boats. He loved to set them in the *koi* pond and splash them about. He also loved to play with *Raisin Cake* and became a favorite with little Butterfly. In that he became a source of contention between the tenant girl and Sapphire, who now lived in the Silver Silence in a room near the main hall. Sapphire continued to be moody, showed temper and pined for her mother. The Old Lady of the House did not know what to do and Lotus did not care for the girl, who also caused trouble between her sisters. So Chi Lin offered to take Sapphire rather than have her put into the cold harbor with her former *amah*. But every time Ming-kuan came into the courtyard and little Butterfly came to play with him by the pool, Sapphire would march in, ordering the girl to stay away from her brother; that Yu Li was nothing but a slave and not to be around him. This started Ming-kuan crying and little Butterfly pouting and Sapphire announcing to everyone that she was in charge of her small brother.

As it happened, when Ming-kuan came to play, Mi Tso-tze would quickly round up little Butterfly, and Po Bo would engage Sapphire, leaving the boy to play with his boats alone, unless his brothers came, which sometimes resulted for sea battles, broken boats and a mess for Lao Lao to mop. Jasmine intervened. She told the Old Lady of the House that it was not appropriate for Ming-kuan to go the Auntie Purple Sage's courtyard unescorted by the *amah*. This was true, and the Old Lady enforced it. Now when the boy came to play, the *amah* was there, chasing the dog away and not permitting Ming-kuan to get wet by the pool. So his point of coming was gone and the boy no longer came. In this, and only this, did Jasmine succeed in addressing Chi Lin's perceived *ji-tzao* snub.

3

Twenty-four summers had changed the scope of the *ji-tzao* inspection. In addition to the tours and the tenant accounting, there was now the scrutiny of the Chi family books, an unusual course of action, which Chi Lin devised to undertake herself. Chi Lin would arrange her *ke-ting* for company with Mi Tso-tze and little Butterfly's help, one grown older and the other a graceful young woman. Mo Li would stand near the door supervising the buns and tea and plates of savories for Purple Sage's guests. The Silver Silence was perfumed with sandalwood and had may fine pieces of furniture. The walls were hung with art acquired as gifts over the years. Today cousin Chi Lu-yi would cross the threshold to review the Chi family books. This had become a normal routine — every three moons. Chi Lu-yi was Chi Fa's son and assumed many responsibilities when his father became the Master of the Chi House upon his father's death. But it had not been always so.

In the days after the restoration of the *ji-tzao*, Chi Fa would come to the Jade Heart Pavilion to review progress. The assembly was always the same — Wu T'ai-po, the journeymen, the grandsons and the women behind the screen. After one such session, Chi Lin surprised everyone by leaving her chair and her position behind the screen. She presented herself to her father-in-law, and then spoke the following words:

"It is with deep humility as a mere woman that I am permitted to speak to you in such company," she said, although no one present remembered when permission had been granted. "The service of my family is as sure as my obedience to my husband to which there can be no doubt. But to doubly assure the compliance to my father-in-law's compact with us, I will undertake to listen to my cousin's accounting once in every three moons as a sign of our bonded trust."

She curtsied first to her cousin, and then to her father-in-law before rising and returning to her chair. In his silence, Wu T'ai-po accepted this bond. In *his* silence, Chi Fa acquiesced in it, but soon visited his cousin in her abode. It had been the first time any of her clan had stepped foot into the Silver Silence and she had it prepared well. It was not as elegant as it would become, but it was enticing enough. The best chair was offered to Chi Fa, who took it unquestioningly. But he did have questions.

"Cousin," he said, chafing. "Was such a display necessary to assure our arrangements with your father-in-law? Do the Chi need to account to you as well as to your brother?"

"My brother accounts for Wu production," she said. "In that, you do the same. But my concern is any extra burden that might press down upon the tenants."

"They benefit from our work," Chi Fa said. "We have no need to squeeze them. We are paid by contract."

"Just so. And it would be an insult if the Wu family oversaw the Chi family accounting. But it would be unfortunate if suspicions grew beyond reach. If I look at the accounting and see no untoward gains, no suspicion can assume the upper hand."

Chi Fa was miffed by the suggestion.

"Surely your brother could do it. This is business, not family politics."

Chi Lin sighed. It was hard to press her kinfolk too harshly, and she would not do it. She raised her tea bowl to soften Chi Fa's manner. He was always pleased when his belly was full, so the bun platter was offered also.

"I mean no disrespect, cousin," Chi Lin said. "I am lost to the world within this big house. But I have managed to make the proposal and gained Wu patronage for the Chi. It rises and falls on . . . on me."

Chi Fa grumbled.

"You will be inspecting the *ji-tzao*. What more could they want?"

"I inspect by proxy. It is the responsibility of the First Wife, Mei Lo, to whom I am not a bright star in the night sky. I will inspect, but she will spark suspicions. As mere women, we know that business is not our affair. But as mere women, we are shaped by gossip that can make the business harder. So, Chi Fa, forgive your foolish cousin. Let her peruse the Chi family accounts once every three moons over buns and tea. It will kill suspicions that gossip spurs. Business will prosper."

4

Chi Lin became a champion of the tenants. She did not speak for them nor incite them, but quietly noted their hardship and tried to aleve it. As tenants, their labor and life would never be free from hardship, but the sight of the touring lady — *the Salt Goddess* they called her, and, after she began wearing a cap of Imperial Crane feathers, *Queen Crane* — gave their hope a lift. Chi Lin did little to effect change, but it came nonetheless. Because the inspection no longer depended on the Journeymen and the Imperial Commissioner's Proxy to make a tally, there was no need for the *squeeze* silver. It was offered at first, but if the tally was incorrect by Chi accounting, the inspection failed and the silver was not returned. Its uselessness became apparent, because the Chi inspectors were salaried and would not take it, especially now that their books were being scrutinized by *the Salt Goddess*. So the *Pao-t'ien* was no longer pressed to bribe their way to success. The families that achieved their quotas stood in line to make the most profit. The wastrel clans got their just due also.

On one occasion, early in the change, the silver ingots *were* offered and the lady basket was filled with seven silver coins. Chi Lin was supposed to take these and give five to Jasmine. Instead, she thanked the elders for their consideration and returned all seven pieces. The silver ingots were also returned by the Journeyman, in this case, Pa Li-tze. Later, when Pa grumbled about it, Chi Lin said:

"The silver was meant to level all faults, but by doing so, it creates faults. Now it will be better to remain in the tenants' hands because we benefit from their increased industry, which is far better, do you not think?"

Pa Li-tze did not know what to think. Everyone in the Wu household knew better than to chide this meddlesome woman, whose intentions were always for the best. Jasmine was a different story. When she sought her five silver coins and was told they were returned, she raged, her fists balled and her demeanor compromised.

"The silver exchange is traditional," she shouted at Chi Lin, who tried not to cower. "It is ceremonial and demanded by the Emperor. How dare you make alterations?"

Chi Lin did no more than curtsy and departed before Jasmine began to throw things. She had expected to be admonished by the Old Lady of the House, but not a word was mentioned. Her mother-in-law was less salty now, sitting quietly, sometime not even undertaking to sew. But she was generally more favorable to Purple Sage than to Jasmine. The lack of chastisement could be construed as favorable. But at the next tour, Chi Lin approached the chair only to find Jasmine in her own chair. So together they undertook the ceremony.

At first, Chi Lin worried, because Jasmine did not acknowledge her and took the lead position in the procession. But soon Chi Lin realized that passers-by did not recall the First Wife. In fact, some just nodded as they would any person in the street. But when they saw Purple Sage in her soft lavender robe and her brilliant Imperial Crane bonnet, they bowed and curtsied, much to Jasmine's annoyance. The tenants recognized the First Wife and acted accordingly, but this did not stop the men from hailing the *Salt Goddess* who followed or the children from shouting *Queen Crane*. By the time the tour reached the *Pao-t'ien*, Jasmine was furious. She bolted out of her chair and marched into the hall taking her place behind the screen. It created a tense atmosphere, but the men went about their business.

Chi Lin sat beside her sister-in-law and watched as the Journeyman (Pang Guo-ta, this time) and the Imperial Commissioner Proxy (Lin Wu-luo still, although there would be others over the years) sip plum wine and oversee Chi Mu and Chi Ma as they reckoned the tallies on bamboo slips. The Elder and the tenant chiefs were tense until the Chi brothers grinned and nodded that all was well. Then they too imbibed the plum wine. A convivial spirit overtook the hall. Chi Lin watched Jasmine staring at the lady basket anticipating the sound of silver jangling to the bottom. But instead, two sweet buns were set inside. Chi Lin took the basket, nodded to the Elder, and then offered her sister-in-law a bun, which she declined. Chi Lin would save them for her own household, little Butterfly being partial to buns steamed by her own clan. Jasmine marched imperiously back to her chair ordering her porters to return her to the Wu House at once.

Although the company was puzzled by the First Wife's conduct, it did not make an impression, not when Mistress Purple Sage was still in their midst, taking a cup of plum wine and nodding to the children. The tour continued to the silk *ji-tzao*, where *Queen Crane* not only inspected the industry, but instructed the women on the best method to feed the newly hatched worms and how to coax them to spin the cocoons to a pure white instead of the more natural tawny. It was taxing to be engaged by so many interested folk, but Chi Lin wanted them to think of her when they worked and remember that she would be there again to encourage their best work.

As for Jasmine, her time for touring was over. She never ventured out again under any circumstances. She never made inquiries on the ceremony or asked for the silver or even paid attention to the Wu House's silk *ji-tzao*. She just kept to her own sphere of influence, which occasionally nipped at Chi Lin's toes, but less often now — now that *Queen Crane* was esteemed by the tenants and the neighbors came to worship *the Salt Goddess.*

Chapter Two

Chi Lin and the Mei-ren

1

"No bound feet," the Old Lady of the House muttered to Chi Lin.

Chi Lin listened intently, and then nodded in consent. The Old Lady was dying and everyone knew it, especially the Old Lady. She had been unwell for six moons, losing weight and occasionally suffering pain. The *yi-sheng* took her pulse and smelled her breath and, although encouraging at first, soon shook his head and told Wu T'ai-po to burn incense and red paper prayers. It was a canker in her belly that consumed her from within. But the herbalists had concoctions to ease the pain and to bring her comfort.

Jasmine deigned to attend her mother-in-law, and even Lotus made an effort to leave her pavilion to pay her respects, but the Old Lady would have none of them. Faithful Willow would attend her needs and, as to company, Purple Sage was her greatest comfort. Chi Lin would sit silently beside the Old Lady and sew, while her mother-in-law watched, smiling at the stitches. Death was never a comfort and Chi Lin had experienced a few recent ones. First, Snapdragon, who passed quietly in her sleep, only to be regaled with a brash interment in the servants' burial grounds – a memorable affair because few servants had an ironwood coffin and a fine silk shroud. Even Lao Lao when he passed, two moons later, was laid in a simple pine box wrapped in a coarse linen liner. Chi Lin would miss these two old faithfuls. Although Snapdragon was fussy and always under foot, her spidery hands were into Chi Lin's hair everyday, despite Mi Tso-tze's need to redo the coif. Chi Lin could not forget that it was Lao Lao who first deigned to speak with her when she came into the cold inner sanctum of the Silver Silence. His cheery voice told her how things were and how they could be. He would be missed. Po Bo was the custodian now, an energetic young scamp, who sprouted to the rafters and sported broad shoulders. Yes, Chi Lin knew death. Even *Raisin Cake* came to an end one day, found dead beside the pool. Although Chi Lin would replace him and rename every replacement *Raisin Cake* (burying seven pets by the southern wall) she was always most fond of the first.

Now it was the Old Lady of the House's turn. She refused to stay in bed, preferring her *ke-ting*. Every day her sewing was set before her and, although she did not work, she patted it as if it would complete itself. As Chi Lin stitched, the Old Lady would grunt and comment on the work, mostly criticism of a kindly nature, but sometimes praise.

"You must teach that stitch to my granddaughter to improve her concentration," she would say.

When the Old Lady referred to *my granddaughter*, she always meant Sapphire. She had no fears for the other two, but worried about the young one's future. Sapphire was growing in body, but not in mind. She remained a frail, moody child, often sitting for hours alone in the shadow of the Silver Silence's walls, twisting the diminutive robes of her dolly. At other times, she fought with Po Bo or little Butterfly, showing a mean spirited side that could only be curtailed by Chi Lin's sterner hand. Purple Sage set aside time each day trying to train the girl up to become a woman – sewing instructions, singing practice and telling her stories, reading from the ever growing collection of books in the Silver Silence. Sometimes the child would smile and caress her auntie. At other times she would throw small tantrums demanding a better story or sweets from the kitchen. It was not an easy course. Sapphire's future was worrisome.

When the Old Lady muttered *No bound feet* this was a different instruction for Purple Sage. Chi Lin had learned that, in the household, marriage arrangements for the children fell outside the sphere of mothers and definitely beyond the realm of men. As such, the Old Lady of the House would be the prime mover, but in her current condition, she could do no more than consider and advise the one person of the house who would manage it – the Fourth Wife.

Chi Lin knew nothing of arranging marriages. Her own was arranged according to plan – the *mei-ren* or broker approached her father stating that Wu Hung-lin decided to take an additional wife and the sky signs were favorable toward the Chi's second daughter. The fact that the first daughter was destined for a life of charity in the monastery quite cleared the way for this new alliance. Chi Ming agreed to have tea with Wu T'ai-po where the bride's price was given, if acceptable. It was declared there was no need for the groom to see Chi Lin before the ceremony and the dowry was sent. Of course, Chi Lin received the purple flower and had to decide on her course to be a ghost bride or retreat to a monastery like her sister had. Beyond this, Chi Lin knew nothing of arranging a marriage. In fact, she had no idea that she would steer this course until Willow took her aside one day before she took up the stitch beside her mother-in-law.

"Mistress," Willow said. She had become Chi Lin's close friend despite the difference in their status. "I shall caution you that today my mistress is in a mood to discuss the First Son's connubial future."

"I will listen with respect," Chi Lin replied.

"You misunderstand me, mistress. She is enlisting you to commence arrangements."

"Me?"

"You are not his mother and you are not a man," she replied. "These are the qualifications for a go-between."

"Oh," Chi Lin responded.

She had never given this much thought. The only time she had considered Wu Lin-kua's marital future was when he bragged that he would have sixteen wives when he was Master of the House. She had also suggested he gain experience in the pleasure house, but she never knew whether Pang Guo-ta ever followed through with her suggestion. So she proceeded to her seat beside her ailing mother-in-law and waited for her cue. It did not come. Nor was it broached on the next day or the next, so Chi Lin assumed the Old Lady had changed her mind and would keep to her own schedule for these things. But finally, the matter was broached.

"No bound feet," the Old Lady muttered.

"Yes, mother-in-law," Chi Lin said. "Our feet are not bound."

"No, child. You miss my meaning. Choose them with no bound feet."

"Choose whom?"

"The wives of my grandsons," the Old Lady replied, annoyed at the missed meaning. "I can give little guidance other than this."

Chi Lin knew the time had arrived, so she listened intently.

"Wu Lin-kua needs to marry. He is inclined to do it, and I fear his inclinations. His mother is useless to guide him well. He listens to me respectfully, but knows my time is near. Respect for a living grandmother is more binding than to an ancestral grandmother to whom he might thank for guidance and honor with red paper prayers, but still do what the living do. As for my husband, it is improper for his intervention in these matters. So it falls to you, his Auntie to guide the arrangements."

Chi Lin nodded reverentially to her mother-in-law. This was the first time she heard that Wu Lin-kua had been considering marriage on his own terms and had no knowledge of this choice. She had not spoken to Jasmine in over a moon and, even if she had, she doubted the First Wife would have broached the matter.

"I am new to such arrangements," Chi Lin said softly.

"You must seek Ying Ling, the *mei-ren*. She is best. There are others, but they have proved misguided in at least one instance in our family affairs."

"Ying Ling will know?"

"You must take care with her, my child. She is a powerful *mei-ren* and can paint pretty words for the right price. But we do not need pretty words. The first wife of a first son must be a connection that lasts for a generation. The sky must be correct, the omens perfect. There can be no question of impropriety and there must be no bound feet."

"No bound feet," Chi Lin repeated.

"My feet are unbound and I gave my husband three sons. Jasmine's feet are unbound and she gave my son two sons. Your feet are unbound and . . . well, you have blessed us. The other wives were dainty-footed and only daughters came forth."

Chi Lin saw the point and the logic, although her own mother had unbound feet and she had two daughters and a crippled son. Still, if this is what was required for the House of Wu, she would follow the course.

"Ying Ling will recommend a score of county daughters, but take care. She is looking for the best commission on her choice. She thrives on silver and, if she makes a good match, it is deserved, but try to think of our family's best interests, even if the girl be one eyed and hunched-backed."

Chi Lin shuddered. She would never saddle Lin-kua with such a wife, but she understood the point and the deep responsibility. What she did not understand was Lin-kua's mind, and for that she needed more than her mother-in-law's guidance.

2

Wu Lin-kua had been introduced to the pleasure house called The Sojourn of Heaven's Eye as had his brother, Wu Chou-fa. Both lads liked the women that they had and compared experiences as only brothers could, with many references to passionate moments and to quirks in women's anatomy. The women they had been coupled with were young at first, but as Lin-kua sprouted, he had the choice of the house having an allowance of silver ingots greater than most patrons. Before he set foot in the place, his teacher P'ing Chin would read him passages from the famous saints of Taoist and Buddhist lore, especially of Ch'ang P'ang, a prolific philosopher who could hold a woman on his lap for hours without becoming aroused. Lin-kua laughed at this as no accomplishment, but perhaps a sign that Ch'ang P'ang's priorities were askew. But P'ing Chin would put it to the point, that it was the priority of a virtuous man to know when arousal was necessary and when not; that knowing the Classics and maintaining the fundamental relationships between male and female was a higher virtue than mere passion and self-indulgence. Lin-kua would acknowledge the point, and then proceed with a journeyman to plow his passions as he saw fit, perhaps thinking of a Classical passage in the culmination – something along the lines of a battle on a parapet releasing vessels of hot oil.

Chi Lin was not averse to men seeking comfort in the pleasure house. It was natural and not for a ghost wife to say otherwise. Had she not encouraged Pang Guo-ta to take the first son to the Soujourn of Heaven's Eye? But now she learned that Wu Lin-kua had fixed his passions on a specific pleasure woman – Cinnamon Rose, a rare treasure who sang like a golden finch and played the *p'i-p'a* like an immortal. These were not faults because she cultivated them to enrich both the Sojourn and her apartment, which had become particularly stellar since Wu Lin-kua's attentions were showered upon her. Such attraction was beyond an Auntie's business unless that Auntie needed to find the first son a wife and that first son announced he had set his cap upon this useless bauble. *No bound feet.* The echo was loud in Chi Lin's head.

Jasmine knew of these things and had argued with her son over his choice. He remained respectful of his mother, but pointed out that her voice did not count in this issue. It would be his grandmother who had the heaviest sway. When he broached the issue with the Old Lady of the House she listened as only a woman in the throes of illness could – in silence and in pain. Her only response was *No bound feet*. Lin-kua respectfully bowed to his grandmother, made no reply or argument, but was ready to follow his own course.

"So, as you can see," Willow said to Chi Lin, "the First Son has already made up his mind on the issue."

"But he cannot arrange it himself."

"Of course not," Willow said. "Even Cinnamon Rose needs to follow the rules."

This was true enough. So, with great anxiety, Chi Lin sent Wu Lin-kua a coin shaped bun. Po Bo delivered it with a message that Mistress Purple Sage had been instructed to call for the *mei-ren* and asked to discuss the matter with the First Son. Lin-kua was to come to the Silver Silence the next day with his usual present for his Auntie – a book; this time a collection of poems by Su T'ai-po, Chi Lin's favorite poet.

The Silver Silence was warm, it being the sixth moon. Her usual course would be to converse on the verandah, but in her new responsibility she wanted to maintain an appropriate atmosphere and meet with Lin-kua inside the hall. She had a chair set under a bower of scented *tzi di-xiang*, the purple beards infusing the pavilion to the exclusion of other aromas. It would put Lin-kua at ease, she suspected and perhaps in the best mood for the subject. Previous interviews between nephew and aunt had been casual, filled with informal banter. Perhaps this would ease him into the connubial subject without the usual male reticence before women.

"This is my favorite poet, master," Chi Lin said, nodding thanks, but putting the book aside immediately.

Wu Lin-kua sat in an unlikely spot, on a cushion purposely placed in the hall for subservience. Mi Tso-tze served him a bowl of rice wine, which he imbibed quickly, his adolescence still evident despite his prowess in the hen house.

"I knew you would like Su T'ai-po, Auntie," he said. He looked about, setting the bowl down. "Why are we sitting in here and in such a manner? It is hot and the scent is overbearing."

"Perhaps so, master," she replied. "But I am representing the household today."

"You are arranging my marriage with Cinnamon Rose," he stated enthusiastically.

"I am arranging your marriage to whomever the gods see fit."

Wu Lin-kua jumped to his feet.

"You are going to side with my mother and grandmother. For that I cannot stand."

"You *are* standing, as I can see. And I did not say you could *not* marry whom you desire. I said Heaven needs a voice and we must consult the *mei-ren*."

Lin-kua frowned, more adolescence breaking through now. He sat again with a thump. Tso-tze filled his cup again and he drank it quickly, almost choking.

"You will call the *mei-ren*, Auntie?"

"It is my responsibility to do it . . . for you, your brothers and your sisters. So accept the practice as you accepted your first top-knot."

Chi Lin waited, and then stood.

"Perhaps it *is* hot in here."

She went to him, gave him her hand, and then walked him onto the verandah, where a warm breeze blew the floral stink away. As warm as it was, it was still refreshing compared with the hall.

"You once told me that when you were Master of the House, you would have sixteen wives, many from the pleasure house."

"I was a child then," he said, almost laughing. "Of course a man cannot afford that many wives."

"But even if you were to have five wives, you would still need a first wife — a woman to give you sons and establish a proper relationship for the ancestors to witness."

This was a truth incontestable – a P'ing Chin truth.

"But who is to say," Lin-kua said, "that a wife from the pleasure house cannot be a fine woman, a bearer of sons and a worthy mate for the master of a great house."

Chi Lin smiled. This was the nub of the issue. What she said next could either anger him or persuade him. But she did not mean to do either. She wanted to set seeds in his mind so he could consider the issue like the future Master of the House. She offered him a seat, which he took. Tso-tze brought the wine bowl, which, this time, he declined. There were distractions now in the courtyard – Po Bo supervising the gardeners stringing rows for pea vines, little Butterfly feeding *Raisin Cake* fried dough and Sapphire singing a melancholy song by the pool. These were distractions slipped into Lin-kua's mind as only a good Auntie could.

"Let us consider these things, Master Lin-kua," Auntie Purple Sage said. "A first wife is for the family, just as the marriage is for the family. It is a contract between families. Now I cannot say that Cinnamon Rose has no family, but will *Heaven* and our ancestors be content with the dowry of a working girl? I will not say that they would not be, because I am not a potent *mei-ren* like Ying Ling. But a pleasure house woman taken as a wife is a good thing, I would say. My husband, your father, took two into his household."

"That is so, Auntie," Lin-kua said. "It is my thinking exactly."

"But consider. Were they first wives?"

"No. But my mother, the First Wife has brought little connection to . . ."

Chi Lin held her hand up, frowning.

"Take care, Master Lin-kua. One does not speak of one's mother in such terms. The First Wife is always the First Wife and must be respected. Her opinions may not be law, but they are to be considered."

"I am sorry."

"Thought sometimes must be confined to private circles attended to by only the spirits of slumber. Now consider Lotus. Think of her. Suppose she were your father's first wife."

Lotus was talented and a beauty, her delicate charms an apparent draw for Wu Hung-lin. Chi Lin recalled the Autumn Moon Festival when Lotus, balanced on her bound feet, climbed the moon tower stairs and sang her song to *Chang-O*. It was unparalleled. But the years had not been kind to Lotus. She rarely left Crimson Blossom Pavilion now. Her delicate palate craved fine foods, beyond the balance she could maintain upon her tiny feet. A steady stream of buns and meats and noodles and rice came to her at all hours of the day and night. She drank much plum wine and found little solace in moving. In fact, she abandoned her chair and reclined on a couch, where her handmaidens waited upon her, feeding her even when the morbid sense to move overcame her. This was the image Chi Lin meant to inject into Wu Lin-kua's mind to weigh in upon his choice of a pleasure house woman as First Wife. Chi Lin loathed to do it because Lotus was a sweet person, useless as a dumpling set on a fine platter, but inoffensive otherwise. She had performed her duties in her time and gave her husband children, albeit daughters.

Wu Lin-kua fell silent. It was clear to Chi Lin that he thought of a gross, inert Cinnamon Rose perched on a grand couch in the Jade Heart's *ke-ting*.

"There is no reason *not* to take Cinnamon Rose as a wife, Master Lin-kua, as *Heaven* admits as much. But if not a first wife, perhaps a second or a fifth."

Chi Lin grinned, nodded, and then stood. The interview was over and on her terms. Wu Lin-kua was deep in thought, no longer distracted by his own force of mind or the clatter in the Silver Silence's courtyard. Chi Lin knew it was time to call the *mei-ren*.

3

Ying Ling arrived in a wide chair carried by four porters and brought to the Blue Fountain Hall, a small communal pavilion used for such matters concerning marriage and funerals and such. Chi Lin had arranged a chair and table for the *mei-ren* and asked Mi Tso-tze to serve and Willow to stand nearby. Jasmine was invited but declined to attend. The Old Lady was not well enough and the Master of House would appear at the door, raise a cup to the *mei-ren*, and then depart, as was the custom. More than likely the rest of the household would eavesdrop from strategic places, but Wu Lin-kua was ordered to stay away.

Ying Ling wore a red and silver robe dotted with orange and green beads. She sported crystal strands in a riot of colors. Her face was powdered white, her lips painted ruby, her eyebrows accentuated in turquoise and her hair, streaked white, draped over her shoulders. Five peacock quills braced her head. Chi Lin was astounded at the sight, but the more color the *mei-ren* wore, the more successful she had been. This was a good sign if Chi Lin could reckon by this rainbow.

Once Ying Ling was seated, several trays of meat and vegetables were served complete with silver *kuai-tze*, which went to work immediate over ruby lips. It was interrupted only once by Wu T'ai-po's wine salute, but then continued as if the woman had not eaten in a fortnight. Once sated, Ying Ling placed the *kuai-tze* aside, and then bowed to Chi Lin.

"Thank you for coming, Mistress Ying," Chi Lin said.

"You are in need of my services, so I hear," the *mei-ren* replied, reaching for her cup. "It has been some time since the House of Wu has called. But now that the flowers bloom and the hair grows thick on the pelvis, my services can be deployed more often."

"Yes, we are in need."

Ying Ling clapped. One of the porters came forth with a bamboo book. She pushed the food trays aside and rolled the scroll before her.

"I have consulted the sticks and the astral charts for the First Son of Wu. He is an interesting case." She tapped the bamboo slip. "Few first sons show more promise to fulfill their responsibilities than Wu Lin-kua, or so says the juncture of stars and the *Yi-ching*. So it is likely that many matches may suit."

"We want the best match."

"Good family?"

"Yes."

"Good looks?"

"If possible."

"Broad thighs?"

"Absolutely."

"Bound feet?"

"No bound feet."

Ying Ling frowned.

"That narrows things."

"The Lady of the House does not want a wife with bound feet to replace her."

"Then we shall respect Mistress Wu." Ying Ling regarded the scroll. "There is a daughter of T'ou and one of Chou that are most propitious."

"None in Gui?"

"Gui daughters are young still, except for one, who has just come of age. She is not pretty and, as for child bearing, she might do, but the bride's price will be low . . ."

"And the dowry high."

"The Gui name counts for much and may curtail the dowry to the bride's brush, bedding and scents."

Chi Lin thought on this. A match between the Gui and Wu House would be more fortunate for the Gui than the Wu.

"But the advantages of marrying into the *ji-tzao* certainly would draw a chest of silver and much silk and horses. But this can be no more than speculation if she has bound feet."

"Her feet are unbound."

"Reach out then and see."

"I must still cast the sticks."

"Cast them and let us know."

Chi Lin sounded churlish in her demand, but Ying Ling was no more than a merchant providing a service; and since there were many more marriages to arrange, Chi Lin wanted the *mei-ren* to know not to take advantage and risk future business. Ying Ling bowed, stood and was helped into her chair.

"One more word," Chi Lin said. "Do you know the pleasure girl named Cinnamon Rose?"

"Yes, mistress. She is a beauty. But her feet are bound and you can expect no dowry from that quarter. I would make inquiries for you on that score for an additional fee, but Cinnamon Rose is already taken."

"Taken?"

"T'ou Chang-la has arranged to acquire her as his fifth wife. The bride price has already been paid."

Chi Lin smiled.

"I thank you."

Once Ying Ling was gone, Wu Lin-kua appeared, released from his restriction. At once, he asked his Auntie for details. She provided none, except the one she needed him to know; the one hardest for him to hear. He wept. There was nothing to be done because T'ou Chang-la was the Master of the T'ou House and could offer Cinnamon Rose much beyond the First Son's allowance. But his Auntie promised him a proper bride, which may not have salved his wounded heart, but kept him on the appropriate course.

Chapter Three

Passing the Torch

1

Honeysuckle, the eldest daughter of the Gui Household proved both available and suitable as determined by Ying Ling. Chi Lin considered this and also Lin-kua's feelings. But the dowry was above expectations, so she announced to Jasmine that a match was set, once Wu Lin-kua sealed it and the bride price paid. A meeting was arranged at the Gui household and a still-sad Lin-kua arrived there with his grandfather and six journeymen to see what he could see. He had told Auntie Purple Sage that if he could not have Cinnamon Rose, Honeysuckle did not matter. Any woman would do if Heaven and the stars demanded it. This did not cheer Chi Lin. She sought Lin-kua's happiness, but not at the expense of a propitious match. But she had little to fear, because once inside the Gui household, and once Lin-kua saw Honeysuckle, he was drawn to her. She was not a brazen pleasure bauble or a radiant beauty, but a girl with a demure countenance who peeked at her possible husband from across the tea table. In fact, she covered her mouth and giggled. He giggled in return, and when the time came to serve the cake, Lin-kua placed a red tea pouch on the saucer. He had approved.

The bride price was paid three moons later, and then Wu Lin-kua went to collect his bride. Her friends and family ceremoniously taunted him, preventing him from entering, but when this custom subsided, the bride's chair was readied, the red robes secured and a procession marched through the salt marsh to the House of Wu. Of course, Wu Chou-fa and his friends ambushed the groom with fireworks, a necessary prank, but this obstacle was overcome also, the bride and her dowry entering the courtyard, the ceremony commencing — short and felicitous — *k'ou-t'ous* to Heaven, a wine cup filled to the brim without spilling, and then the feast — raucous and merry while the wedding couple looked happily on.

Chi Lin was satisfied with the match and the *mei-ren's* work. Honeysuckle was unassuming and gentle — still young and to be molded as the Lady of the House when the time came. The two families, always rivals, were embraced with a new sense of harmony. Then, Lin-kua presented his new bride to the Old Lady of the House. She had been aware of things, but barely. She allowed Willow to dress her in her fine festive robes, which draped over her like curtains on a too-high window. Her face was sunken, her old eyes kept open by the shear force of will.

"Grandmother," Lin-kua said, bowing, Honeysuckle performing a deep curtsy. "My bride pays her respects."

"Gui Lei-la," the old woman said.

"Honeysuckle," came the thin voice of the new bride.

"Sweet as the flower." The Old Lady glanced down at Honeysuckle's feet. "Very sweet, indeed. Welcome to the House of Wu. You are of our family now."

The Old Lady was content, but expressed nothing more until Chi Lin came into her presence. Then she grinned, lifted her hand to her daughter-in-law, and then sighed deeply.

"You have done well, Purple Sage. I know these things are in good hands now."

Chi Lin's heart soared. She even told her husband these things when she visited the shrine, and then turned to the issue of the second son, Chou-fa.

Much changed. Now that Lin-kua had married, he would need a place to live and, in due course, it was decided that the Bachelor Quarters would become the new Pavilion of the Precious Omen. Wu Chou-fa moved into rooms at the Journeymen's Quarters, an arrangement he did not mind because he liked listening to their ribald tales and occasionally joined their games of *Fan Tan*. But Chi Lin knew this could not last. It was inappropriate and only a temporary measure. Wu Chou-fa had now assisted his grandfather with household planning – inventory, transportation and rites, but for the most part he was idle. Therefore, Chi Lin visited Jasmine and broached the prospects of marriage. Once again, Jasmine had pushed a son into a state of non-commitment. Chou-fa had visited the pleasure houses as had his brother, but unlike his brother, he was shy and only chose newcomers, who were not beauties and nearly anonymous. To Chou-fa, the pleasure was a disposal of need and never a dalliance or passionate expenditure. He saw no need to marry yet, and thus resisted his mother's commandment.

Chi Lin planned to meet with Chou-fa and persuade him, but there was little incentive to fire the young man's commitment. She asked Lin-kua to intercede. The brothers were close and she thought perhaps plain speaking would convince Chou-fa, but Lin-kua's efforts were weak, his time invested in his new wife, who was soon kindled for motherhood. Chi Lin's only course was to seek the council of her mother-in-law, but she was not in time.

On the morning the Old Lady of the House passed away, Chi Lin was awakened by Willow.

"You must hurry, mistress," Willow urged. "She calls for you and only you."

Mi Tso-tze quickly dressed Chi Lin and together, Willow and Purple Sage hurried to the Jade Heart Hall, where the *yi-sheng* hovered about the Old Lady's chair. She had refused to be moved to her bed. Wu T'ai-po stood silently in the room's corner, while Wu Lin-kua knelt at his grandmother's side. Jasmine peeked in from the kitchen, while Lotus was no where to be seen. When Chi Lin entered, Lin-kua stood.

"Auntie," he said, tearfully, "she speaks your name."

Chi Lin came to the chair, where her mother-in-law was as cold as the north wind. She stared blankly, but then looked up.

"Purple Sage" she said, barely audible. Chi Lin kneeled, bringing her ear closer to the old one's lips. "You have come."

"You spoke my name, mother-in-law."

"I go, daughter-in-law," she whispered. "A woman's heart is sometimes plagued by things she knows and cannot address. She cannot say it while she lives in the world of men. But I go now and I say now, you are a jewel among the treasures of my heart. Your stitches are the finest and you mend this family. You mend it."

Chi Lin did not know what to say. She hoped no one else heard these words, but she knew Willow had heard them and perhaps Wu Lin-kua.

"Are you comfortable?" she asked. "Can I bring something to ward off this cold?"

"My shroud will do. Your warm hand is a comfort. Knowing you will see the *mei-ren* for my grandchildren, ushers me to *the Yellow Springs* in a calm boat on a gentle tide."

Chi Lin wept, the Old Lady fading in the dewy mist. This woman may not have been encouraging in the way Chi Lin's mother had been, but she was a practical force – the bulwark and pillar for this household, and yet she now conferred such utility on the least of her son's brides. Her mother-in-law squeezed her hand,

and then released her, a half expressed utterance of *Purple Sage* managing across her lips. Then she was gone.

Soon the shadow of Wu T'ai-po crossed the chair. He lifted Chi Lin to her feet, his old arms trembling under the effort. He looked down at his First Wife, and then departed, leaving the family to stand about the Old Lady of the House like silent statues in a wintry temple.

2

Any thoughts of another marriage were postponed for six moons as the household donned the white. By the time Honeysuckle was big with child, she was ensconced in the Jade Heart Hall as the Lady of the House, Wu Lin-kua assuming his grandfather's role. Wu T'ai-po retired to a comfortable pavilion attached to the hall, all but relinquishing the daily business to his grandsons. He meddled to be sure, as any grandsire would amidst the verdant fingers of the semi-taught, but gradually he spent his days reading and sleeping and eating and farting, much to his contentment — nothing in want, all needs subscribed.

With the mourning, all household members returned to pray at the shrine, including Wu Liang-tze's wives, those still surviving, coming from the shambles of the Second Son's vagrant estate. Wu Ming-kuan returned from the port, his apprenticeship having just commenced, but curtailed much to his displeasure. The mourning also brought a visit from Wu San-ehr in all his martial splendor, covered in white, of course.

Chi Lin was happy to see Ming-kuan, but he fretted. He loved learning about the ships and the contours of the sea. He was still too young to set forth across the tides, but his skill with a brush made his studies successful, only to be interrupted by mourning. Chi Lin met with him daily listening to descriptions of rigging and sails, not that she knew the meaning, but it was a pleasure to hear his voice. Like a sea bird surveying the tides, Ming-kuan had found his vocation. As fretful as he was, he was still obedient and observed the rites, attending his brothers in daily prayers to Heaven for their grandmother's *ch'i*.

One afternoon, Chi Lin returned to the Silver Silence to a surprise visitor — Wu San-ehr, who arrived unannounced and, in her absence, made himself comfortable in her *ke-ting*. Mi Tso-tze sent Po Bo to warn her, but it was not timely, the custodian meeting Purple Sage as she entered the courtyard.

"He is here," Po Bo said. "Who would think that he would ever come here? But he marched over the threshold and howled for a bowl of wine and made himself comfortable on your best chair, mistress."

"Who is here, Po Bo? You are speaking too fast."

"The Third Son, mistress."

Chi Lin's eyes opened wide. Her brother-in-law had never commiserated with her. He was a commanding presence in the household when he visited, but he remained in the Jade Heart Hall or took residence in the Bachelor Quarters. He had not crossed over the Silver Silence's threshold since the night of the rape. Chi Lin hastened her pace.

Wu San-ehr sat on the best chair, indeed, and he was calm about it. Chi Lin entered, curtsied to him, and then ordered Mi Tso-tze to have Mo Li prepare dumplings.

"Brother-in-law," she said, sitting opposite him, "this is unexpected, but quite felicitous."

"This Hall is quite felicitous," he remarked looking about. "It has come a long way since I last saw it. You know how to charm the walls and coax the ceilings, Mistress Purple Sage."

"Thank you, my lord."

"I am unaccustomed to see so many books in a woman's household, but I have been told you have crossed the divide on that score. If my father approves, who am I to dispute it?"

"It wiles the time when I am not otherwise engaged."

"And engaged you have been." He leaned forward. "You have proved to be a virtuous go-between — most wise and politic."

"Wisdom has little to do with it, my lord. What is available is available. As for politics, how could a woman know of such things?"

"Know it or not, Heaven has guided you fortuitously."

"I thank you."

"I hope the next matches prove as politic."

Chi Lin was lost on the force of this remark. She knew little of the outside world, the flow of events and Imperial shifts in favor. How political could a connubial match be within a county town?

"Pardon, brother-in-law, but when you say I have acted politically, I do not understand. If it was politic, it was driven more by fate than design."

"Then know this," he said, sipping some wine, and leaning even closer to her. "The salt monopoly is a powerful trust. The Wu hold it, but that does not mean it is ours forever. There are others who would like to take it from us. But only the Emperor can do so. So it depends on political favor, which other families vie for."

"Do you speak of the Gui?"

"I do. They have sent minions to court trying to sway the Emperor and his Heir to allow the monopoly or part of it to slip under their control." He laughed. "But now the alliance between our houses allows them to have a share by proxy, and yet lets my nephew maintain the whole of it. That was your doing, Mistress Purple Sage."

"If it was so, it was not intended, but I am happy to feed destiny."

"You must continue to do so." He sat back and surveyed the room. "Indeed this hall has improved and I shall help improve it more." Chi Lin nodded. "Yes, you must feed destiny again. Wu Chou-fa must marry."

"He is disinclined to it."

"Nonsense. A man must marry as part of his contract with Heaven and Wu Chou-fa must overcome his timidity or whatever objections he may have. Does he like women?'

"Yes."

"It would not matter if he likes men as long as he marries and does his duty."

"He has no ambitions toward it. I believe he knows, in time, it must be done, but . . . ."

"I shall give him two incentives, Mistress Purple Sage. He shall move into Wu Liang-tze's villa. Having a place he can call his domain will make him happier than any wife. But . . . he must marry to have it."

"That would be fine, brother-in-law, but the place, so I hear, is in disarray. The great storm devastated the main hall and it is still in disrepair all these years later. We use the place as a cold palace, the Second Son's wives living in a bitter state."

"Why is this so?" Wu San-ehr barked. "Why have I not been informed of this? My father should have repaired it." He looked askance. "I mean not to speak against him, but it only stands to reason that a good property should be maintained."

"I am not to say it and have no opinions on matters that do not concern me."

"They concern you now. Persuade Wu Chou-fa to a good match and the villa shall be restored. I have an army of personally loyal men who will lend their backs to it."

"And materials?"

"I will donate toward it, and so shall Wu Lin-kua. It is his responsibility as Master of the House. And you shall make a match with the T'ou family."

"But Ying Ling must contrive the match."

"Of course the *mei-ren* must earn her keep, but it must be the T'ou clan. They must bring a mighty dowry to defray the costs of this restoration."

"But they are not as wealthy as the Gui."

"They stand to benefit more, so they shall pay more. You make this so and I will add a second incentive. I will tell Wu Chou-fa that he must marry and marry now or I will take him away from *Yan-cheng* and enlist him my army at the lowest possible rank." He laughed. "That should get the pup's attention."

Chi Lin grinned, not because she wanted to see Chou-fa as a soldier, but she was moved by her brother-in-law's spirit. There was no doubt he could move Mount T'ai if he needed the space to grow rice.

"Yes," Wu San-ehr continued. "All men must marry." He paused. "What about Wu Ming-kuan. I saw him moping about the journeymen's quarters." He paused again, staring at Chi Lin. "I know he is special to you. We cannot speak of it, but great care must be made for his marriage also."

"Ming-kuan has only seen nine autumns," she said.

"He is young, but we still must consider the matter. I hear he is apprenticed at the port, a good notion for a third son."

"He is in love with the sea and with boats. I would . . . we would like to see him well settled on his ambitions."

"He does not know the sea, sister-in-law," Wu San-ehr said, musing on his wine bowl. "Ships he may know from what the books teach him, but the sea is a stern mistress and must be courted like a pleasure girl." He blushed. "Forgive my boldness."

"He is single-minded."

"I will tell you a secret, one that a woman should not know nor gossip." He leaned forward. "Prince Chu Di has a love for the sea also and plans to build many ships and sail beyond the edge of the world . . . if he should become . . . well, I have said too much. But when it happens, we shall take care of our own. Wu Ming-kuan will have the best instruction. He will sail on the first expedition."

Chi Lin's heart leaped. Such a thing would please her because it was Wu Ming-kuan's dream. Any quiet reservations she had about San-ehr dissolved. She stood and curtsied to him.

"Such a thing would settle his heart . . ."

"And your heart also, mistress. A ghost wife is best served when the progeny of a spirit union is honored as Heaven-blessed. I know what I know. I am a man who likes the feel of a horse between his legs and steel in his fist. No ghost tale about that. But the world is what it is and my departed mother is both honored by the white and by her fictions." He stood. "I thank you for your hospitality, sister-in-law. Keep your silent vigil at our family's heart and, when the time comes, our work will be known to the Son of Heaven, whoever He may be."

Chi Lin watched the man strut out to the courtyard. She would recall his words many times over the years, even after he was wounded at the Battle of Chiang-kang and ceased to visit the household. He had, in this one instance, taught her much. It was time for her to apply what she had learned, so she summoned Ying Ling and demanded a match for Wu Chou-fa — with no bound feet and to a woman from the House of T'ou.

Chapter Four

The Cold Palace

1

Abject sadness. Few things broached Chi Lin with deep sorrow, but the Villa was a place which, when first encountered, drew her naturally abundant soft spirit down into her unbound feet. She knew sorrow and, with the exception of her concerns over Sapphire, which always lingered, this first trip to the Villa left an indelible impression on her. She had been diligent until then.

Chi Lin had met with Ying Ling and managed to arrange a meeting between old Wu T'ai-po, Wu Chou-fa and the T'ou clan. The young T'ou maiden, Moon Flower, was more than exceptional and immediately received the red tea pouch from Chou-fa. Moon Flower was older than Honeysuckle, more austere, but a stunning beauty with high rosy cheeks and deep marble eyes. Chi Lin noticed that Chou-fa could not shift his glance away from her, not even for a moment. And her feet were unbound. The bride price was high, but the dowry was nearly twice that of Honeysuckle's, a sign that Wu San-ehr was correct in his assumption that the T'ou greatly desired this match. The only untoward event was that Wu T'ai-po fell asleep during the ritual. But he was an old man now and allowances were made.

By the time Chi Lin set forth with Wu Chou-fa to the Villa, Wu San-ehr's workforce was already shouldering the restoration. The day was rainy — light rain at first, but a harder downpour as the hours crept apace. Mi Tso-tze attended her mistress beside the chair while Wu Chou-fa rode high on his war horse — a gift from his uncle. The Villa was to the east, beyond the Gui estate, which had placed it in the worst position when the great storm had struck during that fateful autumn. Chi Lin had passed the place many times on the tour, but never saw beyond the walls, although she did recall those walls being well maintained when Wu Liang-tze was still alive. Now they were battered, devoid of paint, shy many bricks and patched in odd places. The gate was intact, but the doors were splintered, unpainted and stripped of metal ornamentation.

Once inside, Wu Chou-fa halted, surveying the courtyard from his high horse. He was silent, a cold, wet silence, purporting much disappointment and distress. Chi Lin disembarked, stepping into the mud, Mi Tso-tze sheltering her under a *san-tze*. Despite the rain, the soldiers were heaving debris into pits, their bare backs shimmering with sweat and rain drops. It was a feeble start.

"Does anyone live here?" Mi Tso-tze muttered.

"I am afraid they do," Chi Lin replied.

The main hall's roof was crushed over a sagging verandah, the walls braced by bamboo struts and overgrown with weeds and wisteria gone to seed. There were several other dwellings in better condition, but hardly the product of a great house, although here and there a wink of splendor announced the past. A pool with a rock garden showed that at one time it was a showcase in the far courtyard; and there was a fading blue shrine with a headless Buddha settled in the shadows.

Wu Chou-fa dismounted.

"It needs work," he said, his voice breaking. "Auntie, I remember this place well and it was teaming with fancy pavilions and luxurious boardwalks."

"It shall be so again, my lord," she said, unconvincingly. "Your Uncle is generous and your brother has pledged to make it worthy. The T'ou have contributed mightily to its repair."

Wu Chou-fa turned to her. He was suddenly animated.

"You are getting wet, Auntie. You will catch cold and become ill. Please. Please find shelter from the rain."

Chi Lin took heed and sought an intact pavilion across the courtyard. It was chilled inside, but covered. There was a peculiar odor. Chi Lin was disturbed by ghostly sounds.

"Who is there?" she asked.

"Perhaps we should find another place," Mi Tso-tze suggested.

But before they could, a woman emerged from the shadows. She wore a tattered robe, her hair unkempt and was the source of the peculiar odor.

"Why have you come?" the woman said. "Why are the soldiers destroying our home?"

"They come to repair it."

"But why? This is the Cold Palace. We are the wives of the demon spirit that dwells here."

"We?"

Suddenly, Chi Lin noticed several women. She thought she recognized a few faces, at least glimmers of what she remembered to be Wu Liang-tze's wives. They tottered about on bound feet, their wrapping hardly hiding the hideous contortions of bone and dead flesh. She recalled that since Wu Liang-tze was disowned by the household and since his body was left in pieces, his spirit would naturally roam the neighborhood, never finding his way to *the Yellow Springs*.

Chi Lin girded her nerves and reached out for the woman.
"You were his wife?"
"His sixth wife," the creature said. "We are the later wives. The first wife is already dead. The others fled and some more went back to the Sojourn of Heaven's Eye. They have not fared well there, so we have remained here."
"What do you eat? Where do you sleep?"
"Sleep, when it comes, is best never disturbed. Food, we beg. Some grow beans. Some stew tree bark. Not many trees now, except the Mulberry. But even they are gone now."
Wu Chou-fa entered.
"Auntie," he said. "There are women in every place here."
Chi Lin stepped aside revealing the sixth wife.
"They are the remnants of Wu Liang-tze's misdeeds," she said. "They are in more need of repair than this Villa."
"I agree," he said. "I will ask the soldiers to cease their clearing and gather these women to a single place so we can assess what should be done."
"They need a *yi-sheng*, my lord. And the place needs an army of *fa-shr* before you go any further. While one uncle fosters restoration through his generosity, another uncle haunts the place and needs to be expunged."

Abject sadness. Chi Lin remembered this day, even when she came here later when the halls were restored, the fountain was ripe with *koi* and the courtyard teaming with happy children, the sons and daughters of Wu Chou-fa playing and being taught in a sturdy new school house. She remembered the wives and the children and the remnants of servants, bellies distended, feet racked and exposed to the elements. Some were beyond saving and would need tender guidance to what would prove to be their graves. The redeemable needed shelter, first in the spare quarters in the Wu household, and later in small courtyard houses in town. It had become Chi Lin's private venture to assure that those who survived were maintained for the rest of their lives. Whenever she encountered them, she had only one feeling — abject sadness. Perhaps she should have been angry at Wu Liang-tze. After all, his actions against her would warrant it, an extension of his vile life beyond the grave. But, in truth, it could have been prevented after the bitter harvest of that deadly storm. The Wu household could have mustered its forces to address the Villa's plight even though it had made the restoration of the *ji-tzao* the priority. But who could Chi Lin blame? Wu T'ai-po? It was not her place to blame her benefactor. After all, it was the Old Lady of the House who said *Purple Sage, you mend the household*. Thus from the abject sadness of her first encounter at the Villa, Chi Lin mended the household and mended it well.

2

It was a busy time for Mistress Purple Sage. She still tended the worms and led the household in sewing, repairs and, to her great pleasure, gave Wu Lin-kua advice on gardening, the Master of the House ambivalent to the beautification of the grounds, but enjoying the sight of a blossoming garden nonetheless. When Honeysuckle's time came, Willow, who had remained installed as chief handmaiden, sought Chi Lin's help. Honeysuckle had a difficult delivery and was brought to the kitchen to help bar Ling-kua from the noise of the event. He still paced in the *ke-ting*, but at each attempt to enter the kitchen, Chi Lin quietly blocked his way.

"She must not die," he snapped.

"She is not ill, my lord," Chi Lin replied. "A hundred million miracles happen every day. It is as natural as rain."

"But rain can be a nasty business."

"It is a cleansing business and nourishes the good earth with tears from the dragon. If you must pace, do so in the courtyard. It is better suited to it, my lord."

Wu Lin-kua would argue with anyone else, but Auntie Purple Sage was insurmountable. So he turned and fled to the courtyard.

Honeysuckle howled, much to Chi Lin's chagrin.

"You must suffer in silence," she whispered. "Grasp my hand instead and push steadily."

So Honeysuckle bruised Purple Sage's hand and still howled like a wounded water buffalo. But it came — a son. A whisper ran through Chi Lin's mind as she cut the cord and inspected the tiny penis and swollen testicles. *No bound feet*. It was prophetic. She gathered the child in a blanket and gave it to its mother. She remembered when she had held Wu Ming-kuan for the first time and how wonderful it felt. But Honeysuckle would not be separated from her son. Of course there would be an *amah*, but the mother would remain the boy's *mother*.

Wu T'ai-po was called, Willow helping him into the kitchen, where the child was shown to him, the genitals revealed and the old man raising his hands to Heaven.

"He is the ugliest child I have ever seen."

"Ugly, yes," Chi Lin said. "He is a vision to be shunned."

She laughed, as did the old man. Then, as if the tide could be held back by a bamboo twig, Wu Lin-kua rushed over the threshold to behold his son. He held him in his hands, lifting him to the rafters.

"Such a horrid thing," he laughed. "A terrible gift has been bestowed on me."

Then he too laughed, before rushing away with the child to show the journeymen. Within two days he ordered the school house to be restored and began interviewing for a scholar teacher, now that P'ing Chin had gone to *the Yellow Springs*. The scholar chosen, Lu Wen-wei, was a bit young, but recommended by Chi Sheng, having been a candidate for the National Examinations twice. It would be a few years before the boy (and his two brothers) would be installed in the class room, but Wu Lin-kua meant to mould the teacher along his own lines, that of the *Cheng-chu* school as prescribed by the Sung philosopher Chu Xi, combining practical compositional styles and empirical observations. All this Wu Lin-kua had formulated before his son was three days old.

Jasmine deigned to come see her grandson, and when the child was not in readiness for her viewing, she stomped away. It would be three days before she returned in a more civil mood to chastise her daughter-in-law for keeping such an ugly child from her sight for so long. The *amah* was assigned. But over the many days and moons and seasons, Honeysuckle would not be separated from Wu Tien-po, for so the boy was named. She insisted that the *amah* bring him around twice daily. This endeared Honeysuckle to Chi Lin because, although the child could be viewed as a doll in the hands of a young girl, it kept a circle of love about the boy and blocked any interference from the ever-sour Jasmine.

3

One family concern that never seemed to disappear was Sapphire. She was a pretty child, despite her moods and tantrums, and now budded into a comely young woman with too much time on her hands and not married yet, although the time was coming. Chi Lin already had ideas, but she could not imagine any county family wanting Sapphire. As eccentric as Sapphire grew (she still carried her tattered dolly about on most days), she blossomed early, and the journeymen buzzed about her like bees. Journeymen could be kept away, the gates of the Silver Silence outside their business, but this was not the case with the custodian.

Po Bo outgrew his diminutive wiry monkeyness, sprouting broadly at the shoulders and sporting a handsome countenance. He was more clever than smart and, by the time he assumed the role of custodian, commanded several handy servants and the kitchen staff, although he took care around Mo Li. He loved to lark still, something Chi Lin did not mind because it amused her and added life to the Silver Silence. Po Bo played tricks on the kitchen staff and on little Butterfly, who would feign anger, but had become game enough to follow anger with subtle flirting. Chi Lin was lax with Butterfly, who was helpful to Tso-tze, but otherwise lived an idyllic existence within the Silver Silence. She had her own small alcove and seemed never to have longed to return to her *ji-tzao* roots. She never asked for her family and they never made inquiries after her. Her only aversion was to Sapphire, who had taken it into her head that Butterfly was an interloper. This was Chi Lin's fault, and she knew it. She treated both girls equally, although it was emphasized that Sapphire was a Wu woman of Household, a daughter of Wu Hung-lin, and little Butterfly was nothing more than a lucky waif and, at best, a ward of the Silver Silence. There were several fights between the two girls, mostly provoked by Sapphire, but finished by little Butterfly. These altercations involved small gifts — a hairpin, a button, or a pomade given to little Butterfly by either Chi Lin or Mi Tso-tze. Inevitably the dispute was refereed by Po Bo.

Chi Lin was careful to assure Po Bo had been taken to the pleasure house by the journeymen and introduced to women, if, for no other reason, as a reward for a job well done. Some marriage would be arranged for him, but unlike the clan settlements, servants generally chose their own mates because no families were involved. Chi Lin assumed Po Bo would fancy one of the kitchen staff at some point, or perhaps one of the sewing or silk girls. She even imagined that he might be a good husband for little Butterfly. But Sapphire had other notions and soon Po Bo was tantalized, a dangerous thing for a servant in an established house. Of course, Chi Lin knew of such things, the memory of Gao Lin being more than a memory but manifested in an apprenticed Wu son learning ship's rigging at the port. But Chi Lin was clever and Gao Lin was astute. Sapphire was a silly girl and Po Bo was prone to boasting.

Po Bo was industrious, Chi Lin pleased with his service. She liked the boy now turned to manhood, but would be loathed to lose him to silly notions. So she considered moving Sapphire to the Villa after the renovations were completed. Unfortunately, Chi Lin was in no position to make this decision. She approached Lin-kua on the matter, but he was lost to fatherhood and scarcely paid attention. He referred the issue to Jasmine, who took a position opposite to Purple Sage for no other reason than to be contrary. However, Jasmine's contrary position held sway and Sapphire remained in the Silver Silence.

Chi Lin summoned Po Bo.

"Yes, mistress," he said. "What is needed?"

"Sit, Po Bo," she said. They were on the verandah and in clear view of much activity. "A word on a matter for concern."

With this, Po Bo did not sit, but rather cramped himself into a subservient ball.

"What have I done to displease you, mistress?" he wailed. "Do not send me away, mistress."

"Nonsense. Stop this at once." Po Bo muttered, but came to order. "I asked you to sit."

He did so, but peered at her like a shy calf.

"I did not mean it," he whispered.

"You have done nothing to displease me . . . yet," she replied. "I mean that you should become a man."

"I am a man, mistress."

"Yes. And a man must take a wife."

"I know this to be true, mistress."

"Is there one whom you favor above any other?"

Po Bo paused. His lips trembled. Chi Lin could almost read his thoughts. She saw his lips forming to say a name, a name she did not want to hear.

"You cannot have Sapphire," she said. "She is a daughter of the house and, worthy as you may be, it can never happen."

"She is lovely, mistress."

"And she is unkind to draw you to impossible notions. She will leave some day, to be given to another household as her sisters will be. You must promise me, Po Bo, that you will not hold any hope for Sapphire's company."

She could see he was upset, but, as cruel as it was, it was necessary.

"What shall I do, mistress?"

"Resist her calls, except as custodian. Avert your eyes. I will find you someone suitable."

Po Bo looked up quickly.

"Not Gu Fei or Shan T'o, mistress. I would rather live my life without a wife than have such creatures."

"No," she said laughing. "Leave it to me."

Chi Lin needed to act swiftly, because despite Po Bo's good intentions to avert eyes and be custodian to Sapphire, Sapphire went out of her way to coax Po Bo into compromising situations.

"I will lose him, Tso-tze," Chi Lin complained to her handmaiden. "I would summon Ying Ling today to arrange a marriage for Sapphire, but her sisters must come first."

"Does Po Bo care for Yu Li?" Mi Tso-tze asked.

Little Butterfly was indeed Chi Lin's chief candidate. However, she was younger than Po Bo by four years.

"We shall see," Chi Lin said. "We shall see."

4

Sapphire rarely left the Silver Silence, but one day, when Chi Lin had overheard her toying with Po Bo to the point where the custodian found a corner and wept, she summoned Sapphire.

"You must come with me," Chi Lin said, sternly.

Mistress Purple Sage was not prone to sternness, but in this case she wanted the girl to be stunned by the tone.

"But Auntie, I am not well."

"You are well enough. Yu Li will help you don traveling clothes. You shall see another place within the Wu household."

Sapphire did as she was told. Chi Lin took care as not to stir Jasmine's hive. But the opportunity was ripe — the Villa, still in restoration's flux, presented a formidable face to anyone unfamiliar with the outer world. So, with Mi Tso-tze and Yu Li in tow, the carry chairs took the journey to the Villa's walls. At the sight, Chi Lin had only one feeling — abject sadness. The walls were brighter now and repaired, soldiers on bamboo walks shouldering bricks and cleanser. Still Chi Lin could not shake the sadness.

"What is this place, Auntie?" Sapphire asked.

"It was the house of your uncle, Wu Liang-tze. It will be the house of your brother, Wu Chou-fa. How would you like to live here?"

Sapphire began to weep.

"I have heard of this place, Auntie. There are ghosts here and demons. You would not make me leave the Silver Silence for such a place? You would not?"

"Just take a look," Chi Lin said.

The porters carried the chairs into the courtyard. Roofs were being repaired, the shrine renewed and servants hurried about preparing for the time when Chou-fa would bring his bride across the threshold. Still, the Cold Palace feeling lingered, the remaining wives, clean now and fed, still drifted about in the shadows like wraiths. Sapphire twitched and continued to weep.

"It is not so bad," Chi Lin said. "You could have a pavilion of your own and even one for your dolly."

"And could I come back to visit you?"

"I would try to visit you. Do you like the prospect?"

Sapphire decidedly did not. So Chi Lin gently ordered the chairs turned, but before she ordered their departure, she halted, turning to the daughter of the house.

"Promise me not to abuse my household, Sapphire. Your dolly is a toy, but my custodian is not. He is flesh and blood and sensitive to his duty and loyalty to me. I need his services. But there are places within the house to shelter your moods and fancies other than the Silver Silence. Promise to respect my household."

"I will, Auntie. I am a good girl."

Chi Lin knew that this was not the ultimate conversion, because Sapphire's moods were baked in the marrow, but at least the daughter of the house knew there could be a punishment for her actions despite Jasmine's objections. Mistress Purple Sage glanced at Mi Tso-tze, who moved the porters forward. Her assistant helped. Chi Lin thought: *Yes, it will be Yu Li for Po Bo or the Cold Palace for Sapphire.* Such was her resolve.

Chapter Five

Infringement

1

With the marriage bond to the T'ou household concluded and the Second Son with Moon Flower ensconced within the restored Villa, Chi Lin turned to the marriage arrangements for the Wu daughters. There was no rush, because the household bonds were less crucial, and silver would drain from the household coffers. But Chi Lin nonetheless asked Ying Ling to scout a good match for Pearl. It took five moons.

As Ying Ling explained:

"The men of this county are looking for baubles with bound feet, Mistress Purple Sage. It is the fashion. But Pearl has much going for her."

"Including a large dowry."

"The larger the better."

But Chi Lin knew that unbound feet had better advantages in a marriage, so she held out until Ying Ling put forth a match to the Third Son of the Yuan clan, a moderately wealthy family who owned a fleet of transport barges — a handy alliance for the Wu household, who already used Yuan shipping to the capital and to the northern plain for salt. The dowry was stiff and the groom was ten years older than Pearl, but it would be not long before this daughter of the house departed in her bride's chair as tearfully as Chi Lin had so many years ago. Purple Sage prepared Pearl for the best.

"Your husband is alive," she said. "And although your father has been a warm spirit to me, I never encountered him in the flesh."

Jasmine avoided the event as did Lotus, who sent her felicitations, but was too immobile to walk to the courtyard to bid her daughter farewell in person. Jade was sad to see her sister go. She hinted that she should like to wear the red gown soon, but Chi Lin advised her to be patient, that *beauty such as yours will seize the heart of many gentry sons.*

There were no takers for Sapphire.

On the day when Pearl departed, Chi Lin drifted back to the Silver Silence with Mi Tso-tze and Yu Li in tow. They were greeted on the threshold by Po Bo.

"He is here, mistress."

"Who is here, Po Bo?"

The last time the custodian had made this announcement, Wu San-ehr had taken his comfort in the Silver Silence's *ke-ting*. But it could not be Wu San-ehr, because he was in the north serving Prince Chu Di. Po Bo did not answer, but nodded in the direction of the pavilion. On the verandah sat a wizen man, his head raised and his eyes bright. Chi Lin sighed.

"Tso-tze," she said.

"Yes, mistress."

"Take Yu Li to the kitchen."

Mi Tso-tze curtsied and obeyed. Chi Lin took Po Bo by the arm.

"Where is Sapphire?"

"She is at her place playing with her doll."

Chi Lin noticed that the courtyard was unusually clear, the servants and workman absent. But it was late in the day and things were winding down. She had invested in the digging of a root cellar near the South wall for vegetables, but also as a shelter in case of another *T'ai-feng*. The last diggers were just finishing for the day. But when they approached the pavilion, they gave it wide berth having noticed the man resting there.

"This is unusual," Po Bo said.

"I agree," Chi Lin replied. She reached the edge of the house. "Stay near, but keep your distance."

"Yes, mistress."

With Po Bo hovering on the verge, Chi Lin ascended the verandah, where she paused, and then curtsied.

"Father-in-law," she said. "You have come."

"At long last," he said, his voice broken, shattered by his long life. "It is lovely here. It is as I remember it."

"I have tried to make it hospitable."

"You have succeeded, Purple Sage. You have succeeded."

He nodded. She took the liberty to sit beside him, as she did when he had interviewed her years ago in his *ke-ting*. He smiled and closed his eyes.

"I see her, you know."

"She was fair, I have been told."

"Yes, Snapdragon would have described her beauty to you. Lao Lao would have told you of her kindness." He sighed. "She was a mighty acquisition and gave me my happiest hours, not that the First Wife disappointed as the mother of my sons. But the industry of the Jade Heart Pavilion gives way to the poetry of the Silver Silence. Songs graced the air and the sound of the water cascading from the great rock into the pool eased my days." He sighed again. "Eased my days."

Chi Lin could see the Second Wife, although she had never known her. She could imagine her form, but knew well her robes as they had graced her own body for years. The perfumed air then was as it was now, and Snapdragon combing tresses and Lao Lao telling his tales filled the courtyard with life beyond death.

Chi Lin heard the gentle sighs of her father-in-law give way to snores. He was beyond her now — in the arms of the fairy form who once ruled the Silver Silence. Chi Lin was glad that the place had been restored to his liking and that it pleased him. She tapped his arm, hoping to wake him and offer him some tea, but he did not stir. His snoring was less, and his breathing subtle, if at all. She knew that when the sun set beyond the western wall, Wu T'ai-po would join his lost love. The household would be donning the white once gain.

2

All things come to an end. As it is with the masters of great houses, it is with the rulers of great Empires. Thus the Hung Wu reign period ended when the founder of the Ming perished. The dragon throne passed to his grandson and the Chien Wen reign period commenced. It was declared throughout the land and in Yan-cheng it was no different. Walls were plastered with broadsides proclaiming the new emperor, who was a boy of seventeen summers and quite fixed on keeping his throne against the odds of several uncles, the sons of the Hung Wu emperor. In fact, beside the broadsides were lists of crimes committed by the Imperial uncles and how they were among the worst demons in the land. This included Prince Chu Di. It was clear to anyone who could read that the emperor's uncles were not long for this world.

Although Chi Lin could read, such imperial announcements meant little to her. Emperors came and went. However, a visit to the Ya-men told her a different story. Ai-lo Wun-kua was concerned for the salt monopoly certificates. He explained that the House of Wu was bonded to Prince Chu Di by dint of Wu San-ehr. If the new emperor wanted to disturb his uncle's bailiwick, he could revoke the monopoly certificates and reassign them to another family. This made Chi Lin anxious. Still it was not her business to resolve or even discuss such rumors, even with Wu Lin-kua, who she hoped was astute enough to work out the dangers for himself. In either event, as long as the Wu donned the white, the dynasty would respect them and not bring change.

There had been many changes over the years in Yan-cheng's governance also. P'o T'ai-kuan was no longer the Superintendent. He was reassigned to Hu-t'ai county in An-hui. The new Superintendent, Chou Mai-xin, was of an active breed, keeping regulated hours for his magisterial duties and a sharp review of memorials and other requests. But he was aloof otherwise, never visiting the Wu Household or any other household at Yan-cheng. If you wanted official business transacted, you needed an appointment and a purse for the clerks. Whenever Chi Lin visited Ai-lo Wun-kua and his family, Chou Mai-xin would look down from the parapet and sneer. Clearly a woman in the Ya-men was against his views. But the Imperial Commissioner had the right to guests, so this sanction did not go beyond a sneer.

Chi Lin enjoyed Ai-lo Wun-kua's company. They discussed the classics and sometimes he would allude to the central book of his own beliefs, which Chi Lin did not understand. It was quite unstructured, commencing with four fairy tales about a carpenter's son who became a teacher, but for some unfathomable reason willingly died for his teachings. They were inoffensive teachings, or so Chi Lin surmised, but he died nonetheless and then, like a *jiang-shi*, the hopping corpse walker, came back from the dead. The rest of the book was letters from followers of the invisible god and the *jiang-shi*. She did not care for the book. It lacked the beautiful logic of the Classics, but she respected the Ai-lo for their dedication to it. They did not pray at an ancestral shrine, but prayed when and where they wanted, even in the outhouse. They prepared their food with care and avoided pig flesh and shellfish. Ai-lo Wun-kua only had one wife and would not take another as this strange invisible-god belief forbade him. What mystified Chi Lin most was that the eldest son was not married, and yet the second son sought a wife, and not through the *mei-ren*, but by his own acquaintance. It was a puzzlement, but she respected it.

Ai-lo Wun-kua was worried about the new emperor, who was surrounded, according to court gossip, by eunuchs — eunuchs who mistrusted a Mongol to administer either the salt or iron monopoly. Chi Lin's father once said *Ai-lo Wun-kua should wear an owl on his shoulder*, an anxious but wise course if he wanted to keep his position. Now Prince Chu Di was marching on the capital, presumably to protect the young emperor from the controlling courtiers.

"I have met the Prince," Ai-lo Wun-kua told Chi Lin. "He is not a man to mollify a boy of seventeen summers and leave him sitting on the throne. You must not tell others, but if the Prince controls the capital, the monopoly will be safe."

Chi Lin wished Prince Chu Di well and would burn some red paper prayers for him. He was Wu San-ehr's liege lord after all. But Ai-lo Wun-kua feared that the young emperor would not sit still for control.

"His forces have defeated Prince Chu Chuan and now those armies fight under the Chien Wen banner and might be marching through our county soon. *That* you should tell your Master of the House."

Mistress Purple Sage took the Commissioner's advice. She told Wu Lin-kua about the imperial army and, to her delight, he had already known.

"Do not concern yourself with this business, Auntie," he said. "You arrange marriages and keep us honest in our industrial ventures — you and the Chi clan. I will not expect you to stand guard at the gate with a halberd. I have journeymen for that."

Journeymen he had. Under his father, there were sixteen, but now there were over forty — enough men to defend the Wu walls if need be. Enough men to stave off any incursion into the *ji-tzao*. So Chi Lin retired to her tasks quite content that Wu Lin-kua was indeed the Master of the House.

3

"The sky bleeds, mistress," Po Bo shouted at the threshold.

It was evening and Chi Lin rested, reading a commentary on the *Book of Changes*. She sat with *Raisin Cake* in her lap, the dog yelping upon hearing Po Bo's cry. Soon Mi Tso-tze and Yu Li stirred, rushing to the door and gazing at the sky. The courtyard was filled with much discussion. Chi Lin pushed *Raisin Cake* aside, rolled the book up, carefully tying both fasteners, and then she went to the threshold calmly, but with resolve.

"See, mistress," Po Bo stammered. "The sky bleeds."

Chi Lin peered up, and then moved onto the verandah to get a better view. The sky had turned red, but, near the horizon, just over the wall, it flared orange and tinged yellow.

"It is fire, Po Bo." She looked at her servants huddling in the courtyard. "It is only fire," she announced. "It is too distant to burn us."

But despite her attempt to reassure her staff, her words did not reassure herself. Fire at a distance it may be, but it came from the town and was near enough to be assessed as the Ya-men. The market could catch fire from any number of causes, but the Ya-men had vigorous routines to prevent such calamities. She suspected this was not an accidental fire, but a deliberate act of opportunity.

"It is the Ya-men, is it not, mistress?" Tso-tze said, quietly so as not to alarm Yu Li or the others.

"I cannot speculate, Tso-tze, but let us hope it is some trick of the eyes."

Chi Lin gathered her staff about her, and then went to the Jade Heart. She reasoned that the entire family should be assembled now to assuage fear and consternation. In this she was correct. Wu Lin-kua had already emerged from his pavilion with his journeymen at hand. The new Lady of the House stood by his side. Even Jasmine and her entourage tripped over the boardwalk from the Blue Heaven Pavilion to see what was amiss. She went to her son, curtsied, and then took up a position of authority. Chi Lin could only wait for Lin-kua's instructions. But before they could come, the outer gate opened, revealing the tall form of the Imperial Commissioner on the threshold. His entire family stood behind him. They were scantily clad, their faces smudged with ash. In the street several servants nervously tended two ox-carts.

Wu Lin-kua greeted his visitors, the Wu household drifting into the courtyard behind him, buzzing with discussion.

"What has happened, neighbor?" Wu Lin-kua asked Ai-lo Wun-kua.

"Misfortune," the Commissioner replied, his voice calm as if he was returning a greeting on the street. "Misery visits all lives in each life, and so it has come to my family."

"Enter," Wu Lin-kua said.

"If I enter," Ai-lo said, "accept the recriminations."

"How can it be?" Lin-kua replied. "You are the Commissioner and I am the monopoly holder. What better fit can there be?"

"That is true when times resist change, but I hold my warrant by a thin hair."

"Has the Ya-men burned?"

"Not entirely. But my portion is ruined. Imperial troops have skirmished with the army of Prince Chu Di. I am not sure who has the upper hand, but His Majesty's army retreated and, in their wake, sent me a message from the court."

Ai-lo Wun-kua held up his hand. It was wrapped in green silk, but Chi Lin could clearly see it had been burnt.

"But have they retreated?" Wu Lin-kua asked.

"They have. They may return. Assassins might try their best. Until then, we are free to live in any salt *ji-tzao* that would chance our hiding."

"Nonsense," Lin-kua said.

Jasmine stepped forward. She did not say a word, but stared at her son with venomous intent. Chi Lin saw that the First Wife was dead set against this non-Han family from entering the house. Still, Jasmine dared not speak. But Chi Lin was beyond such feeble restraint. She also stepped forward and stood beside Jasmine. Wu Li-kua frowned — at *both* women, no doubt.

"May I be so bold?" Chi Lin asked, her voice sweet and charming.

"You may not," Jasmine snapped.

Lin-kua shook his head. Such a tense display would bring shame on the house if revealed so openly and before the neighbors.

"It is a mere observation," Chi Lin said. "One of neighborly good feeling."

She curtsied to Wu Lin-kua. Then to everyone's surprise, Honeysuckle stepped forward.

"I would like to hear what you want to say, Auntie Purple Sage."

Wu Lin-kua's breath hitched, but Chi Lin did not allow for his further intervention. She curtsied to Honeysuckle.

"It is just a matter of logistics. Why should we house guests of quality in our courtyard where the nights are cold and the days are brazen? I have nearly completed the cellar in the Silver Silence. It would be happy to accommodate so high a personage as the Imperial Commissioner."

She concluded with a deep curtsey, Tso-tze and Yu Li also following her lead. She even thought Po Bo made a half-bow. Jasmine scrunched her shoulders, and then turned away. Honeysuckle seemed pleased. Wu Lin-kua sighed, but then assumed a hospitable pose.

"Then it is settled," he said. "You are welcome to stay here until your house is repaired and your position is settled. As you can see, I am fortunate to have a stream of useful suggestions from the womenfolk in this household. But the decision is mine, and I have made it."

Ai-lo Wun-kua accepted it. The family entered and the ox-carts rolled in. To Chi Lin's delight, the carts contained mounds of books that would have been otherwise burned. These found a home in the Silver Silence's *ke-ting* which more and more resembled a library than a drawing room. Chi Lin was also happy for Ai-lo Wun-kua's company and for that of his wife. The children were all adults now and none were married yet, following their beliefs — all in good time and when their invisible god saw fit. There were two sons and four daughters, all well behaved, soft spoken and dutiful to their parents and their religious rites. The root cellar was a perfect shelter to keep their practices private and away from curious eyes. Among the carrots and mung beans, they managed to create a temporary household.

Ai-lo Wun-kua explained many things to Chi Lin. She listened and learned, but kept her opinions to herself — mostly. She was not surprised that the superintendent, Chou Mai-xin, had not raised a hand to help the Mongol commissioner, probably assuming that if the Chien Wen Emperor kept his throne, he would not support any superintendent that gave aid to a deposed official. Still, Chou Mai-xin had agreed to help in the restoration of the commissioner's house, a slow task that could bide time while he monitored the political winds. Had the Chien Wen Emperor prevailed, he could claim the house was a guest pavilion, certainly in need of restoration. If the Chien Wen Emperor fell, the superintendent could report to the victor that he was in full support of Ai-lo Wun-kua. Chou Mai-xin was a crafty beast.

"He plays the game," Ai-lo Wun-kua told Chi Lin, "but not well. A new commissioner would see through it and have him reported, and, if Prince Chu Di prevails, he will have his head on the Ya-men gates."

Still, one night an Imperial envoy banged at the Wu House gates demanding information on the whereabouts of a fugitive Mongol official, who was known to be hiding in the county. Of course, Wu Lin-kua denied any knowledge and allowed the envoy and his men to enter and search. And search they did. Po Bo, who happened to be in the Jade Heart, was told to rush to the Silver Silence and give them warning. Wu Lin-kua then summoned his mother to the Jade Heart, where he had Honeysuckle and Willow whisk her from room to room avoiding the envoy and his guard least she speak and reveal the hiding place, which she would have, given the chance. Chi Lin, Po Bo and Tso-tze rushed into the cellar, where Ai-lo Wun-kua and his family were transformed into kitchen servants, donning old robes and sack hats, while their finery was stuffed quickly into the world of turnips and sorghum. The cellar was sealed as best as possible. The envoy, who searched every nook of the above ground Silver Silence, never guessed that Mongol rabbits and voles hid nervously underground awaiting the inspection to be completed.

While Ai-lo Wun-kua survived such infringements, Chi Lin was frazzled by them. She was also shaken by Jasmine's daily visits to the Silver Silence. The First Wife had not visited the pavilion in years, but now she made it a point to come and observe. When she entered the courtyard, the servants would scatter as if a dragon invaded the precinct looking for a sacrifice. Purple Sage could not ask her to leave. It would have been improper. But it was clear that Jasmine did not care about Purple Sage and the Silver Silence. She wanted to monitor the Commissioner and his family.

"Why is your eldest son still unmarried?" she snapped at Ai-lo Wun-kua as he passed her going toward the *ke-ting* for his daily discussion with Chi Lin, who stood quietly on the threshold and listened.

"Good day to you, mistress," he said politely, bowing. "The sun is bright today, do you not think?"

"Is that why he has no wife and why you have only one wife?"

"There is a place for all beliefs under Heaven, mistress."

"When you walk in the open fields and practice heresy, it will be visited upon you and you only. But when you live under a Han roof, that roof is bound to cave in."

"Roofs cave in for many reasons, mistress. Storms, design faults, old age, but in my experience, taking only one wife or not marrying at all is not among them."

"All things depend on all things. You cannot move one rock without disturbing the one above it."

"Then, I promise you, mistress, I shall be careful when I visit a quarry."

He turned his back on her. She spit, but managed a last word.

"Your kind ruled us for too long. We were rid of you. We would be rid of you yet again."

Ai-lo Wun-kua halted. He turned slowly, caching Jasmine's eye.

"My kind never ruled you," he said, more sternly. "We were overcome by the golden river of your culture, but never mastered the black iron of your rule. Our ways conquered, but failed in the governance. But I believe that all under Heaven would fail in governing you."

He turned about and marched to the verandah. Jasmine cursed him, and then left the Silver Silence. Chi Lin emerged onto the porch.

"I wish I could stand up to her like you have," she said to Ai-lo Wun-kua. "But she is the First Wife and I am the Fourth Wife — a ghost bride and Auntie to the children, even to my own . . ." She choked. "No matter. Perhaps your words might scare her away."

"I am afraid she will be back tomorrow looking to engage me again, or my old lady or my eldest son. She is a spider, mistress. She weaves a web for one purpose only. To feed on those beneath her superior eyes. But my invisible God says when you cast buns on the river it returns to you many times over. In the First Wife's case, the bun is stale and the river will dry up leaving her parched in the shallows."

Chi Lin was enlivened by such talk, but she wished it was not inspired by her sister-in-law. Still, despite Ai-lo Wun-kua's rejection of fallen roofs for superstitious reasons, there would be consequences for his infringement on the House of Wu's hospitality.

Chapter Six

A Different Arrangement

1

 Both Ai-lo brothers were handsome, or so Chi Lin assessed, which made them pleasant to observe and gentle company. Neither smacked of Mongol rough house nor the smell of the northlands. Neither had ever been outside the county and, strict to their parent's beliefs, found pride in a quiet existence — studious, pious and industrious, aiding their father in his commissioner's work, obliterating the need for a proxy. Their comeliness also brought anxious moments, because it sparked Sapphire to flirt, especially with the eldest son, Ai-lo Tu-fan. But he showed no interest in her. He was polite, listened to her abysmal chatter about nothing of importance, and then would leave her company — Sapphire sometimes pouting for the rest of the afternoon. This did not escape Chi Lin's attention or Po Bo's. As a result, the custodian performed his duties in relation to the guests, but did so with grumbles and sharp asides. Chi Lin knew the cause.
 Chi Lin wondered about the first son, because he was not married. Although his ways did not insist upon marriage, there were few *yi-shen* families in the county with available daughters. If Ai-lo Wun-kua wanted to continue his line, he would need to send Ai-lo Tu-fan to the capital, where a *yi-shen* enclave thrived. But perhaps Tu-fan was disinclined to do so. Perhaps he preferred a *cut-sleeve affair* and to *share a peach* with a young gentleman. Although Chi Lin never broached the issue, she perceived the Commissioner was not well disposed to such arrangements. She supposed that if he were, as long as his son did his duty and preserved the line, a *cut-sleeve affair* might be sanctioned. There was, however, no question about the second son, Ai-lo Yun-chi.
 Ai-lo Yun-chi was of an easier spirit. When Sapphire failed to provoke a favorable response from Ai-lo Tu-fan, she shifted her attentions to Ai-lo Yun-chi. He played her game to the extent that he told her silly stories and made her laugh. When she flirted with him, he responded in kind, but never to an extent to worry Chi Lin. She could tell a gentleman's banter from overtures of love. However, Sapphire was not as astute. She began to follow the

second son around, until he *did* change his posture to that of his brother's.

"Move her to the Villa, mistress," Mi Tso-tze suggested. "She is sillier by the day and to risk anything more would cause gossip."

Chi Lin wondered. Gossip was bearable. She had learned how to ignore it. But gossip also brought Jasmine on its heels. She thought to ask Wu Lin-kua if perhaps Sapphire could visit her brother at the Villa, at least until the danger to the Ai-lo clan passed. Speaking to Sapphire was useless. She lived more and more in her own world. Then an idea came. Chi Lin visited with her sister-in-law Lotus after an afternoon of feeding the worms. In the Crimson Blossom Pavilion, the hulky Second Wife enjoyed her idyllic existence — ingesting delicacies and basking in sleep's glory. She was courteous to Mistress Purple Sage and most likely enjoyed the deference displayed. But Chi Lin was there to consult with Jade, who managed to find patience under her mother's roof.

"Is it time for my marriage, Auntie?" Jade asked. "Is that why you have come?"

"Your time will come soon. I am here on a different matter."

Jade was a pretty woman, gracious and polite to a fault. She nodded, waiting for the matter to be broached. Chi Lin returned the nod, and then looked toward Lotus, who snored gently.

"I wish you to visit the Silver Silence more often."

"I shall come."

"In fact, if you could come daily and keep your sister company."

Jade frowned, but then recovered.

"I can come, but Sapphire sometimes does not like company. Our conversation will run dry and we will sit in silence until she tires of me."

"To that I have a remedy." Chi Lin moved closer. "You can sew together — shoes are needed for your brother's first son and, now that the Lady of the House is big again with child, more shoes will be needed. Even Moon Flower shows signs. You know many delicate stitches and can teach Sapphire the way. She can stand improvements. And while you sew, you can chatter and sing and even play games. How would you like that?"

"If it pleases you, Auntie. But if it does not please Sapphire . . ."

"When she drifts to her moods, you shall come sit with me. I will read to you."

Jade grinned, and it became so. Jade came the next day and the next and, although Sapphire was disinclined at first, she soon went along with the arrangement, learning the stitches and mimicking her sister's singing.

"The issue is solved," Chi Lin told Mi Tso-tze, who listened, but did not comment, because she had already seen the signs.

After a week, Chi Lin saw the signs also. Ai-lo Yun-chi, who had been avoiding Sapphire suddenly stood at a distance and observed the two sisters as they laughed and sang and worked. He did not approach, at first, but then he introduced himself to Jade one evening as she retreated from the courtyard to her place in the Crimson Blossom. It seemed a harmless dalliance, well within the realm of politeness. Chi Lin thought nothing of it, at first, but as the weeks passed, Ai-lo Yun-chi intercepted Jade more often. When Sapphire had a mood shift and Jade sought her Auntie for some reading, Yun-chi managed to detain her. They walked together near the pool, sitting at the base, with *Raisin Cake* barking about their feet. Their conversation soon turned to laughter.

"Mistress," Mi Tso-tze said, looking out the window. "Here is a picture of domestic life."

Chi Lin knew what she meant. It troubled her. While Sapphire was a vixen with feminine wiles wasted on most men, Jade seemed more impressionable — fragile enough to fall for a handsome face with prospects. However, a Mongol son and worshipper of the *yi-shen* was hardly a prospect.

"I will ask her to come less frequently," Chi Lin said.

"But what of Sapphire?"

Yes, indeed. What of Sapphire? But better one unsolved problem than two. However, before Chi Lin could intervene, circumstances came to her rescue.

2

The Imperial Reign Period changed once again. Chien Wen was gone, the young emperor disappearing into the bowels of protective custody, although some speculated that he dwelled in death's arms. His uncle Prince Chu Di was now Emperor and declared the Yung Lo Reign Period. Once again the broadsides were plastered on walls. Once again the heralds announced the beginning of a great era of peace and prosperity. Once again, politics changed course, but this time in favor of such things as salt and iron monopolies. Superintendent Chou Mai-xin now knew which way the wind blew and announced the restoration of the Commissioner's house inviting Ai-lo Wun-kua to return and inspect his reconstructed quarters. And Wu San-ehr, although wounded in battle, was rewarded by his liege-lord and made the Baron of Jin-kua county with a promise of a villa once the capital was moved from Nan-jing to Yen, a placed now renamed Bei-jing. This was a blessing to the Wu household now that Uncle Wu San-ehr was Baron Ping-an.

    Chi Lin was happy for the household, but was also glad the Ai-lo brothers would be moving from the Silver Silence back to the Ya-men. She would miss Ai-lo Wun-kua's company and his wife's, but it was inevitable. The Imperial Commissioner was a generous man and, as a reward for Wu Lin-kua's hospitality, he increased the Wu's income on the monopoly by twelve percent, which was within his authority to do so. He also gave Chi Lin a great gift.

    "I shall leave my books here in the Silver Silence as a library," he said to Chi Lin.

    "But they are your books."

    "They are your books now — a repository of knowledge to feed your insatiable mind and to flourish in the House of Wu for ten thousand generations. I shall buy more books and, if I need to resort to these for reference, I shall pay you a visit, which will be my great pleasure."

    Chi Lin nearly swooned at this gift. The books were a treasure beyond reckoning. The children would surely benefit, even the girls when they were born, because she meant to petition Wu Lin-kua at the appropriate time to allow all Wu women to learn to read and write. Jasmine would be prejudiced against it, but no matter. Chi Lin would press her cause when the time came. However, the time had come for Ai-lo Yun-chi to depart and, for that, Chi Lin was grateful. She had no dislike for the man, but she wished to avoid the spike of his continued presence.

    One late afternoon, before the Ai-lo had departed, Chi Lin went to inspect the silk *ji-tzao*. She passed the new school house, which was not often in use — Wu Tien-po being still a toddler and teacher Lu Wen-wei in temporary residence. Autumn was nipping at her heels, Mi Tso-tze trying her best to keep a shawl tacked over her mistress' robe. The school house door was covered with a stiff silk drape, the wind shifting it slightly askew. Chi Lin halted and approached, meaning to straighten it. She did so, but then stopped and listened. She heard sounds within.

"What is it, mistress?" Tso-tze asked.

Chi Lin did not reply, but listened to the voices — whispers and soft shifting sounds of silk. Pushing the curtain aside, she was both astounded and embarrassed. Ai-lo Yun-chi and Jade were facing each other in the grips of an embrace. They stirred when Chi Lin entered, pushing each other aside.

"Auntie," Jade said, a quiver in her voice.

Chi Lin remained silent. Then Mi Tso-tze entered.

"What is amiss, mistress? What is . . ."

Mi Tso-tze stammered, turned about, and then returned to the boardwalk.

"Mistress Purple Sage," Ai-lo Yun-chi said, bowing low. "Forgive us. We were compelled."

Chi Lin kept her silence, be approached with measured steps. Jade turned away, but Ai-lo Yun-chi faced her squarely.

"It is not as it appears," he said.

"Can it be anything other than what I see?" Chi Lin replied, finally.

"Do not tell brother," Jade pleaded. "It was merely fondling."

"A gentleman in my household chooses as he will," Yun-chi stated justifying his case. "It is commonplace."

"If it were commonplace, sir," Chi Lin chided, still gently, "you would not have recourse to the shadows. If you were making a choice, you would consult Wu Lin-kua and follow his judgment in the case."

Ai-lo Yun-chi stood.

"It shall be so," he said, nodding sharply.

"I would wait on that course," Chi Lin suggested. "I am the arranger in such matters in the Wu Household."

"Auntie," Jade said, reaching toward her. "Auntie, please. I know you must seek Ying Ling as a go-between and she will find me a husband in a county household. But now I could not bear it. I could not."

She wept. Chi Lin gazed at Ai-lo Yun-chi.

"Does your father know your heart?"

"He will be consulted," Yun-chi said. "He will prefer me to seek a wife in Nan-jing among the believers, but I will have Jade or no other."

"So you will disrespect your father's will?"

"It is *my* choice. It is *his* to bless."

Chi Lin sighed. Her mind raced. The union of a Han woman to a Mongol was acceptable if that family embraced Han ways, Han beliefs and customs. But to join two divergent strands of Heaven under one house might be a precedent the ancestors could not digest. But Chi Lin had no defense against the heartfelt sight she witnessed, an overwhelming spirit of love and affection. Certainly Ai-lo Yun-chi was convicted. He bowed stiffly to Chi Lin, and then left the schoolhouse.

Chi Lin sat beside Jade.

"This is infatuation, surely," she suggested.

"No, Auntie. I am entirely his to command. I think only of him at all watches of the day and night. I long for his touch. And I am sad to think that duty and custom will keep us apart." She shook her head. "If I cannot have him, I shall swallow my earrings and be done with it."

"Foolish talk," Chi Lin snapped, finally moved to anger. "Do you think that such talk will move anyone to believe you are not churlish? This is the kind of thing expected from Sapphire, but not from you."

Jade wept, grasping for Chi Lin's shoulder. Her Auntie gave in. The softness of this beauty nestling in her arms moved Chi Lin to detest her own position as the arbiter of connubial affairs.

"There, there," she said. "Let me ponder these things."

"Then you will allow it?" Jade said brightening."

"I did not say that. If Ai-lo Yun-chi exercises his birthright and chooses you to wife, it must be considered, if not denied. But you must brace yourself for disappointment and follow a course you will not like. You must stay away from him as the events are revealed. Any other course will spoil all chances."

Jade wept again, but Chi Lin would have her way in this. She restricted Jade to the Crimson Blossom until the Ai-lo family departed. However, Ai-lo Yun-chi *did* approach his father, who came to Chi Lin and expressed his doubts, but did not rule against the lovers.

"It will be necessary for the daughter of Wu to embrace our ways," he said.

"I am sure she would cut off her nose and wear a *kang* board to make it so," Chi Lin replied. "Praying to an invisible spirit and following a carpenter's son would be little sacrifice for her. It is how others view it that is worrisome."

This was true enough. Although daughters were lost to the household and an expense until married, the alliance that marriage formed with other families was important, particularly to the receiving family. It would be so for the Ai-lo clan. However, since this version of marriage was not a family contract, but a compact between two individuals, the traditional exchange of gifts and dowry did not apply. Without a dowry, Jade's strange marriage arrangement might entice Wu Lin-kua to regard it favorably. In addition, the bond would be with the imperial commissioner's son, a gesture that would not go unnoticed. It was certainly worthy of discussion. So Ai-lo Wun-kua broached the matter with the Master of the House.

3

Wu Lin-kua listened to the Commissioner, and then summoned his journeymen, who were split on the matter at first. Chi Lin knew of these things from Willow, who attended Honeysuckle within earshot of the *ke-ting*. The journeymen were acquainted with the Ai-lo household and, in most cases, thought it a worthy one. However, it was brought to Lin-kua's attention that a union between the two young people might be misconstrued as a product of the increase in the monopoly take, which, of course, it was not. Still the relief of dowry obligation was enticing and one less mouth the feed in the household, although not an imperative, was judicious. Wu Lin-kua was a good brother and, upon hearing that Jade wanted this union, he could not dismiss his sister's desires, even though her personal feelings did not count in the process.

Wu Lin-kua was inclined favorably to the match until Jasmine heard of it. She demanded an audience with her son.

"Must I remind you, you are your father's son," she said sternly. "The House of Wu is the shining star of Yan-cheng. The tenants look up to you as the preserver of continuity and balance. The Mongols are a curse upon the land. That any should remain among us is odd and unnatural. To donate a daughter of the house to the vipers of the past would sully the honor of our house for a thousand years."

Wu Lin-kua listened silently. His mother had a point, although this was none of her business. He never regarded Ai-lo Wun-kua as any of these things, but perhaps the tenants and his neighbors did.

"It is disreputable," she continued, "most disreputable to be satisfied with only one wife, to prayer to an odd spirit and to ignore the priests and portents when selecting a bride. It is not done, except by these non-Han creatures."

When Chi Lin heard of this exchange, her heart sank. Jasmine could bully her sons. They both showed her respect, but they generally followed their own course. Still, this was Jasmine's most furious argument. To go against it could have consequences. After a time, Chi Lin also had an audience with Wu Lin-kua. She took care not to browbeat him and presented herself as the Auntie, whose business it was to arrange the marriages.

"Auntie," Wu Lin-kua said. "It is a difficult question to resolve, I must admit. But the decision is mine and must be arrived at with care."

"It is yours, my lord," she said. "There are good points on all sides of the argument. Might I suggest you ask the advice of one more senior than you are in our household?"

Wu Lin-kua was grateful for the suggestion and at once dispatched a letter to Wu San-ehr asking for his views. Little did he know Chi Lin had already commissioned her cousin Chi Lu-yi to dispatch her own letter to Wu San-ehr. Chi Lin, in her most flowery hand, composed a poem, and then dovetailed the situation and the advantages of the union with the House of Ai-lo into the word flow. Whereas Wu Lin-kua's request was a humble gesture for his uncle to guide him, Chi Lin's was an outright invitation to make the decision.

Baron Ping-an, if nothing else, was decisive and brief. He knew better than to acknowledge Chi Lin's request, but since it arrived first, it had laid the groundwork for Wu Lin-kua's epistle. Wu San-ehr's reply was short and in large, bold characters:

"Proceed with the marriage. No bride price. No dowry."

Chi Lin was delighted, while Wu Lin-kua was shaken. Of course he followed the directive. Ai-lo Yun-chi was invited to the house, where — in the Blue Fountain Hall, he collected Jade as his wife. Chi Lin and Mi Tso-tze attended to her. The customary red gown had been set aside in favor of a simple red waist skirt, surcoat and shawl, to ward off chill. Wu Lin-kua, Honeysuckle and Willow stood nearby. No priest attended. There was no chair or parade. Bride and groom embraced, and then, lovingly strode back to the courtyard gate and departed for their new life. All the while, Jasmine stood at a safe distance and wailed.

"Shame."

It was a heartless shout, repeated without relent. The season's chill was warm compared to it.

"Shame."

Chi Lin wished to pull her sister-in-law away and shut her in the Blue Heaven Pavilion, but it would provoke an even more heightened and blistering response. So she bore it as did the others. Long after the couple's departure, Jasmine's howls remained, into the evening and through the night. When the sun arose, Chi Lin was glad not to hear it again. She went alone to the shrine, warming her aging hands on the incense pots. She prayed to *Guanyin*, and then turned to her husband.

"My lord and faithful companion," she said. "I know your heart as well as you know mine. Your daughter Jade will be happy and no shame has come because your most honorable brother, the baron Ping-an, has seen fit to bless the arrangement. We are all content except for your first wife. I pray you visit her in her dreams and calm her doubts forever."

She burned her red prayer paper, clapped three times and bowed low. Little did she know that in the darkest hour in the Blue Heaven Hall, her sister-in-law resolved her own doubts and swallowed her earrings, ending her meddling for all times. Once again the House of Wu would don the white.

Chapter Seven

Siblings

1

Chi Lin was sad. She had never meant for Jasmine to take her own life and felt, if the marriage between Ai-lo Yun-chi and Jade had not been pressed, Jasmine would have lived in her own cantankerous way, but lived she would have. No one blamed Purple Sage nor was any shadow cast over the wedded couple. Wu Lin-kua ordered the household to don white for three months. Jasmine was duly buried in the family cemetery, her icon taking its place in the temple shrine. She was honored as the mother of the household. Chi Lin would not deny her that. However, her saddened state concerned Mi Tso-tze and even Willow; and once Willow had discerned her mood, she mentioned it to Honeysuckle, who in turn told Wu Lin-kua.

The Master of the House paid a visit to the Silver Silence, where he partook of hot tea and cold vegetables, as befitting mourning.

"They say you have not visited the silk *ji-tzao* in some time, Auntie," he said. "Am I to be concerned?"

"I will go tomorrow, my lord," she replied.

He gazed about her *ke-ting* admiring the many books stacked on tables and shelves.

"The Silver Silence has become a wonder," he remarked. "Do you still have the first book I gave you?"

"It is a treasure, my lord and a constant companion," Chi Lin replied.

She proceeded to fetch it, but Wu Lin-kua interrupted her.

"No need, Auntie. No need. I know you cherish words and have made much use of them."

She returned to her seat, bowing.

"I am sorry that I wrote to Baron Ping-an about Jade's affair, my lord. It was wrong of me to do so."

Wu Lin-kua grinned.

"I did not know you had written to him."

"Please, do not be cross."

"How can I be? You have been a blessing to this house — a motherly blessing, although you are only my Auntie." He sipped his tea. "But I sense sadness."

"I am in mourning, my lord, as you are."

"True. But my mother was never gracious to my father's other wives. She was hardly gracious to her children. Yet we respect her."

"As we should, my lord. But . . . ." She hesitated.

"Yes, yes."

"I fear that my intercession in this last union angered your mother so much so as to give her only one course of action."

"Nonsense." He set his cup aside. "She had many choices. She chose her earrings. She could not live with what she perceived as dishonor and set her feelings to rest for all times. We must respect her course and acknowledge her feelings. Her act makes it so. Your unwarranted sadness in this should flee to Heaven with the doves."

Chi Lin stood, and then curtsied to the Master of the House. He had grown wise, because he had listened to those about him and never acted rashly. She was proud of him.

"There is the question of the Blue Heaven Pavilion, Auntie," he said. "I know the Silver Silence has become a heart beat in this house, but would you not prefer to move into larger quarters?"

"Forgive me, my lord, but that would insult your mother's spirit."

"Perhaps, so. But I cannot leave it standing barren. Perhaps Sapphire could take up a place there."

"Unwise," she said, and then returned to her seat, contemplating her own manner. She did not want to lecture the man, and yet she knew he would listen to reason. "That Sapphire is a daughter of Wu would make a move into your mother's pavilion appropriate, but she will need to leave the household soon. So a move would be an unkindness, encouraging her to a permanent arrangement within these walls."

"Do you have a match in mind?"

"No, my lord. The matter has fraught Ying Ling. Sapphire's temperament and the joss sticks have stood against her. In any event, she will need to leave the household or bring dishonor upon these walls."

"Do you have a plan?"

"I have a notion and no more. When it is a plan, I will present it for your review. As for the Blue Heaven pavilion, perhaps Lotus could expand to fill it."

Wu Lin-kua laughed.

"I would say Lotus has expanded too much already." Chi Lin grinned. "See, you smile again, albeit at someone else's expense, but there is no need for sadness. I will resolve the issue of the Blue Heaven. I only suggested it because your own household will be expanding."

Chi Lin was taken by surprise. Was he giving her more servants? More cooks? Then she heard his news and was delighted.

2

The Chi clan had become the bulwark of managing the Wu *ji-tzao*. The accounts were in the good hands of Chi Lin's brother, Chi Sheng. However, Wu Chou-fa had taken a keen interest in the accounts and more and more began assuming control of them. The second son had a clever head for figures and a good noggin for business. His own villa had expanded and soon rivaled the Wu Homestead, a fact his brother recognized and encouraged. The monopoly boomed between these twin moons. However, with Wu Chou-fa's increased interest, Chi Sheng's role lessened. This may have been a boon because, in his crippled state, Chi Sheng's business undertakings became increasingly burdensome. With his father dead and both sisters out of the household, the place was falling apart. Reports came to the Silver Silence from Chi Lin's cousins, but there was little Chi Lin could do. She had not seen her brother in over two decades and could not interfere now. So, when Wu Lin-kua announced that her household would be expanding, the last thought she had was that her brother would be coming to live in the Silver Silence.

Workmen were set to converting a portion of the small house adjacent to the root cellar into comfortable quarters. Chi Lin's heart was set on her brother's comfort, although she did not know what to expect. She had not seen or spoken to him in so long, she had forgotten what he looked like. But it did not matter. When he arrived, he had aged considerably and resembled their father, Chi Ming. She received him in her *ke-ting*, but since Chi Sheng could not climb to the verandah without aid, she met him on the porch, Po Bo helping him over the threshold.

"Elder brother," she said, gasping at his sight.

"Little one," Chi Sheng replied, holding tightly to Po Bo's shoulder. Chi Sheng used a crutch and was adept at it, but looked older than his age and was sluggish. "As you can see, the gods have not straightened my legs despite the mountain of red paper burnt to get their attention."

"Come inside," Ch Lin said. "Po Bo, ease him into my best chair. Mi Tso-tze, have Mo Li bring tea and Moon Cakes."

"Moon Cakes?" Chi Sheng snickered. "I am indeed in a fancy house with a mistress of high quality."

"Nonsense, brother. I am the least in this household — the ghost bride. Recall? The passage of time has improved some things, but I am still a servant to my husband's spirit."

"I heard you had a son," he said.

"Hush," Chi Lin said, trembling at the words. "My body was a vessel, but now I am a handmaiden to the men of this household. I am Mistress Purple Sage, Auntie to the children of the house."

"A proper house, indeed," Chi Sheng said, reclining into the chair. "And what a room — a hall of magnificence with fine furnishings and . . . and books. Is this the Wu family's library."

"All that is here belongs to the family, but the books are mine."

"Yours?"

Chi Sheng grinned.

Chi Lin regarded her brother while Mo Li served tea and Mi Tso-tze offered Moon Cakes. Yu Li was at hand with a cushion, while Po Bo took charge of the crutch. Chi Lin missed this man more than she could admit. He had been always at his studies in the old days, but he also had kind words for her — encouragement, where her sister did not.

"It is an indulgence, I know," Chi Lin said. "But the old Master of the House was kind and, although the Old Lady of the House objected, he accepted this ghost bride as one who could read and write."

"Was the Old Lady harsh?"

"She was stern at times, but fair and came to regard me with favor, although I never deserved it."

"Daughters who bear sons always find favor."

Chi Lin did not respond to this. No one ever referred openly to her motherhood. She could see her servants were nervous about its mention, so to pursue it would only make it worse.

"I am skilled at sewing and know the silk *ji-tzao*. My touring has found favor with the neighborhood and the tenants, so I have done my share to maintain the Wu family honor."

"And the Chi family honor also," Chi Sheng said. "I owe you gratitude for my place in that honor."

"Be thankful to Wu T'ai-po and the *tai-feng* for it. I did nothing more than put forth an impertinent idea, which was ignored until time and wind urged it forward. And as for your presence here now, I have had nothing to do with it. That is all on Wu Lin-kua's threshold."

Chi Sheng nodded. He reached for his crutch.

"I do not wish to tire you with my chatter, sister," he said.

"No, no," she said, alarmed. "I am the better for it."

"But still . . ."

"Yes. You must take your ease." She stood, while Po Bo steadied Chi Sheng upon his crutch. "I have had a simple house prepared. The walls are bare, but I am sure it will soon be covered with your brushwork. I have installed a fine writing table and, whatever books you wish, they are here."

Chi Sheng turned to Po Bo.

"You are a fine fellow," he said. "What are you called?"

"I am Po Bo, my lord. I am the custodian of the Silver Silence"

"Tush. I am no one's lord. Your title is higher than mine."

"Yes, my . . . Yes.

"Can you read?"

"No."

"I will teach you the shape of the characters."

"I have no need for them."

Chi Lin wondered about this. Po Bo was too old to start learning, but her brother grinned.

"This *ke-ting* is most likely a long walk away the simple house your mistress has prepared for me. When I need a book, you will need to help me cross the courtyard, push me up the stairs, and float me over the threshold, which will be bothersome. So I will show you a character or three — a book title, so you can take it into your head or on paper and match it to a book here, and then fetch it back to me, if you are so inclined."

"I will do it, my mistress' brother."

Chi Sheng laughed, and then hobbled forward. He turned to Chi Lin as he reached the threshold.

"Our sister could have been a great lady of the house — a ghost bride like you. What she would say if she saw you now?"

"She is settled, brother. We are unlikely to encounter her again."

But here Chi Lin was wrong, because sometimes Heaven moves events to cancel such sureties deemed unlikely encounters.

Chapter Eight

Last Settlements

1

Sapphire had taken to stranger ways. Chi Lin kept a constant watch on this daughter, who would creep about in the shrubbery spying upon the household, particularly Yu Li and Chi Sheng. Yu Li complained to Mi Tso-tze that Sapphire sometimes jumped in her path and tried to block the way, shaking her dolly at her. It quite frightened little Butterfly. Chi Sheng did not mind the girl, because, as he stated, *she is a lost soul and needs to find purpose in this world. If that purpose is to spy on an old cripple scholar, who am I to contradict nature?* Chi Lin did not accept this explanation.

Sapphire would take runs at the servants when they least expected. She sang songs out of tune and would sneak into the kitchen and steal a bun, a thing she could have in plenty and need not steal. Reports came to Chi Lin, several a week, if not a few in any given day. She was perplexed and sent again for Ying Ling.

"Surely there is a place for our Sapphire," she said to the familiar marriage broker.

"Surely," Ying Ling answered. "But not in this county unless she is cast out to fend for herself."

"That would bring shame upon the house."

"No more shame than an unmarried daughter would."

Still, Ying Ling agreed to speak to Gu Sha, the *mei-ren* of adjacent Tai-p'ing County.

Meanwhile, Chi Lin had another marriage in mind, one which Ying Ling was already investigating, when Wu Ming-kuan returned home for a visit. Chi Lin was always thrilled to see her flesh and blood nephew, even if he did not regard her as his mother. He had grown tall, strong from ship work, smart from his able sea master's instruction and ready to command a ship of his own. Still, he was not married; and was overdue.

Wu Ming-kuan arrived on a golden steed who he named *Shore Master*. He kept the beast stabled most of the year, a ship's deck more his metal now. However, his apprenticeship included riding as well as sail craft and map reading. His instructor had not always been a sailor and knew the refinements of riding and husbandry. So

Wu Ming-kuan came ashore once a moon and rode *Shore Master*. When he would command his own ship, he meant to take the beast on board.

"I will construct a stable on *my* ship, Auntie," he declared, "and keep it fresh with hay and stocked with sorghum. When at sea I will not be able to ride him, but we shall explore many lands together, *Shore Master* and me."

Chi Lin was happy that Wu Ming-kuan had not lost his imagination. He wanted this horse and he would have him. If meadows were not on board, he would sail to them and tear up the hillocks ashore. But he would be better to have a wife on board than a horse, if not both. It was inevitable that Chi Lin would broach the topic.

"It is time for me to settle your wedding to a girl of good property, now that you are the only one remaining unmarried," she said.

"I am not the only one," Ming-kuan replied, pouting. "My sister is still in the household. She must be settled first, I would say."

"You would say it, but you would be wrong."

"But, Auntie. I am a man of the sea. I will not be overseeing salt or silk. I am the Third Son and less obliged to do so."

Chi Lin turned away. She could not believe Ming-kuan's thinking.

"You do not stand in line after the daughters of this household," she said, sourly. "And you are obliged to marry as any Wu son. Your wife will bring income to the household; also respect and honor. And, if Heaven wills it, she will bear your sons."

"She will be a burden," he snapped. "I will be away at sea and she will on my brother's hands."

"She could go with you," Chi Lin countered. "There is no reason for a man to be separated from his wives, unless he is a ghost. Your uncle moves from war camp to war camp and his family follow upon his heels."

"To have a woman on a ship would not do, Auntie."
"Is it written?"
"It would be unfair. It would be a hard life for her."

Chi Lin bubbled over, but caught her anger as only a mother could. How much harder would a life aboard a ship be than a life within the walls of a house? A woman's life is hard by nature. For Ming-kuan to use this as an agreement was disingenuous — an excuse to postpone his wedding. Suddenly, Sapphire appeared at the door. She pointed at her brother, laughed, and then ran away.

"What conduct is that?" Ming-kuan asked.

"It is her way, my lord," she said, and then blew a hostile whistle to quell her frustration. "Sapphire has no hope for marriage."

"But she must," Ming-kuan said. "She will bring dishonor upon the house."

"Yes, and then where would your chances be?" Chi Lin patted the air, and then took solace in a tea cake. "I will discuss your wedding with your father. I will employ a priest to divine his will. And you must go to the shrine and ask his guidance."

Wu Ming-kuan bowed low at this suggestion. It ended all discussion and put him in his place. He departed quietly, leaving his Auntie to her frustration. She knew he would come around. He had no choice. If *fa-shr* and prayers at the shrine did not move him, his elder brother would lay down the law. And if that failed, there was always Wu San-ehr.

"Mistress," Tso-tze said, coming to her side. "Do you mean to visit the silk *ji-tzao* today?"

"No. Nor will I sew or mend chairs. The older children of the household have always been a revelation to me. But the younger ones prefer to do as they please."

"You are too good to them."

"Perhaps, so. But can you blame me with Wu Ming-kuan?"

"Surely, he will come around."

"He needs a stern hand when out of sight. I pray to *Guan-yin* that he has one. As for Sapphire, she must be settled before the Moon Festival — before the smaller ones begin to follow her example."

And so it came to pass.

2

The settling of Sapphire went beyond Chi Lin's arrangements, into a zone where men had *say* and women had none. Wu Lin-kua was a thoughtful man and sensitive of the family's honor and how it would reflect on his ever-growing family. Respectability was a key to success with his tenants and the maintenance of the monopoly. So, to have an unmarried sister would not do.

Since Auntie Purple Sage had failed to arrange things as they should be arranged in Sapphire's case, Wu Lin-kua considered another path. It was not a casual path, but one that his newly arrived guest — Chi Sheng, had inspired. As it happened, Wu Lin-kua admired his former accountant and would visit the invalid's simple house in the Silver Silence. Chi Lin's brother was a keen *xiang-chi* player. Wu Lin-kua missed playing the game with Wu Chou-fa, now that his brother lived in the Villa, and the journeymen were poor at the game or would let him win because he was *The Master of the House*. Chi Sheng had held no such deference when it came to strategic board games. He would lose as many times as he won, which made for an enjoyable afternoon for both men. During such gaming, Sapphire sometimes peeked in and made animal noises to distract them. While Chi Sheng found it amusing, Wu Lin-kua did not — a reminder that his sister was not only still on his hands, but was also a handful. It was during a game of *xiang-chi* that Chi Sheng suggested an honorable solution, a strategic way to solve the Wu family's problem.

Chi Lin had not known of her brother's suggestion or that Wu Lin-kua entertained it until it was no longer a suggestion but a fact. However, the course of action did not surprise her entirely. It was a common course known to her already. But when it came to it, she *was* surprised.

On afternoon, Chi Lin's brother hobbled on his crutch to the pavilion with Po Bo's aid, but did not enter. He sent word to his sister.

"Mistress," Mi Tso-tze said. "Someone has arrived in the courtyard. Your brother has sent me to ask you to attend. The Master of the House is here also."

Chi Lin could not imagine who had come and why both Wu Lin-kua and Chi Sheng would attend. But her wondering was worth nothing while her curiosity piqued. She was summoned. So she donned her common robe — the purple one that marked her as the ghost bride, and emerged into the sunlight.

Standing in the courtyard was a thin figure dressed in black, a bamboo basket strapped on the back. The person's head was shaved and, at first, Chi Lin could not tell whether this was a man or a woman. But when she drew closer she could see it was a woman — a nun, the beggar kind, who wore straw sandals and saffron-dyed undergarments.

Chi Lin's heart leaped. As she approached the woman, she recognized the face, albeit a gaunt version of a former ample visage and, now, with a bald head, quite avian in appearance.

"Sister?" Chi Lin whispered, her voice hitching. "Chi Tsai, is that you?"

The nun clasped her hands together, raised them to her forehead and bowed.

"I am now known as Sister Marsh Wren," Chi Tsai replied. "Because I am formed by the salt plain, my chapter has renamed me so."

Chi Lin turned to her brother. She did not need to ask.

"She is here at our request," Wu Lin-kua explained.

"She is here for Sapphire," Chi Sheng added.

Chi Lin understood. She could see Sapphire in the distance, peeking from behind a barrow, trying to discern who had come into the courtyard, no doubt. Chi Lin also sensed Po Bo's distress as he realized that Sapphire was destined for the monastery.

"Sister," Chi Lin said, confused whether she should embrace her. "Come into my *ke-ting* and be refreshed."

"Although it is good to see you and see you thriving," Chi Tsai replied, "I cannot renew our acquaintance on such terms. I am here to take the girl. I have my begging bowl for cold fare. It is our way. I cannot trouble you without breaking my vows."

"But you have come so far and on foot."

"Only two days, mistress. Only two days. Such a stroll is mild for the handmaidens of Lord Buddha." She turned to Wu Lin-kua. "Where is the girl, my lord?"

Wu Lin-kua, who had also spotted Sapphire's hiding place, nodded in her direction. Chi Tsai bowed again to her sister and brother, and then walked to the barrow, where Sapphire stirred.

What transpired amazed all present. Sister Marsh Wren approached the girl, who cowered at first. The nun spoke, and then sat at the barrow's edge, Sapphire entranced by whatever was said. Chi Lin could not hear the words and dared not ask. In fact, Chi Sheng and Wu Lin-kua kept their silence also.

After two watches — late in the afternoon, the nun returned to the foot of the verandah, now with Sapphire in hand. The daughter of the house appeared bewitched — calm, but lucid, her dolly dangling from her hand. She looked to her brother and her Auntie, and then smiled.

"We have come to an understanding," Sister Marsh Wren said, bowing again. "She shall come to the temple. We shall send her robes and shoes back after her induction, but she may keep her play doll for three moons after which she will present it as a cherished gift to Lord Buddha. Your household will be blessed if you honor your arrangements."

Wu Lin-kua stood.

"Holy sister," he said, "the House of Wu will send your temple two cold feasts each year on the second day of the second moon and the tenth day of the tenth moon. We will also donate a silver ingot each year to the poorest of our tenants in the name of my sister."

"It is good," the nun replied. "We shall go."

Chi Lin was stunned. She watched her sister depart with Sapphire through the gates of the Silver Silence never to see either again. She was disquieted by her sister's pious chill and Sapphire's strange calm. Mistress Purple Sage suddenly felt old — her age, perhaps, and no place to breathe in life's narrow disparity.

As the sun set, no one moved. Silence reigned upon the verandah, the settlement thus completed. Silence reigned except for Po Bo's gentle weeping as he inherited silence itself.

Chapter Nine

The Grand Director

1

The Yung Lo Emperor, the former Prince Chu Di, had a grand scheme for his Ming Dynasty. His father, the Hung Wu Emperor, ruled with an iron fist and secured the realm from the Mongol predecessors, but more so from a wave of rebellions at the Yuan Dynasty's collapse. Hung Wu's successor, the Chien Wen Emperor was small peas compared to the ambitions of his uncles, the founding emperor's sons and, although Chien Wen managed to defeat many intrigues, he succumbed to Prince Chu Di's occupation of Nan-jing, ostensibly to protect his nephew, but ultimately to eradicate him. Then the new Emperor raised his sights on five projects. He would move the capital north to his former stronghold at Yen-chou, rename it Bei-jing and construct a great palace there — a forbidden city of nine thousand, nine-hundred and ninety-nine halls and pavilions. He would restore the Grand Canal so this new capital could be supplied with the grain wealth of the south. He would repair and reconstruct the long wall to the north to maintain the boundary between the civilized Han peoples and the wild folk of the steppes and forests. He would lock his nephew away in a monastery and formally eradicate the Chien Wen year period from the history annals. Finally, he would build a great fleet of one-thousand one-hundred and eighty ships, including sixty-two ocean-going vessels, each five-hundred *chi* in length — veritable palaces on the sea. To these he appointed General Cheng Ho, a favored palace eunuch and war hero, to become the Grand Director of the Seas, to sail forth as envoy to the kingdoms and islands to the south.

Chi Lin knew nothing of these great doings until it was announced that the Grand Director was coming to the ports of Po-hai bay to inspect the shipping in preparation for a voyage from Su-chou. Cheng Ho would be stopping in Yan-cheng and the Wu household was selected to entertain the Grand Director on his course toward the ports.

Chi Lin had been busy at other pursuits. There were repairs in progress at the silk *ji-tzao* and also a tour of the salt works. Chi Lin was feeling the effects of the tour, her joints beginning to ache more and more with the jostling. But as Queen Crane, in her feathered hat, her presence among the tenants raised spirits and secured stability. With the boom in ship building at the port towns, many tenant sons were drifting to the coves and learning to be joiners and sail makers. Hemp spinning and resin making kept many employed and much silk was transformed from the looms into sails.

Chi Lin also had domestic issues to settle. Po Bo moped after Sapphire. In fact, Chi Lin was saddened by the abrupt departure of the daughter of the house. Honor may have been preserved, but the sight of the pretty girl dashing about making faces and swinging her dolly was missed. As necessary as it was, Chi Lin felt it was unfair. She also felt failure. She was unable to broker a match for Sapphire, while the men, in a more direct design, removed embarrassment by literally removing the source. As for Po Bo, he was slack in his duties. Chi Lin made allowances, but her high hopes for the new custodian forced her to confront the situation.

"You must marry, Po Bo," she said to him, a commandment, not a suggestion.

"If it must so, mistress," he said. "But my mind will always be distracted."

"If it must be so," she replied. "But be fair to your new wife as she will be the mother of your children."

Po Bo sighed, but did not protest. He knew who was selected before being told. Yu Li, the selected, was more willing to the arrangement. She had expressed fond feelings for Po Bo both directly to him and to Mi Tso-tze, who favored the match also. With Sapphire out of sight, it was assumed Po Bo's misplaced feelings would settle into something more appropriate. Despite his distraction, Yu Li was willing to earn her place. Chi Lin reasoned that, unlike family, servants could bond before their marriage. There was never any contract at stake. It was always a matter of proximate arrangement and convenience.

Before Po Bo and Yu Li could be join, however, the announcement came that the Grand Director was coming. So it was decided to wait on the marriage ceremony until after the distinguished guest's visit. Po Bo was content in this. With the flurry of activity in the household now, such an event as a servants' wedding would be missed entirely. Yu Li was distressed, but was consoled.

"Child," Chi Lin said. "Neither you nor Po Bo are going anywhere. You will be too busy to settle into married life while we are preparing for the great visit, so it is better to wait. Then you can savor that which should be savored."

Of course, Chi Lin did not speak from experience, but she had managed enough weddings to know the tug and pull it could have on couples, especially if they already had each other's acquaintance. Yu Li just sighed and accepted the postponement. What else could she do?

2

In honor of Cheng Ho, Wu Lin-kua ordered a feast be set in the Jade Heart Pavilion and invited prominent neighbors to dine with the Grand Director. Of course, Wu Chou-fa shared a place of prominence with his brother as did Ai-lo Wun-kua and his sons, and the superintendent, Chou Mai-xin. As a special dispensation, Lotus was hauled there on her chair and Chi Lin was allowed a place at the hall's far end beside Honeysuckle and Moon Flower. Wine flowed freely, as did tea and buns. Plates of pork, chicken, dolphin, pangolin, eels and blooded veal were served in plenty. Cheng Ho ate heartily and complimented every dish by drinking a bucket of wine.

Chi Lin thought well of this man, even from afar. He was praised and yet did not stand on ceremony. He toasted his hosts and challenged the journeymen *to down their wine bowls in one go, if they dared.* After the meat course, the vegetables came — stacks of melon, cowcumbers, and glistening peas in their pods, mung beans and bamboo shoots in chili sauce. Then came the sweets. Chi Lin had not eaten so much in years, not even at the family annual festivals. She looked to Lotus, who had no difficulty eating everything served to her, and then looked for more. Chi Lin did not begrudge Lotus her due, but somehow sensed that if she grew any fatter, they would need to build a larger carry-chair.

"Let us drink to my liege-lord, His Majesty," Cheng Ho shouted, standing on a raised platform to give him prominence, not that he needed it. "May He live ten-thousand years."

Everyone stood and echoed the sentiment, raising their bowls, the journeymen certain to follow the Grand Director's example and down them in one go. Wu Lin-kua and Wu Chou-fa remained standing when the others were reseated. It was clear that they would make speeches, each in turn. But Cheng Ho raised his hands.

"No fuss, please," he said. "This has been a fine meal, one which makes me fond of Yan-cheng and the House of Wu. I am sure it will remain with me long before it seeks to add luster to the surrounding fields." He laughed, drawing a round of frivolity from the guests. "I am a plain fellow — renown for my battle prowess, but that is on hill and dale. But now my lord wishes me to rule the fishes and the sea beasts. Of course, there is no fiercer sea beast than his Majesty's navy, which stands in several ports waiting for me to haul it together into a single fleet on the crest of the Su-chou tide. What I shall find beyond the horizon matters little if it does not *k'ou-t'ou* to my Lord. So I am the envoy to the peoples of the South Seas. I will bring them gifts and take their tributes for His Majesty's honor. That is what I am about. I shall bring back rare gems and oddities of men and animals, while my Lord builds his vast city in the north. Thus I am charged and I mean to succeed. But when I sit at the tables of the away folk beyond the touch of my native land, I will always remember this great feast and the folk of Yen-chang."

He raised his bowl again, and then tipped it. But it was empty. He frowned, and both brothers were upstanding to remedy the fault. Chi Lin did not regard it as a fault, because she could discern that Cheng Ho was jesting. But Wu Lin-kua and Wu Chou-fa were apologetic and had the bowl filled to overflowing. Cheng Ho downed it in one go, and then smacked his lips.

"You will have me drunk, yet," he bellowed. "But remember . . . I sleep alone."

He was a eunuch, after all.

3

The feast went past sundown and, when the time came, Lotus was lifted sound asleep in her carry-chair and taken to the Crimson Blossom Pavilion. Chi Lin was concerned for her sister-in-law, who snored, but also gasped for air. So she followed the chair to assure the servants did not dump their burden in the hall and leave without preparing her for bed. Chi Lin stood vigil, Willow also coming to watch.

"It would not matter," Willow said, "if they set her in the hall and retired. She will sleep until dawn and beyond."

"It may not matter," Chi Lin replied, "but it would be disrespectful."

"I agree. I am here, but your presence weighs far more with them. See, they comb her hair and prepare her bed."

It was true. The servants pampered Lotus, who stirred briefly, but was soon asleep in her vast bed. Chi Lin, satisfied that they complied with proper conduct, retreated, heading for the Silver Silence. As she strode under the gate, Po Bo met her, agitatedly.

"Mistress," he said. "He is here?"

"Who?"

Her brother, perhaps, or the Master of the House?

"His lordship," Po Bo said. "He marched into the *ke-ting* and ordered us all out of the place. We dared not obey."

Chi Lin hurried to the pavilion as fast as her legs could manage it. Yu Li and Mi Tso-tze were outside, pacing.

"I could not stop him, mistress," Tso-tze said. "I told him it was not a proper course to take, but he just grunted and told us to leave him alone."

Chi Lin glanced up the stairs, and then took her resolve. No one would keep her away from the Silver Silence. She reached the threshold and peered in. Inspecting her book shelves and tables was Cheng Ho. His back was turned, but she knew by his bright yellow robe and his tall stature who it was.

"My lord," she said approaching him. "It is not proper to be alone in a lady's *ke-ting*."

He did not turn, but kept perusing the books.

"You are the one called Mistress Purple Sage — the ghost bride. I know your brother-in-law Wu San-ehr, well."

"I *am* Mistress Purple Sage, my lord."

"Do not worry your head about propriety in my case," he replied, turning. "I am a eunuch and have dwelled among court ladies since I was a lad with never a fear to stir Heaven's head."

"Truly, my lord."

"And no need to address me as *my lord*. My father was a ditch digger and my mother, a basket swinger. I ate spoiled beans and boiled tree bark when I was a child; and was sold into the great house when I could hardly know where the sky was or that lobsters had claws." He laughed. "I am embarrassing you."

"No," Chi Lin said, curtseying.

"That was then, but I know things now. I grew tired of shining tiles and cleaning pisspots. I learned to build things and draw my designs in the sand pits. The Prince, who is now His Majesty, had me tutored for better use — to read and write and sit a horse. So, although I am a eunuch, I have led an army and won battles. But I am no such thing as a *lord* — just a director, and a *grand one* at that."

Chi Lin did not know what to say or how to proceed. She curtsied again.

"Shall you take tea, sir?"

"After that feast? I am fit to fart. I am here because Ai-lo Wun-kua told me he had a particular rudder in his Library — a detailing of the shoal water off Pi-ch'u cove. And since his library is now your library, I would like to . . ." He stopped, his hand darting to a scroll. "I believe I have found it."

Cheng Ho snatched the scroll, read its label, and then spread it on the low table.

"Is it the one?" Chi Lin asked.

"I believe it is," he said perusing it, his hands tracing the line work. "This is a handy thing to know. May I borrow it, Mistress Purple Sage?"

"What would I do with a map, sir?" she asked. "It is yours."

"Fine," he said, rolling it up and popping it into his robe sash. "You have done a service for me and His Majesty, may He live ten-thousand years."

"You will not have a bucket of wine, sir, before you leave?" Chi Lin asked.

"Rid of me, you would be," Cheng Ho said, grinning. "Yet I still have something to say to you."

"Please sit on my finest chair."

"What I have to say can be said standing." He placed his hands on his hips and stood tall. "Your son is in my service, Mistress Purple Sage."

Chi Lin's breath hitched. How could this man know such things?

"You are mistaken, sir," she said, whispering.

"No, no. Wu Ming-kuan is a fine sailor and will make a seasoned seaman when he sets to sail. Have no fear. I, like Ai-lo Wun-kua, am not bound by family fiction — a ghost child, indeed.

But for your honor, I will say no more on that score. If you must be his Auntie, I understand, but my roots are too raw for such refinements."

"Thank you, sir."

"Think nothing of it. I am commissioning Wu Ming-kuan. He shall be the captain of the *Zenith Star*, a fine bark of good length and girth — a tailgater for my own flagship."

"Thank you, sir."

"He deserves it. Now I shall leave you to your domestic bliss." He tapped the scroll. "Again, I thank you for this. I will retire to a place called the Blue Heaven Pavilion, where I am told the best bed in the house has been reserved for this mountain I call a body."

Cheng Ho headed for the threshold, a swaggering presence. Chi Lin was glad to see him leave. She had never encountered a man like this before — a being untrammeled by rule or regulation. Yet, as she watched him depart, she had a notion and needed to entertain it.

"Sir," she said. He turned, waiting impatiently for a question. "Forgive me, but I need to ask your advice on a matter of the sea."

"Fishes and waves are good companions," he said. "What more is there to know for a land bound lady?"

"Just one thing. Wu Ming-kuan is yet to marry and fears the prospects of taking a wife aboard a vessel. So he hesitates. Is it uncommon for a man to take his wife to sea?"

Cheng Ho roared, quite disarming Chi Lin and probably anyone within earshot.

"I see your point," he said. "As an unmarried man, I cannot give you much advice on what a husband and wife can or cannot do aboard a ship that they cannot do on the shank of a hill. But as the Grand Director of this fleet, I can say this. As a condition of Wu Ming-kuan's commission, he shall marry at once and take his prize to the decks of the *Zenith Star*." He bowed to Chi Lin, touching the scroll again. "Again, I thank you Mistress Purple Sage. If you disagree with my commandment, I am sorry for it. But so it shall stand."

Chi Lin curtsied to the Grand Director as he left. She could hear his merry chuckling through the courtyard, even after Mi Tso-tze, Yu Li and Po Bo returned to the hall. She was happy she had asked for advice and happier still with the conditions. She could now set about arranging Wu Lin-kua's marriage over his objection and hesitation. Cheng Ho had commanded it, if the *Zenith Star* was to have its new captain.

Chapter Ten

Serenity

1

Ying Ling had already assessed the available candidates to marry Wu Ming-kuan in anticipation of the inevitable. However, she did not take into consideration the conditions, both Cheng Ho's and Chi Lin's. The first required a wife willing to go to sea, and the second required the most perfect paragon ever to be born in the county. Chi Lin reviewed the candidates, a list of ten daughters, and when she dismissed each for one flaw or another, Ying Ling reached over the border to T'ai-p'ing county, the *mei-ren* there most willing to split the commission. It was in the House of Fei at Guo-lin-shr that a daughter was found who satisfied Chi Lin.

In order to confirm the beauty of the second daughter of Fei, called Morning Glory, Chi Lin paid the household a visit. It was a necessary inconvenience, which tired her greatly. But she did not want Wu Ming-kuan to place the red tea pouch on the saucer for expediency, his ship more important than his wife, although that might become the case. So Chi Lin traveled to Guo-lin-shr where she was paid the highest respect by the Master of the House, Fei Tang. While the *mei-ren* conferred with each other, Chi Lin observed the girl.

Morning Glory was the most beautiful creature Chi Lin had ever beheld and was surprised that her feet were unbound. She was further surprised when she learned that Fei Tang was liberal in his views of daughters, much like her own father. Morning Glory could read and write and even paint fans. Then came the question.

"The groom is a man of the sea," Chi Lin said bluntly. "It would be required that you travel with him over the waves. Is that acceptable?"

Morning Glory smiled, and then nodded to Mistress Purple Sage.

"I have known only these walls, mistress," she replied. "But I have gone beyond them in my books. To see the world beyond these shores would make me a lucky girl, indeed."

"It is a hard life," Chi Lin cautioned. "Consider the sickness you might experience. Consider the harsh language you might hear."

"Words are but words, mistress. A woman can dismiss them by shutting her mind to them. As for the sickness, will I not be sick when I bear my husband a son? Perhaps I can combine the two and never know the difference."

Chi Lin's heart soared. This was the one. Before the next moon she had Wu Ming-kuan in the House of Fei for see for himself. Never had a man so hesitant to marry made such a turnabout. Whether it was Morning Glory's beauty or her charm, her wit or intelligence, the red pouch was practically thrown on the plate. The pact was sealed. Wu Lin-kua agreed to a fair bride price and the dowry was settled, half to go to the household and half to go to sea.

Chi Lin was content — weary from the travel, but content. Upon returning, she set her daily chores aside for weeks while the wedding preparations went apace. She read and even slept, but mostly she sat by her rock pool and reminisced.

2

"It is time, mistress," Mi Tso-tze said. "The porters are approaching and you have not even made an effort."

Chi Lin was drifting to another time and place, her hand stroking the cool pool water. Mi Tso-tze tried again.

"Do not sleep, mistress," Mi Tso-tze nagged. "The priest will scowl."

"Let him scowl," Chi Lin muttered. "Let him wait. He has waited before."

"When?"

"Ah, yes. Before you had entered my service."

Chi Lin could hear Mi Tso-tze's chuff, but ignored her. Chi Lin snored.

"Mistress, Wu Ming-kuan waits in the Jade Heart. The bride will be in the courtyard. Honeysuckle and Moon Flower will be greeting her."

Chi Lin heard the farty priest horn and the drum. It stirred her. She looked at the sky — a grey sky portending rain, but that was a lucky thing for a wedding, a gift from the dragon-king.

"I do not know why I am so tired, Tso-tze, but it is so."

"You have been doing too much, not that I should say."

"But you say it anyway." Chi Lin stood, her knees stiff. Tso-tze steadied her. "It is an auspicious day — a day to end all days. I am content, but . . ."

"I know, mistress. I know. Yu Li will help dress you, but we must hurry."

Chi Lin was beyond hurrying. The day needed to be savored. After it, she would never see her Ming-kuan again. His happiness would be her fretting — a melancholy touched with satisfaction. Suddenly, *Raisin Cake* scurried about her feet. So many *Raisin Cakes,* almost as many as weddings arranged. Po Bo approached, ushering Yu Li in his wake. The whole crew meant to get their mistress ready for the event. All she needed to do was enter the Silver Silence and stand still. The rest would happen, much like the day when she was a bride standing in her father's house, her sister wrapping the undergarments tightly and draping the heavy red gown and harsh veil over her entire being. How was this different? This time Chi Lin knew what to expect, while on her journey as the ghost bride everything was a mystery. This time life was an open scroll.

3

Chi Lin listened. She sat in the Jade Heart Hall — the Lady of the House's *ke-ting,* Honeysuckle yielding the place of honor to her — the Old Lady's chair. Chi Lin did not refuse the offer. Lotus was carried in and placed at the far end of the room, where she promptly fell asleep. Moon Flower joined Honeysuckle on the couch. Mistress Purple Sage was content as she listened, first to the rain, which, as promised, gently kissed the roof, and then to the chanting priest and the cup ceremony. There was a constant hum from the men folk attending the couple as Wu Ming-kuan said his prayers to *Guan-yin* and the ancestors. Then came raucous rounds of toasting. Chi Lin recognized the voices — Wu Ling-kua, Wu Chou-fa and Ai-lo Wun-kua. Some voices were familiar, but she could not place them exactly as they praised the moment but insulted the bride's ugliness.

When the feast began, the voices returned to a low constant hum. Dishes were brought into the *ke-ting* for the ladies. Chi Lin was pleased by the exquisite care taken in the preparation of the pigeon, Wu Ming-kuan's favorite dish, and the peppery flavor of the steamed dolphin, which danced on her tongue. She could not remember when she enjoyed a dish more. Honeysuckle and Moon Flower tended to Lotus, who awoke for the feast, but resorted to using her fingers, as the *kuai-tze* were too thin for her to manipulate.

Chi Lin sighed as the voices arose again, almost drowning the sound of the rain. The guests were about to lead the happy couple to their wedding bed. Suddenly, Wu Ming-kuan appeared before Chi Lin, bowing deeply. Morning Glory stood behind him.

"I have come, Auntie," Ming-kuan said. "You see before you a married man, just as you wanted."

"And the captain of the *Zenith Star*," Chi Lin crowed.

Wu Ming-kuan beamed.

"And this is my wife," he said, as if it was the first time Chi Lin had encountered the woman.

Morning Glory curtsied, and then kissed Purple Sage's hand.

"When I am at sea," she said, "I will not forget your diligence in this match, Auntie."

"I am glad to be of service," Chi Lin said. "But do not forget to greet Lotus and your brother-in-law's wives. You must recall them when you are far away in the realm of the fishes."

Morning Glory curtsied again, and then approached Lotus.

"And this, Auntie," Ming-kuan announced. "This is my mentor, who taught me about ships and maps and the wonders of sailing."

Wu Ming-kuan moved a tall man forward, but was then taken by the elbow, tugged by his brothers, who announced it was time to prepare for bed. Chi Lin heard the commotion. It was as noisy as New Year. Distracted for the moment, she finally gazed at Wu Ming-kuan's mentor, the man who had taught him seamanship. She trembled. The world of the *ke-ting* moved in circles about her as Ming-kuan was dragged away and Morning Glory was ushered quickly under a *san-tze* to be in bed before her husband arrived. Lotus was lifted, a chance to take her home. The men folk howled — singing bawdy songs. But none of this mattered to Chi Lin now — nothing except this tall man. She sighed.

"Gao Lin," she whispered.

Gao Lin bowed gently. He had grown older and sported a short white beard, but age was kinder to him than to most. Chi Lin shivered.

"Gao Lin," she said again. "Odd, but happy that you are here." She suddenly thought. "You know, Ming-kuan must never know."

"His ignorance matters not," Gao Lin said. "I have watched him since he was born. I would sneak in at night or with a bamboo delivery. I would observe him at play and with the *amah*. He has always been within my sights. And when he took to playing with boats, so did I — the big kind, preparing for the day when he would come to the port and seek guidance. So, I was there — Master Chou K'ai-lin as I am called now."

Chi Lin reached for his hand. He kissed hers, and then went to one knee. They had the *ke-ting* to themselves — only these two and the sound of the rain.

"It matters not that you are only his Auntie and I just his mentor," Gao Lin said gently. "We have loved him and he has come to regard us as we are. You have managed the best for him, and I shall continue to watch over him as long as I live."

Chi Lin closed her eyes, the tears welling from the deepest happiness within and also the deepest sorrow. How she wished she could embrace this man again and disregard the fiction of the ghost bride, but this was a special day and she would not dampen it with personal desires. Instead, she opened her eyes and drank in the sight of the man she loved, while he gently wiped away the tears cascading over her cheeks.

"He must never know," she whispered.

"And yet he has always known, gentle heart, and will remember both of us as such although Heaven has set our places as they are." He kissed her hand again. "I must go. I must knock on the bedroom door and vilify the institution of marriage like any good groom's guest would."

"Yes, Master Chou K'ai-lin," she said, grinning slightly. "Remember me."

"I have never forgotten."

Then, he was gone, and soon Mi Tso-tze stood before Chi Lin toting the *san-tze*.

4

The return trip to the Silver Silence went unspoken, although Mi Tso-tze chattered, asking many questions. Chi Lin just nodded, deflecting them.

"Shall we visit the shrine, mistress? It would be proper."

"Tomorrow is soon enough. The rain is sweet and gentle, but enough to make me damp."

So they passed the shrine, went through the gate and crossed the courtyard to the Silver Silence, where Yu Li and Po Bo waited on the verandah. Chi Lin climbed the stairs, but stopped at the stone bench. Here she sat as she did on the day when she had arrived here so many years ago. She listened again. The wedding sounds had ended — only the rain sang soft on the cobblestones and balustrade. She sighed again.

"I shall sit here awhile."

"But, mistress," Mi Tso-tze chided. "You will catch cold and suffer for it tomorrow."

"I will not be long. Yu Li, fetch my comb and, Lao Lao, in the chink under my bed is my last silver ingot. Bring it here."

Yu Li departed, but Po Bo did not.

"Is there a fault?" Chi Lin asked.

"You called me Lao Lao."

"Ah, yes," she said. "Did I call Yu Li Snapdragon also? But no matter. You are the custodian as much as Lao Lao was. Fetch the ingot. Fetch the ingot. Bring it here."

"Mistress," Mi Tso-tze reproached.

"Turn down my bed, Tso-tze. Do not be tiresome."

Mi Tso-tze grumbled but did as she was told. Yu Li returned and began removing the pins and combing her mistress' hair. Chi Lin closed her eyes. She imagined Snapdragon's spindly fingers dancing through her tresses. But this was Yu Li, who was competent and trained up for it. It must be the rain's magic that made Chi Lin nostalgic.

Po Bo returned, holding the silver ingot in his palm. Chi Lin opened her eyes, the gray light reflected on the silver's edge. She closed Po Bo's hand around the ingot.

"Take this to the market tomorrow. Go to the carpenters and order me a strong ironwood coffin, and then see the draper for a fine silk shroud."

"But mistress," Po Bo said, alarmed. "You are not leaving us?"

"No," Chi Lin said. "But there is comfort in such things when the work becomes less and the days grow shorter. This ingot should cover the cost, but if you get a good price, you may keep the balance and buy a sturdy chair for your quarters."

Po Bo appeared stunned, especially when Mi Tso-tze returned.

"Enough, Yu Li," Chi Lin said. "I shall come inside momentarily." She spotted a distant light in her brother's house. He was unable to attend the wedding. "Po Bo, see how my brother fares. Attend to his comfort before you and Yu Li retire."

Po Bo hesitated, but bowed curtly before darting away. Mi Tso-tze grumbled, and then entered the hall. Yu Li curtsied, and then followed her.

Chi Lin sat alone now on the stone bench with the rain lulling her to fine thoughts.

"Gao Lin," she whispered.

She sighed again.

"Wu Ming-kuan."

She gazed through the rain, laughing gently.

"And yet he has always known and will remember us both as his parents, although Heaven has set our places as they are."

Again she sighed, but then smiled. The rain danced in her mind now, the Silver Silence in her soul and, although she came into this place as a ghost bride, the fourth wife of Master Wu, she had grown beyond such things. She was Chi Lin — Mistress Purple Sage and Auntie to them all.

Ch'i-lin and the Cup

A Flash story originally published at *Whim's Place*

By *Edward C. Patterson*

She reached out and took the cup, her eyes closing, shutting the world out. She would not see the edge as it touched her lips and made bitter the sweetened rice brew that sealed this pact. Her red veil was raised, but her heart was far from the moment. As the acrid cooling brew washed bitter over her tongue, she recalled her childhood—a recollection that had ended with that brutal cup and this heartless pact.

"Ch'i-lin," came the voice. "Are you here Ch'i-lin?"

She was here. She felt the gentle breeze of the kitchen on her cheek, although she stood in the parlor surrounded by guests. She had left her father at the door with the many gifts for Master K'ung—gifts that matched the family's expectations. She had left her mother down the road, peering over the wall, tears of mixed-joy standing in eyes like water bags on a mule's back, stubborn to flood her arroyo cheeks. Ch'i-lin was content behind her father's walls, content to be just a girl, flowering and useful to mother's chores, her sister's games and her father's doting. Life for those who have the misfortune to be born bereft of testicles are distracted by those who had them; and those that had them had cash and good connections.

Ch'i-lin felt the kitchen's breeze and she knew that her *new* mother stood in the portal planning the life of her *new* charge. Life for a childless woman was set, even at the age of thirteen; and childless Ch'i-lin would be. They all knew that. She heard that voice again—*Ch'i-lin*, but instead she heard the call of the kettles and woks, the buckets and the carry-poles. She had a strong back—her gift to the union as no issue would be coming. She shuddered and for a moment she wanted to answer the voice. "I am not here. I am in my father's gardens sewing daisies to my mother's skirts. I am singing to the willow and making my *erh-hu* sigh to the west wind. I am watching the rain kiss the bean fields and praying to the radishes as they quake from the soil. I am there, but never here. Never here."

The kitchen breeze and her new mother's voice cawed. "Drink and make it so."

Ch'i-lin opened her eyes and swallowed. It was a hollow choke—a bitter vision. Beyond the toil of her new life, her husband sat slumped in a muddle beside his mother. The rice wine slurped to his chapped, blackening lips; the drops beading down his sallow cheeks like grease from a roasting duck.

The corpse wore crimson raiment, silks much finer than its skin. Soon it would wear white funeral robes hosting another ceremonial. But first—this one; the one bonding two properties in peace and civility. Ch'i-lin shuddered and her childhood and maidenhood passed along with the cup—the cup that made her the widow K'ung and a mule to her new mother.

Copyright 2006, Edward C. Patterson

Also Available

No Irish Need Apply
Cutting the Cheese
Bobby's Trace
The Closet Clandestine: a queer steps out
Come, Wewoka & Diary of Medicine Flower
Surviving an American Gulag
Turning Idolater
Look Away Silence
The Road to Grafenwöhr
Are You Still Submitting Your Work to a Traditional Publisher?
A Reader's Guide to Author's Jargon and Other Ravings from the Blogosphere
Oh Dainty Triolet
The Academician - Southern Swallow Book I
The Nan Tu - Southern Swallow Book II
Swan Cloud – Southern Swallow Book
The House of Green Waters – Southern Swallow Book IV
The Jade Owl
The Third Peregrination
The Dragon's Pool
The People's Treasure
In the Shadow of Her Hem
Belmundus
Pacific Crimson: Forget Me Not
The Sapphire Astonishment
The Twinning of Vincent Cassidy
Mother Asphodel
Boots of Montjoy

Edward C. Patterson has been writing novels, short fiction, poetry and drama his entire life, always seeking the emotional core of any story he tells. With his eighth novel, The Jade Owl, he combines an imaginative touch with his life long devotion to China and its history. He has earned an MA in Chinese History from Brooklyn College with further postgraduate work at Columbia University. A native of Brooklyn, NY, he has spent four decades as a soldier in the corporate world gaining insight into the human condition. He won the 2000 New Jersey Minority Achievement Award for his work in corporate diversity. Blending world travel experiences with a passion for story telling, his adventures continue as he works to permeate his reader's souls from an indelible wellspring.

His novel *No Irish Need Apply* was named Book of the Month for June 2009 by Booz Allen Hamilton's Diversity Reading Organization. His Novel *The Jade Owl* was a finalist for The 2009 Rainbow Awards.

Visit Dancaster Creative — www.dancaster.com
Contact author at edwpat@att.net — Feedback is always appreciated
Amazon Author's page — http://www.amazon.com/-/e/B002BMI6X8

Made in the USA
San Bernardino, CA
30 July 2017